Kiss

The 87th Precinct Novels by Ed McBain

1956: Cop Hater • The Mugger • The Pusher
1957: The Con Man • Killer's Choice
1958: Killer's Payoff • Killer's Wedge • Lady Killer
1959: 'Til Death • King's Ransom
1960: Give the Boys a Great Big Hand • The Heckler •
    See Them Die
1961: Lady, Lady, I Did It!
1962: The Empty Hours • Like Love
1963: Ten Plus One
1964: Ax
1965: He Who Hesitates • Doll
1966: Eighty Million Eyes
1968: Fuzz
1969: Shotgun
1970: Jigsaw
1971: Hail, Hail, the Gang's All Here
1972: Sadie When She Died • Let's Hear It for the Deaf Man
1973: Hail to the Chief
1974: Bread
1975: Blood Relatives
1976: So Long as You Both Shall Live
1977: Long Time No See
1979: Calypso
1980: Ghosts
1981: Heat
1983: Ice
1984: Lightning
1985: Eight Black Horses
1987: Poison • Tricks
1989: Lullaby
1990: Vespers
1991: Widows
1992: Kiss

Kiss

A NOVEL OF THE 87th PRECINCT

ED McBAIN

William Morrow and Company, Inc. · New York

Library of Congress Cataloging-in-Publication Data

McBain, Ed, 1926–
    Kiss : a novel of the 87th Precinct / by Ed McBain.
      p.   cm.
    ISBN 0-688-10220-4
    I. Title.
PS3515.U585K54   1991
813'.54—dc20   91-15908
                                                                                CIP

Printed in the United States of America

First Edition

1 2 3 4 5 6 7 8 9 10

BOOK DESIGN BY LINEY LI

This is for
my wife
Mary Vann—who worked
so very hard for it

The city in these pages is imaginary.
The people, the places are all fictitious.
Only the police routine is based on
established investigatory technique.

1.

She was standing at the center of the subway platform, waiting for the uptown train to come in, when the man stepped up to her and punched her.

She felt shocking pain and then immediate outrage, how *dare* he? And then she remembered that this was the city in which she'd been born and bred, and in this city crazy things happened, and when they happened you tried to protect yourself. So she stepped back and away from him—a glimpse of red, he was wearing a red woolen hat—and was swinging her handbag at his head when he shoved her toward the edge of the platform.

He's crazy, she thought, he's a lunatic, and she said out loud, "*Stop* it, are you crazy?" but he grabbed her arm and pulled her toward the very edge of the platform, trying to throw her over, struggling with her. She screamed, she pulled away, tried to pull away, heard her coat tearing up the back when he reached for her again. Each time she moved away from the edge of the platform, he shoved her back again. The red hat, a brown jacket, blue jeans—she saw all these in almost subliminal flashes. He was only an inch or so taller than she was, but he was much stronger, and when finally he put all his strength into what seemed a last, desperate shove, she lost her balance and fell backward onto the tracks. In the moment before she went over, she saw his boots. Brown leather boots with a white—

A train was coming.

She heard its thunder up the track, and from where she was

crouched on her knees she turned to see its lights in the distance. She scrambled to her feet, tried to get back onto the platform, it was almost waist high, put her hands flat onto it, and tried to hoist herself up as if she were in a swimming pool and bouncing up out of the water. But there was no water here, there was no buoyancy to help her, there was only the high platform and the rattling sound of the train coming closer. Help me, she said to no one, Oh dear God, help me, and grabbed the edge of the platform with both hands, the train rumbling closer, thrusting herself up from the elbows, swinging one leg over the rim, scrabbling for purchase, the other leg over and up now, she was on the platform now, the train not thirty feet away and screeching out of the darkness.

Her pantyhose were laddered, her coat split up the back seam. She was wearing only a light wool dress under the coat. Shivering from the cold, or her fear, or perhaps both, her eye throbbing where the man had punched her, both hands bruised from trying to cushion her fall to the tracks, knees scraped raw and bleeding, she lay flat on the platform, hugging the platform, sobbing, sucking in great gobs of air.

She did not know how long it was before a Transit Authority policeman came to her.

2.

Five feet eight inches tall, blonde and buxom and blue-eyed and bursting with red-cheeked health, Birgitta Rundqvist marched into the station house at three o'clock on the afternoon of December 28, the Friday before the big New Year's Eve weekend. It was eight degrees Fahrenheit outside, but she was wearing only a lightweight red parka over a red reindeer-patterned sweater, a short black mini, red pantyhose, and little cuffed black boots. The desk sergeant thought she looked like Little Red Riding Hood. Birgitta told him she wanted to talk to a detective. When he asked her why, she said she had just witnessed a murder attempt.

This was a rarity. Someone in this city actually coming to the police to report having witnessed a crime. The desk sergeant figured if you lived long enough, you saw everything. He buzzed the squadroom.

Upstairs, Detective Meyer Meyer was sitting at his desk, minding his own business, typing up a report. Across the room, Andy Parker and Fat Ollie Weeks were talking about the new police commissioner. Parker and Weeks got along fine together. That's because they were both bigots. Weeks was perhaps a bigger bigot than Parker, but nobody can be only a little bit pregnant, although Weeks did in fact look a little bit pregnant—in fact about three months gone.

Obese and a trifle smelly, his belly hanging over his belt buckle, his fat, round face set with little pig eyes, Weeks was here visiting his good old buddies at the Eight-Seven, his own bailiwick being the Eight-Three, all the way uptown in Diamondback. Parker was always happy to see him. In Weeks's presence, and by comparison, Parker seemed nattily dressed— even though he was sporting a three-day beard stubble and a wrinkled suit. Whenever anyone questioned Parker's appearance, he told them he was on a stakeout. Whenever anyone questioned Weeks's appearance, he told them to go fuck themselves. Parker liked him a lot.

"The new commissioner's a scholar," Weeks said.

"A professor," Parker said, nodding in agreement.

"Used to teach criminology down there in that shitty little town the mayor snatched him from."

"He always refers to himself as *we*, you notice that? *We* this, *we* that. *We* feel the number of policemen on the street has nothing to do with crime prevention . . . ."

"*We* have learned over the years that community interaction is paramount. . . ."

"*We* this, *we* that."

"Like he's two people," Weeks said, and turned suddenly to look at Meyer. "You listening to this?" he asked.

"No," Meyer said.

"You ought to," Weeks said. "You might learn a few things about this new commissioner we got."

"I know enough about the new commissioner," Meyer said.

"Without your people," Weeks said, "there wouldn't *be* this new commissioner."

The new police commissioner was black.

So was the new mayor.

Weeks was saying that if it hadn't been for the Jews in this city, a black mayor wouldn't have been elected, and if a black mayor hadn't been elected, there wouldn't now be a black police commissioner. Meyer himself hadn't voted for the new mayor, but neither the new mayor nor the new commissioner was on anyone's Top Ten list at the moment, and it was always easy to blame the failings of one minority group on yet another minority group. Crouched behind his typewriter, pecking out his report with the index fingers of both hands, blue eyes squinting at the page in the roller, bald head gleaming in the late afternoon light that streamed through the grilled windows, Meyer wanted nothing less than an argument about either the new commissioner *or* the new mayor. He busied himself with indifference.

"Maybe the new commissioner can show your people where Bethtown is," Weeks said, and nudged Parker with his elbow.

Bethtown was the city's smallest sector, across the River Harb and reached either by ferry or bridge. Weeks was making a joke. The new commissioner had been quoted in yesterday's papers as asking his driver where Calm's Point, one of the city's *largest* sectors, was located. Meyer agreed that the man was a small-town hick in bib overalls, so why was Weeks virtually *insisting* that Meyer defend him? He was about to tell Weeks to stuff the new commissioner up his ass when the telephone rang.

"Eighty-Seventh Squad," he said, "Detective Meyer." He listened for a moment, raised his eyebrows in surprise, said, "Send her up," and then put the receiver back on the cradle. Birgitta came into the squadroom some three minutes later. Weeks looked her up and down. So did Parker. Meyer offered her the chair alongside his desk.

She told him who she was, told him she worked as a nanny for a Mrs. David Feinstein on Barber Street in Smoke Rise . . .

"I'm from Stockholm," she said.

Which was why she was dressed for the tropics, Meyer supposed.

. . . told him she was just wheeling the baby into the house when she saw this automobile come roaring around the corner . . .

Across the room, Parker burst out laughing at something Weeks had just said. What Weeks had just said was that he loved eating Danish. He had overheard the girl's faint accent and had mistaken her for Danish. Parker found this hysterical.

". . . aiming straight for this woman," she said.

"What woman?" Meyer asked.

"This woman walking on the sidewalk."

"The car was *aiming* for her?"

"Yes, sir," Birgitta said. "It jumped onto the curb, it tried to run her over."

"When was this?"

"Just before lunch. I had to wait for Mrs. Feinstein to get back before I could come here."

"What kind of car was it?"

"A Ford Taurus."

"What color?"

"Gray. A sort of metallic gray."

"Did you notice the license plate number?"

"I did."

A proud little nod. She watched television a lot, Meyer guessed. He supposed they had television in Sweden, didn't they? They certainly had it in Smoke Rise.

"Can you tell me the number, please?" he said.

"DB 37 612," Birgitta said.

He wrote it down, showed it to her, and said, "Is this it?"

"Yes," she said. "Exactly."

"It wasn't an out-of-state plate, was it?"

"No, no."

He wondered if they had states in Sweden. Sweden had Volvos, that he knew.

"Did you see who was driving the car?"

"I did."

"Man or woman?"

"A man."

"Can you tell me what he looked like?"

"Not really. It all happened very fast. He turned the corner, and aimed the car at her, and tried to hit her. And she threw herself over this low wall in front of the house next door to ours, and he just drove off."

"Was he white or black, did you notice?"

"White."

"Can you tell me anything else about him?"

"He was wearing a red woolen hat."

Big day for red, Meyer thought.

"How about the woman?" he said. "Anyone you know?"

"No."

"Not anyone you might have seen in the neighborhood? Before this, I mean."

"No, I'm sorry."

"Did you talk to her at all?"

"No. I took the baby inside the house, and when I came out again, she was gone."

"What'd she look like, can you tell me that?"

"She had blonde hair. Like mine. But longer. And she was a little shorter than I am."

"How old would you say she was?"

"In her thirties."

"Did you notice the color of her eyes?"

"I'm sorry."

"What was she wearing?"

"A mink coat. No hat. Dark boots. We still have snow on the ground up there."

Smoke Rise. Like the country up there. Hard to believe it was part of the Eight-Seven, but it was. Big, expensive houses, rolling woodlands, even a stream running through some of the choicer lots. Smoke Rise. Where a man driving a gray Ford Taurus had tried to run down a blonde woman in a mink coat.

"Anything else you can tell me?" Meyer said.

"That's all," Birgitta said. "He was trying to kill her. Will you do something about it?"

"Of course," he said.

The first thing he did was call Motor Vehicles to request a computer check on the license plate number Birgitta had given him. The MVB reported that the car in question was registered to a Dr. Peter Gundler who lived downtown in the Quarter. Meyer wrote down the doctor's address and then called Auto Theft. The detective he spoke to there took down the license plate number, the name and address of the registered owner, asked for the year and make of the car, settled for the make alone, and told Meyer he'd get back to him in ten minutes. He got back in seven to report that the good doctor's car had been reported stolen on Christmas Day, nice present, huh? Meyer thanked him and hung up.

Easy come, easy go, he thought.

There were times when Detective Steve Carella looked positively Chinese. As he sat in the sunlight that angled through the grilled squadroom windows, the light touching his face in a way that made his dark eyes appear more slanted, pondering the Ballistics report on his desk like a Buddhist monk studying a prayer scroll, it seemed conceivable that he'd been left on his parents' doorstep by a silk merchant from the Orient. He looked up from the report, glanced at the clock. Five minutes to eleven. Ballistics wouldn't be out to lunch yet. He was picking up the phone to dial, when she came down the corridor and stopped just outside the gate in the slatted-rail divider.

His first impression was one of paleness.

A tall, slender blonde woman wearing a long gray cavalry officer's coat. Taking a crumpled tissue from her pocket now, blowing her nose, returning the tissue to the pocket, hesitating outside the gate.

"Mrs. Bowles?" he said.

"Yes?"

"Come in, please," he said, and put the phone back on its cradle.

She had found the latch on the gate. She opened it and walked to his desk. Long, firm strides, pale horse, pale rider. He asked if he could take her coat . . .

"Yes, please."

. . . and then carried it to the rack in the corner, near the water cooler. Under the coat, she was wearing a black sweater, a pleated watch-plaid skirt, and black stockings. She resembled a student at a private girl's school.

"Please sit down," he said, and offered her the chair along-side his desk. She looked very grave. Straight blonde hair sitting on her head like a burnished helmet. Dark eyes solemn. Face raw from the wind outside.

"Someone's trying to kill me," she said.

"Yes," he said, and nodded.

She had called not a half hour earlier. When a woman on the phone tells you someone has made two attempts on her life, you ask her to come in immediately. She was here now. And now she was telling him how she'd been coming from a baby shower on Silvermine Oval and was waiting on the subway platform at Culver and Ninth to take a train uptown to Smoke Rise, the Barber Street station up there, do you know it? In Smoke Rise? Waiting for the train when a man pushed her onto the tracks. This was two weeks ago, a little more than two weeks ago. And then, yesterday, he'd tried to kill her again. Tried to run her over with an automobile. The same man. Closer to home this time.

This was all news to Carella.

The Transit Authority cop to whom Emma Bowles had sob-bingly poured out the information on the night of December twelfth hadn't filed a report with the Eight-Seven, and Meyer hadn't told Carella about his visit from the Swedish nanny yes-terday. So he listened now while Emma told him that she'd gone out for a little walk before lunch yesterday, strolling up Barber Street and into Smoke Rise, and suddenly this gray car that might have been a Lincoln Continental came tooling around the corner and climbed the sidewalk chasing her, and would have hit her if she hadn't jumped over this little stone wall bordering one of the houses.

"The same man was driving the car," she said. "The one who pushed me off the platform."

"Are you sure?"

"Positive," she said. "And I know who he is."

Carella looked at her.

"It came to me yesterday, when he tried to run me over," Emma said. "I suddenly remembered."

"Who is he?" Carella asked.

"He used to drive my husband."

"Drive him?"

"Martin is a stockbroker. He works all the way downtown, a car picks him up in the morning and takes him home again at night."

"When you say this man *used* to drive him . . . "

"Yes. He doesn't any longer."

"When did he stop?"

"Last spring. I don't know what happened then, but Martin got another driver."

"You're sure this is the same man?"

"Yes, he drove us to the theater once. I *know* it's the same man."

"But you didn't recognize him when he shoved you off that subway platform."

"No, I didn't make the connection. But yesterday he was in a *car*. And it rang a bell."

"Good," Carella said. "What's his name?"

Martin Bowles was a man in his late thirties, tall and slender, with thick dark hair, deep brown eyes, and the solid build of someone who worked out regularly. Every New Year's Eve, he wore a dinner jacket. Didn't matter where they were going, big party, small one, private home, restaurant, didn't even matter if they were going anywhere at *all*. They could be staying home, just the two of them, enjoying a quiet candlelit dinner, Bowles would nonetheless put on a dinner jacket. To him, New Year's Eve was an occasion. To Emma, it was like any other day of the year. She therefore found it mystifying that her husband went through the ritual of dressing up each year, and she was somewhat amused by the way he preened before a mirror each time he put on his ruffled shirt and black tie. His posturing might have appeared foolish on any other man, but he was truly strikingly handsome, and never as good-looking as when he was wearing formal attire. Tonight, he looked spectacularly elegant.

"I've hired a private detective," he said.

She was sitting at the bedroom vanity, fastening a pearl earring to her ear. She almost dropped it.

"A private detective?" she said. "What for?"

"To get to the bottom of this," he said.

She looked at him. He had to be kidding. The bottom of this was Roger Turner Tilly, the man who used to drive him to and from work. Once the police found him . . .

"The police don't seem to be doing anything about this," he said. "A man pushes you off a subway platform, and the same man . . . "

"Well, yes," she said. "But I know who he is, I told you who he . . . "

"Well, you don't know for certain," he said.

"But I *do* know," she said. "It was Tilly."

"The thing is, the police are treating these two incidents . . . "

"Incidents?" she said. "He tried to *kill* me."

"I know that. Why do you think I'm so concerned? The thing is, they're treating attempted murder like any ordinary occurrence. When was the first time? How long ago was that?"

"The twelfth."

"Exactly. And again last week. So what have they done, Emma? Nothing. Man tries to push you under a subway train," he said, and shook his head in disbelief. "Same man tries to run you over. Well, I don't want to wait for a *third* attempt. I've hired a private detective."

"I really don't think we need..."

"Man named Andrew Darrow, supposed to be excellent."

"A private detective," she said, and shook her head. "Really, Martin, let's leave this to the police, okay? The man I spoke to up there seemed..."

"The police are underpaid and overworked," Bowles said, as if quoting from an editorial he'd read. "I don't want to trust your life to them."

"That's very sweet of you, darling, really," she said, and stood up and turned to him. "But..."

"You look beautiful," he said.

She was wearing a shimmering white gown cut low over her breasts. Her long blonde hair was piled on top of her head. Drop pearl earrings dangled from her ears.

"Thank you," she said. "But, Martin, what would this man *do*? I mean..."

"Stay with you. Protect you. Try to get to the bottom of this."

"Let's go on a vacation instead," she said. "Use the money you're paying him..."

"We can do both," he said. "Soon as we resolve this thing, we'll take a nice long trip to the Caribbean, how does that sound?"

"I can taste it," she said.

Smiling, he put his arm around her and walked her out to the entrance foyer. He took her mink from the closet, helped her into it, put on his own coat, and draped a white silk scarf around his neck.

"I don't want anything to happen to you," he said.

"Nothing will happen to me," she said.

"I love you too much."

"I love you, too."

"He'll be starting next week," Bowles said. "Case closed."

The intercom buzzer sounded from the lobby downstairs. He went to the wall speaker, pressed the TALK button.

"Yes?"

"Your car's here, Mr. Bowles."

"Thank you," he said. "We'll be right down."

"The car," he said, and came back to her and took her in his arms, and offered her his lips.

"Kiss?" he said.

When Carella was a kid, his mother used to serve lentils shortly after midnight on New Year's Day. It had something to do with an Italian tradition her grandparents had brought over from the Old Country. Louise Carella didn't know what the tradition was—"Something to do with good luck," she explained to her son with a shrug—and neither did Carella's father. For that matter, Carella's grandparents couldn't remember, either. His mother and father, his grandparents on both sides of the family, had all been born here; the ties to forebears who had arrived at the turn of the century were already dim and uncertain. But after midnight, when the New Year was scarcely minutes long and everyone had already banged away to his heart's content on pots and pans at open windows, his mother used to serve cold lentils. She didn't know why they had to be cold, either. Cold lentils with a little olive oil. "For good luck," she said.

And on New Year's Day, they would all go over to Grandma's house for the big feast prepared by all the women in the family. There'd be Grandpa and Grandma and his mother's sister Josie and her husband Mike, and his mother's brother Salvatore, whom everybody called Salvie, and his wife Dorothy, whom Carella loved to death. And the kids, all Carella's cousins, and sometimes Uncle Freddie who lived in Las Vegas and who was a casino dealer who occasionally came East on the holidays and who once gave Carella a silver ring with a turquoise stone, which he said he'd won from a wild Apache Indian in a poker game. This was the old neighborhood—Carella's parents had already moved out of it to Riverhead, but Grandma and Grandpa refused to leave, even though more and more often you saw signs announcing BODEGA or LECHERÍA rather than SALUMERIA or PASTICCERIA.

Carella's father used to bring the pastry.

Baked in his own shop.

The meal would start with antipasto—sweet red peppers his grandmother had roasted over the gas jets on the kitchen stove, and ripe black olives, and anchovies and eggplant and crisp celery stalks and imported olive oil into which you dipped the crusty bread his grandfather sliced from a big round loaf. And then there was the pasta, always with a delicate tomato sauce, either spaghetti or rigatoni or penne, which he loved to smother with the grated Parmesan cheese he spooned from the bowl passed around the table—"Take a little more cheese, Stevie," his grandmother used to say sarcastically, scowling at him with a smile, he always wondered how she managed that trick.

And then there'd be the roast chicken and the roast beef and the potatoes and the green beans and the fresh peas he'd seen the women shelling in the kitchen, the Italian part of the meal magically seguing into what was essentially American, the way the immigrants had magically segued into their new lives here, I pledge allegiance. And there'd be fruit and cheese and coffee—and the pastries his father had baked in his own shop and carried downtown in little white thin cardboard boxes fastened with white string.

His Uncle Salvie was a great storyteller. He used to drive a cab all over the city, and he had a thousand stories about all the crazy passengers he carried. Grandma kept saying he should have been a writer. Salvie used to shrug this aside, though Carella suspected this was really a secret ambition of his, the stories he told. It was Carella's sister, Angela, who was always scribbling away. She seemed to have more homework than anybody in the entire world. Any holiday they spent at Grandma's house, Angela had books with her. All the cousins would be running around the apartment chasing each other and yelling at each other and laughing, and Angela would be curled up in a chair in the living room, reading a book, and then writing into her notebooks. "The Homework Kid," Uncle Mike called her. She always smiled shyly when he said this, he was her favorite.

Aunt Dorothy had a ribald and bawdy sense of humor. She was always telling jokes Carella at first suspected, and later realized, were sexual in content. Every time she started to tell one, Grandma would warn, "*I creaturi, i creaturi*," scowling at her without a smile, gesturing with her head in the direction of the children. Aunt Dorothy would wave aside Grandma's warnings and plunge right ahead with whatever joke she'd started. When Carella turned twelve, thirteen, whenever it was that he began seriously noticing girls and realizing what his aunt's jokes were all about, he would grin in knowledgeable embarrassment whenever she delivered a punch line, and she would wink at him in defiance of Grandma's disapproving scowl.

He never could understand how she'd learned about Margie Gannon. But she'd sensed unerringly—or perhaps his mother had tipped her to the fact—that he was enjoying what to him at the time was a wildly erotic relationship with the little Irish girl who lived across the street from him in Riverhead, and she teased him mercilessly about her, referring to her as Sweet Rosie O'Grady, God alone knew why.

The family would sit around the table, joking and laughing, drinking coffee and eating the pastries his father had baked. The cannoli and the sfogliatelli and the zeppoli and the strufoli and the Napolitani and the sfingi di San Giuseppe.

Aunt Josie was the one who always suggested, "Why don't we play a little poker?"

"Good idea," Uncle Freddie would say.

Uncle Freddie always won, even though they only played for pennies. Aunt Josie was a sore loser, Louise could never understand how her sister had developed such a temper. If she drew to an inside straight and failed to pull the card she was looking for, she'd throw her cards on the table and start swearing at whoever was dealing. *"Vergogna, vergogna,"* Grandma would scold, another of the few Italian expressions she had picked up from her mother, long dead. Grandma herself was dead now. Grandpa, too. Aunt Josie and Uncle Mike had moved to Florida, and they never came North anymore. Uncle Salvie died of cancer shortly after Carella joined the force. Aunt Dorothy remarried almost immediately afterward, and the family lost touch with her. Carella missed her and her dirty jokes.

At his father's funeral last July, there were no uncles or aunts who'd known Carella when he was small. There were a handful of cousins he hardly remembered, all of them expressing condolences over this terrible thing that had happened, one of them asking if Carella could fix a speeding ticket for him, the jackass. Behind their sad countenances, there lurked the unspoken thought that if such a thing could happen to a *cop's* father . . .

On New Year's Day this year, there were no pastries baked by Tony Carella. Tony Carella had been gunned down in his shop on the night of July seventeenth, and never again would there be pastries baked by him. Carella's mother was still in mourning. Black dress, black stockings, black shoes, honoring a tradition virtually gone in the land from which it had come; except in the most remote sections of Italy, widows rarely wore black for very long. But Louise was a woman who still served cold lentils after midnight on New Year's Day.

This was not a joyous Tuesday. The weather, chill and bleak and gray, seemed to echo the sense of loss that pervaded the house in which Carella and his sister had both grown up. A fierce and icy wind rattled the windows in the old house. There were cooking smells, yes, just as there had been on all the holidays Carella could remember, but there was no laughter, and even the children seemed oddly hushed. Only the immediate family —and not even all of it—was here today. The feast seemed somehow paltry; you did not celebrate when the funeral meats were not yet cold upon the table.

His mother was a blunt, plainspoken woman.

"I want to come to the trial," she said.

This was after the midday meal. Carella was due in the squadroom at a quarter to four; the Police Department had no respect for holidays. The family was sitting at the dining-room table under which he and Angela used to hide when they were children. Long tablecloth hanging almost to the floor. Giggling because they thought the grown-ups didn't know they were listening. *I creaturi*. The dishes had been cleared, they were drinking coffee. His mother dressed in black, her hands folded on the table, her slender gold wedding band tight on the ring finger of her left hand. Carella and his sister sitting side by side, both of them dark-haired and dark-eyed, the eyes slanting downward, their father's legacy. Teddy Carella sat beside her mother-in-law, raising her eyes from the knitting needles in her hands; she was knitting sweaters for the new twins in the family. Cynthia and Melinda, Angela's daughters, born on the twenty-eighth of July last year, eleven days after his father's murder; what the Lord taketh away, the Lord giveth back. Carella didn't much care for either name. He visualized one of them growing up as Cindy and the other as Mindy. He knew that his sister had unilaterally named them. His brother-in-law, Tommy, was conspicuously absent today. There were problems here, too. Carella sometimes felt overwhelmed.

Louise was waiting for an answer. She saw her son's eyes click with her daughter's, brown against brown, in the secret communication she recognized from when they were children. Teddy was watching Carella's lips.

"I don't think that's such a good idea," he said.

"Why not?"

"Mom, there's going to be testimony . . ."

"I want them to know he had a wife. I want the jury to know that."

"They'll know that anyway, Mom."

Teddy's eyes flashed from lips to lips, reading the words on them. Her world was a silent one. She had been born deaf and had never uttered a word in her life. Teddy knew how to sign, but her mother-in-law tried it only occasionally, both she and Angela preferring to speak with exaggerated lip motions they hoped Teddy could decipher. Except at times like now, when they were intent on the urgency of their own messages.

"Mom," Angela said, "Steve's . . ."

"No, don't *Mom* me. . . ."

"But he's right. There's going to be stuff you won't want to hear."

"I want to hear it all. I want them to know I'm there listening to it all."

"Mom . . ."

"Especially that *sfasciume* who killed him."

Carella automatically looked to see where the children were. He was never quite certain what the word *sfasciume* meant, but he suspected it was obscene and something *i creaturi* shouldn't hear coming from their grandmother's lips. His daughter was curled up with a book, reminding him of Angela at that age, and in fact resembling her somewhat. His son was working intently on a model airplane that had been a Christmas gift. Mark and April. Sensible names for twins, never mind Miffy and Muffy or whatever his sister's kids would grow up to be called. Angela's three-year-old, Tess, her brow furrowed in concentration, was working on a coloring book.

Bringing Teddy more completely into the conversation, signing as he spoke, Carella said, "Mom, this is a decision you have to make for yourself, but . . ."

"I know it is. . . ."

". . . but I've testified in cases where the victim's spouse was present . . ."

"The victim's *spouse*," Louise said, almost spitting the word.

". . . and I can tell you it's not an easy thing to live through."

"He's right, Mom," Angela said.

"They'll be showing pictures, Mom. . . ."

"I saw what he looked like, the pictures can't be any worse."

"Mom, that was a long time ago, you don't have to relive it all over again."

"It was yesterday," Louise said.

"It was last . . ."

"It'll always be yesterday," she said.

Teddy missed this. Carella signed it to her. She nodded.

"Until I can look that bastard straight in the eye," Louise said.

Carella had already looked that bastard straight in the eye. Had rammed the muzzle of his service revolver into the hollow of Sonny Cole's throat, had heard Detective Randy Wade whispering beside him, "Do it." He had not squeezed the trigger, although in the narrow corridor of a house surrounded by vacant lots this would have been the easiest thing in the world to do. He had not done it. Now, seeing the look in his mother's eyes, he wondered if he'd been right.

"I'm coming to the trial," she said, and nodded curtly.

"Mom . . ." Angela started.

"What time next Monday?" she asked.

"Nine o'clock," Carella said, and sighed heavily. "The Criminal Courts Building downtown."

3.

Even though Henry Lowell had received his undergraduate degree from Duke and his law degree from Harvard, locker-room gossip maintained that he'd once gone to Oxford University. Either way, his record was an impressive one. Since starting work at the District Attorney's Office three years ago, he'd racked up twenty-six convictions as opposed to a sole acquittal. He had never tried a murder case.

Six feet four inches tall, beanpole thin, lank dust-colored hair hanging on his broad forehead and crowding his hazel-colored eyes, Lowell stood with Carella just inside the massive bronze doors that opened onto the marbled lobby of the Criminal Courts Building on High Street downtown. It was ten minutes to nine on Monday morning, the seventh day of January. It had taken almost two weeks to select the jury; this morning the trial would begin in earnest.

Carella again wondered, as he had the first time they'd met, why Lowell sported a British accent rather than a Southern one, or for that matter *any* regional American one. He also wondered how the accent would sit with a jury composed of three white males, four black males, two Hispanic males, one white female, one Hispanic female, and one Asian female; you heard plenty of exotic accents in this city nowadays, but hardly any of them were British.

"I must tell you straightaway," Lowell said, "that I hope

this doesn't break down into a trial of issues rather than of substance.''

Carella didn't know what he meant.

"I don't need to mention," Lowell said, "that in this city there have been recent incidents of Italian-Americans attacking and harming African-Americans . . ."

Carella hated *both* those labels.

". . . and conversely there have been incidents of African-Americans attacking and harming Italian-Americans. Point is, we have here a case of two *African*-Americans attacking an *Italian*-American . . ."

My father, Carella thought.

". . . and in fact inflicting upon him the most grievous bodily harm."

Killing him, in fact, Carella thought.

"One of the perpetrators is still alive, and will be tried today and in the days to come. I'll do my best, of course, to convict him, but I don't want this trial to disintegrate into an ethnic contest. Point is, I'd be much happier if your father's name were Smith or Jones, but unfortunately it isn't.''

Wasn't, Carella thought.

"I don't have to tell you, I'm sure, that there is still a lingering prejudice in this country against people of Italian descent. The *paisans* in your own precinct didn't help matters any when they . . ."

"If you're referring . . ."

". . . when they chased a black kid into St. Catherine's and later went in there and made a mess of the place."

"They're no *paisans* of mine," Carella said.

Lowell looked at him.

"Do you ever get over to England?" he asked.

"No," Carella said.

He wondered what that had to do with the price of fish.

"I was there a short while ago," Lowell said, "I love it there, well, Oxford, you know." He smiled in reminiscence. He had a good smile. Carella imagined he had used that smile to great advantage in the twenty-six cases he'd successfully prosecuted. "Point is . . ." he said.

Bad verbal tic, Carella thought. Point is.

". . . during my stay, I ran across an interview in a newspaper called *The Guardian*. If you're not familiar with it . . ."

"I'm not."

". . . it's a liberal newspaper, quite respectable. The piece was written by a man named John Williams. Its title was 'Of Wops and Cops.'"

"Uh-huh," Carella said.

"As I recall, the subject of the interview was some cheap American thriller writer of Italian descent. Point is, neither Mr. Williams *nor* his newspaper seemed to realize just how offensive the use of the word *wops* was. They could just as easily have titled the piece *Of Niggers and Triggers*, do you catch my drift?"

"No, I'm sorry, I don't," Carella said.

"It's unconscious. Even there in England, thousands of miles away, a presumably respected journalist like John Williams . . . is the name familiar to you?"

"It is now," Carella said.

"John Williams . . ."

"I'll remember it."

". . . can feel free to slant an interview into an ethnic attack. Point is, however much you may deplore it, there'll always be people who'll find satisfaction in equating you with those *paisans*, those *guineas*, those *wops*, yes, who invaded St. Catherine's Church."

"I see," Carella said.

"So if we allow this trial to become a name-calling contest . . ."

"Uh-huh."

"One minority group against another . . ."

"Uh-huh."

"An Italian-American victim versus . . ."

"I find *that* word offensive, too," Carella said.

"Which word?"

"Italian-American."

"You do?" Lowell said, surprised. "Why?"

"Because it *is*," Carella said.

He did not think that someone with a name like Lowell would ever understand that *Italian*-American was a valid label only when Carella's great-grandfather first came to this country and acquired his citizenship, but that it stopped being descriptive or even useful the moment his *grand*parents were *born* here. That was when it became *American*, period.

Nor would Lowell ever understand that when we insisted upon calling fourth-generation, native-born sons and daughters of long-ago immigrants "*Italian*-Americans" or "*Polish*-Americans" or "*Spanish*-Americans" or "*Irish*-Americans" or—worst of all—"*African*-Americans," then we were stealing from them their very American-ness, we were telling them that if their forebears came from another nation, they would never be *true* Americans here in this land of the free and home of the brave, they would forever and merely remain wops, polacks, spics, micks, or niggers.

"My father was American," Carella said.

And wondered why the hell he had to say it.

"Exactly my . . ."

"The man who killed him is American, too."

"That's how I'd like to keep it," Lowell said. "Exactly the point I was trying to make."

But Carella still wondered.

"And thank you for the insight," Lowell said. "I won't use either of those words during the course of the trial. Italian-American, African-American . . . gone from my vocabulary as of this moment." He smiled again, and then abruptly looked up at the clock. "It's time we went upstairs," he said. "I hope your mother hasn't got lost."

Carella looked up the corridor. His mother had gone to the

ladies' room some fifteen minutes ago. He saw her coming toward them now, dressed in black, moving with a slow, steady pace over the marbled floors and between the marble columns. There was a white, lace-edged handkerchief in her right hand. Her dark eyes looked moist. He wondered if she'd been crying.

"Mom?" he said, going to her and putting his arm around her.

Just that single word.

"I'm fine," she said, and lifted her chin.

Together, they went upstairs, the son and the wife of the victim, and the man who would present their case to a jury *not* composed of Sonny Cole's *peers*—the word meant *equals*, and none of these men or women were murderers—who would determine whether the man who without question had shot and killed Anthony Carella had, in fact, actually shot and killed him. In the sunswept, wood-paneled second-floor courtroom that was General Sessions, Part III, twelve men and women would seek justice. Carella prayed they would find it.

Up close, Emma Bowles was even prettier than in the photograph her husband had shown him. The black-and-white picture hadn't even hinted at the peaches-and-cream complexion or the luster of her dark eyes. Blonde hair cascading long and straight to her shoulders, aglow in the Monday morning sunlight that slanted through the blinds. She was wearing a jumpsuit the color of her eyes, flat sandals with gold thongs that echoed her hair and the slender gold clip that swept it back on the right side of her head. She had a full-lipped mouth, the tented upper lip revealing a wedge of white.

"It's just that . . . well, I'll tell you the truth," she said, "a bodyguard would embarrass me."

"I'm not a bodyguard, Mrs. Bowles," Andrew said. "I'm a private investigator."

"Whatever. But, don't you see, Mr. Darrow? The police are

already working on this, there's no need . . ."

"Mrs. Bowles," he said, "your husband hired me to do a job, and with your permission, I'd like to try doing it."

She was thinking he seemed pretty confident of himself. Tall, slender blond man wearing a brown turtleneck shirt and a corduroy jacket that matched the amber color of his eyes, dark brown slacks, brown socks, brown highly polished loafers. Easy, pleasant smile, soft, well-modulated voice, not the sort of man she had expected. Not the sort at all.

"What exactly does he want you to do?" she asked.

"Two things," Andrew said. "First, he wants me to protect you. . . ."

"Which is bodyguarding, isn't it?" she said.

"Well, no, not exactly. Because he also wants me to find out who's trying to kill you."

"How much is he paying you for this?"

"Well, I think that's between me and your husband."

"No, I don't think so," she said.

"Well," Andrew said, and shrugged. "The going rate for a private detective is thirty-five dollars an hour."

"I see."

"In Chicago," he said.

"And what's the going rate *here*?"

"I don't know what it is here," he said. "I'm charging your husband what I'd charge him in Chicago. Thirty-five an hour. Plus expenses."

"I'm not sure I know what you're saying. What's *Chicago* got to do with any of this?"

"That's where I'm from. Chicago. That's where I'm licensed to operate."

"I still don't understand," she said. "If you're from Chicago . . ."

"Your husband called me there and asked if I'd like to do this work for him."

"Called you all the way in Chicago?"

"All the way in Chicago, yes."

"You must be good," she said.

"I am," he said, and smiled. "Your husband hired me to find out who's trying to hurt you, and I'm pretty sure I can do that."

"I already *know* who's trying to hurt me."

"You do?" he said, opening his eyes wide in surprise.

"Yes, I do."

"Well . . . who is it?"

"His name is Roger Tilly. My husband *knows* who this man is, I *told* him who this man is, he *knows* this man, he used to *drive* for him. It's just that he doesn't trust the police to find him. So he goes all the way to Chicago to hire a bodyguard, when really . . . "

"A private investigator," he said, gently correcting her. "Not a bodyguard, ma'am."

She said nothing for several moments.

She was wondering if perhaps he *might* be able to help, after all.

"Well," she said, and hesitated.

He kept watching her expectantly.

"I suppose we can give it a try," she said.

Fat Ollie Weeks kept shaking his head.

Not because he'd found a dead man hanging from an asbestos-covered pipe in the basement, but because he could hear a record player going somewhere upstairs, and the song being sung was a little item called "Fuck tha Police." This was a fine way to teach respect. Black people singing a song like that. Rapping out a song like that. Ollie shook his head again. Ollie hated black people even more than he hated Jews.

He did not wonder what a white man was doing all the way up here in Darkest Africa, because he knew that a lot of goddamn white fools came up here to get their crack thrills. He also didn't wonder how come this particular white man had ended up with a rope around his neck, because he further knew that a lot of goddamn white fools came up here to Zimbabwe West and went back home in body bags. He didn't even wonder how all this had come about. All in good time, he thought, and first things first. Ollie Weeks was a terrible bigot, but he happened to be a good cop. He phoned in the shit and sat back to wait.

By six-thirty that Monday night, his stomach was grumbling and his patience was running out. He had come on at a quarter to four and had caught this stupid squeal at five-ish, ten minutes after his partner had gone down for coffee and burgers for both of them. Now his partner was only Christ knew where while Ollie was here in this fuckin basement with dripping pipes on the ceiling and a dead man hanging from one of them and a lot of cops in heavy overcoats hanging around freezing cold with their hands in their pockets and Monoghan and Monroe from Homicide just coming down the steps and still no fuckin M.E.

"What've we got here, Weeks?" Monoghan said.

"A little lynching?" Monroe said, looking up at the dangling man, his witticism missing fire in that the victim was white.

Ollie pulled a face nonetheless.

"Where's the fuckin M.E.?" he asked no one. "I called this shit in an hour ago."

"Busy night tonight," Monoghan said.

"Yeah, why's that?" Ollie asked.

"Guy Fawkes Day," Monoghan said.

"What the fuck's that, Guy Fawkes Day?" Ollie asked.

"Lots of parties tonight," Monroe said, picking up on the gag. "Guy Fawkes Day."

"I never heard of no fuckin Guy Fawkes Day," Ollie said.

"Anyway," one of the blues said, "Guy Fawkes Day is in November."

"Who asked you?" Ollie asked.

"Anyway, it ain't," Monroe said.

"November the fifth," the uniformed cop insisted.

"No, it's in January," Monroe said, shaking his head. "It's today. The seventh of January."

"Be sure to remember the fifth of November," the cop said.

"Who gives a fuck *when* Guy Fawkes Day is?" Ollie said. "Where the fuck's the M.E.?"

"My mother was born in England," the cop explained.

"Who gives a fuck *where* your mother was born?" Ollie said.

"I'm only saying. Guy Fawkes Day," the cop said, and shrugged.

"Dumb fuck hangs himself from the ceiling," Ollie said, "I got to wait for my fuckin supper."

"How do you know somebody else didn't hang him there?" Monroe asked.

"How do you know Guy *Fawkes* didn't hang him there?" Monoghan asked, and both Homicide detectives burst out laughing. They were both wearing black overcoats and black fedoras. Monoghan had taken to wearing a white silk scarf lately. So had Monroe. They stood with their hands in the pockets of their coats, hats tilted raffishly. They thought they looked like Fred Astaire and Cary Grant in the same old black-and-white movie, going to a party together on Guy Fawkes Day. Actually, they looked like two fat penguins.

"Who gives a fuck *who* hung him?" Ollie said, and just then the M.E. came down the steps. "Where the fuck you been?" Ollie asked. "Some fuckin Guy Fawkes party?"

"What?" the M.E. said, and looked up at the hanging man.

"Somebody get him a ladder," Monoghan said.

"Go get him a ladder," Monroe said.

Two of the blues went off looking for a ladder. The blue whose mother had been born in England stood around looking offended.

"What do you think killed him, Doc?" Monroe said, and winked at Monoghan.

"Assuming he *is* dead," Monoghan said, and winked back.

The M.E. glanced at them sourly, and lighted a cigarette.

"That's bad for your health," Monroe said.

The M.E. kept puffing away.

Ollie lighted a cigarette, too.

The corpse kept twisting overhead. He was wearing a long blue overcoat, black leather gloves, blue earmuffs, and a gray fedora. The blues finally came back with a tall ladder. They opened it for the M.E., who watched them nervously.

"I've got acrophobia," he said.

"What the fuck's that, acrophobia?" Ollie asked.

"Intense fear of heights," the cop whose mother was born in England said.

"This one's a mine of information," Monroe said, glaring at him.

"I'm not going up that ladder," the M.E. said. He was beginning to turn a little pale.

"Then how the fuck you gonna examine him?" Ollie asked.

"Take him down," the M.E. said. "I'll examine him down here."

"What shall we do with this ladder?" one of the blues asked.

"Shove it up your ass," Ollie said. "We ain't allowed to touch him till you pronounce him dead," he explained to the M.E. "That's the rules."

"I know the rules."

"So if you won't go up the ladder and pronounce him dead, how the fuck can we take him down? We have to *touch* him to take him down, don't we?"

"I can tell he's dead from down here. He's dead. I pronounce him dead. Now take him down and I'll examine him."

"I ain't going up that ladder," Ollie said.

"Me, neither," Monoghan said.

"Go on up that ladder and take him down," Monroe told the cop with the English mother.

"I don't go up ladders on Guy Fawkes Day," the cop said.

The other two blues went up the ladder. One of them hoisted

the body a bit while the other one loosened the rope from where it was wrapped around the asbestos-covered pipe. Carefully, slowly, they walked the victim down the ladder and lowered him to the ground on his back. The rope was wound tight around the corpse's throat. Somebody had done a very good job on him. The M.E. put his stethoscope to the man's chest.

"You still think he's dead?" Monoghan asked, and winked at Monroe.

"Or should we get a second opinion?" Monroe asked.

The M.E. looked at them sourly. They watched as he examined the body.

"What do you think killed him?" Monroe asked, still running with the gag.

"You think cause of death might have been hanging?" Monoghan asked, winking at his partner.

"I think cause of death might have been a gunshot wound," the M.E. said, possibly because he had just rolled the victim over and found a bullet hole at the base of his skull.

"Oh," Monoghan said.

Ollie tossed the dead man.

That was when he learned his name was Roger Turner Tilly.

Carella got there half an hour later. Ollie was waiting for him outside the building, sitting on the front stoop, eating. He had sent the blue with the English mother out to get him a bagful of hamburgers and a large Coke, and he was eating his dinner upstairs here because he didn't like to eat where there were dead bodies. Also, he already figured this wasn't his case. That's why he'd called the Eight-Seven and asked them to beep Carella.

Carella was wearing two sweaters under his heavy overcoat, and he was wearing a woolen muffler and a hat with earflaps, and he was still cold. Ollie was wearing only a sports jacket over his trousers and shirt, but he looked toasty warm.

"Your man's downstairs," he told Carella, and bit into his

sixth hamburger. "Tilly, am I right? Ain't that what you said on the phone?"

"Tilly, right," Carella said.

He had spoken to Ollie late last week, on the offchance he'd have some fresh information on the man Emma Bowles said was trying to kill her. According to Identification Section records, Tilly had stopped driving Bowles last spring because he'd left the city in March—for a prison named Castleview, all the way upstate. He'd been sent up there because he'd assaulted a man who'd called him *un maricón*. Tilly wasn't *un maricón*. Besides, he didn't understand Spanish, and he didn't even know what he'd been called until someone later translated it for him. That was when he went looking for the other driver. So that he could break his nose and both his arms, in that order.

The other driver was Hispanic. Or Latino. Or whatever other label was being hung on people of Spanish descent these days. That was why he knew what *maricón* meant. He had called Tilly *maricón* because Tilly was small and compact and light on his feet. He didn't know that the reason Tilly was light on his feet was that he'd once been a welterweight boxer. Hence the broken nose and arms.

The dispatcher at Executive Limousine, which was the limousine company for which both Tilly and the Spanish-American Hispanic Latino worked, called the police and also the hospital. The police got there first. Tilly punched one of them while they were putting the cuffs on him. This could have made matters worse for him, but the judge who heard his case thought that anyone with a name like Roger Turner Tilly couldn't be all bad. The judge himself hated minority groups of any stripe or color. He sentenced Tilly to a mere year and a half upstate. Tilly got out in six months.

The address he'd given his parole officer was 335 St. Sebastian Avenue, right up here in Ollie's bailiwick. But no one there had ever heard of him, hence the call to the Eight-Three.

Ollie promised Carella he'd listen around. Now, as it turned out, he wouldn't have to anymore.

"Are you sure it's him?" Carella asked.

"Never saw the man in my life," Ollie said, chewing. "I'm only telling you what his ID shit said. Roger Turner Tilly."

"Is the M.E. still here?"

"Nope."

"What'd he say?"

"Gunshot wound."

"Where?"

"Back of the head. He's still layin' on the floor down there, go take a look."

"Who else is down there?"

"Just a couple of blues. We been waiting for the ambulance. It's been a busy night," Ollie said, and shook his head. "Fuckin Guy Fawkes Day."

"Who'd Homicide send?" Carella asked.

"Monoghan and Monroe. They're already gone. So are the techs. I told you, there's just the stiff and a couple of blues down there. Now that you're here, I can go home."

"What do you mean?"

"I'll turn over all the paper, you can sit and wait for the meat wagon."

"What do you mean?" Carella said again.

"I mean it's all yours, Stevie."

"All *mine*?"

"Right. You can take it from here."

"Take *what* from here? What the hell are you talking about?"

"You can pick up where I left off," Ollie said.

"Where you left *off*? You haven't even *started* yet. All you've done . . ."

"The case is yours, Steve."

"Oh, really? How do you figure that?"

"You told me you were looking for Tilly, didn't you? You

said you wanted him for attempted murder.''

"No, I said I wanted to *question* him about an attempted . . .''

"Same thing. So now you got him, Stevie baby. He's down the basement.''

"Uh-uh,'' Carella said. "This one's yours, and you know it.''

He was thinking that if Tilly was in fact the man Emma Bowles had identified as trying to kill her, then she was no longer in any danger from him. So why should he take on a homicide from another precinct? Ollie had caught it, the case was his. Ollie felt otherwise.

"They're related,'' he said. "First Man Up, Stevie, you know the rules.''

"First Man Up is when a *previous* homicide investigation is in progress. That doesn't apply here.''

"You were investigating an *attempted* murder, Stevie. That's the same thing.''

"No, it's not.''

"Besides, you can close this one out in a minute. It's a suicide. The man hung himself from the ceiling.''

"I thought you said there was a head injury.''

"That's what the M.E. said. *I'm* saying he hung himself.''

"Either way, it has to be investigated as a homicide. You know that, Ollie. That means the whole nine yards.''

"So be my guest,'' Ollie said, and took another bite.

"No,'' Carella said. "It's your case.''

"You think so?''

"I know so.''

"Well, maybe so, who knows?'' Ollie said. "But I wonder what my lieutenant'll say about that. 'Cause I'll tell you, Stevie, the Eight-Three is up to its ass in homicides right now, and what we don't need is a fuckin *'nother* one that's related to a case the Eight-Seven is already working. You know what *I* think the Loot'll say? I think he'll say this is *your* case, even if he has to talk to the Chief of Detectives about it, who by the way he plays poker with every Tuesday night.''

Ollie bit into another hamburger.

Carella looked at him.

''Yep,'' Ollie said.

I was beginning to wonder if I still had a husband, Teddy signed.

''I'm sorry I'm late, honey,'' Carella said, signing and speaking and trying to take off his overcoat at the same time, his fingers and his words getting lost in the sleeves, ''something of an emergency.''

Teddy wasn't buying emergencies tonight. Teddy had eaten alone with the children, her husband nowhere in sight, her TDD calls to the squadroom—*four* of them—going unanswered. On her last call, she'd typed, WHERE THE HELL R U? GA. The GA stood for GO AHEAD, but no one was going ahead, no one was answering her calls. She stood fiery-eyed and beautiful, arms folded across her chest, waiting for him to go ahead now. Carella tried to kiss her on the cheek, but she turned away.

''I really am sorry,'' he said. ''Are the kids in bed already?''

Yes, the kids were already in bed, the kids had in fact been asleep for the past hour or so, this was now ten-thirty on a Monday night, and tomorrow was a school day. He knew he should go down the hall to look in on them, but he didn't dare turn his back on Teddy for fear she would clobber him with a hammer or something, in which case he would have to arrest her for assault. He had never seen her quite this angry. Well, yes, maybe two or three times, but in those instances *he* hadn't been the object of her anger. He wondered what she was really angry about. He'd come home late before, he was a cop, cops were *always* coming home late. And *this* time, there really had been—

''We almost had a riot,'' he said, and signed the word to

her, spelling it out letter by letter, R-I-O-T, giving it emphasis so that she'd know he hadn't been hanging around downtown, frivolously putting away a few brews with the boys. She still wasn't buying it. Her blazing eyes were telling him that anything short of World War III was unjustifiable cause for him being late tonight. But why? What had happened to bring *this* on?

"I mean it," he said, "the whole damn station house was out there in the street trying to contain it," not daring to mention that he hadn't had dinner yet, and was starving to death.

What had happened . . .

And he told this to her as his stomach rumbled and roared, fingers flying in the sign language she had taught him, mouth exaggerating each word in support of his hands . . .

. . . was I went back to the precinct after I left the courthouse, and then Ollie called 'cause he had a stiff hanging in the basement, and he claimed it was rightfully mine, it's a long story, honey, but anyway I didn't get finished up there in Diamondback till eight-thirty, and then I had to go back to the squadroom to talk to the lieutenant about it, and what happened was some guy decided not to take the parkway uptown because the traffic was too heavy, big fat white guy driving a Caddy, decided to come uptown on the precinct streets instead. So he was stopped at a traffic light when a black guy with a pail of water, a greasy sponge, and a squeegee came over to the car, ready to wash his windshield for him, and the white guy waved him away . . .

Slow down, Teddy signed.

But at least she was listening.

. . . but the black guy kept on coming. So the white guy rolled down his window—this is how he reported it to us later—and told the black guy his windshield was clean, he didn't need it washed, and the black guy slapped the sponge onto it, anyway, and wiped a big smear of grease all over it, and started walking away. The light had changed by then, but the white guy got out of the car and yelled, Hey, *you*, wiseguy, or something like that, and when the black guy kept on walking he went after him and yanked him by the back of his collar and almost pulled him off his feet. He dragged him back to the car and was trying to force him to clean off all that *shmutz* he'd left on the windshield, when all at once there was a crowd in the streets, and the next thing you knew the white guy was running for his life.

David-Car happened to be cruising by, and the two cops in it—one white, one black—saw what appeared to be ten thousand black people chasing a fat white man through the streets in what looked like a bona fide lynching. So they got out of the car and took the white man in custody and started making the usual cop noises, okay, let's break it up, nothing here anymore, let's all go home, move it on now, let's go, but the usual noises weren't washing tonight. The crowd wanted blood, and the cops were the only thing preventing the satisfaction of this desire. So the crowd started surging forward, rocking the police car, at which point the shotgun cop, who happened to be the black one, got on the pipe and called in a 10–13. This was at a quarter to nine, while I was still talking to the lieutenant . . .

You must be hungry, she signed. *Let me put your dinner in the microwave*.

. . . about the guy hanging from the basement ceiling, re-member I told you about Fat Ollie's homicide? Anyway, I had to get out in the street with everybody else because we had this riot about to erupt over one fat white guy who'd chased one skinny black guy away from his car and then got annoyed when the guy messed up his windshield. Cleaning windshields is a form of extortion, anyway, you know, in that the driver's trapped inside his car and anybody approaching it—this one happened to be a skinny little guy, but some of them are this tall and this wide—appears threatening. But try to explain that to a bunch of people who are festering over all the bad things the black people in this city have to live with, just try to explain it.

"This is delicious, honey," he said, gobbling down his food and at the same time signing with his free hand.

Anyway, we finally got everybody to go home before one of

those professional-agitator black ministers arrived on the scene, in which case the damn thing would have gone on all night or all week or all month. The fat white guy drove off steaming because his windshield was still dirty and he was now late for a dinner party in the bargain. The skinny black guy pranced for the television cameras while all his pals made faces in the background, all of them famous for five minutes. By the time we all got back to the station house, it was past ten o'clock—

"I came straight home," he said. "Why are you so angry?"

Because I thought something had happened to you, she signed, and then rolled her eyes as if this were something any *idiot* should understand. He was taking her in his arms when the telephone rang. He went to it at once, and picked up the receiver.

"Hello?" he said.

"Steve?"

His mother. In tears.

"Mom?" he said. "What's the matter?"

"That lawyer," she said, sobbing. "All those things he said."

"Mom . . ."

"You heard him."

"Yes, but . . ."

"That the man who killed Papa *didn't* kill him. That there's no proof he did it, the gun wasn't even his, there's no case against him . . ."

"They always say that in their opening statements. We've got everything we need, believe me."

"I wanted to kill him," she said. "Sitting there with that look on his face while his lawyer was telling everybody he didn't do it."

"We'll see what kind of look he . . ."

"He worried me. The lawyer."

"No, Mom . . ."

"He did."

"No, there's nothing to worry about."

"Suppose they let him go?"

"They won't."

"But suppose they do?"

"Mom, you shouldn't have taken the lawyer so seriously. That's all part of the hype, the way they soften up a jury. So the jury'll believe whatever they see and hear."

"Suppose they *do*?"

"Mom . . ."

"Believe everything he tells them? Suppose they believe it?"

"They won't."

"Do you trust this Englishman?"

"He's not an Englishman, Mom."

"Then why does he sound so English?"

"He went to Oxford. That's the way they talk there at . . . "

"He sounds phony."

"Well . . ."

"I hope the jury doesn't think he sounds phony."

"They won't, Mom, don't worry."

"The other lawyer looks like Santa Claus. He talks right to the jury, he tells them his man didn't do it, I'm afraid they might believe him."

"Mom, really, don't worry, okay?"

He heard her sighing on the other end of the line.

"Will you pick me up tomorrow morning?" she asked.

"Angela said she'd come by for you. I'll meet you both downtown."

"I wish I liked him better," Louise said.

"Well," Carella said.

"I'll see you tomorrow."

"Yes."

"At the courthouse."

"Yes. And don't worry about what the lawyer said."

"I worry," she said, and hung up.

4.

Bloody murder would be the subject of this trial.

Bloody murder seemed to rage in the fierce January wind that rattled the tall windows on one side of the courtroom. The windows were shut tight against the winter cold, but you could still hear the high, shrill whistle of the wind outside, more insistent than the muted sounds of traffic in the streets below. The walnut-paneled courtroom was far too small for the crowd it contained. An expectant hush seemed to shrink the room further as Assistant District Attorney Henry Lowell called his first witness.

"I would like Dominick Assanti to take the stand, please," he said.

A tall young white man with wavy black hair and brown eyes came through the doors at the back of the courtroom, nodded to a man sitting in the back row—undoubtedly his father, judging from the remarkable resemblance—and walked down the center aisle to the witness chair. The clerk of the court swore him in. Lowell approached.

"Could you tell me your name, please?" he asked.

"Dominick Assanti."

"How old are you, Dominick?"

"Eighteen."

"How old were you on July seventeenth last year?"

"Seventeen."

"You had your eighteenth birthday between then and now, is that it?"

"Yes, sir. On the sixth of December."

"Mr. Assanti, on July seventeenth last year, do you recall going to a movie with a girl named Doris Franceschi ... "

"Yes, I do."

". . . who was your girlfriend at the time, wasn't she?"

"Yes. But we broke up. She's not my girlfriend no more."

"But she was at that time."

"Yes."

"At the time, did she live at 7914 Harrison Street?"

"I think that was her address, yes."

"Mr. Assanti," Lowell said gently, "if you can remember the exact . . ."

"Objection."

Harold Addison, attorney for the defense. A white man in his early sixties, sporting a Santa Claus beard and a potbelly to match. Ruddy-cheeked and twinkly-eyed, he gave the impression of a kind and generous grandfather whom it pained even to use the word *objection*, but if justice was to be served . . .

"Yes, Mr. Addison?"

"He's answered the question, Your Honor."

"I don't believe so. Please read back the question."

"At the time, did she live at 7914 Harrison Street?"

"Do you mean Frankie?"

"Is that what you called her?"

"Frankie, yes. That's her nickname."

"And is that her address?"

"Yes, that's where she lived," Assanti said.

From where Carella was sitting with his mother and sister in the third row right, he saw Addison smile in his Santa Claus beard, as if he'd won a major victory. Carella could not for the life of him imagine why. Judge Rudy Di Pasco was frowning, as if displeased by whatever it was that Grandpa Addison had done. To nail it all home, Lowell said, "Then on July seventeenth last year, Doris Franceschi *was* living at 7914 Harrison Street, in Riverhead, was she not?''

''She was, yes,'' Assanti said.

''Thank you. Now tell me, Mr. Assanti, on that night, after the movie, did you not walk Miss Franceschi back to her home at 7914 Harrison Street?''

''I did.''

''Would you remember what time this was?''

''It was after the movie.''

''Yes, but what time was that? Would you remember what time the movie let out?''

''It must've been about eight-thirty. Around then.''

''Did you go directly from the movie to Miss Franceschi's house?''

''Yes.''

''Arriving there at what time?''

''I don't remember.''

''Well, isn't the theater you went to only ten blocks . . . ?''

''Your Honor?''

Santa Claus. On his feet again. Head tilted to one side as if he'd just come down the chimney and was apologizing for all the soot he'd trailed onto the carpet.

''Yes, Mr. Addison,'' Di Pasco said.

''I hate to interrupt the orderly flow of an examination,'' Addison said, ''and I realize that Your Honor has already ruled upon an instance where Mr. Lowell was insisting on certain knowledge rather than on conjecture. But, Your Honor, when the witness says he cannot remember something, then surely this may be taken as a direct answer to a direct question. I do not remember . . . it is impossible for me to recall . . . whatever language the witness may choose to use, it means the same thing. He cannot remember. And not remembering something is a valid answer and not, to my knowledge, a crime in this sovereign state.''

Murder *is*, Carella thought.

"Mr. Lowell?"

"It was my hope, Your Honor, to refresh the witness's memory by providing significant facts relating to time and distance."

"Perhaps you can find another way of getting to that."

"Your Honor . . ."

"I've ruled, Mr. Addison."

"Thank you, Your Honor. But . . ."

"I said I've *ruled*."

"Thank you," Addison said, and rolled his eyes as he sat down, clearly transmitting to the jury that something rotten was afoot in a court of American law where a witness wasn't allowed to say he didn't remember something.

"What was the name of the theater you went to?" Lowell asked.

"The Octagon."

"Thank you. And the Octagon is on what street?"

"Benton."

"And how far is that from Harrison, would you say? From the house Miss Franceschi lived in on Harrison."

"About ten blocks."

"So how long did it take you to walk those ten blocks? Would you say five minutes?"

"Longer than that."

"Ten minutes?"

"More like fifteen or twenty."

"Is it fair, then, to say that it took you fifteen or twenty minutes to walk to her house from the movie theater?"

"That's about what it took."

"Which would have placed you there at a quarter to nine, ten to nine, around that time."

"Yes, it was around that time."

"What time did you leave Miss Franceschi?"

"Around twenty after nine."

"Mr. Assanti, do you have any knowledge of a bakery shop

at 7834 Harrison, a shop called A&L Bakery, are you familiar with this shop?''

"I've seen it, yes. It's out of business now."

"Would you know if it was still in business on the night of July seventeenth last year?"

"It was."

"After you left Miss Franceschi, did you pass this shop on your way home?"

"I did."

"What time was this, do you recall?"

"It was about nine-thirty, give or take a few minutes."

"Mr. Assanti, can you tell us what happened as you were walking home?"

"I heard shots."

"Where?"

"I didn't know where at first. I thought it was from the liquor store."

"What liquor store?"

"There's a liquor store next door to the bakery."

"How many shots were there?"

"Three. One right after the other."

"Were these shots, in fact, coming from the liquor store?"

"No."

"Where were they coming from?"

"The bakery."

"Tell us what happened next."

"Two guys came running out of the bakery."

"Describe them."

"They were both black. Very big. Both wearing jeans and black T-shirts."

"Were they armed?"

"One of them had a gun."

"And you say they came running out of the bakery shop . . . "

"Yes, and almost knocked over a man who was coming out of the liquor store."

"So you heard these three shots . . ."

"Yes."

"One right after the other."

"Yes."

"In rapid succession, would you . . . ?"

"Your Honor, he's putting words into the witness's mouth."

"Sustained."

"You heard these three shots one after the other, and you saw two men come running out of the bakery shop . . ."

"Yes."

"And one of them was carrying a gun."

"Yes."

"Did you get a look at the gun?"

"I did."

"Do you know what kind of gun it was?"

"No, I don't know anything about guns."

Lowell walked to the prosecutor's table, picked up a tagged pistol, and carried it back to the witness stand. "Mr. Assanti," he said, "I show you a nine-millimeter assault pistol, and ask if the gun you saw on the night of July seventeenth looked like . . ."

"Objection!"

Addison was on his feet again, a chiding smile on his bearded face, as if he were saying that *surely* Lowell knew better than even to *begin* posing such a question. Shaking his head in reprimand, he said, "Your Honor, is the district attorney asking whether Mr. Assanti saw this *particular* pistol on the night of July seventeenth . . ."

"My question . . ."

"Let him finish, please, Mr. Lowell."

"Thank you, or a pistol merely *like* this one," Addison said. "Because if we are discussing this *particular* gun, which the district attorney now . . ."

"We are discussing this particular gun," Lowell said, "but only as . . ."

"Then of course the question becomes of paramount importance."

"I am asking . . . if I have a chance to get the question out," Lowell said in a sly aside to the jury, "whether a pistol *like* this one was seen by Mr. Assanti . . ."

"Then, Your Honor . . ."

"Approach the bench, please."

The two attorneys stepped up to the bench. Di Pasco looked down at them.

"I don't like this kind of showboating," he said to Addison.

"Your Honor, surely . . ."

"Surely me not," Di Pasco said. "You heard Mr. Lowell's question as well as I did. Now if you're going to keep jumping up every three minutes with objections designed to confuse the jury . . ."

"Perhaps I myself was confused, Your Honor."

"Yes, perhaps you were."

"In which case, I apologize for taking up the Court's valuable time."

"Spare me," Di Pasco said, and rolled his eyes.

Addison went back to the defense table, a slight, small smile hidden in his beard. Lowell went back to the witness chair.

"Mr. Assanti," he said, "did the gun you saw on the night of July seventeenth *look* like this gun?"

"Yes, it did."

"Same size and shape . . ."

"Yes."

"Same sight and trigger guard . . ."

"Yes."

"Same muzzle . . ."

"Yes."

"Same grip . . ."

"Yes."

"In fact, a gun that looked *exactly* like this gun, isn't that so?"

"Yes."

"Your Honor," Lowell said, "I would like this pistol marked and moved into evidence subject to connection by a subsequent witness."

"So moved," Di Pasco said.

Lowell seemed mildly surprised that Addison hadn't objected. He hesitated a moment before asking his next question. Or perhaps that was only for dramatic effect.

"Mr. Assanti," he said, "can you please tell us which of the men was carrying a gun that looked like this one?"

"The one called Sonny."

"How do you know what he was called?"

"The other one called him Sonny."

"When was this?"

"When they were running by me."

"They came running out of the bakery shop . . ."

"Yes."

"And almost knocked over a man coming out of the liquor store . . ."

"Yes."

"By the way, would you recognize this man if you saw him again?"

"I think so, yes."

"And then they ran by you, is that it?"

"Yes."

"Tell me what you heard as they came running by."

"The other man . . . not Sonny, the one *with* him . . . yelled, 'Come on, Sonny, *move* it.'"

"Meaning what?"

"Objection."

"Sustained."

"Did you get a look at both of these men?"

"I did."

"The one carrying the gun?"

"Yes."

"You got a look at him?"

"Yes."

"Would you recognize him if you saw him again?"

"I would."

"I ask you to look around this courtroom and tell me if you see the man who was carrying a gun exactly like this one on the night of July seventeenth last year."

"I do."

"Would you point him out to us, please?"

"He's there. He's sitting right there."

"Is he sitting at the defense table?"

"Yes."

"Is he the black man sitting next to Mr. Addison?"

"He is."

"Let the record show that the witness is pointing to Mr. Samson Wilbur Cole, also known as . . ."

"Objection."

"His name is noted as such on the indictment, Your Honor. Samson Wilbur Cole, a/k/a Sonny Cole. Which, of course, means 'also known as Sonny Cole.' "

"Overruled. Proceed, Mr. Lowell."

"I have no further questions."

He didn't much enjoy being with her.

She didn't say a lot, she wasn't a talkative woman, but she did manage to express—with a rolling of the eyes, or a heavy sigh, or an almost imperceptible shake of the head—enormous impatience whenever he revealed his ignorance of the city. Hesitate before crossing a street or turning a corner, show the slightest puzzlement about which way was east or west or north or south, confuse the subway or bus lines, head off uptown when he'd meant to go downtown, and her face would flash the now-familiar look that told him he was just a hick from Second City, U.S.A., fumbling his way through M*E*T*R*O*P*O*L*I*S!

That Tuesday—this was already the eighth of January, the new year seemed to be flashing by—he told the doorman downstairs that he was here, and the doorman buzzed up and said, "Mr. Darrow's here, madam," and her voice came over the speaker, "I'll be right down, George." Didn't ask him to come up. Well, why should she? He was hired help.

He waited in the ornate marble lobby. Chatted with the doorman about the weather. The temperature outside this morning was twelve degrees Fahrenheit. He'd read *USA Today* while he was having breakfast in the luncheonette around the corner from his building. Twenty-nine in Chicago. It was like the Caribbean up there, but he was freezing to death down here. The doorman told him a warm front was headed this way. He'd believe it when he saw it. Meanwhile, the wind was howling outside. Nice and warm here in the lobby though. He hated having to go outside again. Maybe she'd be heading someplace warm.

"Good morning," she said.

Stepping out of the elevator, walking toward where he was sitting. A raccoon coat hung open over a yellow leotard, black tights, and black aerobic shoes. He said, "Good morning," his eyes studiously on her face and nowhere else. She pulled the coat closed, fastened it, took a woolen hat from one of the pockets, and yanked it down over her ears. Together, they stepped out into the cold.

She walked at a brisk pace, saying nothing, vapor pluming from her mouth. They were heading in what he now knew was a southerly direction, toward the wide avenue that skewered this part of the city east and west. Its proper name was Stemmler Avenue, clearly visible on the corner signposts, but the natives here called it The Stem, something he had discovered only yesterday, live and learn. He recognized the manicure shop he'd passed on the way to the apartment yesterday, recognized other little landmarks along the way, the laundromat, the deli, the Christ the Redeemer Billiards Parlor, the herbal shampoo store, the statue of the Civil War hero General Julian Pace sitting astride a rearing bronze horse on the center island. He was getting to know this city.

The aerobics studio was upstairs in a building that housed a Chinese restaurant on the ground floor. Emma led him up a long, narrow flight of stairs that terminated at a glass-paneled door lettered with the name of the place, Body Language, and decorated with its logo, a woman in silhouette leaping into the air with arms and legs impossibly spread-eagled. The door opened onto a room with a wooden bench on the wall to the right, a row of pegs on the wall to the left, a counter directly opposite the entrance door, with a doorless doorframe just beside it. A blonde wearing a pink aerobics outfit looked up as they came in.

"Hi, Mrs. Bowles," she said.

"Hello, Ginger," Emma said, and went directly to the row of wall pegs and hung the raccoon coat alongside a long down parka. She glanced at the clock hanging over the bench—it was now twenty minutes to nine—and then turned to Andrew. "It's over at ten, ten-fifteen," she said. "If you want to go for a cup of coffee or anything . . ."

"Too cold out there," he said. "I'll wait here, if that's okay."

"Sure," she said, and shrugged as if to say there was no accounting for the odd ways of bodyguards hired by a person's husband. "This is Mr. Darrow," she said to Ginger. "He'll be with me for the next little while."

"Nice to meet you," Ginger said, and didn't question why he'd be with her for the next little while. Andrew wondered how many men accompanied women to their aerobics classes. Emma disappeared through the doorless doorframe. He could hear her greeting other women inside there. He took off his coat, hung it on the rack alongside hers, and then went to sit on the bench. A small end table was cluttered with magazines like *Vogue, Mademoiselle, Vanity Fair*, and *Cosmopolitan*.

"I can get you some coffee, if you like," Ginger said.

"That'd be very nice, thank you," he said.

"How do you take it?"

"Light with one sugar, please."

"Do you mind instant?"

"Not at all."

"Back in a jiffy," she said, and smiled at him, and then walked out of sight somewhere behind the counter.

He was wearing a black cashmere jacket over worsted trousers in a small houndstooth check. Gray broadcloth shirt with white collar and cuffs. Simple silver cuff links. Matching silver tie tack fastening a wine-colored silk tie. Black loafers shined early this morning at the shoemaker's two blocks from the apartment he was renting. He knew he looked casually but elegantly dressed, but he also knew he'd have attracted little Ginger here even if he'd been wearing mud-covered jeans and a ketchup-stained T-shirt. He had that effect on women.

Well, most women.

"Here you go," she said. "I hope it's light enough."

Still smiling. Tightly packed into the pink leotard and tights. A beautiful body.

"Thank you," he said, and accepted the cup.

She did not immediately go back to the counter.

"What'd Mrs. Bowles say your name was?" she asked.

"Andrew," he said.

"I'm Ginger," she said, and extended her hand.

"Yes, I know."

He took her hand. The palm was fleshy, slightly damp. He wondered where else she might be damp.

"Nice to meet you," he said.

"Hi, Ginger!"

Through the doorway with the leaping-lady silhouette came a woman herself in silhouette and fairly leaping with energy. She bounded into the room, looked up at the wall clock, gave Andrew a cursory but appreciative glance, and then hung her coat on one of the wall pegs. She was tall and very slender, a woman in her late forties who'd obviously taken very good care of herself. Good, firm breasts in the molded leotard, long, shapely legs in the black tights. She glanced at Andrew again. She smiled at him, and he smiled back. She gave a slight, barely perceptible acknowledging nod and then went through the doorframe into the other room, where a tape now began playing.

He listened to the jolting music.

His eyes closed, he visualized them leaping around in there.

When at last they began flowing out through the doorframe again, he imagined each and every one of them in bed, knowing this was the way they would look after sex, out of breath, clothes sweaty and clinging, faces flushed, hair disarrayed, bodies pushed to the limit of exhaustion. They knew—or at least he *thought* they knew—that he was stripping them naked with his eyes. Emma seemed to sense this as well; she put on her coat with seemingly unnecessary haste.

"I hope you weren't bored," she said dryly.

"Plenty of magazines," he said, and they went down into the cold again.

They walked back to the Butler Street condo, and this time she asked him to come up. They rode the elevator in silence. They walked down the twelfth-floor corridor in silence. She unlocked both locks, the Medeco and the one below it.

"I'll only be a little while," she said, "make yourself comfortable." An airy hand gesture toward the living room. "There are magazines." Little note of sarcasm there? For having appreciated all those pretty aerobics ladies? He watched her as she went through a door into what he supposed was the master bedroom. The door whispered shut behind her. There was a click. She had locked it.

He went into the living room, sat on a stainless-steel tubular sofa with vanilla leather cushions and back, and picked up a magazine from the similarly tubed glass-topped coffee table. *Forbes*. Undoubtedly her husband's choice. The magazine under it was *Fortune*. And beneath that, *Business Week*. He wondered where all the women's magazines were. In the bedroom?

He looked at his watch.

Twenty to eleven.

He began reading *Fortune.*

Lots of rich people in this country.

He wondered how many of them paid income tax.

He was deeply absorbed in a story about corporate takeover when she came out of the bedroom. She was wearing a gray cable-stitched turtleneck sweater and snug tailored slacks. Black boots. A red beret tilted low on her forehead.

"Ready to go?" she asked, and took her mink coat from the hall closet.

It was ten minutes to eleven.

The doorman hailed a taxi for them. She told the driver she was going midtown, and gave him an address. To Andrew she explained, though it seemed to pain her to have to do so, that she was going to Gucci's to leave a handbag for repair.

"Have you got a Gucci in Chicago?" she asked.

"Oh, yes," he said, "on Michigan Avenue. I buy all my shoes there."

Proud of the way he dressed. Wanting her to know that he spent money on clothes. Took care in selecting his clothes. Bought his clothes at only the very best shops.

"Incidentally," he said, "I thought you might like to have my home number."

"Why?" she asked.

"Well, I can't be with you twenty-four hours a day, and if anything happens . . ."

"Once the police find Tilly, nothing will happen," she said.

"In the meantime, they haven't got him, have they?"

"No, but . . ."

"Then take my card," he said, and handed it to her. "I've written a number here on the back, it's where I'm staying while I'm in town. You can call me anytime you need me."

She looked at the card:

"Darrow Investigations," she said aloud.

"Yes."

"South Clark Street."

"Yes."

She turned the card over, studied the telephone number he'd scrawled in ink.

"Where is this?" she asked.

"All the way downtown. Near the Calm's Point Bridge."

"I used to live down there."

"Oh?"

"Long ago. Before I met Martin."

"What were you doing then?"

"Dreaming," she said, and fell silent for the rest of the trip downtown.

The police cars here in the center of the city were marked on their sides with the words MIDTOWN NORTH PCT. Andrew wondered where the Midtown *South* precinct started. Was there a dividing line? The stores lining the avenue had already taken down all the Christmas decorations, their windows were showing cruise wear. Hall Avenue was the name of the big shopping street here, it reminded him of The Miracle Mile in Chicago, except that it wasn't as wide. Everything here in this city seemed cramped and stingy. You didn't have the feeling of extravagant *space* you had in Chicago. Well, Chicago had been carved out of the prairie, and this place was an island, but even so, they could have made their avenues a bit wider. At *least* their avenues. He really hated this fucking city.

She spent about half an hour upstairs at Gucci, first waiting to see someone about the bag and then explaining what had happened to its clasp. The woman she spoke to was in her late forties, Andrew guessed, an attractive woman with jet-black hair pulled into a bun at the back of her head. She spoke with an accent Andrew found charming. He wondered what Rome was like. He was willing to bet they had wide avenues in Rome.

It was a little past twelve when they came out into the street again. The sidewalks were thronged with people on their lunch hour. That was another thing about this city. It always seemed so *crowded*. No wonder people's tempers were short.

"Shall we have some lunch?" Emma asked.

"About that time, isn't it?" he said.

She led him to a little French restaurant on one of the side streets. He didn't know exactly where he was, but he gathered this was a neighborhood with a lot of restaurants in it, most of them expensive from the looks of them. The *outside* looks, anyway. The canopies, the thick wooden entrance doors, some of them elaborately carved, the polished brass doorknobs. He won-' dered at once who'd be paying for lunch. He'd told her that his fee included expenses. Would they be going Dutch here? He certainly hoped she didn't expect him to pay for *her* lunch. In the Bad Investment Department, that would be an indisputable winner.

Emma ordered a glass of white wine. He ordered an Absolut on the rocks.

"I only drink the best," he said. "Cheers."

"Cheers," she said.

She sipped a little of the wine, and then put her glass down.

"Wine okay?" he asked.

"Fine," she said.

And fell silent again. He hated these silences she fell into.

The restaurant was tiny and intimate, small square tables with pristine white tablecloths, polished silver, sparkling stemware glasses on each table, a small one for the white wine, a large for the red, a yet-larger water goblet. People kept drifting in; the place was gradually filling up. There were good aromas in here. Andrew suddenly felt ravenously hungry. The headwaiter brought their menus and padded off. Andrew studied his.

"I'm going to need help," he said.

"Sure," she said.

He thought at first that she was going to translate for him, but instead she signaled to the headwaiter, who patiently recited the day's specials and then answered Andrew's specific questions about several items on the menu. He ended up ordering the grilled salmon *without* the mousseline sauce. She ordered the chicken special. The waiter asked him if he would care for another drink. He said he'd just have a glass of white wine, please.

"*Madame?*" the waiter asked.

Her glass was still three-quarters full. She covered it with her hand.

"I'm fine," she said. "Thank you."

And fell silent again.

What the hell was wrong with her?

"When *was* that?" he asked abruptly.

She looked up.

"When was *what?*"

"When you lived downtown. Near the bridge."

"Oh. When I was very young."

"How young?"

"Nineteen. A long time ago."

"Not so long ago," he said, and smiled.

"Long enough," she said.

"What were you doing back then?"

"I was in school," she said.

"Best time of my life," he said, and smiled again.

It was tough to get this woman to return a smile. Her thumb and forefinger kept working the stem of the wineglass. She was looking down into the glass again. No eye contact. The waiter brought Andrew's wine. He lifted it in a toast she did not see, and took a small swallow of it.

"Nice," he said.

"Yes," she said.

"Studying what?" he asked.

"What? Oh. I wanted to be an artist."

"Really?"

"A painter," she said. "I was studying at the Briley School of Art. Do you know where that is?"

"No."

"Well . . . downtown. Near the bridge."

"Were you any good?"

"I thought I was."

"But?"

"Things change." She looked up. "I met Martin."

"Uh-huh."

"And we fell in love. And we got married. And . . . "

"And?"

She shrugged and picked up her wineglass. She took another sip, but that was all. Put the glass right down on the table again. Began toying with the stem again. Big drinker, this lady.

"How'd you meet him?" he asked.

"In the park. There's this little park outside the school, I used to bring a sandwich to school and eat it in the park. And after lunch, when the weather was good, I'd sit there and sketch. . . . I was very serious about becoming an artist, you see. The war in Vietnam was over by then . . . "

. . . well, it had been over for several years by then, and most students were settling down and trying to prepare themselves for whatever the future might hold. Nobody was even sure there'd *be* a future; the kids used to sit around and talk about the big blast coming any day now. Telling Andrew about it now, Emma remembers that there seemed to be constant trouble all over the world, heads of state being murdered everywhere, countries getting invaded or overthrown, and all of this might have been completely unsettling to a nineteen-year-old girl—had it not been for her art.

Back then, Emma saw everything with a frame around it.

Her careful eye searched out the details of city life, and her quick pencil recorded them. When later she worked these sketches into charcoal drawings on canvas, enlarging them, expanding upon them in oils, giving them full-bodied life in riotous color, she felt like an essential part of this tremendously exciting thing that was happening here in the big, drafty room on the top floor of the school; the skylights spilling northern light, the kids in paint-smeared smocks standing behind their easels, touching brushes to pallet and canvas, the smell of turpentine and linseed oil, the serious looks on all the faces; Mr. Grayson standing with his hands on his hips, a stub of a cigar clenched between his teeth, squinting at the canvas, Nice, Emma, very nice, oh Jesus, it was so beautiful. Vibrating with energy and talent and ambition, she took images from this city and made them her own and gave them back again enriched.

That day in the park outside the school . . . that bright spring day . . . she remembers there was a man playing an accordion . . . yes . . . and a bird . . . a green-and-yellow parrot . . . and the parrot would dip his beak into this tray of cards and take out one of the cards, and there would be a fortune printed on it. She made a series of quick sketches—the man playing his organ, the parrot dipping into the tray, the grinning faces of the boys and girls in the crowd—and was working on several more careful studies of the parrot's claws gripping the perch, and the parrot's bright, intelligent eyes . . . when . . .

"That's very good," he said.

Startled, she looked up.

The man standing there looking over her shoulder was perhaps five or six years older than she was, a tall, slender man with dark hair and brown eyes, his pleasant mouth turned up in a smile. He was wearing a dark pinstriped business suit with a white button-down collar shirt, and a silk rep tie.

"Really, it's quite good," he said.

"Thank you," she said.

He sat beside her on the bench. Crossed his long legs. Looked over at the accordian player and then at the parrot. Looked down at her sketch pad and the busily working pencil.

"Do you go to school here?" he asked.

"Yes," she said.

He looked up at the building as if discovering it for the first time.

"The Briley School of Art, hm?" he said.

"Yes," she said. Eyes on the parrot's eyes. Those difficult folds around the eyes.

"I'm Martin Bowles," he said.

"Hello, Martin," she said. "Let me get this, okay?"

He watched her silently. Pencil shading in those folds around the eyes. Bright, piercing parrot eyes.

"Very nice," he said.

"Shhhh," she said.

And kept working. When at last she turned to him, he said, "All done?"

"For now," she said. "I have to go back in."

"Let's go for a walk instead."

"No," she said, "I can't."

She closed the pad, rose from the bench. Holding the pad against her breasts, she said, "I'm Emma Darby," and smiled and walked back into the school.

"That's how we met," she told Andrew now. "He was the handsomest man I'd ever seen in my life."

"Mr. Assanti," Addison said, leaning into him affably, like a department-store Santa Claus wanting to know what a terrified kid would like for Christmas, "you've testified that you walked Miss Franceschi home from the movies . . ."

"Yes."

". . . and got to her house at about a quarter to nine, ten to nine, isn't that what you said?"

"Yes."

"And you've also testified that you left her at about nine-twenty . . ."

"Yes."

". . . which is how you happened to be in the vicinity of the A & L Bakery at or around nine-thirty . . . I believe you said it was nine-thirty, give or take a few minutes, please correct me if I'm wrong."

"No, that's what I said."

"Thank you. Now, Mr. Assanti, what were you doing between a quarter to nine, when you arrived at Miss Franceschi's house, and nine-twenty, when you left her? Isn't that what you said? Nine-twenty?"

"Yes. It only took me ten minutes or so to . . ."

"Yes, so what were you doing between a quarter to nine and nine-twenty, can you tell me?"

"We were in Frankie's hallway."

"Doing what?"

Assanti looked at the judge.

"Answer the question," Di Pasco said.

"We were necking."

There was mild laughter in the courtroom. Di Pasco glared out over his bench. The laughter ceased.

"You were necking for thirty-five minutes, is that right?" Addison asked, looking amazed.

"Yes."

"Mr. Assanti, do you remember talking to Detectives Randall Wade and Charles Bent on the night of July twenty-fourth last year?"

"I do."

"Do you remember telling them that as you walked home, all you could think of was Frankie?"

"Yes, I think that's what I told them."

"Well, did you, or didn't you?"

"I did."

"In fact, didn't you tell them you felt sort of dizzy after being with Frankie?"

"I may have said that, yes."

"Well, those are your exact words, aren't they?" Addison asked, and walked to the defense table and picked up a stapled sheaf of papers. "Here, I'll refresh your memory."

"What is that?" Di Pasco asked.

"The Detective Division report written and filed by Detective Randall Wade of the Forty-fifth Detective Squad, recounting the conversation with the witness on the night of July twenty-fourth last year."

"Proceed."

"Now, Mr. Assanti, isn't this what you said? 'I guess I was feeling sort of dizzy after being with Frankie all that time. I was walking along wiping her lipstick from my mouth . . .' "

"Well, that's okay, you don't have to . . ."

"I'd like to go on, if I may. 'Wiping her lipstick from my mouth and thinking about what happened in her hallway.' Isn't that what you told Detectives Wade and Bent?"

"Yes."

"And isn't that when you heard what at first you thought were backfires? While you were wiping her lipstick from your mouth and thinking about what had happened in her hallway?"

"Yes."

"What made you decide they weren't backfires?"

"There were no cars on the street."

"Ah. In your delirious state, you were able . . ."

"Objection. He's characterizing the witness's . . ."

"Sustained."

"Anyway, I wasn't delirious," Assanti said.

"You told the detectives you felt dizzy. That is the exact word you used. Dizzy."

"I guess I was being poetic."

"Ah. A poet. How nice."

"Objection. Counsel is harassing . . ."

"Sustained."

"Anyway, I was in love with Frankie at the time," Assanti said.

"But you're no longer in love with her."

"No, I'm not."

"And now, in your more stable, nonpoetic condition . . ."

"Objection, Your Honor."

"Sustained. *Really*, Mr. Addison."

"Mr. Assanti . . . would you here and now *still* say you were dizzy on Frankie when you left her that night?"

"Well . . . yes."

"But not so dizzy that you couldn't distinguish gunshots from backfires . . ."

"They were gunshots."

"You realized later."

"Yes."

"Because there were no cars on the street."

"Yes."

"*Not* because you were able to distinguish them as gunshots, but only because they couldn't have been backfires since there were no cars on the street."

"Well, yes, I figured . . ."

"Actually, it was a sort of reasoning process, wasn't it?"

"Yes, I suppose . . ."

"Even though your reason, at the time, was somewhat distorted, wasn't it? You were in love with Frankie, your head was full of Frankie, you were dizzy with thoughts of Frankie, wiping her lipstick from your face, remembering what you'd done together in her hallway. And in this condition, you saw two black men coming out of the bakery . . . are you sure they were black?"

"Positive."

"And you're sure there were two of them?"

"Yes."

"That's what you told Detectives Randall and Wade a week *after* the incident, isn't it? That you saw two black men coming out of that bakery, isn't that so?"

"Yes."

"But on the *night* of the incident . . . on July seventeenth . . . just minutes after you'd witnessed the incident, you told Doris Franceschi that you saw some guy running out of the bakery shop with a gun in his hand. Isn't that what you said?"

"I may have said that, I'm not sure."

"Well, weren't those your exact words? Some guy with a gun?"

"Maybe, but what I meant was . . ."

"He's answered the question, Your Honor."

"Let him explain."

"I meant I saw two guys but only one of them had a gun."

"I see. But that's not what you actually *said* on the night of July seventeenth, is it?"

"No."

"That is what you're saying *now*, isn't it?"

"Yes."

"With complete confidence."

"Yes."

"And you are also able to say—now, with complete confidence—that you saw Samson Wilbur Cole that night, and that he had a nine-millimeter semiautomatic assault weapon in his hand."

"Yes."

"Mr. Assanti, do you recall being shown some photographs by Detective Randall Wade on the twenty-fifth of July last year?"

"I do."

"How many photographs were you shown?"

"I don't remember. There were a lot of them."

"Well, by a lot of them . . . would you say twenty?"

"More than twenty."

"Well . . . fifty?"

"More than that."

"A hundred?" Addison said.

"No, not that many."

"Somewhere between fifty and a hundred then?"

"Yes."

"Does seventy-two sound like it might be a correct number?"

"Yes, around that."

"Were you informed that these were mug shots of known criminals?"

"Yes."

"Were you told that all of these known criminals had the nickname Sonny?"

"Yes."

"What were you looking for, Mr. Assanti?"

"I was trying to pick out the man I saw running out of the bakery shop."

"On July seventeenth last year?"

"Yes."

"Were you successful in picking him out?"

"No."

"You looked at upward of seventy photographs of known criminals named Sonny, but you could not find one who even *faintly* resembled . . ."

"Objection."

"Sustained."

"Did you find a single photograph of anyone who resembled the man named Sonny, whom you say you saw running out of the bakery shop?"

"No, I didn't."

"*Seventy* some-odd photographs!"

"Yes."

"But now—five, almost six months after the event—you can look across the courtroom and point a finger at the defendant sitting there, and say without question that he is one of the men you saw running from that bakery with a gun in his hand."

"That's right, yes."

"No further questions."

Lowell rose from the prosecutor's table, consulted some notes in his hand, and walked toward the witness chair.

"Mr. Assanti," he said, "when you were shown those photographs last July, did Detectives Wade and Bent tell you what you were looking at?"

"Yes, they did."

"What were you looking at?"

"Pictures of people convicted of felonies in this city."

"And you say you could not find Mr. Cole's photograph among those that were shown to you, is that correct?"

"That's correct."

"His photograph was not among those of known felony offenders in this city."

"It was not."

"Known offenders whose nickname was Sonny."

"Yes, sir."

"Not among those."

"No, sir."

"Were you shown pictures of anyone who may have committed a felony in California, for ex . . ."

"Objection!" Addison shouted. "May we please approach the bench?"

"Come on up," Di Pasco said.

The attorneys moved to the bench.

"Your Honor," Addison said, "at this time, I would like to move for a mistrial."

"Denied," Di Pasco said.

"Your Honor, the assistant district attorney's question implies that Mr. Cole has been convicted of felonies elsewhere . . . "

"Yes, I know. And *you* know that in the pretrial *Sandoval* application . . ."

"Yes, Your Honor, but . . ."

". . . I ruled that I'd allow questions about the defendant's prior murder conviction, based on your representation that Cole would testify and put his credibility into issue. Nothing has changed my mind about that. Moreover, you opened the door by bringing in the photographs in the first place. Resume your questioning, Mr. Lowell.''

Lowell went back to the witness stand.

''Mr. Assanti,'' he said, ''*were* you shown photographs of known felony offenders in California?''

''Not to my knowledge.''

''You were only shown pictures of felony offenders in this city.''

''Yes.''

''And Sonny Cole's picture was not among them.''

''It was not.''

''Thank you, no further questions.''

''I should caution the jury at this time,'' Di Pasco said, ''against accepting questions as *evidence*. Questions are *not* evidence. Only *answers* are evidence. You must not read anything into questions, you must accept them solely as vehicles for eliciting responses.''

At the defense table, Addison smiled.

5.

The Property Clerk's Office occupied the entire basement of the new Headquarters Building on High Street downtown. This was a vast improvement over the cubbyhole that until recent years had served as a repository for recovered stolen goods or confiscated narcotics or clothing and jewelry removed from a victim or, in many instances, huge quantities of cash seized as evidence in an arrest. But despite its size and its enlarged staff—six police clerks where there used to be only two—the drafty basement room was crammed to overflowing, and the clerks seemed adrift on an ocean of flotsam and jetsam.

The filing system was now computerized, and so it was a relatively simple matter to punch up TILLY, ROGER TURNER and pull out the list of goods that had been bagged in his name at the morgue. It was quite another thing, however, to *find* all these things. The storage arrangement seemed to make sense when the clerk explained it to them . . .

"Clothes are on the open shelves, jewelry and such in the locked mesh cages, cash in the steel, double-key lock boxes, like a bank has . . ."

. . . but once he'd unlocked the grilled inner door and let them into that vast warehouse, it became almost immediately clear that locating Tilly's worldly goods would be akin to zeroing in on *Rosebud* deep in the caverns of Xanadu.

"There's a system, believe me," the clerk kept telling them.

The name on his little plastic tag was J. DI LUCA. He also

kept telling them he wasn't too familiar with the system because he was just filling in for one of the regulars who was out sick. Where he normally worked was in the Identification Section upstairs. Up there, it was easy to find things because it was all paperwork. Even the fingerprints were paperwork. Down here in the basement, it was *things,* you follow? All these fuckin *things.*

Meyer had been at the crime scene almost all day, canvassing tenants and shopkeepers, trying to get a lead on what anyone might have seen or heard on the day of Tilly's murder. Carella had come here directly from the courthouse, leaving just as Lowell was beginning his recross. It was now almost four o'clock, and both men were bone-weary, but they were nonetheless eager to see all the miscellaneous papers and cards found in Tilly's wallet. His shoes and socks, his Jockey shorts, they could do without. Ditto the other articles of clothing and jewelry. But those miscellaneous papers and cards sounded like something they should look at.

"How does this work?" Meyer asked. "Do you take the money out of the wallet and put it in one of the lock boxes? Or do you . . . ?"

"You're askin' *me*?" the clerk said. "I just started here this morning. And I'll be glad to get out of here, I'm tellin' you."

" 'Cause what we'd like to take a look at," Carella said, "is the wallet."

"But not the cash, huh?"

"No, we're not particularly interested in the cash."

"They got lock boxes down here with millions of dollars in cash in them, would you believe it?"

"I believe it," Carella said.

"From dope raids," Di Luca said. "Somebody wants to get smart, he should hold up this joint, he'd get more than he would in a bank heist."

"It's been done," Meyer said.

"Everything's been done," Di Luca said sadly. "Let me see

if I can find somebody knows what the fuck is goin' on here.''

He came back some five minutes later with another clerk in blue uniform. This one knew the system. He told them he'd been working for the Property Clerk's Office for fifteen years, and, if they wanted to know, he liked the old one better than this one, however crowded and cramped it might have been. His name tag read: R. BALDINI.

"They call me The Great Baldini," he said, " 'cause I'm the only one in this office can *find* anything. So what is it you're interested in? The man's billfold?"

"Actually, the papers that were in it," Carella said.

"What we do," Baldini said, "there are thieves in the Police Department, I guess you know that. Plenty of them."

"You better believe it," Di Luca said.

"So what we do, we got the mesh cages for jewelry and such, and the lock boxes for cash. Because of all the sticky fingers we get down here. But usually, we don't separate cash that's in a person's wallet or handbag. Because that's like a package, you understand? We don't break up the package."

"Uh-huh," Carella said.

"So what we have to do is go back to the computer again, and get the index number for this guy's shit. It's the index number we follow all the way through. It's like the Dewey Decimal System, you familiar with the Dewey Decimal System?"

"No," Carella said.

"No," Meyer said.

"No," Di Luca said.

"I used to be a lib'arian," Baldini said. "What we used was the Dewey Decimal System. It works the same here, only we got what we call these index numbers. All the guy's shit will be under the same index number. Whether it's clothes, jewelry, money, whatever, it'll have the same index number in different locations here. You understand what I'm saying?"

"No," Di Luca said.

"You must do great up there in the I.S.," Baldini said dryly, and led them back to the computer again. Once again, they punched up TILLY, ROGER TURNER. But this time Baldini showed them a letter-and-number sequence somewhat to the right of and slightly above the name: RLD 34–21–679.

"I'll be damned," Di Luca said.

Baldini led them back through the rows and rows of open shelves, indicating the index numbers that defined each folded pile of clothing, showing them similar identifying numbers on the locked mesh cages with their little gray plastic trays of wristwatches and wallets, necklaces and rings, bracelets and earrings, all separately identified inside the cages, stopping at last before a cage marked RLD 34–21 and on a separate line below that 650–680. From a ring hanging on his belt, Baldini found the key he wanted, and unlocked the cage.

"It may be in here," he said, "or it may be in one of the boxes. Depends how much money was in the wallet."

"According to the list, four hundred and thirty-five bucks," Meyer said.

"Usually, we'll put five-hundred or over in the boxes."

In a gray plastic tray tagged with the sequence RLD 34–21– 679, they found Tilly's watch, ring, tie tack, and pen, an open package of Marlboro cigarettes, a matchbook, a plastic bag with three subway tokens, two quarters, four dimes, one nickel, and three pennies in it, an open package of Wrigley Spearmint chewing gum, *and* a brown leather wallet.

"Okay to look through the wallet?" Carella asked.

"Take the whole tray with you, if you like," Baldini said. "There's a room back there you can sit in, make yourself comfortable. No smoking, please. When you're done, take the tray back to the counter, and we'll check the inventory against the computer list."

"Thanks," Carella said.

They carried the tray to the door Baldini had indicated, and went into a windowless room behind it. There was a long wooden table with a dozen or more wooden chairs around it and a row of cheerless fluorescent lights above it. Two men in suits were sitting at the far end of the table, poring over the contents of another gray plastic tray. Carella recognized one of them as a detective from the Tenth. He nodded hello, and then he and Meyer took off their coats, draped them over one of the chairs, and sat down to look through Tilly's wallet.

All of the cash was still there. Just so that no one could later accuse them of dipping into the cookie jar, they counted out the bills and made a list of the serial numbers on them. Four hundred and thirty-five dollars exactly, in hundreds, fifties, twenties, tens, and singles. In this city, that seemed like a lot of cash to be carrying around.

His chauffeur's license was made out to Roger Turner Tilly and it gave his date of birth as 10/15 . . .

"Birthdate of great men," Carella said, but did not amplify.

. . . and the license expiration date on the same day and month three years from now. They calculated that Tilly would have been only twenty-seven years old when he was shot and killed. He had given his address as 178 St. Paul's Avenue in Isola, smack in the heart of *L'Infierno*, the city's most densely populated Hispanic sector. The blue field behind his photograph indicated to any policeman that he was licensed to drive a motor vehicle only while wearing corrective lenses. The inventory list of his possessions had not included eyeglasses, but perhaps he'd been wearing contacts.

The miscellaneous papers and cards included a laminated card from a video rental store called Videodrome, bearing the serial number MRL 06732 and the name Roger Tilly hand-lettered in blue ink; a slip of paper with the name *Arthur* written on it, and below that *64 Charlesgate East, Boston 02215*, and below that *Sweater—Large, Shirt 16–32, Belt 32*; and similar little scraps of paper listing addresses and sizes for another male named Frank and two females respectively named Paquita and Gerry. All of the little notes were written in the same bold hand, presumably Tilly's. There was also a booklet of first-class postage stamps and a card that gave the address and telephone number of a gypsy cab company.

There was only one other business card in the wallet.

For an investment firm called Laub, Kramer, Steele and Worth at 3301 Steinway Street.

In the lower right-hand corner of the card was the name *Martin Bowles*.

There was the certain knowledge that death had been to this place.

The police padlock on the door, yes, and the yellow plastic crime-scene tapes, and the black-and-white sign tacked to the wall, advising that the area was closed to all but Police Department personnel, all these, yes. But more.

They unlocked the door, and Meyer flicked the light switch on the wall to the right, and the two men went down the steep staircase into the basement where a naked light bulb dangled at the bottom of the steps, everything dark beyond its circle of illumination. Now there was the lingering chilling sense that death had passed this way and left behind its sullen shadow.

They were experienced detectives, these two, they knew the feel of a place where death had visited, they had shared together on far too many occasions the exact feeling they shared now. They stood in the circle of light like two stunned vaudeville performers spotlighted from the balcony, forgetting the lines to their comic routine, forgetting the steps to their soft-shoe dance. Coats open, mufflers hanging loose, breaths pluming on the cellar's dank air, they peered into the darkness waiting for a cue, stared into the gloom that death had left behind, one trying to see what was to the left, the other studying the grayish void to the right—was there another light switch?

Neither of them said a word.

Meyer fanned out to the right, feeling along the wall for a switch. Carella was already moving to the left, groping along

the wall there. Sudden light spilled into the basement room behind him. He turned. Meyer had found a wall switch. And now,
with the room lighted somewhat better than it had been, Carella
found yet another switch in the area he was searching, and he
snapped the toggle and more light flooded the room, a stage
coming to life, the performers on it moving toward each other
now to survey what their efforts had revealed.

Doors stretched along the entire wall that faced the stairs.
Padlocks on all of the doors. Each door marked with an apartment
number. 01 for the super on the ground-level floor, then 11, 12,
and 13, for the first floor, on up to the fifth floor, three apartments
on each floor for a total of sixteen in the building, sixteen doors
locked with padlocks, sixteen narrow storage cubicles on a wall
some sixty-five or seventy feet wide. The width of the building,
more or less.

The padlocks hung open on the hasp eyes; this was the scene
of a crime, and no one needed a court order to search for a
weapon here; a man had been killed, an investigation was under
way. The Crime Scene Unit had already been through the place
with a fine-tooth comb. Now it was the turn of the detectives
handling the case.

In this city, any murder case normally belonged to the detective team catching the squeal. Homicide Division consulted
and supervised, but that was it. The two men rummaging through
this musty, damp, death-reeking basement should have been
Detective/Second Grade Jasper Loop and his partner, Fat Ollie
Weeks. Instead, operating on the First Man Up rule—sometimes
known as the First Man Up Your *Ass* rule, because of the many
inequities it fostered—Meyer and Carella were the lucky cops
sifting through all this dusty shit in these crowded little storage
cubicles. Looking for whatever had put the bullet hole in Roger
Tilly's head.

They found bicycles and lamps and folding beach chairs and
an old television set and a clown's costume and a floor fan and
a thirty-set edition of the *Encyclopaedia Britannica* and a deflated

inflatable rubber doll with a blonde wig and stacks of old *Life* magazines corded together and a pay telephone with a coin box that had come from God knew which corner phone booth and rubber tires and tools and a winepress and ironing boards and a folding bridge table and chairs and all the stored and forgotten flotsam and jetsam of crowded urban living, stacked here out of sight and out of mind, most of it covered with dust, some of it covered with mildew. They did not find anything that even remotely resembled a pistol.

There was an oil burner at the far end of the basement, humming into the stillness of the afternoon, clicking on and off as the thermostat dictated, filling the basement with a sound death would have denied it if possible. Death was everywhere here. From the bloodstain where Roger Tilly had been lowered to the gray and cracking concrete floor . . . to the rope indentations in the asbestos-covered pipe from which his murderer had hanged him . . . to the dark silences in corners and coves.

"I wonder why," Meyer said.

"Why what?"

"Why he bothered hanging him from the ceiling. He had to know we'd find the head wound."

"*If* it was a man."

"Had to be a pretty strong woman to hoist him all the way up there," Meyer said, and looked up at the overhead pipes running close to the ceiling.

"Lots of strong women in this city," Carella said.

"Oh, sure. But even so . . . why bother? Dead is dead, no?"

"Dead is dead, all right."

Meyer kept looking up at the asbestos-covered pipe.

"Maybe he wanted us to think it was a crazy," he said at last. "Shoot Tilly in the back of the head and then string him up. Make us think a crazy did it."

"Maybe it *was* a crazy," Carella said.

"Maybe."

Both men fell silent again.

"I wonder if the killer followed him down here," Carella said.

"He also could've been waiting down here," Meyer said.

"Could've been somebody he knew, in fact."

"Some kind of meeting down here."

"Some kind of prearranged meeting."

"Why would anyone meet in the goddamn basement?"

"Well, up here . . ."

"Dope," Meyer said.

"Could be."

They were both thinking it could have been dope *anywhere* in this city, not only up here. A man got killed, you automatically thought dope. That was the saddest fact of life in America these days.

"Think he maybe had dope stashed in one of those cubbies?" Meyer said.

"Maybe."

"Comes down here to visit his dope."

"Unlocks the cubby, makes sure it's still there, guy comes up behind him, nails one into his skull."

"Runs off with the dope."

"Could be."

"It's a scenario, that's for sure."

"Didn't take anything else from him, though. More gold on him than there is in Fort Knox. Killer left all that behind."

"Too many questions, Steve."

"Not enough answers."

There was an old cast-iron coal-burning furnace in one corner of the basement, obviously unused for some time now. Its main steam pipe had been disconnected at the first elbow, the pipe running up out of the boiler and ending abruptly in midair. On the other side of the boiler, the water-return pipe had been similarly disconnected. It ran out horizontally for some two-and-a-half feet, and then right-angled upward to the air vent, where it, too, abruptly ended. There was a coal bin to the left of the furnace, chunks of shiny coal still piled loosely against its rear wooden wall. An overhead light bulb illuminated a shovel still thrust into the coal at an angle. They might not have opened the furnace door if Carella hadn't caught the faintest tint of red on the handle that hung from it. Just a wink of red. But enough to make him think . . .

"Blood," he said.

Meyer turned from where he was peering into the coal bin, walked over to where Carella was examining the handle, and bent to look at it.

"Could be," he said.

Carella went into the bin, picked up the shovel, and carried it back to the furnace. Using the flat blade, he lifted the handle on the heavy iron door. They still couldn't see anything inside there. Meyer went rummaging in one of the storage cubbies and came back with a flashlight.

That was when they found what looked like a .32-caliber revolver.

The bar at five o'clock that Tuesday afternoon was relatively empty, but then again it wasn't near any of the big office buildings that were letting out around this time. Andrew had been tracking around with Emma Bowles all day long, and he was glad to be rid of her now. Have a few drinks, get himself a good steak dinner, forget the damn job Bowles had given him. He was lifting his glass to the bartender to signal that he wanted a refill when the girl sitting on his right turned to him and said, "Hi, I'm Daisy."

He thought at once he would like to pluck this daisy. Nineteen, twenty years old, brownish-black hair, blue eyes, a cute little nose, a mouth made for sin. She was wearing a white long-sleeved silk blouse, high-heeled black pumps, and a black mini riding up to Alaska. Her legs were crossed. She kept jiggling her right foot.

"I'm Andrew," he said, and took her extended hand.

He figured her for a hooker.

Pretty young girl sitting at a bar, opens a conversation with "Hi, I'm Daisy," that's a hooker, right?

She told him she worked for the telephone company. He believed her. He could imagine her with a headset on, jiggling that right foot, how may I help you, please? He asked her why none of the pay phones in this city worked. The other day, he had to try eight phone booths before he found one with a working telephone. Two of the booths had coin boxes but no telephones. The telephone receivers were simply missing, cut from their connecting wires. The only thing left was a sort of shiny metallic cable with a spray of narrow, colored wires blooming from its end. No telephone receiver. The next two booths had receivers, but the coin slots were plugged, and you couldn't insert your quarter. The last four were simply dead. You lifted the receiver from the hook and you put in your quarter, and you got nothing but dead air, and when you hung up, the coin box swallowed your quarter. He wasted a dollar trying to make a call, without getting so much as a beep.

"It's terrible, I know," Daisy said.

"And there are no phone books in these booths."

"They tear them up, I know," Daisy said.

"Who tears them up?"

"Who knows? Vandals."

"Why would they tear up phone books?"

"Who knows?" she said. "Why would they spray graffiti on walls? It's the breakdown of civilization."

She kept jiggling her foot. He felt a sudden urge to slide his hand up under that short mini, break down a little civilization on his own.

"Do you like New Year's Eve?" she asked, and without waiting for an answer started telling him how much she hated New Year's Eve because it was always such a big disappointment. Nineteen, twenty years old, Andrew figured she'd had just *worlds* of experience with disappointing New Year's Eves. She told him she'd stayed home this past New Year's Eve, watched it all happening on television. She was in bed by twelve-thirty, she told him.

"Alone," she added, and rolled her blue eyes.

She was drinking a Campari with soda, something Andrew had never tasted. It looked like cherry soda.

"I've done everything a person can possibly do on New Year's Eve," she said, "and it's always . . ."

"How old did you say you were?"

"I didn't," she said. "But I'm twenty-four."

"Uh-huh," he said.

"How old are you?"

"*Thirty*-four."

"I like older men," she said.

Older men, he thought.

"Also, I'm partial to blond men."

"Lucky me," he said.

"Yes, with cat's-eyes," she said, and smiled. She had a nice wide smile. Good teeth, extravagant, brightly painted mouth. "*Anyway*," she said, "as I was saying, I've gone to small parties and big parties, and I've stayed home and had quiet candlelit dinners for two, and I've gone out to fancy restaurants and had dinner with three other couples, and I've gone to bed alone, and I've also gone to bed together with someone, and it's always the same, it's always a bore, New Year's Eve is really a fucking bore."

He wondered if she'd had one too many Camparis with soda.

"What do *you* do?" she asked.

"Well, this year I went to bed early, too," he said.

"No, I don't mean on New Year's Eve. I mean what do you *do*?"

"Oh, for a *living*," he said. "I'm a private investigator."

"Really?" Daisy said. "I thought that was only in books and movies."

"In real life, too," he said, and smiled.

"Well, well," she said, and looked him over. Jiggling her foot. He leaned in closer. He touched her knee only briefly, as if to emphasize what he was about to say, and then casually removed his hand, put it on the bartop, rested it there alongside his second Absolut martini on the rocks, couple of olives, please. She looked at his hand, as if wondering why it was no longer on her knee.

"I've been working a case uptown," he said. "Near Smoke Rise. Are you familiar with the neighborhood?"

Only neighborhood he himself was vaguely familiar with, since it was up there that Emma Bowles lived. Well, he knew *this* neighborhood, too, more or less. One day, he'd have to really *learn* this city. It was frustrating not knowing a place.

"Where's that?" Daisy asked. "The Butler Street stop?"

"You've got it."

"The G train, right?"

"Yes."

"I know a girl who lives up there. She works for the telephone company, too. You have very nice hands, did you know that?"

"Well, no, I never noticed," he said, and held up both hands as if just discovering them on his wrists, and turned them this way and that under the soft light flooding the bar.

"Nice long fingers," she said. "And you take good care of your nails, I can see that."

"Well, thank you," he said, and pulled back his hands as if embarrassed. Actually, he'd been told before that he had good hands. Beautiful hands, in fact. He'd once passed himself off as a concert pianist. This job he had in Seattle. Gained access to an impresario's office by claiming he was a concert pianist.

"So what's it like being a private eye?" Daisy asked.

"Same as any other job," he said, and put his hand on her knee again, and left it there this time. She gave no indication that she knew it was there. But neither did she ask him to take it away.

"I wish we had a private police force in this city," Daisy said, " 'stead of what we've got now. I called the police the other day, it took them three hours to get there. I'm not complaining, you understand, but when a girl calls to say there's somebody outside her door yelling obscenities at her, you'd think the police could get there a little faster than three *hours*. You should hear some of the things he was saying. You must know cops, aren't they supposed to respond, whatever you call it, to something like that?"

"Oh, sure," he said.

"A girl calls 9–1–1 to tell them somebody's outside her door yelling all kinds of filth at her, isn't that something they should check on right away? Instead they come three hours later. Long after he was gone."

"They sometimes figure that's exactly what'll happen," he said.

"What do you mean?"

"That he'll get tired and go away."

"But suppose he hadn't? I mean, suppose he'd broken down the door or something? I mean, you should have *heard* the things he was saying."

"What sort of things?"

"Well, all the things he wanted to *do* to me. It was like getting an obscene phone call right through your front *door*!" she said, and burst out laughing.

He laughed with her.

His hand was still on her knee.

He squeezed her knee.

"Speaking of obscene phone calls," she said, raising her eyebrows, "I guess you know that's pretty exciting."

"What is?" he asked.

"Your hand on my knee that way. You have very nice hands," she said.

"Thank you," he said, and moved his hand higher on her leg, off the knee, up toward the hem of the skirt where it rode high on her thighs. She covered his hand with her own, stopping its upward glide. "You have very smooth hands," she said. Moving her hand on his. Touching his hand. Exploring his hand. "Are you married or anything?" she asked.

"No."

"I didn't see a ring, but you never know."

"I'm not married," he said. "How about you?"

"Don't be ridiculous," she said, and took her hand from his and reached for her drink. He watched her drinking. Eyes closed, face lifted, the long, clean sweep of her throat.

"What's so ridiculous about that?" he said. "Pretty girl like you . . ."

"Oh sure."

"You are, you know."

"Sure, sure."

"I wouldn't say so if I . . ."

"My mouth is too big."

"No, it's a beautiful mouth," he said, and slid his hand higher on her thigh.

"People say I look like Carly Simon," she said, and made no move to stop his hand.

"You have her mouth, that's for sure."

"Yes, that's what I meant."

"Exactly her mouth," he said.

"Mmm," she said.

He was working her leg now. Hand very high on her leg, the warm, soft, slightly moist feel of her flesh under the nylon high on her thigh.

"I don't plan to get married for a while yet," she said.

Looking into her drink. Ignoring what his hand was doing under her skirt.

"You know . . ." she said.

"Yes?"

"I don't normally let men get this familiar with me."

"If you want me to stop . . ."

"In a public place," she said. "I mean, I just don't."

Their eyes met.

"I live right around the corner," he said.

She didn't say anything for what seemed a very long time. Then she said, "You're a very attractive man, you know."

"Thank you."

"Very," she said. Her eyes studying his face. He waited.

"Why don't we just go to a movie or something?" she said.

"If you like."

"No, what I'd like . . . never mind."

"Tell me what you'd like," he said.

"I'd sound like that guy yelling in the hallway."

"Tell me what he said."

His voice a whisper. His hand under her skirt.

"I'll tell you later," she whispered. "Maybe."

"Tell me now."

"What do you think he said?"

"He probably said he wanted to kiss that Carly Simon mouth of yours."

"He said he wanted to do *something* to it, that's for sure."

"What did he want to do to it?"

"What do you think he wanted to do to it?"

"Why don't we go up to my apartment?"

"Why should we?"

"Too public here."

"Doesn't seem to be hampering you any."

"I don't want to get arrested," he said, and smiled.

"Do they arrest private eyes?"

"All the time," he said.

Especially if you've got your hand this high up a woman's skirt, he thought. Bust you for molestation or disorderly conduct or trying to find a trade route to China.

"Are you carrying a gun?" she asked.

"No," he said.

"Do you have one?"

"Yes."

"Where?"

"In the apartment. Want to come see it?"

"I've never seen a gun," she said.

"Right around the corner," he said.

She looked at him.

"You really want to do this, huh?" she said.

"Yes, I think it might be nice," he said.

"Nice," she repeated, nodding.

"Yes."

"I guess it would be."

"But that's up to you."

"Oh sure, that's up to me."

"It is."

"We know each other ten minutes . . ."

"Longer than that."

"And you've got me all . . ."

She let the sentence trail. She shook her head. She picked up her glass again, drained it, took an ice cube in her mouth, sucked on it, let it fall back into the glass.

"You do this a lot, don't you?" she said.

"Do what?"

"Get women all . . ." She shook her head again, and then lifted the glass to her lips and tilted another ice cube into her mouth. Rolled it around inside her mouth again. Let it drop into the glass again. "How do I know you haven't got something I wouldn't want to catch?" she asked.

"I haven't got anything."

"How do I know?"

"I tested negative."

"So did I," she said.

Still looking at him, studying him. Jiggling her foot. Nodding. Thinking it over. Eyes locked with his. Nodding.

"Incidentally," she said, "I'm not sure I can stand much more of this."

"Shall I stop?"

"It's getting sort of excruciating, if you know what I mean."

"Mm-hm."

Smiling at her. Working her.

"I mean . . . did you see that movie *Harry and Sally*?"

"*When Harry Met Sally*," he said.

Correcting her. Smiling. Working her steadily.

"Remember that scene in the restaurant?" she asked.

"Yes?"

"What she did in the restaurant?"

"Yes?"

"Well, either you quit what you're doing . . ."

"She was faking," he said.

"*I* won't be faking," she said. "I promise you."

"Let's go look at my gun," he said.

"Let me go pee first," she said, and took his hand away and rolled her eyes as if to say *Whooo*, and slid off the stool, her skirt riding up higher on her thighs. He watched her as she walked toward the rest rooms. And thought *How easy, how perfectly goddamn easy*. And at the same time wondered why he'd bothered—when really, you know, he didn't give a damn anymore about any woman in the world.

At a little past six that Tuesday evening, Fat Ollie Weeks walked into the squadroom.

"You still mad at me?" he asked.

It was twelve degrees Fahrenheit outside, but he was wearing only blue jeans, a white shirt, a tan sports jacket, dark blue socks, and brown loafers. The shirt had either a ketchup stain or a bloodstain on its front, and it was unbuttoned at the throat. A tuft of black hair sprouted at the opening, curling up over it. Bread crumbs or cake crumbs, some kind of crumbs, were caught in the tangled hairs. Ollie needed a shave. *And* a bath.

" 'Cause you won't be mad once I tell you what I found out," he said.

"What'd you find out?"

"I found out why this Tilly character was uptown on Ainsley."

"Why?" Carella asked.

"Why was he up there? Or why was I doing you a favor?"

"What favor was that, Ollie?"

"The favor of asking around about your case. On my own time."

"Gee," Carella said.

"You *are* still mad, ain't you?"

"No, I'm very happy to have my caseload increased."

"What you think is I dumped a homicide in your lap, ain't that right?"

"No, what would give me that idea?"

"I don't *know* what, since it's an open-and-shut FMU."

"Then don't worry about it."

"Who's worried about it? You want to know why Tilly was up there, or not?"

"Why was he up there?"

"He was boffin' the broad in apartment 22."

"How do you know that?"

"I told you. I been asking around. Tilly used to know this broad from before he went to the slammer on an assault rap, did you know about the assault rap?"

"Yes, Ollie."

"What he done, Tilly, he nailed this fuckin spic who called him a fag. Which he ain't, by the way, since he was up there boffin' this broad the night before some other spic hung him from the ceiling after smoking him."

"Who says?"

"The spic? I'm guessing. This neighborhood the building's in is strictly San Juan nowadays. They finally took over from the niggers on that section of Ainsley, you don't know what fuckin headaches it's causin' us. Anyway, you want to talk to this broad, she's in apartment 22, her name is Carmen Sanchez.''

"Have *you* already talked to her?"

"No, I got all this from askin' around.''

"Who'd you ask?"

"You got your people, I got mine.''

"An informant?"

"What else is there?"

"In Diamondback?"

"No, on the fuckin French Riviera.''

"Want to give me his name?"

"I would be happy to give you his name, except it ain't a him, it's a her. There *are* ladies in this city, you know, who sometimes fall afoul of the law, ah yes,'' Ollie said, and fell into his dreaded W. C. Fields imitation. Carella winced.

"Did your informant mention how Tilly happened to end up on the ceiling?"

"All my informant told me, m'dear, is that Tilly was upstairs boffin' the Sanchez girl all night long, who I wouldn't mind boffin' myself, from what I hear she looks like.''

"Did your informant actually *see* Tilly up there?"

"I do not know, m'friend, I do not know. What I suggest you do is go up there yourself and talk to the lady in 22, who according to what I've been told is something to observe, ah yes.''

Carmen Sanchez was a woman in her late twenties, tall and loose-limbed, with a mop of curly black hair, eyes to match, and a mouth made for singing. Or so she told them at once. Carmen was on her way to a singing lesson. Just putting on her coat, in fact, when the doorbell rang. The coat was as red as her very snug, long-sleeved sweater. A long striped muffler around her throat was the color of the snug sweater and her very snug jeans. Carmen said she had to leave immediately, she did not have time to talk to the police. Meyer said this would only take a minute.

"Sure, I know a police minute," Carmen said, and looked at her watch. "Okay, five minutes, that's all I've got. I'm not kidding you. I have to be there at eight."

"Five minutes," Carella promised.

"I mean it," Carmen said. "I have to pay her for the full hour no matter *how* late I am. So let's do this fast, okay?"

"Roger Tilly," Carella said, getting straight to the point.

"I figured."

"Was he here the night before he got killed?"

"He was here."

"This would've been Sunday night, the sixth."

"I know when it was."

"What time did he get here?" Meyer asked.

"He was here when I got home."

"What do you mean? In the apartment?"

"Yes."

And now the two men—mindful of the five-minute time limit Carmen had put on the questioning but ready to violate it if they had to—began working her as a team, firing at will, asking questions willy-nilly, trying to find out just what had happened in those hours before Tilly's death.

"Does he have a key?"

"No, I left it with the super. I knew he was coming over."

"Home from where?"

"I was working that night. I got home around two o'clock."

"Working where?"

"A club down the Quarter."

"On a Sunday?"

"Why not? You religious or something?"

"Doing what?"

"I'm a singer. I thought I told you."

"Which club?"

"Why?"

"Just curious."

"I didn't kill him."

"Who said you did?"

"Why do you want to know which club? So you can check if I was there, right?"

Both detectives looked at her.

"It's called Clancy's, it's a jazz club," she said.

"How come Tilly came *here* instead of going to the club?"

"He doesn't like jazz. Anyway, he's heard me sing a hundred times already."

"So he came here to wait for you."

"Yeah. This was Sunday night. *Murder, She Wrote* was on."

"He liked that, huh?"

"Never missed it."

Carmen looked at her watch.

"Three minutes," she said.

"What was Tilly doing when you got here?"

"Sleeping."

"Was he here all night?"

"All night."

"What happened yesterday morning?"

"We got up, it must've been ten, ten-thirty. We had some coffee, and then went back to bed for a while."

"Uh-huh," Carella said.

"Then what?" Meyer said.

"I started getting dressed."

"What was Tilly doing?"

"He was talking on the phone."

"Did he make the call? Or did someone call him?"

"The first one he made. The second one came in."

"There were two altogether?"

"Yes."

"Did he mention any names while he was on the phone?"

"I've got to get out of here in one minute flat."

"Did you hear him say anyone's name?"

"He asked for a Mr. Steinberg. He was buying a new car, that was the salesman he was dealing with."

"Was this the call *he* made?"

"Yes."

"How about the second call?"

"He was talking to somebody about money."

"Yeah, go ahead. What'd he say?"

"He said he wanted the rest of his money."

"What'd he mean by that?"

"I don't know. But he was really angry. Yelling in the phone—look, I have to leave."

"Just sit tight a minute, Miss Sanchez," Carella said.

"No, I'm not sitting tight a minute or even thirty seconds," she said, and began putting on the red coat. "I'm out that door...."

"Just a few more questions," Carella said.

"You promised me..."

"Promises, promises," Meyer said.

Their eyes locked.

"Cops," she said, and shook her head, and took off the coat, and draped it angrily over one of the kitchen chairs. "All right, let's get it over with," she said, and sat in the chair, and stretched her long legs and folded her arms across the tight red sweater.

"This second call," Carella said.

"Yeah," she said, and nodded curtly, fuming.

"Give it to us in detail."

"What kind of detail?"

"What's the first thing he said?"

"He said, 'Yeah, this is me.'"

"Then what?"

"He said something like, 'Well, when *am* I gonna get it?'"

"Yeah, go on."

"Then he . . . how do *I* know? How do you expect me to remember . . . ?"

"Try."

"He said something about No, I want the rest of it *now*, not tomorrow, I want it right this minute. He said that a couple of times, about getting the rest of his money *now*. He said that was the deal, and he was tired of asking for it. He wanted the rest of it *now*."

"He specifically mentioned the word *money*?"

"Yes. Well, the money, or the bread, whatever."

"How'd the conversation end?"

"They made arrangements to meet downstairs."

"How do you know?"

" 'Cause I heard Roger giving the address here, and then he . . ."

A look suddenly crossed her face. She was remembering. They waited.

"Yeah," she said, nodding. "That's right."

"Yeah *what's* right?" Meyer said.

"He *did* say a name."

"What name?"

"Bowles. 'I'll give you half an hour, Mr. Bowles.' "

"Are you sure about that?"

"Yeah, that was the name. Bowles."

"Then what?"

"He listened for a minute, and then he said, 'All right, make it twelve sharp.' "

"And you say he gave him this address?"

"Yeah, and said he'd meet him on the front stoop."

"At twelve o'clock sharp."

"Yeah. And he said he'd better have the money with him."

"What time was this, would you remember?"

"It must've been around eleven-fifteen."

"What'd Tilly do then?"

"He took a shower, and then he got dressed and went down-stairs."

"What time was that?"

"Well, I guess it was around twelve."

"Did he come back up here after his meeting?"

"No, he never came back up here," Carmen said.

6.

In an American court of law, the prosecuting attorney is always the first to present his case. In what is called a direct examination, he questions the witnesses he has called, and then the defense attorney questions them in what is called a cross-examination. The D.A. then gets a second shot at these witnesses in what is known as a redirect. After which the defense attorney gets his turn once again in a recross. Once the prosecutor has paraded all his witnesses, he tells the judge that he is resting his case, and the defense calls *his* witnesses, and the same ritualistic procedure starts all over again: direct, cross, redirect, recross. It is sometimes tedious and confusing.

On Wednesday morning, the ninth day of January and the third day of the Carella murder trial, Henry Lowell called his second witness, a Ballistics Section detective named Peter Haggerty. Short and squat, with a thick black mustache and eyeglasses with matching rims, Haggerty took the stand, swore to tell the truth, the whole truth, and nothing but, so help him God, and then looked out comfortably over the rows of benches, conveying the impression that a courtroom was second home to him. When Lowell asked him how many times he had been called to testify as an expert witness, he said, "This is my forty-eighth time."

"In how many courts have you testified as an expert witness?"

"Eleven."

"In how many counties?"

"Four."

"How long have you been working with the Ballistics Section?" Lowell asked.

"Twelve years."

"Can you tell me what sort of training you've had in identifying and . . . ?"

For the next ten minutes, Haggerty paraded his credentials, telling the court about the extensive training he'd had, the seminars he'd attended, the lectures he himself had given on ballistics to various police departments all over the nation. At the end of that time, Di Pasco accepted him as an expert witness, but instructed the jury that whereas his expertise should be considered, it was not necessary that they *accept* it either wholly or in part.

"During the course of your everyday duties," Lowell asked, "are you called upon frequently to identify the makes and calibers of various firearms?"

"I am," Haggerty said.

"And during the course of your everyday duties, are you also called upon to identify bullets fired from various firearms?"

"I am."

"Does your work also involve comparing bullets and cartridge cases against other bullets and cartridge cases in order to determine whether they were fired from the same gun?"

"I do that every day of the week, as a matter of routine."

"I show you a pistol previously marked and moved into evidence and ask if you performed certain examinations on this pistol?"

"I did."

"Can you tell me what kind of pistol it is?"

"It's a nine-millimeter Uzi."

"And what is that? If you'll explain to the jury . . . "

"It's an Israeli-made assault pistol, a shorter and lighter version of their Uzi submachine gun."

"When you say 'lighter . . . ' "

"It weighs about four-and-a-half pounds fully loaded."

"What constitutes 'fully loaded'?"

"Well, it carries a twenty-round magazine. That means you can fire twenty bullets without having to reload. That's what fully loaded means. Twenty bullets."

"Now, when you say it's a nine-millimeter pistol, what does that mean?"

"It means that the gun fires a nine-millimeter Parabellum cartridge. That's the caliber. Nine millimeters."

"And when you say it's a shorter gun than the submachine gun, what *are* its dimensions, actually?"

"Its overall length is two hundred and forty millimeters."

"Perhaps inches would be more understandable to the jury. Can you translate that into inches for us?"

"Well, without a slide rule . . ."

"Approximately. So the jury will understand it."

"The overall length would be about nine-and-a-half inches."

"And the length of the barrel? Again, in approximate inches, please."

"About five inches."

"Can this gun be held in the hand?"

"Oh, yes, it's *designed* to be held in the hand. It's what is known as a hand-held, semiautomatic pistol."

"What does semiautomatic mean?"

"It means that a separate pull of the trigger is required for each shot. As opposed to a *fully* automatic weapon, where the gun will continue firing as long as pressure is exerted on the trigger."

"Would you say that this weapon is capable of firing a great many shots in rapid succession?"

"Well, as many as twenty. That's the magazine capacity."

"But in rapid succession?"

"Yes. The gun is designed to absorb recoil. This enables

rapid fire with enormous control and therefore accuracy.''

"Would this gun be capable of firing, say, three shots in rapid succession?''

"Oh yes. Certainly.''

"Your Honor, I would like to offer in evidence, three nine-millimeter Parabellum bullets recovered during autopsy on the body of Anthony John Carella.''

"Mr. Addison?''

"No objections.''

"Mark them Exhibits Two, Three and . . .''

"Your Honor, since there'll be more evidence of this nature, may I suggest that it might be simpler to mark the three bullets as a *single* exhibit rather than . . .''

"Yes, fine. Mark them Exhibit Two.''

Carella cut a glance at his mother. She was sitting erect, her face impassive, watching Lowell as he walked back to the prosecutor's table and picked up another sealed plastic bag with a Police Department EVIDENCE tag on it.

"Your Honor,'' Lowell said, "I would also like to offer in evidence three spent nine-millimeter Parabellum cartridge cases recovered by Detectives Wade and Bent in the A&L Bakery Shop at 7834 Harrison Street on the night of July seventeenth last year.''

"No objection.''

"Mark them Exhibit Three.''

"Lastly, Your Honor, I would like to offer in evidence three cartridge cases and three bullets recovered in test firings in the Police Department's Ballistics Section.''

"Mr. Addison?''

"No objection.''

"Mark them Exhibit Four.''

"Detective Haggerty, I ask you now whether you performed comparison tests on all of these bullets and cartridge cases?''

"I did.''

"Can you tell me now whether all of these bullets were fired from the same pistol?"

"They were."

"Can you tell me whether all of the cartridge cases were ejected from the same pistol?"

"They were."

"Detective Haggerty, which pistol did you use in your test firings?"

"The assault pistol you showed me just a few minutes ago."

Lowell picked up the gun.

"Are you referring to this nine-millimeter semiautomatic Uzi assault pistol marked Exhibit One in evidence?"

"I am."

"And are you willing to say without qualification that the bullets recovered from the body of Anthony John Carella were fired from this gun?"

"They were. The markings on the recovered bullets and the test bullets are identical."

"Similarly, were the cartridge cases found on the floor of Mr. Carella's bakery shop ejected from this gun?"

"Without question. The markings on the recovered shells and those examined after the test firing are identical."

"Thank you, no further questions."

"Mr. Addison?"

Addison rose ponderously, shaking his head even before he approached the witness chair, conveying to the jury the certain impression that somebody was being hoodwinked here, but that he intended to set that little matter straight as soon as possible.

"Detective Haggerty," he said, "when did you receive the bullets allegedly recovered from the body of Anthony John Car . . . "

"Objection, Your Honor!" Lowell shouted, leaping to his feet. "Unless the integrity of the Medical Examiner's Office is being challenged here, then there is no *question* that those bullets *are* the ones recovered from the corpse. There's nothing *alleged* here, Your Honor. Dr. Josef Mazlova signed the necropsy report and also signed the evidence tag attached to the three bullets. Those are the bullets. I ask that you instruct Mr. Addison . . .''

"Question withdrawn," Addison said, and again shook his head as though the entire world—including his opponent and the sitting judge—were against seeing justice done in this courtroom. "Detective Haggerty," he said, "when did you receive these bullets?"

"Do you mean the ones recovered from the corpse?" Haggerty asked; he had worked with Carella on many occasions, and he was damned if he'd now let a shyster lawyer pull the kind of stuff he was attempting here today.

"The bullets marked Exhibit Two," Addison said, refusing to repeat what he hoped the jury would still believe was a slander.

"I received them on July eighteenth last year. The day after the murder."

"Who sent you those bullets?"

"Dr. Josef Mazlova, assistant medical examiner. At the request of Detective/Second Grade Charles Bent of the Forty-fifth Precinct."

"Was there any direct communication between you and Dr. Mazlova?"

"None."

"Between you and Detective Bent?"

"Yes."

"What was the nature of that communication?"

"He asked me to determine the make and caliber of the firearm from which those bullets were fired."

"And did you supply this information?"

"I did."

"What did you tell him?"

"That the bullets had been fired from a nine-millimeter Uzi pistol."

"You were certain of this?"

"I was positive."

"So you knew all the way back then—long before you fired any test bullets from the Uzi—that the bullets recovered from Mr. Carella's body . . ."

Beside him, Carella saw his mother flinch.

". . . had been fired from a nine-millimeter Uzi."

"I did."

"And you so informed Detective Bent."

"I did."

"So that everyone was looking for a nine-millimeter Uzi as the murder . . ."

"Objec . . ."

"I don't know what *everyone* was looking for. I know . . ."

"Your Honor, objection, please."

"Yes, Mr. Lowell."

"There is no way that Mr. Haggerty could know what *everyone* was looking for."

"Sustained."

"Detective Haggerty, did you tell Detective Bent that the murder weapon was a nine-millimeter Uzi?"

"I told him that the evidence bullets had been fired from a nine-millimeter Uzi."

"And you determined this by performing certain routine tests . . ."

"Yes."

"That are, so far as you know, performed by every ballistics section in the United States . . ."

"In the *world*."

"In the world, thank you. Tests examining lands, and grooves, and twists, and what-have-you . . ."

"These are all highly scientific . . ."

"I haven't asked my question yet, Mr. Haggerty. Are these tests infallible?"

"The tests are infallible, yes."

"And are *you* also infallible?"

"What?"

"Have you never in your life made a mistake?"

"Not where it concerned determining the caliber and make of an unknown firearm."

"Other mistakes, though? You have made other mistakes in your lifetime?"

"Everyone makes mistakes in his lifetime. I'm saying . . ."

"No further questions."

"Mr. Lowell?"

Lowell came to the witness chair, looped his thumbs into his jacket pockets, leaned into the chair, and said, "Is it not an indisputable scientific fact that the caliber and make of an unknown firearm can be determined by examining a bullet fired from that weapon?"

"Indisputable."

"Is it not also indisputable that the Ballistics Section in this city maintains the largest and most comprehensive classification of weapons anywhere in the entire world?"

"That is indisputable."

"And that it maintains up-to-date records on any gun known to exist, including specimens of bullets *fired* from those guns?"

"Yes."

"Did you compare the evidence bullets recovered from Mr. Carella's body with a specimen bullet fired from a nine-millimeter Uzi?"

"I did."

"And what did you discover?"

"All of the bullets were of the same caliber, with the same twist, and the same number and width of lands and grooves."

"And is that how you knew they'd all been fired from a nine-millimeter Uzi?"

"Exactly."

"Thank you, no further questions."

Addison rose again and came to the witness chair.

"Mr. Haggerty, are you saying that *any* bullet fired from *any* nine-millimeter Uzi would have the same markings?''

"No, sir, I'm not saying that at all."

"Because I got the impression here that the bullets recovered from Mr. Carella's body could have been fired from *any* nine-millimeter Uzi, and not necessarily . . ."

"No, sir, the impression would be a false one. What I said . . ."

"Thank you, you've answered the question."

"Your Honor?"

"Yes, Mr. Lowell?"

"May the witness explain what he *did* mean?"

"Your Honor, I'm satisfied with his answer."

"I'm not," Di Pasco said. "Finish what you were saying, Detective."

"I was trying to say that *initially* I examined the bullets recovered from Mr. Carella's body only to determine the caliber and make of the pistol that had fired them. But *later*, when I received the evidence pistol, I was able to conduct test firings that proved the evidence bullets were fired from that very gun. *That's* what I was trying to say, Your Honor."

"Does that answer your question, Mr. Addison?"

"I felt my question had already been answered, Your Honor," Addison said dryly. "But I thank the witness nonetheless for his further elucidation." He turned from the witness chair, seemed about to walk back to the defense table, and then said, "Oh, yes," and walked back to Haggerty. "Tell me," he said, "when *did* you receive the evidence pistol?"

"On the second day of August."

"How did it come to your attention?"

"It was sent to Ballistics for examination."

"Sent by whom?"

"By Lieutenant Nelson."

"Do you mean Lieutenant James Michael Nelson of the Forty-fifth Detective Squad?"

"I do."

"Was there a so-called Chain of Custody tag attached to it?"

"There was."

"Was there any other name on that tag? Aside from Lieutenant Nelson's?"

"There was."

"Can you tell me what that name was?"

"Detective Randall Wade."

"Thank you, no further questions."

Carella thought he noticed a thin triumphant smile hidden in Addison's beard.

This was the Old City.

He walked swiftly through City Hall Park, pigeons strolling even in the bitter cold, hands behind their backs like little old men, passing freshly painted green benches; here among the formidable, pillared buildings of government, there was still a sense of law and order, of civilization functioning, even though the city proper was a shambles. He continued walking steadily downtown, the day cold and bright and sunny, Lowell's words ringing in his ears, Addison's humming in secret counterpoint. And now the towers of big business loomed suddenly ahead, not too distant from the impressive gray structures of the law, where Carella had stayed only long enough to hear Addison's recross, and then had kissed his mother on the cheek and hurried off to meet Meyer. There were obligations, and not all of them were in that courtroom.

The ocean-battered seawall still stood where the Dutch had built it centuries ago, the massive cannons atop it seeming even now to control the approach from the Atlantic though their barrels had long ago been filled with cement. If you looked out over the wall at the very tip of the island, you could watch the Dix and the Harb churning with crosscurrents where the two rivers met. The wind howled in fiercely here, ripping through streets that had once accommodated horse-drawn carts but that were now too narrow to allow the passage of more than a single automobile. Where once there had been two-story wooden taverns, a precious few of which still survived, there were now concrete buildings soaring high into the sky, infested redundantly with lawyers and financiers. And yet—perhaps because the Atlantic was right there to touch, tumbling majestically off toward the Old World that had given this city its life—there was still the feel here of what it must have been like when everyone was young and innocent. Well, not so innocent that they couldn't steal the place from the Indians.

They had tried to reach Martin Bowles at home last night, but there'd been no answer on the phone. When Meyer called his office this morning, he was told that Mr. Bowles could not see him until eleven A.M., after his morning meeting. Now, as Carella and Meyer walked through the narrow streets of the Old City, they went over it one more time. Police work was ever and always a matter of going over it one more time. And then one more time after that. And again and again after that, until it began to make sense.

"I admit it looks different with money involved," Meyer said.

"*Very* different," Carella said.

"It eliminates a crazy."

"It also eliminates a dope angle."

"What it gets down to is Bowles owed Tilly money."

"One of the two basics, Meyer. Love or money. Now why do you think Bowles owed Tilly money?"

"Ask me a hard one."

"Okay, how do these contracts work?"

"It's usually half on agreement, remainder on delivery."

"Usually."

"But Tilly didn't deliver. He fumbled two attempts."

"And *still* wanted the rest."

"Which is maybe why he ended up in a basement with a bullet in his head and a rope around his neck."

"Which is why we're here to see Bowles," Carella said.

The offices of Laub, Kramer, Steele and Worth seemed a trifle cold and modern. A foot-high electronic ticker tape ran incessantly on the wall opposite the thick glass entrance doors, racing from right to left with symbols neither Carella nor Meyer understood. Lower on that same wall were paintings Carella recognized as enormously valuable, even though he could not for the life of him have identified the individual artists. A very beautiful black woman in a severe black dress sat behind a rosewood desk trimmed with stainless steel. One slender hand was resting on a console that looked as if it could launch nuclear weapons to any nation on earth. The nails on that hand were very long and very red. Her lips were painted the same color as the nails. As the detectives came into the reception area, she turned languid brown eyes toward them. Behind her, the ticker tape kept spilling quotes across the narrow electronic screen on the wall opposite.

"Mr. Bowles, please," Carella said, and flipped open a small leather case to show her his shield and his ID card.

"Do you have an appointment?" she asked.

"Yes, we do," Meyer said.

"May I have your names, please?" she said, and tapped a button on the console and picked up a telephone receiver.

"Tell him Detectives Meyer and Carella are here."

The woman nodded noncommittally.

"Two gentlemen to see Mr. Bowles," she said into the phone. "A Detective Meyer and . . ."

Slight arching of one eyebrow . . .

"Detective Carella," Carella said.

". . . Detective Carella," she said into the phone, and listened. "Thank you," she said at last, and put the phone back on the console. "Someone will be out to show you in," she said. "Won't you have a seat, please?"

They both took seats.

They felt uncomfortable here, these cops.

They didn't know what all those symbols meant, running across that high-tech electronic thing up there . . . AGC and BHC and FAL and JNJ and DIS . . . what the hell *were* all those letters? They were cops who didn't have disposable income to invest anywhere. The way they disposed of their income was in feeding and clothing their families and maybe taking them out to a movie every now and then. So they sat there feeling uncomfortable. And because they were uncomfortable, sitting there in their cop clothes and feeling like cops, they didn't say anything to each other until a statuesque blonde wearing a business suit and high heels suddenly appeared in the reception area and said, "Mr. Carella, Mr. Meyer?" and they both leaped to their feet as if called upon by an arithmetic teacher to recite a solution to a long-division problem—"Yes," they both said together—and the glacial blonde said, "This way, please, gentlemen," and led them past the desk where Nefertiti with her long red nails and her languid look and her luscious red lips sat deciding whether she should throw her brother to the crocodiles. And down those long, mean corridors they followed the blonde until she stopped at a door with a little brass plaque on it etched with the name MARTIN J. BOWLES.

She knocked.

"Come in," he said.

Martin J. Bowles.

Some six feet one, six feet two inches tall, a good-looking man with dark hair and brown eyes, a smile on his face, hand extended, wearing what looked like a designer suit.

"Gentlemen," he said, "how are you?"

Hand still extended.

"Mr. Bowles," Carella said, taking his hand, "I'm Detective Carella, this is my partner, Detective Meyer."

Still feeling clumsy.

"How do you do?" Bowles said, shaking hands vigorously. "How can I help you? Is this about the attempts that were made on my wife's life?"

"Yes, sir, it is," Carella said.

"I thought so," Bowles said, and nodded.

"We understand a man named Roger Turner Tilly once worked for you as a chauffeur," Carella said.

"Well, he worked for a limousine company, actually," Bowles said. "Executive Limousine. But he was my regular driver, yes."

"Until last spring sometime, isn't that so?"

"Yes. He got into some kind of trouble . . ."

"Yes, and was sent to prison."

"Yes, that's my understanding of what happened."

"Have you seen him since his release from prison?"

"No, I haven't."

"You know that he's dead, don't you?"

"Yes. My wife mentioned that you'd called yesterday morning . . ."

"Yes."

". . . to inform her."

"Yes. When's the last time you saw him alive, Mr. Bowles?"

"Before he went to prison. Must've been last February sometime."

"Did you know he'd been released on parole?"

"Yes."

"How'd you happen to know that, Mr. Bowles?"

"Well, I've spoken to him."

"When would that have been?"

"The first time was last week sometime."

"Last week?" Carella said, surprised. "When last week?"

"Friday, I guess it was. I remember I was just on my way out at the end of the day. Emma and I . . . my wife . . ."

Carella nodded.

"Had theater tickets, and we were going to dinner beforehand. Tilly called at around five-thirty, it must have been."

"What was the purpose of his call?" Carella asked.

"He said I owed him money."

"Oh?" Carella said, surprised again. "For what?"

"He said I'd hired him to take me to a seminar upstate last year—hired him *personally*, you understand, not through Executive—and that I'd only given him half the money for the trip and still owed him the rest. I told him I was on my way out, and he gave me a number where I could reach him. I didn't call him back until Monday morning."

The day Tilly got killed, Meyer thought.

"Why'd you call him?" Carella asked.

"To settle this thing. I had, in fact, hired him to drive me up there—he'd rented a limo someplace, I really don't know the details, I'm sure he made more than if I'd gone through Executive. But I'd paid him in full, and I wanted to clear this up. I didn't want the man thinking I'd stiffed him."

"What time did you call him?"

"Eleven, eleven-thirty, somewhere in there."

"What'd you talk about this time?"

"Well, it was ridiculous. He kept insisting that I owed him money, virtually *demanded* that I go up there to Diamondback, meet him uptown at twelve sharp with the rest of the money. I never heard such nonsense in my life. As if I'd go to Diamondback under *any* circumstances."

"But *did* you go up there to meet him?"

"Of course not!"

"Did you *tell* him you'd be there?"

"Yes, I did. To get him off my back."

"Did you plan to let us know you'd had these two telephone conversations with him?"

"Frankly, no."

"Did you mention them to your wife?"

"No, I didn't."

"Mr. Bowles, I suppose you know that your wife identified the man trying to kill her . . ."

"Yes, I know all . . ."

". . . as Roger Tilly."

"Yes. But I don't know where she got that idea. The man had no reason to . . ."

"You don't think he was the man she saw, huh?"

"I think she was mistaken. He had no reason for wanting to do anything like that."

"How about this money he claimed you owed him? Could he have been angry about that?"

"That occurred to me, but then why didn't he talk to me *before* these attempts were made on Emma's life? It just doesn't jibe, you see."

Carella was thinking that *none* of it jibed. He was thinking Bowles was lying in his teeth.

"So you don't think this money you owed him . . ."

"Money he *said* I owed him."

"Yes, excuse me, you don't think that had anything to do with whoever was trying to kill your wife."

"Nothing whatever."

"How'd you get along with Tilly personally?" Meyer asked, taking another tack. He, too, thought Bowles was lying. There was a feel here. It came from years of talking to killers and nonkillers alike. You just knew when someone was leading you down the garden.

"We got along fine," Bowles said. "He was one of the best drivers Executive ever sent me. Well, that's why I kept him as a regular. I didn't know he was going to go crazy in prison."

"You think he went crazy in prison," Meyer said, nodding.

"Well, this whole business about the money," Bowles said, and shook his head.

"You *didn't* owe him any money, right?"

"Not a penny."

"Before these two phone conversations," Carella said, "had there ever been any harsh words between you?"

"Never."

"Did you have any reason to think he may have been harboring a grudge?"

"No, nothing like that."

"Yet your wife felt certain he was the man who shoved her off a subway platform . . ."

"I know, but . . ."

". . . and later tried to run her over."

"I'm sure she was mistaken."

"And you're sure you didn't owe him this money he claimed you . . . ?"

"Yes, how many times do I have to . . . ?"

"Did you have reason to give him a business card lately?" Carella asked.

"No. I told you, I hadn't seen him since last February."

"Mr. Bowles, can you tell us where you were this past Monday at noon? That would've been the day before yesterday, the seventh."

Bowles looked at him sharply.

"Am I going to need a lawyer here?" he asked.

"Not unless you feel you need one."

"I mean, what is this, where *was* I? What the hell *is* this?" Bowles said, pulling his appointment calendar to him, and angrily leafing through it. "Here it is," he said, snapping the page, and then looking up. "I had a client with me until eleven or so," he said, "after which I placed the call to Tilly. Then I left the office . . ."

"To go where?"

"I had a lunch date."

"With whom?"

"Another client."

"What's his name?"

"It was a woman."

"Her name then."

"Lydia Raines."

"What time was your date?"

"Twelve noon."

"Where?"

"A restaurant called Margins."

"Where's that?"

"On Zwaan."

The word was Dutch, a holdover from the days of Peter Stuyvesant. Bowles pronounced it the way most natives of this city did: Zwayne.

"Where can we reach this woman?" Carella asked.

"She's a valuable client, I don't want her . . ."

"Mr. Bowles, I'm not sure you understand the serious . . ."

"I do indeed. I also understand the importance of . . ."

"Do you know this is a *murder* case?" Carella said.

"Yes, I do," Bowles said. "I'm merely suggesting that there may be some other way to confirm that I was there with her. I don't want her to know that a police investigation is under way. Investors hear *police*, they immediately believe the firm's involved in some wrongdoing. I expect to be promoted in May. If a client as important as Ms. Raines . . ."

"What other way are you suggesting?" Meyer asked pleasantly.

"I just don't want to get her involved in this."

"But she's already involved," Meyer said gently. "Don't you see?"

"I suppose so."

"So can you tell us where she lives, sir?"

"Well . . ."

"Please," Meyer said. "It'll make it a lot easier for all of us."

"She lives on Chase. 475 Chase Avenue."

"Thank you, sir," Meyer said.

"I'd appreciate it if you didn't mention you're investigating a murder."

"We'll try not to," Meyer said, and again smiled pleasantly.

Lydia Raines owned a flower shop called The Raines Forest, on Davidson and Parade. The name of the place might have worked as a cutesy-poo pun, except for the fact that none of Lydia's customers knew her last name. As a result, not too many people gave a passing thought to the cleverness on the front plate-glass window. Most passersby figured the middle word had been mis-spelled. As a matter of fact, the doorman at her building on Chase had told the detectives that the name of her shop was The Rain Forest.

The window was full of exotic blooming plants, surprising at any time of the year, absolutely startling for January. Carella recognized the orchids, but there were other plants he could not have guessed at, all purple and yellow and orange and gold, most of them looking phallic. Meyer was thinking about the name of the place and wondering what other businesses Lydia Raines could have gone into, and what other variations she might have worked on her name. If she imported venison from the Wild West, for example, might she have called her business Home on the Raines? Or if she made bridles and such for the horsey set, would her business be called Saddles and Raines?

"Or how about It Never Raines?" he asked Carella out loud.

"Huh?" Carella said.

"For a salt manufacturer," Meyer said.

"Huh?" Carella said again, and opened the front door to the shop.

"But it pours," Meyer explained, and shrugged.

Once, a long time ago, Carella and Meyer had gone together to Puerto Rico, to extradite a man wanted for a double murder. The moment they'd stepped off the plane in San Juan, they'd known they were in the tropics. Their perception had nothing to do with the brilliant sunshine, or the heat, or the humidity. It came instead from the heady scent in the air, a fetid mix of mildew and perfume, rot and riotous growth, an aroma neither of the men had ever before inhaled. There was the same aroma here in Lydia Raines's private little forest. Mist should have been rising from the giant leafy plants that crowded the walls and cluttered the narrow aisles of the shop. Tiny bright birds should have been twittering about the open blooms that stridently trumpeted their colors. There should have been the incessant sound of insects. And in the distance, the lazy whisper of the ocean.

Lydia Raines—if such the lady was—stood behind the counter at the rear of the shop, fussing over an arrangement, tucking in a purple flower here, moving a red to another position, fanning out a spray of fern. Carella guessed she was in her mid-forties, a tall, slender woman who resembled one of her own exotic plants. Golden hair tufted close, green eyes sparkling in leafy imitation, a skirt the color of a tropical sky, a blouse and sweater that seemed in pink and crimson bloom, high-heeled pumps that echoed the pale blue of her skirt. She looked up as the bell over the door sounded, smiled as they came down the crowded center aisle, brushing past the variegated leaves on one of the giant plants—"May I help you?"

"Miss Raines?" Carella said.

"Yes?"

"Detective Carella," he said, showing his shield and his ID card, "Eighty-seventh Squad. This is my partner, Detective Meyer."

Her hands hovered like birds over the flower arrangement, flightless now.

"Yes?" she said again.

"There's no need to be alarmed," he said, "we're . . ."

"But I'm not alarmed," she said.

And yet her hands still hung motionless over the arrangement, and her welcoming smile seemed frozen on her lovely face. Only the green eyes were in motion. Darting. Apprehensive.

"Miss Raines, do you know a man named Martin Bowles?" Meyer asked.

"Has something happened to him?" she asked.

"No, no," Carella said.

"Then . . . ?"

"This is just a routine investigation," Meyer said.

To a criminal, this meant run for the hills. But Lydia Raines was not a criminal.

"*Do* you know him?" Carella asked.

"Yes, he's my investment broker," she said. "With Laub, Kramer, Steele and Worth."

"When did you last see him?" Carella asked.

"Is he missing or something?"

She looked puzzled now. Nothing had happened to him, or so they'd just told her. But now they wanted to know when she'd seen him last. Why? Unless he was missing or something. All of this showed on her face and in her eyes. She was either a very good actress or else Bowles hadn't called her in advance to warn her about their impending visit.

"No, he's not missing," Meyer said, smiling pleasantly, nodding. "In fact, we just saw him . . . when was it, Steve? Half an hour ago? Forty minutes?"

"About then," Carella said.

Putting her at her ease. They still hadn't told her that Bowles had used her as his Monday alibi. They wanted to hear this from her.

"Can you tell us when you last saw him?" Meyer asked.

Still smiling pleasantly. Nodding. Come on, darling. Tell your baldy-bean uncle when you last saw the nice man.

"I had lunch with him on Monday," Lydia said, "I'm sure it's in my book."

She gave the arrangement a last loving touch, almost petting one of the flowers, glanced at it appreciatively and admiringly, and then walked to a small desk nestled into a nook alongside a pair of double-doored, glass-fronted refrigerator cases. She sat in the chair behind the desk, crossing what Carella now saw were very shapely legs, and opened the drawer over the kneehole. Her appointment book was one of those thick black leather-covered things that shrieked efficiency. She opened it swiftly to where a heavy paper clip marked the current day, removed the clip, and began flipping back through the pages.

"Yes, here it is," she said, and looked up.

Exactly the words Bowles had used when he'd consulted his own calendar.

"It was Monday," she said. "The seventh."

"You had lunch with him that day," Carella said.

"Yes," she said. "Well, here it is," she said, and turned the book to show him the page. In a sprawling handwriting Carella presumed was her own, he read the words:

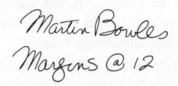

"Is that the name of a restaurant?" Meyer asked, already knowing the answer. "Margins?"

"Yes. It's down near the Exchange. On Zwaan."

She, too, pronounced it Zwayne. But there was in her voice a regional dialect that identified her as originally coming from someplace else.

"Was Mr. Bowles there when you arrived?" Carella asked.

"Yes, he was."

"You didn't have to wait for him or anything, did you?"

"No, he was sitting at the bar."

"Is it a big place? Margins?"

"Fairly big."

"Were there many people there?"

"I suppose. I really didn't notice. Why? What's he done?"

They were both wondering when she'd get around to that.

"Nothing that we know of," Meyer said, and again smiled pleasantly. Old Uncle Meyer here. You may not be able to trust the one with the Chinese eyes, but me you can bet your life on.

"Then why all these questions?" she asked.

"Just routine," Carella said.

"Sure," she said. "And I'm Princess Di."

"When did you make this lunch date?" Meyer asked.

"I have no idea. Martin and I meet periodically to discuss my investments. I may have called him, he may have called me. I simply don't remember. What is it he's done?"

"As I told you . . ."

"Or *supposed* to have done?"

"Nothing. That we know of."

"What do you *suspect* he's done?"

"Nothing," Carella said.

"Sure," she said again. Her eyes locked on his. Meyer had never seen such an eye-lock in his life. The Green Lantern, this one was, shooting a laser beam at Carella. Defying him to tell her why they were really here. For a moment, Meyer was tempted to lay it all on the table. He resisted the temptation.

"Where are you from originally?" he asked.

"Chicago," she said. "Why?"

Carella went to see her personally—and alone. There were matters he needed to discuss with her, and he wanted to afford her at least a semblance of privacy. He did not want this to be a visit from two police goons in heavy overcoats. She told him she'd just got home a few minutes ago, and she offered him a drink. This was now four in the afternoon. He told her he was still on duty, and she took his coat and hung it in the hall closet, and then they moved into the living room that was all leather and steel, and he got down to brass tacks.

"Mrs. Bowles," he said, "do you have any reason to believe your husband might want you dead?"

She looked at him in stunned silence.

"Mrs. Bowles?" he said.

"No. Of course not. No. What do you mean? *Martin*?" she said.

"Yes, ma'am. Have you been having trouble lately?"

"No, we . . ."

"In your marriage, I mean."

"Yes, I know. No, positively not. We're . . ."

"Has he ever mentioned divorce . . ."

"No, no, we're very . . ."

"Or even obliquely suggested it?"

"No, we're very happy."

"Have you had any violent arguments recently . . . ?"

"No."

". . . anything like that?"

"No."

"He hasn't ever abused you, has he?"

"No. Do you mean . . . ?"

"I mean has he ever *hit* you. Physically abused you."

"No. Never."

"Or threatened abuse?"

"No."

"Mrs. Bowles, I'm sorry I have to ask this, but it's important. Does your husband have another woman?"

"He does not. Mr. Carella, really . . ."

"I'm sorry, but I have to ask these questions. There's not another man in your life, is there?"

"Definitely not!"

"Your husband has absolutely no reason to distrust you . . ."

"None."

"Or to want you out of his life . . ."

"None."

"How do your wills read, Mrs. Bowles? I'm sorry," he said, "I'm not enjoying this, either, believe me. But two attempts were made on your life . . ."

"Why would you imagine *Martin* . . . ?"

"Because he telephoned Tilly on the morning he was killed . . ."

"Tilly?"

"Yes. To discuss money Tilly said he owed him."

She looked at him.

"Yes," he said.

She kept looking at him. It was beginning to sink in.

"I'm sorry," he said.

"It's just . . . I've never had reason to believe . . . "

"I appreciate that."

"I just never . . ." she said, and let the sentence trail.

She was thinking now. Wondering about everything he'd told her. Considering whether or not it was even remotely possible that . . .

"There are prenuptial agreements," she said. Very softly. "We signed prenuptial agreements."

"What did they say, Mrs. Bowles?"

"If . . . if we ever got divorced . . . I'd get half of everything he owns. Now and forever."

"I see."

"And . . . we're in each other's wills as well. As sole beneficiaries. Whoever goes first . . ."

She shook her head.

"There's lots of money involved," she said.

Carella waited.

"His father left him something in excess of a million dollars . . . and, of course, he's done very well on his own. He'll probably be made a partner this spring."

She shook her head.

"I just can't believe this, really. If you say he called Tilly . . ."

"Yes, he's admitted that."

"Then, well . . . I suppose he did. And I suppose if he was considering a divorce, he might have given it second . . . but he *wasn't*, he *isn't*, I know that. We *love* each other. And if you're suggesting . . . I mean, I don't know *what* you're suggesting, but I guess you're trying to say Martin got this Tilly person to . . ."

"Yes, Mrs. Bowles, I'm suggesting that's a possibility."

"But that's just it. If that were the case, why would he have hired Darrow?"

"Who's Darrow?" Carella asked, puzzled.

"A private investigator."

"A *what*?" Carella said. He was thoroughly surprised. "Why'd he hire a private . . . ?"

"To get to the bottom of this. To find out who was trying to hurt me. So you see . . ."

"When was this?" he asked.

"He started on Monday."

"I wish you'd have told me."

"I didn't see any reason why I should. The man's legitimate, he's . . ."

"How do you know that?"

"I checked."

"I wish you'd have let *me* do the checking."

"It seemed such a simple thing to do. He gave me his card, I simply called the number in Chicago . . ."

"Your husband hired a private investigator from *Chicago*?"

"Yes."

"Why? Don't we have enough of them here?"

"I don't know why. He's supposed to be very good."

"And you say you called him in Chicago?"

"The number, yes. On his card. It's a real detective agency."

"Why'd your husband hire him, do you know?"

"I just told you. To protect me. And to find whoever was trying to kill me."

"Well, now that Tilly's dead, he won't have to do *that* anymore, will he? Tell me this man's name again."

"Andrew Darrow."

"How do you spell that last name?"

"D-A-R-R . . ."

Carella was already thinking it was a phony. A private eye named *Darrow*? As in Clarence?

"...O-W."

"And the name of his company?"

"A. N. Darrow Investigations."

I'll bet, Carella thought.

"Have you still got his card?"

"Yes."

"Can I see it, please?"

"It's in my bag," she said.

She went out of the room. When she came back, she handed him what seemed to be a bona fide business card—but no one ever asked for identification when you had these things printed up. He copied down the name, address, and telephone number printed on the face of the card, and then handed it back to her. It was beginning to get dark outside. He thanked her for her time, and told her he'd stay in touch. What she'd told him about the prenuptial agreement worried him considerably, but he tried not to reveal this. Nor was he too terrifically pleased that Martin Bowles had hired a stranger from Chicago to protect his wife from harm.

The moment he got back to the squadroom, he dialed the number he'd copied from the card. A recorded message said:

"You've reached Darrow Investigations. I'm out of town just now, but if you'll leave a message when you hear the beep, I'll get back to you as soon as I return. Thank you."

Darrow Investigations, he thought, and dialed 1–312–555–1212.

"Directory Assistance," a voice said.

"In Chicago," he said. "A listing for Darrow Investigations on South Clark Street."

"How are you spelling that?" she asked.

"D-A-R-R-O-W," he said.

As in Clarence, he thought.

"One moment, please," the operator said.

He waited.

"I'm sorry, sir, I don't have a listing under that name."

"Can you try A. N. Darrow?" he asked.

"Is that N as in Nancy?"

"Yes, please."

"Moment, please."

He waited again.

When she came back, she said, "Nothing under that name, either, sir."

"Are you sure?"

"Yes, sir."

"Thank you," he said, and hung up.

He thought for a moment, and then looked through his personal directory for the number of the telephone company's P.A. line. When he got through, he identified himself to the woman who answered, told her he was investigating a homicide and needed a name and address for a telephone number in Chicago. She said she'd call back in a moment. It actually took her three minutes to punch up and dial the number her records showed for the 87th Precinct. When she got Carella again, she asked him for the number in Chicago, said she'd contact her equivalent there, and called back ten minutes later to say the number he'd given her was an unpublished number.

"I don't understand the problem," he said.

"I just told you, sir. It's a nonpub."

"Am I talking to a P.A. operator?"

"Yes, sir, you are."

"And do those letters still stand for Police Assistance?"

"They do, sir."

"I've had cooperation on nonpubs in the past," he said.

"I'm sorry, sir," she said. "You're probably thinking of a nonlist."

"No, I'm thinking of a nonpub. This is a homicide I'm working."

"Yes, sir, I appreciate that. But I can't let you have a nonpub . . ."

"Did Chicago give you a name and address for that number?"

"No, sir, Chicago did not."

"Who'd you talk to there?"

"I can let you have the number at Illinois Bell, sir, but they seemed pretty adamant about it."

"Let me have the number, please," he said.

"Yes, sir," she said, and gave him the number.

Carella dialed it.

"Subpoena Group," a woman's voice said.

Carella figured he was already in trouble.

"Yes," he said, "this is Detective Carella at the 87th Precinct in Isola?"

"Yes?" she said.

"Who am I speaking to, please?"

"Mrs. Fisher."

"Mrs. Fisher, I'm working a homicide down here, and I have a Chicago telephone number I understand is unpublished . . ."

"Yes, sir?"

"I'd like a name and address for that number."

"You'll have to get a court order . . ."

"This is a homicide," he said.

"You'll still need a subpoena ordering us to release that information."

"Well, that might be a little difficult . . ."

"Yes, sir."

". . . seeing as I'm all the way down here, and you're . . . "

"Yes, sir, but that's the way it's done here."

"Are you talking about an *Illinois* court order?"

"Yes, sir. This is Illinois, sir."

"That's just what I mean. A man's been killed down here . . ."

"Yes, sir."

"And normally, when we're investigating . . ."

"*All* of our requests come from law-enforcement officers, sir."

"What I'm saying, in a situation like this one, the telephone company will usually . . ."

"Illinois Bell handles some eight- to nine-thousand such requests every year, sir. You'll still need a court order."

"Don't you have some sort of liaison with the Chicago PD?" he asked. "Down here, we . . ."

"Are you with the Chicago PD, sir?"

"No, I told you . . ."

"Then you'll need a court order, sir."

"Thank you," he said, and hung up.

He went back to his personal directory, found a listing for Police Headquarters in Chicago, dialed the number there, and told the sergeant who answered the phone what he needed. The sergeant put him through to a detective named Riley. He explained it to Riley all over again. Told him all about his conversation with Mrs. Fisher.

"Yeah, they can get snotty when they want to," Riley said. "But here's what you do. You get in touch with our Field Inquiry Section. Look up the teletype number in your Leads Network directory. Tell them what you're working and why you need the information. The Chief of Detectives'll turn it over to the Detective Division, and somebody'll take care of it."

"You'll get that subpoena for me?"

"No, no, that's bullshit."

"She said . . ."

"Yeah, but we got a special guy in their security office, he works with us all the time. In an active investigation . . . you did say homicide, didn't you?"

"I said homicide."

"He'll usually give us the information right on the phone."

"Good," Carella said. "How long will it take?"

"Later this afternoon sound okay?" Riley asked.

* * *

The teletype from the Chicago PD came in half an hour later. It told Carella only two things:

The unpublished telephone number printed on Andrew Darrow's supposed business card was billed to a man named Andrew Denker at an address not on South Clark but instead on West Wellington.

7.

The meeting took place in Lieutenant Byrnes's corner office on Thursday morning, the tenth day of January.

Meyer and Carella sat side by side in hard-backed wooden chairs near the windows, winter-backlighted, ready to make their presentation, both of them looking spruce and chipper. It was snowing behind them. Byrnes hated it when it snowed. It made response times longer and often gave criminals an edge they didn't need.

Cotton Hawes looked pinkish from a skiing vacation in Colorado, his red hair seeming to reflect onto his cheeks. He was badly in need of a haircut; Byrnes wondered if he should mention it. Hawes sat on one corner of Byrnes's desk, partially blocking his view of Arthur Brown, who stood hulking near the door as if blocking entrance to any unwanted arrival. If Byrnes had to walk unarmed down any dark alley at two in the morning, he would choose Brown as his partner. Andy Parker sat in a chair next to him. Unshaven, as usual. Plant him on a park bench, you'd think he was one of the city's homeless. Plant him in Miami, you'd think he was with Vice.

Bert Kling leaned against the wall beside him, no doubt trying to figure out how to get his girlfriend back. Eyes a hundred miles away, Byrnes felt like kicking him in the ass. He knew the full story. Knew Kling was the reason Eileen had lost her backups on a job tracking a serial killer. Knew she'd had to shoot the man to death. One in the chest, another in the shoulder, and then emptying the gun into his back for good measure. Tough lady, Eileen Burke. Good cop. Working with the Hostage Negotiating Team now. Byrnes wanted to kick Kling in the ass, tell him to get on with *life* again.

Bob O'Brien sat in a chair to Kling's right, arms folded across his chest, long legs stretched toward the desk. Bad Luck Bob. Respond to a call with him, and there'd be shooting nine times out of ten. Go figure. You got yourself partnered with O'Brien, some dumb bastard was going to pull a gun and start shooting at you. He'd killed six men in the line of duty. Byrnes thought he ought to ask O'Brien to sit down with Eileen Burke one day, pour out his Irish heart to her, mick to mick, tell her what it was like to *really* kill people. You want killing people? Try six for size. Tell her how he cried inside every time it happened. Tell her just what he'd told the lieutenant one rainy day, right here in this office. I cry inside, Pete. Every time. I cry inside.

"Ready to start?" Byrnes said. The clock on the wall read ten minutes past eight. The Graveyard Shift had been relieved twenty-five minutes ago. It had been snowing since midnight. "I want to make this fast, Steve has to get downtown to the courthouse. This is the case him and Meyer've been working since the end of December. It turned into a homicide this past Monday."

"What was it before then?" Hawes asked.

"Attempted murder," Carella said.

"Of the homicide victim?"

"No. He was the guy trying to kill her. Or so she says."

"I'm lost," Hawes said.

"Go back to Aspen," Parker told him.

"Vail."

"Wherever."

"I wish I could."

"Tell him he can go back, Loot."

Byrnes glared at both of them.

"Why don't you take it from the top, Steve?" he said, and leaned back in his swivel chair and laced his fingers across his chest. Carella filled them in. Every now and then, Meyer broke in to correct a time or a date, but for the most part it was a solo recitation, Carella telling them everything that had happened on the case since the twenty-ninth of December, when Emma Bowles walked into the squadroom to report two attempts on her life, taking them through the murder of Roger Turner Tilly and the First Man Up dispute with Fat Ollie Weeks . . .

"Yeah, that's Ollie for you," Parker said, chuckling.

. . . and the discovery of the gun in the basement, and the conversations with both Martin Bowles and the client he was presumably lunching with on the day of the murder, and the news that he'd hired a private eye who was using a phony name.

"That's it so far," Carella said.

"Questions?" Byrnes said.

"Have you got anything on the gun yet?" Hawes asked.

"Ballistics is supposed to be getting back to us today."

"It's a thirty-two for sure," Meyer said.

"A Hi-Standard Sentinel," Carella said.

"That the one with the snub barrel?"

"Yes."

"What was this guy's name again?"

"Roger Turner Tilly."

"Sounds black," Parker said.

"No, he's white."

"Only people in this city who have white names anymore are black," Parker said. He seemed not to realize that Brown was standing near the door, looking as tall and as wide as a mountain. Brown said nothing. He felt like throwing Parker out the window, but he didn't say a word.

"So what's your thinking?" O'Brien asked. "That the husband is involved?"

"Yes. We found his card in Tilly's wallet. . . ."

"Well, there's your positive link," Parker said.

"And we've got him talking to Tilly on the morning he was killed."

"At the scene, you mean?"

"No. On the phone."

"What about?" Brown asked.

"Tilly claimed he owed him money."

"Uh-oh."

"Yeah. According to Bowles, Tilly drove him upstate last year sometime . . ."

"Now we're into ancient history, right?" Parker said.

". . . and still owed him the rest of the money for the trip. This was before he got sent up for assault last spring."

"I hate stories with ancient history in them," Parker said.

"The victim was in the slammer?" Hawes asked.

"Pay attention," Parker said.

"I didn't know if it was the husband in the slammer or the victim."

"The victim, the victim," Parker said.

"I just wanted to get it straight."

Parker nodded sourly and turned to Carella. "It's the husband," he said. "Go arrest him."

"He's got an alibi," Meyer said.

"Right," Brown said, nodding. "The flower-shop lady."

"Did you go to that restaurant?" Byrnes asked.

"No, not yet."

"Better do it right away. See if anyone saw them there together."

"Meyer'll be going down there this morning," Carella said.

"Not enough days in the week, Loot," Parker explained.

"Who's this other guy?" Byrnes asked.

"Denker? We don't know yet. No make on him in the computer. He's supposed to be a private eye."

"Why would anyone in his right mind want to say he's a private eye if he ain't one?" Parker said.

The detectives all laughed.

Even Byrnes laughed.

"All right, all right," he said at last.

But the men were still laughing.

"All right, let's calm down," he said.

"But the husband hired him, is that right?" Brown asked.

"Yeah."

"To protect her."

"Yeah."

"What bullshit," Parker said.

"She'd better watch her ass," O'Brien said.

"That's what we figure," Carella said.

"Gee, no kidding?" Parker said. "You guys must be masterminds to dope that out. Wake up, Farm Boy," he said to Kling. "I'm about to explain police work to you."

Kling hadn't said a word thus far.

Now he said, "Fuck you, Parker."

"Thank you," Parker said, and stood up and bowed to him. "But be that as it may, this is the way this thing is shaping up. Bowles . . . is that his name?"

"Bowles, yes," Meyer said.

"Bowles hires this one jerk to kill his wife, and the guy fucks up. Twice, no less. So Bowles tells him to get lost, and he hires himself *another* jerk, this time from Chicago. Only the first jerk isn't going away so fast, he wants the rest of his money."

"His delivery payment," Brown said. "Pay or play."

"Thank *you*, Dr. Watson," Parker said, and grimaced and shook his head in sour acknowledgment of the simpletons surrounding him. "So he calls Bowles and tells him to pay up or else, and Bowles pays him off with a bullet in the head."

"You're forgetting that Bowles has an alibi," O'Brien said.

"Alibi, bullshit. Lean on the flower-shop lady, the alibi goes down the toilet."

"Maybe," Carella said.

"Maybe, my ass. She's fucking Bowles, what do you *think* this is? So he tells her I have to run uptown to take care of something, sweetheart. If the cops ask you where I was on Monday, such-and-such a time, you tell them we were having lunch together. She says, Certainly, darling, let me suck your cock."

"Maybe," Meyer said.

"No maybes. Why do you think Bowles wants the wife dead? 'Cause he's already got the flower-shop lady on the side. Meanwhile, we now got this *second* jerk joined to the wife at the hip, ready to smoke her the minute he finds the right time and place. There's your case, gentlemen. Arrest Bowles for the fuckin murder, and the flower-shop lady as an accessory-after. Then run that phony private eye out of town on a fuckin railroad tie."

The room went silent.

"Sounds good to me," Byrnes said.

Carella hated to admit it, but it did.

Detective/Third Grade Randall Wade looked as mean as tight underwear. Tall and black, with narrow shoulders and a lean, muscular body, he stepped up onto the witness stand, raised his right hand, and placed his left hand on the Bible the clerk of the court extended. He seemed uncomfortable in a suit and tie. His hand on the Bible showed the oversized knuckles of a street fighter. His face was badly pockmarked, and an old knife scar over his left eye made him appear particularly threatening. Louise Carella gave him the once-over and hoped the jury wouldn't find him as frightening as she did; she was having trouble believing he was truly a cop.

"Detective Wade," Lowell said, "I show you this nine-millimeter Uzi assault pistol and ask when first you saw it."

"On the night . . . well, let me correct that," Wade said. "It was still dark, but it was morning already. The morning of August first last year."

"*Where* did you first see this pistol?"

"In the hallway of a house at 1143 Talley Road."

"Where is that, Detective Wade?"

"In Riverhead. The Four-Six Precinct."

"What were you doing there?"

"We were there to apprehend a pair of suspects in a murder case we were investigating."

"Which murder case was that?"

"The murder of Anthony John Carella."

"And which suspects were you there to apprehend?"

"Desmond Whittaker and Samson Cole."

"Is Samson Cole the same Mr. Cole who is the defendant in this trial?"

"He is."

"Was Mr. Cole in that hallway at 1143 Talley Road when first you saw this pistol?"

"He was."

"Where was the pistol when first you saw it?"

"In Mr. Cole's right hand."

"Can you tell me how the pistol came into your possession?"

"It was seized as evidence after Mr. Cole was subdued and apprehended."

"When you say 'subdued' . . ."

"He had raised the gun into a firing position. It was necessary . . ."

"This gun?"

"Yes, the gun in your hand. He had turned it on us and was about to fire. It was necessary to take him by force."

"When, exactly, did you seize the pistol as evidence?"

"After Mr. Cole was in handcuffs."

"What did you do with the pistol then?"

"Tagged it as evidence and gave it to my superior officer."

"May I have your superior officer's name?"

"Detective-Lieutenant James Michael Nelson," Wade said, "commander of the Forty-fifth Detective Squad."

"Detective Wade, what is the usual procedure when evidence is passed from one individual to another in the Police Department?"

"There's what we call a Chain of Custody tag attached to the evidence."

"Can you tell me what is printed on these tags?"

"First there are the words *Received From* and then the word *By* and then the words *Date* and *Time*. There's room on the tag for three people to write in the information. After that, you have to use a supplementary tag, which is usually stapled to the first one."

"So that when you passed this tagged pistol on to Lieutenant Nelson, for example, he would have indicated that he'd received it from you, and then he would have signed it after the word *By*, is that correct?"

"That's correct."

"Would you know what happened to the pistol after you passed it on to Lieutenant Nelson?"

"Yes, sir. It was sent to the Ballistics Section for test-firing."

"Your Honor," Lowell said, "I would like this so-called *Chain of Custody* tag marked in evidence."

"No objection," Addison said.

He was stroking his beard, Carella noticed. Idly stroking his beard. Seemingly throroughly bored with all this stuff about the pistol.

"Mark it Exhibit Five for the prosecution," Di Pasco said.

"Detective Wade," Lowell said, "would you please take a look at this tag?"

Wade accepted the tag, glanced at it, nodded.

"Can you tell from that tag who after Lieutenant Nelson was next in possession of the pistol?"

"Yes. Receipt of the pistol was signed for by Detective Peter Haggerty at Ballistics Section, on the morning of August first at eleven twenty-seven."

"The chain of custody, then, as indicated on the tag was from you to Lieutenant Nelson and from Lieutenant Nelson to Detective Haggerty."

"That's correct."

"Are there any other names on that tag?"

"None."

"Would anyone else have been in possession of this pistol at any time? Other than the persons whose names appear on that tag?"

"No one else would have had possession of it."

"Then there is no question in your mind that the pistol you seized from Samson Cole on the morning of August first is the same pistol received by Detective Haggerty later that morning."

"No question whatever."

"After Detective Haggerty received this pistol, did you have any conversation with him?"

"I did."

"Can you tell me the nature of that conversation?"

"I told him we wanted him to test-fire the gun and compare the bullets and spent shells with the ones my partner had sent him earlier. The bullets and casings in the Carella murder."

"Did he do that?"

"He did."

"Did you have a subsequent conversation about his results?"

"I did. He gave me a verbal report on his findings."

"What did he say?"

"The bullets and casings matched."

"That is to say, the test-firing showed that the gun you had seized from Mr. Cole was the same gun used in the Carella murder."

"Yes."

"Was this later confirmed in writing?"

"We received the Ballistics report the very next day. It confirmed what Detective Haggerty had told me on the telephone."

"Which was what?"

"That the gun recovered from Mr. Cole was the same gun used in the Carella murder."

"Thank you, no further questions."

Margins was a restaurant large enough for a bar mitzvah celebration, but small enough to provide privacy for any couple seeking a quiet little nook in a hidden corner. It was entirely possible that Bowles and the so-called flower-shop lady had been here on Monday without anyone having seen them. If that turned out to be the case, then the alibi held, and Parker was probably right in thinking that the next thing to do was lean on the lady.

The headwaiter was a man named Frank Giglio.

Jacketless, wearing black trousers, a ruffled white shirt, a black bow tie hanging loose around his neck, black suspenders, black socks, and highly polished black shoes, he pushed open one of the swinging doors leading from the kitchen and immediately apologized for having kept Meyer waiting so long.

"I was getting ready for lunch," he said, and looked at his watch.

It was ten minutes to eleven. The tables were set with pristine white tablecloths and sparkling glassware. Sunlight streamed through the leaded windows, touching with a cold, flat silvery light the silverware set at each place.

"Mr. Giglio," Meyer said, "I wonder if I could see your reservations book for this past Monday, the seventh of January."

"Why, yes, certainly," Giglio said. "Was there anything in particular you were looking for?"

"Yes, a twelve o'clock reservation for a Mr. Martin Bowles."

"Oh, yes, of course," Giglio said.

Meyer looked at him.

"Mr. Bowles of Laub, Kramer," he said. "Yes, he was here on Monday. I took the reservation myself."

"Are you sure?"

"Positive," he said. "But let me check my book."

He went to a podium near the entrance, where two brass stanchions some four feet apart supported a red velvet rope. Reaching into a little shelf under the slanting top surface of the podium, he pulled out a long book bound in black, opened it wide, and ran his finger down the page for Monday, January 7. His finger stopped.

"Twelve noon," he said. "Martin Bowles. Reservation for two."

"Do you know who was with him?" Meyer asked.

"A woman," Giglio said. "I don't know her name. He's been here with her before."

"What did she look like?"

"A tall, very pretty blonde woman."

"How old would you say?"

"In her forties."

"What time did they leave?"

"One-thirty? Two o'clock? I can't say for sure."

"Thank you," Meyer said.

He was thinking none of them are ever easy.

"If you don't mind, Mr. Wade," Addison said affably, "I'd like to go over this one more time."

"Objection, Your Honor," Lowell said, unfolding his long body, and coming to his feet, and managing to convey to the jury the impression that he was exceedingly weary and beginning to lose patience. "Detective Wade has answered the same questions, by my count, at least three times now. The same questions over and over again, Your Honor. Now I don't know what purpose it serves to keep going over the same ground *incessantly . . .*"

The way he says that word makes him sound very British, Carella thought.

". . . except to harangue the witness, which I hope is not my learned colleague's . . ."

Those words, too.

". . . intention. But unless . . ."

"Want to come up here, please?" Di Pasco said.

Both attorneys approached the bench.

"You do seem to be covering the same ground repeatedly, Mr. Addison," Di Pasco said.

"I am merely trying to make the facts clear to the jury, Your Honor."

"Begging my colleague's pardon, Your Honor, and not wishing to impute an ulterior motive to him . . ."

"Well, thank you for that," Addison said.

"But it seems to me his insistence on reliving the arrest of Mr. Cole on the night of August first is merely an attempt to circumvent . . ."

"Oh, come now," Addison said.

"Yes, go on," Di Pasco said.

". . . to circum*vent*, I was about to say, Your Honor's pretrial finding on admission of the pistol as evidence. I think Mr. Addison is trying to plant doubt in the jury's mind as concerns the legality of the seizure, despite the fact that Your Honor found . . ."

"*Do* you intend to put questions as to the legality of the seizure?" Di Pasco asked.

"I intend to put questions that go to the officer's credibility."

"But as his credibility pertains to the seizure of this weapon?"

"As it may or may not pertain, Your Honor."

"Then I would have to object," Lowell said.

"The issue here is credibility," Addison insisted.

Shaking his head, raising his eyebrows in disbelief, Lowell said, "Your Honor, I would like a ruling on this, please."

"It's not up to any jury to discount evidence because they may *believe* it was illegally seized," Di Pasco said. "The jury

finds only on *facts*. You know that, Mr. Addison. It's the judge
who makes the legal findings. And in this case, I've already
found that the pistol was legally seized and could be admitted
as evidence. My pretrial finding stands. I'll allow the questioning
to continue, but only as it pertains to credibility. Justice doesn't
require or allow the relitigation of a suppression issue.''

"Thank you, Your Honor," Addison said, and smiled sourly.

Carella saw him smile, and wondered what they'd been talking about up there.

They were in the museum when she asked him what the middle
initial in his name stood for: Andrew *N*. Darrow. A new exhibit
had opened yesterday, and though she'd told him there was no
longer any need for his services now that Tilly was dead, he'd
insisted that until he was dismissed by Martin Bowles himself,
he intended to stick to her like glue.

As they moved through the galleries, he mentioned that Chicago had a very good museum called the Art Institute, but he'd
never been to it. There was something totally disarming about
his confessions of ignorance. The new exhibit concerned itself
with adventurous forms of sculpture, one of which he almost
stepped onto, or into, because it did sort of resemble a ladder,
a pile of bricks, and a trowel lying there on the floor. Some ten
minutes later, as they wandered through the permanent collec-
tion, he stopped before a massive Seurat, and said it was completely amazing how a man could make a whole painting from
just all those little colored dots. When she asked if he'd seen
Sunday in the Park with George, he looked totally bewildered,
and she realized he didn't know what on earth she was talking
about.

Changing the subject, she said, "What does the *N* stand for?"

"The what?"

"In your name."

"Oh. Nelson," he said.

"Like the admiral?"

"Exactly."

"How come?"

"My mother liked the ring of it."

"Is she British?"

"No, but my father used to be a sailor."

"Was *he* British?"

"No. American."

"Then why didn't she name you after an *American* sailor? Like John Paul Jones?"

"I'll have to ask her one day," he said, and shrugged.

They came out of the museum at a little past three, into blustering winds and a day already ominously dark. The weather forecasters had promised more snow for the weekend, and the sky overhead was leaden, but so far they'd been lucky. She asked if he'd like a hot chocolate, and said she knew a nice little tearoom nearby. Her long mink coat flapping about her ankles, gloved hand holding the collar closed at her throat, she rushed him toward the avenue up ahead, thronged with pedestrians and passenger cars, taxis and buses. He was wearing a belted camelhair Burberry that he'd told her he'd bought in Chicago but that had been manufactured in England, was she familiar with the Burberry label? Smiling, she had said Yes, she'd heard of the label.

"Where'd the Darrow come from?" she asked.

"Darrow?" he said. "I have no idea."

"You know there was once a famous lawyer named Darrow, don't you?"

"Oh, sure," he said. "The Leopold-Loeb case. That was a Chicago case."

"Yes," she said, and guessed she felt relieved. She was never quite certain *what* he knew.

"But I don't think we're related to him," he said. "My father was originally from Rhode Island."

Approaching the corner, stopping for the red light there.

Scaffolding overhead, the inevitable razor wire running along its upper edge, windows being replaced in the corner building. Put up a scaffold in this city, somebody would climb it. And if it was climbed, and there was no wire on it, then whoever climbed it would get into the first-floor windows. If you worked for the window company, you had to watch out for the damn razor wire. It was like everything else in this city. The honest citizens paid for what the thieves were doing.

"Do you have any brothers or sisters?" she asked.

"Nope. I'm an only child. How about you?"

"I have a sister in Los Angeles."

"Older? Younger?"

"Younger."

"If she looks anything like you," he said, "she must be a beauty."

The light changed to green, sparing her an answer. She stepped off the curb, took two steps into the gutter, glanced automatically to her left to check on traffic—and saw the bus.

"Emma!" he shouted.

She would remember later that this was the first time he'd used her given name.

The bus was shiny and metallic and huge, and it was racing to beat the light, but the light had already changed. She stopped dead in her tracks, not knowing whether to move forward or backward, it was coming at her so fast. She heard the squealing of brakes. And then he shouted her name again—"Emma!" And suddenly she was being pushed at from behind, his hands on her back, shoving her, almost knocking her off her feet. She staggered forward, struggling to keep her balance. The brakes kept shrieking at her, and now a woman on the sidewalk was screaming. She realized all at once that he was still immediately behind her, the bus hurtling past them, missing them by what had to be a scant six inches. They kept stumbling forward, both of them carried by their own momentum. She felt herself falling. She put her hands out ahead of her. He reached for her, missed her, and she tumbled to the pavement, hitting her knees as she went down, but managing to break her fall before she landed on her face. He picked her up at once. Lifted her to her feet. Held her for just an instant. The woman on the sidewalk was still screaming.

"You okay?" he asked.

"Yes," she said, and caught her breath.

The bus was already half a block away, approaching the next corner. "You stupid bastard!" he yelled after it, and then he turned to her and said, "I'm sorry. I hope I didn't hurt you."

"No," she said. "I'm fine."

Her heart was pounding.

"Let's talk about that morning of August first again, shall we?" Addison said pleasantly.

Wade said nothing.

He had been talking about the morning of August first all afternoon. It was now almost three-thirty, and they were *still* talking about the fucking morning of August first.

"You told me that you went to the house on Talley Road on information provided by . . ."

"Yes."

". . . a prostitute named Dolly Simms, now deceased."

"Yes."

"Tell me, Detective Wade," Addison said, "on the morning of August first last year, had you obtained either an arrest warrant or a search . . . ?"

"Objection, Your Honor!"

"Sustained. And please come up here."

The attorneys approached the bench.

"Now what is this?" Di Pasco said.

"Sir?" Addison said.

"You argued this business of the warrants at the pretrial hearing, and I found that the circumstances that night did not *require* warrants. Your question now implies to the contrary. You know very well that this is not a jury question. So what are you doing?''

"Well, sir, I thought . . ."

"Leave it alone. Do you understand me?"

"Yes, sir."

"Good. No more shenanigans, please."

Lowell smiled. Addison went back to the witness stand.

"So, Detective Wade," he said. "On the night of August first, you went to this house . . ."

"Yes, sir."

". . . on information supplied by a *prostitute* . . ."

"Yes, that the two men we were looking for . . . "

"A prostitute told you . . ."

"Yes, that was her trade."

"Told you that Desmond Whittaker and Samson Cole were inside that house . . ."

"Yes."

"So you went there with . . . how many other officers were there?"

"Before the hostage situation broke out?"

"I want to know how many police officers accompanied you to the house on Talley Road?"

"There were ten of us altogether."

"In how many cars?"

"Two."

"Ten detectives. All from the Forty-fifth Precinct?"

"No. Not all."

"Was there a detective there who was *not* from the Forty-fifth Precinct?"

"Yes."

"Who was that detective?"

"Detective Stephen Carella."

"What precinct is he from?"

"The Eight-Seven."

"What was *he* doing there?"

"I called him."

"Why?"

"I thought he would like to be in on the arrest."

"Why did you think Detective Carella might like to be in on this arrest?"

"These men had killed his father . . ."

"Your Honor . . ."

"Strike that," Di Pasco said. "You know better, Officer."

"Was Detective Carella related to the victim in the case you were investigating?" Addison asked.

"Yes, he was."

"What was his relationship to the victim?"

"He was the victim's son."

"So included among the detectives who were about to make an arrest was the *son* of the victim, is that right?"

"That's right."

"Were there any other detectives involved in this arrest?"

"Yes."

"How many of them?"

"Eight."

"Also from the Four-Five?"

"No. From the Four-Six. Talley Road is in the Four-Six."

"So that altogether, there were eighteen detectives involved in this raid."

"It wasn't a raid."

"Then how would you characterize it? Eighteen detectives descending upon . . ."

"It was an *arrest*, not a raid. We knew from Dolly Simms where these two men were, which was why we were there to make the arrest. We already *had* specimen bullets and casings that were fired at us by these men during the course of our investigation. And these had compared positively with the bullets and casings from the murder weapon. So we knew that these men were in possession of the murder weapon. It was as simple as that. This was what you might call hot pursuit in that . . . ''

"Now, *really*, Detective Wade . . ."

"Yes, sir, in that we knew where they were and we went there as soon as we could to make the arrest. As it was, by the time we got there, the girl had already told them we were on the way, and we walked into a hostage situa . . ."

"That's the subject of another trial," Di Pasco said.

"I wasn't going to talk about that in detail, sir," Wade said. "I was only trying to explain why we felt time was of the essence, that's all, Your Honor."

"Are you familiar with Police Department guidelines regarding the use of deadly force?" Addison asked.

"I am."

"Do those guidelines dictate when a pistol may be unholstered?"

"They do."

"And when a pistol may be fired?"

"They do."

"You testified earlier that the first time you saw the Uzi pistol was in a hallway at 1143 Talley Road . . ."

"That's correct."

". . . and that it was in the right hand of the defendant."

"That's also correct."

"Had you already unholstered your pistol by that time?"

"Yes, sir. A felony was in progress. The guidelines specifically state that a pistol may be unholstered if it is evident that a felony is in progress."

"Had you already *fired* your pistol by that time?"

"Yes, sir. As a defensive measure."

"Were you being threatened by the defendant at that time?"

"The defendant was holding an Uzi assault pistol in his hand. This was the same make and caliber pistol that had fired the murder bullets."

"So, naturally, you *assumed* this was the murder weapon."

"Well, it seemed logical to me that if here's the man Dolly Simms told us had fired at us six nights ago . . ."

"*Did* you assume this was the murder weapon? Yes or no?"

"Yes."

"And on that basis, you fired your pistol at the defendant."

"On the basis that we were confronting a man holding a weapon that was used in a previous felony, yes."

"By 'we,' whom do you mean?"

"Me and Detective Carella."

"You and Detective Carella were both in the—by the way, how did you come to be in that hallway?"

"We were waiting in the basement for the signal to assault."

"The signal from whom?"

"Inspector William Cullen Brady, commanding officer of the Hostage Negotiating Team."

"Your Honor . . ."

"Your Honor, I'm sorry," Wade said, "but it *was* a hostage situation there, and it's impossible for me to talk about it without *saying* what it was. The two men were holding this young girl hostage. That was the felony in progress, Your Honor. That was what gave me the right to draw my gun."

"Are you allowing that, Your Honor?"

"Let it stand."

Addison sighed heavily.

"So you were waiting in the basement," he said, "you and Carella . . ."

"Yes, sir."

". . . for the signal to assault."

"Yes."

"I expect you got that signal . . ."

"We did."

". . . and came out into the hallway."

"Yes."

"Was the defendant surprised?"

"I don't know what he was."

"Well, did he *look* surprised?"

"He looked surprised, yes."

"He wasn't *expecting* you, was he?"

"No, he wasn't expecting us."

"Then he was surprised, isn't that correct?"

"I suppose he was surprised."

"Surprised to see you."

"Yes."

"You and Detective Carella, in that hallway, with guns in your hands. Had both of you unholstered your guns by then?"

"Yes."

"Did both of you assume that the man there in that hallway with you was a murderer?"

"I don't know what Carella assumed. I know what I myself thought."

"Yes, what *did* you think, Detective Wade? Tell us what you thought in that split second before you shot Samson Cole."

"I thought here's a man with a deadly weapon in his hand, I better take him out before he hurts somebody."

"Take him *out*?" Addison asked, looking astonished. "Am I to understand that you shot to *kill*?"

"No, sir, I shot to take him *out*. That's not to kill him, I didn't shoot to waste him, I didn't shoot to box him. I shot to take him out. Knock him down before he could hurt anybody."

"Where did you shoot him?"

"In the leg."

"Were you aiming for his leg?"

"I was."

"And that's where you got him."

"Yes. His right leg."

"You must be a good shot."

"I am."

"Took him out with that single shot, is that right?"

"Yes, sir."

"Knocked him down."

"Yes."

"Then what?"

"He sat up and turned the Uzi on us. I kicked it out of his hand and we subdued him."

"How?"

"I don't remember."

Carella remembered. Sitting there in the third row of the courtroom, watching Wade as he recited impassively the events of those empty hours of the night on that early August morning last year, he remembered it all, Wade's bullet catching Cole in the right leg and knocking him off his feet, Wade kicking the Uzi out of his hand as Cole tried to sit up and raise the gun into a firing position, Carella kneeing him under the chin and slamming him onto his back on the linoleum-covered floor in the narrow corridor. Green linoleum, he remembered now. Yellow flowers in the pattern. Green and yellow and Sonny Cole's wide-open brown eyes as Carella put the muzzle of his gun in the hollow of his throat, and beside him Wade whispered, "Do it."

". . . aware, are you not, Detective Wade, that the guidelines specifically prohibit using a weapon as a means of apprehension?"

"I did not use it to apprehend the defendant."

"Then what do you call it when the man has not threatened you, the man is surprised by you as you burst into that hallway, the man does not even turn the gun on you until *after* you've shot him, what do you call that if not using your weapon as a means of apprehension?"

"Sir, when a man has a semiautomatic pistol in his hand, that is threatening, sir. And in a situation such as that, firing in self-defense is permissible."

"Even if the man makes no threatening gesture with the pistol?"

"Sir, I consider a pistol in a man's hand to be very threatening."

"Well, that's for the jury to decide, isn't it?"

158

"Yes, sir, but it was also for *me* to decide right there on the spot. I know what the guidelines say, I'd *better* know what they say. I had maybe five seconds to make my decision, and I made it."

"No further questions," Addison said.

Lowell rose and walked toward the witness chair.

"I just wanted to clear up one point," he said. "You testified that you had already recovered bullets that had been fired at you . . ."

"Yes."

". . . and spent cartridge casings as well."

"Yes."

"Under what circumstances had you recovered these bullets and casings?"

"An informer had told us that two men—who might've been the ones we were looking for—were holed up in an abandoned building on Sloane. So we went there to check it out."

"When was this?"

"On the twenty-sixth of July."

"What happened when you got there?"

"We were shot at, which enabled us to recover the four casings, but only three bullets. We couldn't find a fourth bullet."

"What did you do with these?"

"My partner bagged them and tagged them and sent them to Ballistics."

"When?"

"The next day. July twenty-seventh."

"Why did he send them to Ballistics?"

"To compare against the bullets and casings we had in the Carella homicide."

"How did they compare?"

"Positively. They had been fired from the same gun."

"And this gun was what?"

"A nine-millimeter Uzi."

"And only five days later, on the first of August, you saw

a nine-millimeter Uzi in Sonny Cole's hand.''

"I did.''

"Thank you,'' Lowell said.

Nodding, Addison rose and walked toward the stand again.

"Detective Wade,'' he said, "when you burst into that hall-
way, did you at that time know for certain that the pistol in
Samson Cole's hand was the same pistol that had killed Mr.
Carella?''

"No, I didn't know that at the time.''

"Did you even know it was an Uzi?''

"Not until I saw it.''

"When you saw it, did you then know it was an Uzi?''

"Yes, I'm familiar with Uzis.''

"Was that when you fired? When you saw the Uzi and assumed it was the murder weapon?''

"I fired when I saw a man with a semiautomatic pistol in
his hand.''

"Even though you had no proof at the time that the gun in
his hand was, in fact, the weapon used in the Carella homicide.''

"I had no proof.''

"You merely made that assumption.''

"I made that assumption.''

"Thank you, no further questions.''

"Let's recess till tomorrow at nine,'' Di Pasco said, and
rapped his gavel.

As enforcer for the Benalzato crime family, it was charged—
but never proved in a court of law—that Jimmy the Blink had
ordered the murders of some fourteen people, all of whom had
turned up in the river in assorted bits and pieces. Some responsible and normally reliable detectives in this city maintained that
Jimmy had once eaten the heart of a rival gangster, yanking it
still bleeding from his chest and swallowing it raw like some
Indian in the Wild West. This, too, had never been substantiated.

At the age of sixty-seven, Jimmy looked as if he'd never in his lifetime eaten anything but well-done steaks and French fries. Corpulent just short of obesity, he looked like a bald Sumo wrestler with unexpectedly piercing green eyes. His true name was James Albert Biondi, but he'd been called Jimmy the Blink ever since he was eight years old, when he developed an unfortunate tic that kept yanking his left eyelid out of kilter every ten or twenty seconds. Some law-enforcement people in this city claimed that Jimmy had developed the tic at that tender age because that was when he'd committed his first murder. The cops would have liked nothing better than to ship him back to Sicily. The trouble was they couldn't do that because Jimmy wasn't Italian, or even Italian-American. He'd been born right here, folks, and was therefore a one hundred percent Yankee Doodle Dandy.

And dandy he was, make no mistake about it. Wearing a white shirt and a dark blue nailhead suit with a silk rep tie as red-white-and-blue as his birthright, he sat at a table in a restaurant named Colucci's—known for a fact to be mob-owned—and greeted Carella cordially, just as if he weren't interrupting an honest citizen finishing an early dinner. The clock on the wall read twenty to six. Carella had come here directly from the courthouse. Sitting with Jimmy was a man he introduced as Senator Ralph Antonelli. Carella knew that Antonelli had just got out of the slammer. That he was now sitting here openly with a known gangster was evidence of Jimmy's influence and power.

"I was hoping we could talk alone," Carella said.

"Then maybe you should have telephoned first, huh?" Jimmy said, and the left eye blinked.

"Ah, if only I had your number, Jimmy."

The double entendre was not lost on him. He burst out laughing and then said, "The senator here only stopped by to say hello, he was just leaving. Give me a call, Ralph, huh?" he said, blinking, and extended his meaty hand to him. The senator, graying and on a cane, took Jimmy's hand, said he was happy to have met Carella, and then hobbled off to a booth at the far end of the long room.

"Haven't seen you in a long time," Jimmy said.

"Well, you know. Busy."

"I was sorry to hear about your father."

"Thank you."

"When does the trial start?"

"It started Monday."

"How's it going?"

"Good, I think."

"They don't nail that jig, you let me know, huh? There are people in this city like to see justice done."

"Uh-huh," Carella said.

"So what can I do for you, *paisan*? You want something to drink? Or is this a duty call?"

"I wouldn't mind a Coke."

Jimmy signaled to the waiter.

Carella tried not to look at that blinking left eye. He picked up a matchbook and began toying with it. But the eye was hypnotic. His gaze kept drifting back to it.

"You want a lemon in that?" Jimmy asked.

"No, just plain," Carella said.

"Bring my friend here a plain Coke, no lemon," Jimmy said to the waiter, and then turned to Carella and said, "So how you been?"

"Fine, thanks. You're looking good."

"Well, I could stand losing a few pounds. What brings you here?"

"Ever hear of a Chicago hitter named Andrew Denker?"

"No," Jimmy said at once, and blinked. "What am I, a stoolie? Come on, willya? Hey, waiter, cancel that Coke," he shouted, and burst out laughing. "Asking me such a question," he said to Carella. "You know better than that."

"Excuse me, Mr. Biondi," the waiter said, coming over.

"Did you really wish me to cancel that Coke?"

"No, bring it, bring it, I'm a big spender," he said. "Anyway, I haven't seen my friend here in a long time."

"Maybe too long a time," Carella said.

Jimmy looked at him.

"Maybe your memory's going, Jimmy."

Jimmy blinked.

"How's your son?" Carella asked.

So that was it.

"Fine," Jimmy said.

Now it was on the table. You do me a favor, I do you a favor, that's the way it works, friend. In politics or in crime, which were maybe synonymous, sooner or later all the markers got called in. Carella had done the favor a long time ago, but he'd never taken advantage of it till now. Maybe he should have saved the marker for something more important. But if anyone in this city knew whether a hitter from Chicago was in their midst, it was Jimmy the Blink.

"At long last, huh?" Jimmy said.

Carella shrugged.

"A hitter from Chicago, huh?"

"Andrew Denker," Carella said, and nodded.

"Let me think," Jimmy said. "Here comes your Coke."

The Coke came with a complimentary cognac from the house. Jimmy nodded a pleased acknowledgment and then picked up the snifter. He warmed the glass between his hands, just like an expert. He inhaled the bouquet. He nodded again and took a swallow, and rolled the cognac around on his tongue. Carella sipped at his Coke.

Back then, Jimmy's son was eighteen years old. As handsome as his father had been when he was that age, with the same curly black hair, astonishing green eyes, and a face kissed by angels. He'd been riding in an automobile with a pal of his who'd carelessly smoked four marijuana cigarettes before hitting the road, and who'd even more carelessly rammed his Cadillac Seville head-on into a VW Bug, instantly killing the driver and sending the only passenger to the hospital.

There was no question but that James, Jr., hadn't been driving and was cold sober at the time of the crash. There was nothing with which the police could charge him, nothing for which he could be booked. But the cops downtown at the Twelfth, where the accident occurred, recognized that the handsome young kid they had here was the son of Jimmy the Blink Biondi, the cocksucker who'd beaten more raps than Al Capone ever had. So they thought it would be comical if by mistake they ran cherubic little Jamie here through the city's lovely legal system, sent him along in the wagon with his hophead friend, let *both* of them spend the night in the pen downtown while waiting for arraignment.

With the one call allowed him, Jamie naturally telephoned his father. Jimmy the Blink sent a lawyer to the Twelfth at once, but the kid was already on his way downtown to the Criminal Courts Building, the wheels of justice grinding exceedingly fast in this singular case. Jimmy then called Carella at the Eight-Seven uptown. Carella owed him nothing. In fact, he had once arrested Jimmy, only to see him walk when the case came to trial. But the first thing Jimmy said on the phone was, "I know you don't owe me a thing." Which Carella knew, anyway. Unless Jimmy was talking about a long prison term, in which case Carella—and every other cop in this city—owed him a lot.

"So what's up?" he asked.

Jimmy told him.

Carella said, "So?"

"I want him out of there," Jimmy said.

"He's eighteen," Carella said. "That makes him . . . "

"I'm not talking legal here," Jimmy said. "If you want legal, he wasn't even charged or booked."

"Then what *are* you talking?"

"Human. You know what'll happen to him in that pen."

"Not if they find out you're his father."

"They already *know* I'm his father. That's why he's *in* the fuckin pen."

"I'm talking about the people in there with him."

"You're talking about *animals* in there with him," Jimmy said. "You're talking about junkies and rapists and misfits who don't know how the system *works*. Don't you know what this city *is* nowadays? For Christ's sake, don't you *know*?"

"I know," Carella said.

"All right then, help me. To them, my son's only fresh meat. You got to get him out of there."

"Why?" Carella asked.

But, of course, he knew why. Unless you subscribed to the theory that the sons were accountable for the sins of the fathers, then the police—if Jimmy was telling the truth—had no right to lock up his son overnight. Jimmy was right; he would not come out of that pen the way he'd gone into it. And whereas a lot of dumb people might later find themselves with their throats slit as a lesson on how the system *really* worked, it would be too late then to save an innocent kid. Carella had no reason to want to help Jimmy. For all he cared, Jimmy could rot in hell. But Jimmy's son was something else again. And Jimmy had mentioned the key word: *human.*

So Carella went all the way downtown to the County Courthouse and talked to the sergeant who was the jailer there and asked him to pull Jamie out of the pen.

"The fuck for?" the sergeant asked. "You know whose kid that is?"

"Yank him out," Carella said.

"You on Biondi's ticket?" the sergeant asked.

"How'd you like a broken nose?" Carella asked.

"I'm a fuckin *sergeant*," the sergeant said, reminding Carella that he was outranked.

"Okay, *Sergeant*," Carella said, "the kid hasn't been charged or booked. You're asking for a lot of grief down the line, believe me."

"My middle *name* is grief," the sergeant said, but he was beginning to look doubtful.

"My lieutenant wants him out," Carella said. "Is that high enough up for you? Or you want to call my precinct commander? There's the phone, *Sergeant*. The number's 377–8034."

The sergeant looked at the phone.

"Go ahead, call," Carella said.

"Only to check it out," the sergeant said, letting Carella know he wasn't backing down.

Lieutenant Byrnes told him the prisoner should be released in his detective's custody. They were both going way out on a limb—but they both had sons of their own. With a great show of reluctance and indignation, the sergeant unlocked the pen door and let Jamie out. He seemed unaware that the police had pinned a hand-lettered sign to his back. The sign read: SHORT EYES. This meant that the wearer of the sign had eyes only for short people— in other words, children. The police were telling the assembled crew of law-breakers in the pen that Jamie was a child-abuser. If this did not guarantee his rape, nothing would have. Apparently, Carella had got there just in time. The other prisoners had already taken Jamie's gold Rolex from him and ripped open his custom-made silk shirt.

Jimmy the Blink's lawyer was waiting outside with a subpoena ordering that the prisoner either be charged or released. There was some further red tape about the commanding officer of the arresting precinct having to sign the official release, but the acting officer at the Twelfth—this was now eleven o'clock at night, and Carella should have been home three hours ago— was happy to drop this potentially hot potato. By eleven-fifteen James Biondi, Jr., was stepping into a limousine his father had sent downtown for him. Jimmy's lawyer shook hands with Carella and told him that Mr. Biondi never forgot a debt.

The next morning, a case of Glenfiddich scotch arrived at the squadroom.

The card inside the carton read:

Thanks.

Jimmy

Carella resealed the carton and asked Charlie-Car to run it by the whiskey store that had delivered it.

His card read:

No, thanks.

Stephen Louis Carella

Detective / 2nd Grade

But now it was payoff time.

"There was some guy from Chicago looking for a piece," Jimmy said, and blinked, and took another sip of cognac.

"When?" Carella asked.

"Around Christmas sometime. Right after Christmas," Jimmy said. "I forget exactly."

What had happened was that one of his people who owned a candy store, and incidentally a numbers drop, out in Majesta, called to say some guy from Chicago was in looking to buy a gun. Guy came recommended by a Cicero bookie named Danny Gerardi, who was into horses and football and such. Jimmy knew the name only vaguely, a small-time book reported to be a bit hotheaded and heavy-handed. But professional courtesy was professional courtesy, and so he told his man in Majesta to see what he could do for him. He was figuring a guy comes in from

Chicago, he can't carry a gun on an airplane, can he? So you try to lend a hand. Professional courtesy, right? This can be a big city when you're a stranger.

"It can," Carella agreed. "Did this stranger happen to leave a name?"

"I'll tell you the truth, I never asked further."

"Or an address?"

"I'll have to find out," Jimmy said.

He was thinking he'd got off cheap.

8.

Four detectives, two to a car, were waiting up the street from the Bowles apartment building at seven-thirty that Friday morning. It had been snowing all night. The world was white. The sky was crisp and clear and achingly blue. The temperature was five degrees Fahrenheit. The car engines were running, and the heaters were on.

At twenty past eight, a black limo pulled up to the curb in front of the building. A uniformed driver got out, went into the building, and emerged again a moment later. Meyer got on the pipe.

"Cotton?"

"Yeah?"

"This may be the pickup."

"We spotted him."

"Be ready to roll."

"Yep."

Some five minutes later, Martin Bowles came out of the building . . .

"There's your man," Meyer said.

"Got him," Hawes answered.

. . . wearing a dark overcoat and a fur hat with earflaps. He walked over the shoveled sidewalk to the limo, said something to the driver who was holding open the rear door on the passenger side, and stepped into the car. The door slammed shut behind him . . .

"Stay with him," Meyer said.

"Yep," Hawes said.

. . . and the limo pulled away from the curb. Hawes gave it barely enough time to reach the corner and then pulled out after it. He did not even look at O'Brien or Meyer as he drove by. Kling's eyes, too, were intent on the road ahead.

At ten minutes to nine, a man answering Emma's description of Denker came walking up the street from the direction of the subway kiosk two blocks away. He was hatless, his blond hair blowing in the wind. A long brown-and-green-striped wool muffler was draped around his neck and hanging loose down the front of his camel-hair coat. His hands were in his pockets. He paid no attention to the faded blue Dodge across the street. But Meyer wondered if he'd spotted them.

"Good-looking guy," he said.

"Yeah," O'Brien said.

"With Tilly dead, how's he justifying his existence?"

"Beats me," O'Brien said.

"I mean, who's he protecting her from *now*?"

"Himself?" O'Brien said.

"I would like Dr. Josef Mazlova to take the stand, please," Lowell said.

This was the moment Carella had been dreading.

"Mom," he whispered, "I don't want you to hear this."

"I want to hear it," she said.

". . . truth and nothing but the truth, so help you, God?"

"I do."

"Angela, take her outside."

"I don't want to go outside."

"Mom . . ."

"Dr. Mazlova, can you tell me where you are currently employed?"

"I work for the Medical Examiner's Office here in this city."

Heavy Middle-European accent of some sort, the word *work* coming out *vork*. Thin white hair combed across a balding pate. Thick-lensed eyeglasses. Wearing a brown suit and vest, a gold chain hanging on it.

Carella took his mother's hand.

"In what capacity?"

"Mom, please . . ."

"I'll be all right."

". . . to the Deputy Chief Medical Examiner."

"Do you have occasion to teach forensic medicine?"

"I am Associate Professor of Forensic Medicine at Ramsey University."

"And do you also have occasion to lecture on the subject?"

"I have lectured on forensic medicine at the College of Physicians and Surgeons at Carlyle University, and I have lectured on Criminologic Medicine at the Police Academy here."

"Have you often testified as an expert witness in homicide trials?"

"I have testified, I would guess, some twenty or thirty times."

"And in which courts and which counties . . . ?"

And now came the credentials again, flatly and dryly, all the courthouses and the counties, all the honors and awards. And now came Lowell again asking the court to accept Mazlova as an expert witness, and the judge doing so with his subsequent customary instruction to the jury.

"Now then, Dr. Mazlova," Lowell said, "does working as assistant to the Deputy Chief Medical Examiner sometimes entail performing autopsies on trauma victims?"

"Not very often. Only occasionally. In cases considered of unusual importance."

"Dr. Mazlova, did you on the morning of July eighteenth last year . . ."

"Mama, please, I wish you'd go outside."

". . . perform an autopsy on the body of Anthony John Carella?"

"I did."

"Please, Mom."

"*Shhh!*" someone sitting behind them said.

His mother covered his hand with her own. Patted it. Nodded. Don't worry, the nod said. I'm all right. I'll be all right.

"Can you show us on this body chart what your findings were that day? If it would help you to consult your notes, you may do so."

No photographs, Carella thought. Thank God, no photographs. Not yet, anyway.

"There were three entrance wounds," Mazlova said, looking at the top sheet on the clipboard in his lap, "bullet wounds, that is, all of them described by an area some thirty-three centimeters in diameter in the region between the lower end of the manubrium . . ."

"Excuse me, Doctor, but for the laymen on the jury . . . "

"That is the upper part of the breastbone or sternum . . . "

"Thank you."

". . . between the manubrium and the ensiform cartilage," Mazlova said, indicating the area on the chart. "The defining lateral boundaries . . ."

Carella held tight to his mother's hand. Sitting on her right, Angela took the other hand. Together, hands clasped, all three sat listening as Dr. Mazlova told of having found two bullets in the victim's left lung . . .

Carella squeezed his eyes shut.

. . . and another in the anterior abdominal wall.

The doctor's voice droned on.

. . . bone fragments from a perforated rib . . . blood in thoracic cavities . . .

Our Father who art in heaven . . .

. . . perforated pulmonary artery . . .

... *hallowed be Thy name.*

... dark red in color ...

Thy kingdom come ...

... likely that the same bullet ...

Papa, he thought. *Oh God, Papa.*

"... as a result of asphyxia and profuse hemorrhage," the doctor concluded.

"Dr. Mazlova," Lowell said, "did you subsequently recover the bullets that had caused these wounds?"

"I did."

"Is it usual to find bullets still inside the body in wounds of this type?"

"I would say the bullets do *not* pass through in sixty, perhaps sixty-five, percent of such cases."

"What did you do with these bullets after you recovered them?"

"As per instructions from the Forty-fifth Precinct, I bagged them and sent them to the Ballistics Section for identification purposes."

"From whom did these instructions come?"

"Detective-Lieutenant James Michael Nelson."

"Were the bullets addressed to anyone in particular at Ballistics?"

"I addressed the Chain of Custody tag to Detective Peter Haggerty."

"How did you send these bullets to Detective Haggerty?"

"By messenger. A police officer picked up the sealed package for delivery to him."

"How was the package sealed?"

"With red plastic tape marked in white with the words *Evidence—Medical Examiner's Office.*"

"Is it your belief that Detective Haggerty received this package?"

"I'm certain he would have signed the Chain of Custody tag when he accepted the package. That is usual procedure. In any event, he telephoned to say he was in receipt of the bullets and wanted to know what the priority was.''

"Thank you, Doctor, I have no further questions," Lowell said.

Addison rose, stepped up to the witness chair, and immediately asked, "What did you tell him?"

Mazlova cocked his head to one side, puzzled.

"About the priority," Addison said. "What did you say the priority was?"

"I told him exactly what Lieutenant Nelson had told me."

"And what was that?"

"That a police detective's father was the victim."

A police detective's father, Carella thought.

My father.

"No further questions," Addison said, smiling.

"I have no other witnesses, Your Honor," Lowell said. "The prosecution rests its case."

Di Pasco looked up at the wall clock.

"It's been a long and difficult week for all of us," he said. "If the defense has no objections, I'd like to recess until Monday morning. Will you be ready to call your first witness at that time, Mr. Addison?"

"I will, Your Honor. And on behalf of the jury, I thank you for the respite."

"Yes, well," Di Pasco said dryly, "this court is adjourned till Monday morning at nine," and rapped his gavel once, sharply.

"All rise!" the clerk of the court shouted, and Di Pasco came up off his chair like a bat spreading its wings, and glided out of the courtroom, his black robes trailing.

At five minutes past ten that morning, Martin Bowles came out of his office building at 3301 Steinway, and immediately hailed a taxi. Hawes and Kling—who had parked the unmarked sedan

in an underground garage four blocks away—were waiting outside 3303. The moment they spotted Bowles, they flagged another cab and told the driver to follow the taxi up ahead. This
was the first time the driver had ever had cops in his automobile.
He looked bored.

The streets and most of the sidewalks down here in the fi-
nancial section had already been cleared of snow. But many of
the people who worked down here lived in the outlying reaches
of the city, where the plows would not be through for weeks, if
then. This was a city in decline. The cabbie knew it because he
drove all over this city, and saw every part of it. Saw the strewn
garbage and the torn mattresses and the plastic debris littering
the grassy slopes of every highway, saw the bomb-crater potholes
on distant streets, saw the black eyeless windows in the abandoned tenements, saw public phone booths without phones, saw
public parks without benches, their slats torn up and carried away
to burn, heard the homeless ranting or pleading or crying for
mercy, heard the ambulance sirens and the police sirens day and
night but never when you needed one, heard it all, and saw it
all, and knew it all, and just rode on by.

The police also knew what was happening to this city.

The only difference was they couldn't just ride on by.

Bowles was heading uptown. Not *too* far uptown, as it turned
out, because his cab made a left at the Collins Building with its
spectacular curving glass front, and then continued crosstown
for several more blocks before taking a right and then a left into
a tree-lined street of snow-capped brownstones. The sign on the
corner streetpost read JACOB'S WAY. Both detectives were familiar with the street. It was one of the city's block-long sur-
prises, a little jewel pincered between two avenues narrowing
toward an imminent intersection. Bowles's cab was stopping in
the middle of the block.

"Pull in right here," Hawes said.

"Who you following?" the driver asked. "Jack the Ripper?"

"Yes," Hawes said.

Up ahead, Bowles was getting out of the cab, pulling on his gloves. He went up the steps of the three-story brownstone ahead of him, pulled off his right glove again, and pressed the bell button set in the doorjamb. A moment later, he reached for the doorknob and let himself into the building. Up the street, Hawes and Kling were just getting out of their taxi. The wind was sharp, their eyes were already beginning to water. Hatless, they stood on the sidewalk and waited. The taxi pulled away. The wind keened through the narrow little street.

"Give him a few minutes," Hawes said.

"Yeah."

Breaths vaporizing on the air.

Hands in their pockets.

Hawes looked at his watch.

"Should be settled in by now," he said, and both men walked quickly down the street. The address on the building Bowles had entered was 714. Kling went swiftly up the steps, stooped to read the name under the doorbell, and came down again just as swiftly. The men began walking toward the opposite corner.

"What'd it say?" Hawes asked.

"Moorthy," Kling said.

"What?"

"Moorthy. M-O-O-R-T-H-Y."

"Is that a name?"

"I don't know."

"I never heard of a name like that," Hawes said.

An hour and a half later—by which time both men were almost frozen solid to the sidewalk—Bowles came out of the building. He was not alone this time. Clinging to his arm as they came down the front steps was a tall blonde wearing a dark fur coat.

"Enter the bimbo," Hawes said.

"Coming this way," Kling said, and both men ambled around the corner like two gents out for a stroll on a balmy afternoon. A moment later, Bowles and the blonde approached the corner, talking animatedly. The blonde laughed. Bowles hailed a taxi, opened the door for her, and then waved goodbye as the taxi pulled away from the curb. The detectives, facing the reflecting plate-glass window of a store selling handbags, watched Bowles flag a second taxi for himself and get into it. They turned from the window as the cab pulled away.

"I want to take another look at that doorbell," Hawes said.

"I'm telling you it said Moorthy," Kling said.

Which was what it did say.

"Well," Hawes said, and shook his head in disbelief.

"Let's get some coffee," Kling said.

He had put his mother into a taxi and sent her home, figuring there was only so much of this she could take in any one day, and now he sat with his sister and Henry Lowell, who was trying to explain to both of them what game plan he'd been following all during the past week.

The dining room at the Golden Lion was a faithful replica of what one might have found in an English coach house, circa 1637. Huge oaken beams crossed the room several feet below the vaulted ceiling, binding together the rough plastered walls. Here and there throughout the room there hung portraits of Elizabethan gentlemen and ladies, white-laced collars and cuffs discreetly echoing the whiteness of the walls, rich velvet robes or gowns adding muted touches of color to the pristine candlelit atmosphere. At a little past noon, the dining room was busy and bustling, the muted hum of voices and occasional laughter drifting into the adjacent bar where the three of them were sitting in a corner booth.

Carella had been in this place only once before, a long time ago, with an attorney named Gerald Fletcher, who'd been trying to tell him he'd killed his own wife. He'd felt uncomfortable that day because the place was too rich for his blood, and he hadn't known what the hell Fletcher was up to. Today he felt uncomfortable because he had the distinct impression that Assistant District Attorney Henry Lowell was hitting on his sister.

Angela.

His kid sister.

A married woman, albeit tentatively, in that the outcome of her husband's commitment to shake a deeply embedded cocaine habit could very well determine whether or not she *stayed* married to him.

Nonetheless, a married woman with three kids.

Sitting there beside Carella, same slanting brown eyes as her brother, giving her an exotic Oriental look, hair an inky black as opposed to his merely dark brown, hanging on every word Lowell said.

"What I tried to do was link the gun irrefutably to Cole," he said. "My first witness . . ."

"Assanti," Angela said.

"Yes," he said, nodding, "Assanti. He told the jury he'd seen Cole coming out of your father's bakery with the gun in his hand. . . ."

"Or a gun *like* it," Carella said.

"Exactly, but I think I got that point across, don't you?" he said directly to Angela. "That the gun he saw looked exactly like the gun I introduced in evidence?"

"What was *that* all about, by the way?" Angela said.

"Well, in the sidebar, Addison was trying to have the gun evidence excluded all over again. No gun, no case. But Di Pasco refused to fall for that, he'd already ruled in the pretrial hearing. Which is why Addison came back later with all that garbage about a search warrant and an arrest warrant . . ."

Angela nodding.

". . . and firing his gun outside the guidelines, all that. Point is, I don't think that'll wash with the jury. Because I think I *did* show, through subsequent witnesses—the Ballistics expert, and the medical examiner, and Wade himself . . ."

"Wade was important," Carella said.

"*Enormously* important," Lowell said to Angela. "He's the one who *took* the gun from Cole, he's the one who sent it to Ballistics for test-firing . . ."

"That was very good, what you did," Angela said. "Showing all the names on the tag . . ."

"Yes, the Chain of Custody," Lowell said, smiling.

"Yes, that was very good. So there'd be no mistake about who *got* the gun and the bullets and all that."

"Point is," Lowell said, again addressing all this to Angela, "we now have Assanti saying he heard the shots, and saw the . . ."

"Three shots in rapid succession," Carella said.

"Exactly. To establish the gun as a semiautomatic," Lowell said to Angela.

"Yes," she said, nodding.

Was she flirting with him? Carella wondered.

His little sister?

His little married sister with a husband and three goddamn kids?

"Heard the shots," Lowell said to her, "and saw the killer, and saw the gun in the killer's hand. And next we have Haggerty from Ballistics saying he tested the gun and it's definitely the gun that fired the murder bullets . . ."

"I thought he was very good, too," Angela said.

"Excellent witness," Lowell agreed, nodding, and all but patting her left hand where it rested on the tabletop, her gold wedding band and diamond engagement ring clearly in evidence for any and all to see. "Addison couldn't get anywhere with his cross, he knew there wasn't a damn thing he could do to shake him. And then we had Wade saying this was the very gun he'd taken from Sonny Cole, which of course establishes a direct line from the gun to Ballistics . . ."

"He seems like a very good cop," Angela said to her brother.

"He is," Carella said.

"Strong witness, very strong," Lowell said. "Addison went

at him hammer and tongs, but he wouldn't be shaken, either. He'll score well with the jury, wait and see. It doesn't hurt that he's black, by the way.''

"Does that bother you?'' Angela asked. "The number of blacks on the jury?''

"Well, I discussed this with your brother before the trial began. What I've been trying to do is stay away from the black-white angle . . .''

"I don't think it's been brought into the trial at all,'' Angela said.

"And I hope it *won't* be. But Addison's still to be heard from, you know. Point is, we then had Dr. Mazlova saying the bullets he sent to Ballistics were the bullets he'd recovered during autopsy. The last link in a clear and direct chain. I merely hope the jury followed it all.''

"Oh, I'm sure they *did*,'' Angela said. "It was all very clear and . . . well, direct.''

Carella looked at her.

"Addison's star witness is Cole himself,'' Lowell said, "and of course he'll lie about everything that happened. He's a habitual criminal being tried for Murder Two, and what*ever* the verdict in this trial, he'll be standing trial later for the murder of that little girl. I argued initially that both counts be tried together, you know, because there *are* overlapping transactions, you see, and the evidence in one case would appear to be probative evidence in the other. Cole's taking of a hostage, for example, when confronted by the police . . .'' He turned suddenly to Angela and said in explanation, "He and his partner were holding a sixteen-year-old girl hostage . . .''

"Yes, I know.''

"And the partner killed her. Guiltlike flight would be admissible as evidence, you see, the hostage-taking. On the other hand, trying both murders at the same time would obviously be prejudicial to the accused, so perhaps the decision was a fair one, who knows? In any case, we're stuck with *two* trials, and my job is to win *this* one.''

''Yes,'' Angela said, and smiled encouragingly.

''My job is to make sure he never sees another sunrise without bars in front of it.''

He thinks that's poetic, Carella thought.

And realized with amazement that *Angela* thought so, too.

''Point is,'' Lowell said, ''Cole's going to lie to save his neck. The only people who tell the truth in court are law-abiding citizens. The murderers and thieves lie. Always.''

Angela nodded as if she were hearing wisdom dispensed by a guru on a mountaintop.

''I *want* Addison to lead him down the garden,'' Lowell said, almost gleefully. ''I want Cole to parade all his damn lies, so I can knock them over one by one.''

''Are you confident you can do that?'' Carella asked.

''Oh, *am* I!'' Lowell said, and grinned in evil anticipation. And then, suddenly, he turned to Angela again and said, ''Were either of you planning to have lunch downtown? Because the food here is marvelous, and I'd be delighted if you'd join . . .''

''I have to run,'' Carella said.

Angela hesitated. Her eyes met Carella's. There was nothing in his eyes that she could read, but they'd been brother and sister for a good long time now.

''Thank you,'' she said, ''I have to get back home.''

And could not resist adding, ''Maybe some other time.''

They wandered from gallery to gallery, walking along Hopper Street toward the Scotch Meadow Park, the area taking its name from the fact that Hopper ran parallel to the park, hence Hopscotch, trendy and memorable. O'Brien and Meyer followed at a respectable distance behind them, enjoying the sunshine but not the fierce cold, turning to look into a window whenever

Denker and Emma did, moving on again past art gallery and boutique, glancing now and again at windows displaying sandals, or jewelry, or antiques, or drug paraphernalia imported from Bombay, trying to make themselves look like tourists browsing a tourist area, rather than detectives following a possible killer and his prey.

At a little before two o'clock, Denker and Emma went into a little soup-and-sandwich joint on Matthews. Meyer and O'Brien bought hot dogs and Cokes from a street-corner cart, and stood outside in the cold, eating and drinking, waiting for them to emerge again.

They hoped it would not be a long lunch.

It was.

They did not come out onto the street again until close to three-thirty.

"Let's go home, kiddies," Meyer whispered.

But they were not going home. They continued wandering the area all afternoon, seemingly impervious to the cold. Shivering, the detectives at last saw Denker hailing a taxi and putting Emma into it. He himself caught another cab. He was their prey; they followed him.

At twenty minutes to five that afternoon, the four detectives converged outside Bowles's office building. Hawes and Kling were already in a car parked across the street, ready to follow Bowles's limo, which was waiting for him at the curb. O'Brien and Meyer had followed Denker downtown, surprised when he led them to Bowles's building, but unsurprised—now that he was here—to see Bowles come out and walk directly toward him. The stock market had closed at four; they guessed that Bowles had asked Denker to meet him here at four-thirty, and had been a little late getting downstairs.

The two men did not shake hands. All four detectives watched as they walked toward the limo at the curb. O'Brien and Meyer stood there as the limo moved off. Across the street, they saw Hawes pull the unmarked Dodge away from the curb and into a wide U-turn. A moment later, the Dodge fell in some four car-lengths behind the limo.

Like a submarine in murky waters, the limo nosed its way through late afternoon traffic. Dusk was upon the city; knife-edged towers loomed against a sky turning purple to the west. It had been a sunny day; it would be a spectacular sunset. There were things in this city that still caused the heart to leap in something other than fright.

The men sat in a black leather, tinted-window cocoon. The glass privacy panel was up, and the driver could not hear what they were saying. Nonetheless, Andrew spoke in a voice almost a whisper; he did not trust limos with their little toggles and switches, and he especially did not trust men who drove limos for a living.

"Do you own a gun?" he asked.

"No," Bowles said. "A gun? No. Of course not."

"I thought you might."

"No, I don't."

Bowles had lowered his voice, too. The limo purred gently in the encroaching darkness. Outside, there was a city waiting to pounce. But the limo was impervious. The limo spoke the same language in every nation on earth. The limo said, Here is wealth, here is power.

"Is there a safe in the apartment?"

"Yes."

"Where is it?"

"In the master bedroom. Why?"

"I plan to do a burglary."

Bowles looked at him.

"Can you let me have the combination?"

"I'm not sure that's such a good idea," Bowles said.

"I think it'll work."

"A burglary and *then* what?"

"Do the job," Andrew said.

"That's what I thought."

"Make it look like a felony murder."

He glanced at the separating glass partition. He could perceive the driver only dimly through the tinted glass.

"Do you know what a felony murder is?" he whispered.

"I think so."

"A murder committed during the commission of a felony." Still whispering.

"A burglary is a felony."

"Yes, I know that. Why didn't you let that *bus* hit her yesterday? She told me she almost got hit by a bus, but you . . ."

"Suppose it only sent her to the hospital?"

"Well . . ."

"You know a more public place than a hospital? You want me to do this thing with hundreds of nurses and doctors and . . . "

"Well . . ."

". . . visitors all over the place? The reason I'm asking about a gun, I want to make this thing look like a burglar picked up a weapon of convenience. Do you know what that is? A weapon of convenience?"

"Of course I know what that is."

"It's a weapon that just *happens* to be there."

"Yes, I know."

"A weapon *convenient* to the . . ."

"Yes, yes," Bowles said impatiently. "But I just told you, I don't have a gun."

"What I thought," Andrew said, "is the burglar gets surprised while he's in there, has to kill the lady in self-defense."

"Well," Bowles said, and shrugged.

"Which is why I'd need the combo to the safe."

"Why?"

"To open it. To take what's in it. Because this is supposed to look like an interrupted burglary."

"Well," Bowles said again.

"So what's the combo?"

"I don't think I like this," Bowles said.

"Why not?"

"Because it'll come right back to me."

"How?"

"My wife's already been to the police . . ."

"I know."

". . . told them someone was trying to kill her."

"Yes, I know."

"So now a burglar *conveniently* . . ."

"Happens all the time."

"Maybe so. But if it happens to *Emma*, the police will automatically . . ."

"Let them."

"Sure," Bowles said, and nodded sourly. "This is *some* accident you've arranged, I've got to tell you."

"I think it's better than an accident."

"I told you I wanted this to look like an accident. So you're arranging a fake . . . what do I tell the police when they get there?"

"You'll be in Los Angeles," Andrew said.

Bowles looked at him.

"Far, far away," Andrew said, and smiled.

Bowles kept looking at him.

"In fact, you can leave for Los Angeles . . ."

"Why would I go to L.A.?"

"It doesn't have to be L.A., I don't care *where* you go. Where would you *like* to go? You can go anyplace but Chicago. The point is, you'll be out of town when it happens. You'll leave three, four days before it happens, the police'll call you and tell you all about this terrible tragedy."

"They'll know right off," Bowles said.

"Knowing is one thing. Proving is another."

Bowles was silent, thinking.

"I'm sure Emma told them about you," he said at last. "That I hired a private eye. I'm sure she'd have reported that."

"So what? Let them find A. N. Darrow."

"Well . . ."

"Who doesn't exist."

Bowles was still thinking, trying to find holes in it. Andrew didn't mind that. Sometimes a devil's advocate was valuable.

"They'll know the burglar had the combo," Bowles said.

"No, I'll rough up the box, make it look like I worked it."

"What'll you take from it?"

"Whatever's in it. What's in it?"

"Lots of stuff."

"Like what?"

"I'm still not sure I want to go along with this."

"Okay, forget it. I'll find another way. Only, I have to tell you, you and your fucking *accident* clause are turning this job into . . ."

"You knew what you were getting into."

"That's true. But I don't like you shooting down a perfectly good idea. It's *me* who has to do this, not you. What is it? Don't you trust me going into that box?"

"The price we agreed on was a hundred thousand. There's at *least* that much in the safe."

"In what?"

"Jewelry, treasury bills, cash . . ."

"If you don't trust me . . ."

"I didn't say that."

"If you don't *trust* me, then take out anything negotiable. Just leave the jewelry. Just leave what a woman would normally keep in a bedroom box."

"That'd still come to something like fifty thousand dollars' worth of stuff."

"I'm not a jewel thief, I don't want the goddamn jewels. I'll put them in a pay locker someplace, you pick the place. A bus terminal, a railroad station, whatever. The minute you pay me the second half, I'll hand over the key. Is that fair?"

"If I'm out of town, how can . . . ?"

"I'll wait for you, but I don't want to come anywhere near you till the police get through questioning you."

"I'll have to think about where," Bowles said.

"Yeah, well, think about it fast, okay? I want to get this thing done. Your wife's starting to give me a pain in the ass."

"Tell me all about it."

"Also, I have business to take care of in Chicago. I didn't intend making this job a lifetime career."

"Well, I'm sorry about that. But you knew what . . . "

"Yeah, yeah. Incidentally . . . "

He turned to Bowles.

"Did you kill Tilly?"

"No," Bowles said.

"Have the cops been around?"

"Yes."

"To ask about the Tilly hit?"

"Yes. They wanted to know where I was. And so on."

"And did you tell them?"

"I did."

"Where were you?"

"I didn't kill Tilly."

"That's not what I asked."

"I was having lunch with a client."

"Did the cops buy that?"

"They went to see her. She confirmed what I'd told them."

"Uh-huh. A lady, huh?"

"Yes."

"Who is she?"

"That's none of your business."

"You're right," Andrew said, and smiled. "So have you thought it over yet?"

"I want you there when I open the locker," Bowles said.

"Fine," Andrew said. "Just pick a place convenient to both of us. We're making a federal case out of this fucking . . . "

"Wherever," Bowles said.

"Fine, what's the combo?"

"My birthday," Bowles said. "September twenty-third."

"You're a Virgo, huh?"

"Yes."

"No wonder you don't trust anybody. So what is that? Nine, two, three?"

"Yes."

"What's the right-left sequence?"

"Four to the right, three to the left, two to the right."

Andrew was writing this down. He looked up and said, "Four to the right, stop on nine. Three to the left, stop on two. Two to the right, stop on three. Is that it?"

"That's it. When do you plan to do this?"

"As soon as possible. Few things to figure out yet. I'll let you know."

The intercom erupted with an audible click.

"We're on Lewiston, Mr. Bowles," the driver said. "May I have that address again, please?"

"Pulling in," Kling said.

"I see him."

The limo was nudging its way gently toward the curb.

"Roll it by," Kling said.

Hawes drove past the limo as it maneuvered into what seemed to be the only free parking space on the block.

"Better let me out."

Hawes double-parked only long enough to let Kling out. Up the street, Denker was just getting out of the limo. From a distance, Kling watched him. He leaned over, said something into the car, and then straightened up and closed the door. Turning away from the car, he walked to a building some two doors up from where the limo had parked. The limo was pulling away from the curb now. Kling started up the street. By the time he reached the building, Denker had already gone inside. He wrote the address into his pad, waited a moment or two, and then stepped into the small entrance hallway.

There were thirteen mailboxes on the wall to the right. One of them was marked SUPER. The other twelve were numbered for each floor of the building, three to a floor, starting with 1A, 1B, and 1C on the first floor and ending with 4A, 4B, and 4C on the fourth floor. 4C was the only mailbox without an identifying name on it. A plastic stick-on label above the boxes, black lettering on a silver field, gave the name, address, and telephone number of the real estate company managing the building. Kling copied down the information. When he came out of the building, Hawes was just pulling the sedan into the space the limo had vacated.

"What've we got?" Hawes asked.

"Nothing yet," Kling said. "We've got to make some phone calls."

"Tomorrow," Hawes said. "It's already ten after five."

"No, today," Kling said.

The telephone company gave Hawes a listing for a Dr. Kumar Moorthy at 714 Jacob's Way and advised him that the unpublished number had been in service for the past four years now. The supervisor Hawes spoke to outdid herself by informing him that this was the only telephone listed for that address. Which meant single occupancy for the three-story brownstone. Too bad he didn't know who Dr. Kumar Moorthy was.

"Got to be Indian," Parker said, looking at the pad on Hawes's desk. "That's an Indian name, for sure."

"Which tribe?" Hawes asked him.

"I'm talking *Indian* Indian."

"No kidding?"

At his own desk, Kling was on the phone with a woman from Bridge Realty. He motioned for them to tone it down. She was telling him that apartment 4C at 321 South Lewiston was rented to a man named Raymond Androtti. Kling wondered if the absence of a nameplate in the 4C mailbox meant anything at all.

"Do you have a renter named Andrew Denker?" he asked.

"Denker? No, sir."

"Or Darrow?"

"No, sir. I can give you the names of all the renters in the building . . ."

"Yes, would you do that, please?"

She ran down the list for him. As she'd told him, there was neither a Denker nor a Darrow. Nor was there anyone with the initials A. D. or A.N.D.

"How long has Mr. Androtti been renting the apartment?" Kling asked.

"Since last July."

"On a lease?"

"Yes, sir. A year-long lease."

"Well, thank you very much," he said.

"Not at all," the woman said, and hung up.

Kling looked up the name Raymond Androtti in the directories for all five sectors of the city. There was a listing for an R. Androtti in Majesta. He dialed it.

"What you should do," Parker told Hawes, "is try every hospital in the city. If this guy's an Indian doctor, that's where you'll find him. We got more Indian doctors in this city than they got in all Bombay."

Hawes was thinking that wasn't such a bad idea. How the hell was Parker coming up with all these good ideas all of a sudden?

"Hello, Mr. Androtti," Kling said into his telephone.

"Yes?"

"Raymond Androtti?"

"No, this is Ralph Androtti."

"Is there a Raymond Androtti at this number?"

"No, I'm sorry, there isn't."

"Thank you," Kling said. "Sorry to bother you."

He hung up and began dialing down the list of all the other people named Androtti, although not Raymonds. It was not a common name, there were only eight of them scattered throughout the city. Hawes had already begun dialing down the list of hospitals in his personal directory.

"Hello, I'm trying to locate a man named Raymond Androtti," Kling said. "Can you tell me . . . ?"

"Wrong number."

"Hello, this is Detective Cotton Hawes, 87th Squad? I'm looking for a doctor named Kumar Moorthy, I wonder if . . ."

Kling was finished with his comparatively short list before Hawes had made even a small dent in his. Parker, who had relieved at a quarter to four, and who was enjoying a relatively quiet night watch, did not offer to help either of them when they split the list and continued dialing. By twenty minutes past seven, they had called every hospital in the city and had not located a doctor named Kumar Moorthy.

"Call the Indian Consulate," Parker suggested.

Hawes looked at him in something close to wonder.

Parker shrugged as if to say Elementary, my dear Watson.

The consul Hawes spoke to was a man named Ajit Sakti Vedam, and he spoke with a marked British accent. He told Hawes that indeed they were familiar with Dr. Moorthy, and then explained that the doctor taught Sanskrit, Hindu, Bengali, and Nepali at Ramsey University and was a frequent and honored guest here at the consulate.

"As well as seminars on Modern India, Indic Studies, and Hindu and Buddhist Controversies," Vedam said.

"Would you know how I can reach him?" Hawes asked.

"I believe I have an address for him in New Delhi," Vedam said.

"New Delhi?"

"Yes, sir. He is there enjoying a sabbatical."

"When will he be back, would you know?" Hawes asked.

"I believe he left in September," Vedam said.

"Did he mention how long he'd be gone?"

"I'm sorry, sir."

"Would you know what he's doing with his apartment meanwhile?" Hawes asked.

"I have no idea, sir."

"Renting it? Or whatever?"

"I'm sorry."

"Thank you very much, Mr. Vedam," Hawes said, and put the receiver back on its cradle. "Any other ideas?" he asked Parker.

"Sure. Go on the earie."

The request for a court order to begin surveillance of the telephone equipment installed at 714 Jacob's Way stated that the detectives of the 87th Squad were actively engaged in an ongoing homicide investigation and had good and reasonable cause to believe that the current occupant or occupants of the building might have knowledge valuable to the investigation, which knowledge might be revealed through aforesaid surveillance.

The simultaneous request for a court order to begin surveillance of the telephone equipment installed in apartment 4C at 321 South Lewiston stated that the detectives of the 87th Squad had good and reasonable cause to believe that the current occupant of the apartment had entered into a conspiracy to commit murder, and that sufficient cause for arrest might be divulged through aforesaid surveillance.

Both petitions asked for a No-Knock provision granting permission to enter and install listening devices on whatever telephones discovered therein.

Both petitions were denied in their entireties.

This being America, that was the end of that.

Parker suggested that they go in, anyway. Plant their bugs, get what they needed, worry about the rest of it later. He was just whistling in the wind; he knew as well as the others that anything they uncovered through an illegal wiretap would be considered fruit of the poisonous tree and would be kicked out of court in a minute.

They were right back where they started.

Until Jimmy the Blink called on Saturday morning.

9.

"We never had this conversation," Jimmy said.

"What conversation?" Carella said.

"Good," Jimmy said, and Carella visualized him blinking. "This is what I understand from my people. There's this guy in no way connected to us who before now was running girls, very low-level, two or three in his stable, maybe four tops, from what I understand. Nobody to worry about, a flyspeck on a sand dune, you follow? Okay. Two, three months ago he starts another little enterprise."

"And what's that?"

"Housing for the homeless."

"How very kind of him," Carella said.

"Not the crazies you see on the street," Jimmy said. "What this person does, he provides like a safe house for anybody who needs it and can pay for it. You read spy novels?"

"No."

"Some of them are good."

"I'll bet."

"Anyway, he tucks these people in this pad while they're hiding, or working a job, or whatever. Charges them plenty, covers his overhead and then some. A small-time player, working every shitty little angle."

"Where's the pad?"

"On Lewiston. 321 South Lewiston. Apartment 4C."

"What's his name?"

"Ray Androtti."

"For Raymond?"

"I guess. It don't ring a bell with me," Jimmy said. "A small-time player all around."

"What's his connection with Denker?"

"My people think he recently rented the pad to this guy from Chicago who was looking to buy a gun. Now whether or not this is your man, I don't know."

"Where do I find Androtti?"

"That's another thing. He comes and goes like the night."

"If he *did* rent to Denker, do your people have any idea who the target might be?"

"None."

"Is Androtti from Chicago?"

"Not that I know of."

"Then why would a Chicago hitter be going to him?"

"Well, there are roads and byways that lead to everyone and everyplace," Jimmy said philosophically. "I'm sure you know that."

"Do *you* know any Chicago hitters? Off the top of your head?"

"I know hitters *everywhere* off the top of my head."

"But you tell me Androtti's very small-time."

"True."

"So how would he know a Chicago hitter?"

"Maybe the man was recommended to him."

"But your people don't know anything about him, huh? Denker?"

"Nothing."

"And you don't, either."

"I don't."

"Even though you know hitters everywhere off the top of your head."

"I don't know any Denkers," Jimmy said, and paused, and probably blinked. "You want me to call Chicago?"

"Could you?"

"Sure. But that's the end of the favor."

"That's the end of it. Andrew Denker. Or maybe Andrew Darrow."

"Which one?"

"Take your pick."

"I'll get back to you. It's still early in Chicago."

There was a click on the line.

Carella pressed the cradle-bar rest, got a fresh dial tone, and called the I.S. The detective he spoke to up there listened to his request for whatever they had on a Ray-possibly-Raymond Androtti and then said, "I got a call on this already."

"What do you mean?" Carella said.

"Ain't this the Eight-Seven?"

"Yes?"

"So talk to your people up there every now and then, okay? I already got a call from somebody named Kling. You know anybody named Kling?"

"Yes?"

"He called me yesterday. This is Saturday, ain't it? He called me yesterday, Friday. I got it written down right here."

"Are you saying you've already *given* us this information?" Carella asked.

"No, Rome wasn't built in a day," the I.S. detective said.

"Well, when do you think you can get back to us?" Carella asked. "This is a homicide we're working."

"Yeah, homicide, homicide, everybody's working a homicide in this city. I'll get back to you soon as I pull anything up, okay?"

"I'd appreciate . . ."

"Yeah, yeah," he said, and hung up.

He got back a half hour later.

There was quite a lot.

* * *

It seemed that Androtti's given name wasn't Raymond, as both Carella and Jimmy had surmised, but was instead Ramón. Nor was his last name even Androtti. It was Andros. This truly surprised Carella. It was not unusual in this country for someone with an ethnic name to change it to something more Anglo-Saxon. Carella could think of at least a hundred people who had done that, and not all of them were criminals. But to drop *one* ethnic name only to adopt *another*? Unheard of. Nonetheless, Ray Androtti was the only listed alias for Ramón Andros.

Ramón, or Ray, or whatever he called himself in the privacy of his own mind, had been a very busy fellow since his arrival from Puerto Rico some six years back. His B-sheet had him charged with a various assortment of crimes, starting with a couple of Dis Conds, and then graduating to a B&E and then doing a Burg-Three before something finally stuck and he was at last convicted and sent away on a 230.25, a Pros-Two, defined in the statutes as: "Advancing or profiting from prostitution by managing, supervising, controlling or owning, either alone or in association with others, a house of prostitution or a prostitution business or enterprise involving prostitution activity by two or more prostitutes."

This was a Class-D felony, for which Andros could have taken a fall for a max of seven years. But he was sentenced instead to a year in prison, and served only four months of it before he was paroled. His alma mater was Castleview State Penitentiary. He had been there from March through June of last year. It occurred to Carella that the late Roger Turner Tilly had been up there at about the same time.

Andros's most recent Parole Board address was 1134 Barnstable, in a section of Riverhead that once had been largely Italian-American and was now almost exclusively Hispanic. The building in which Andros lived was a two-story clapboard house alongside an empty lot. The lot had a wooden fence around it, but this hadn't prevented anyone from tossing garbage over it. The fence was covered with graffiti, like many of the buildings and walls in this city. Maybe that was because if you couldn't get rich here, you could at least get famous by writing your name in spray paint all over town.

As if reading his mind, Meyer said, "I blame Norman Mailer."

Carella looked at him.

"For calling it an art form," Meyer said.

They climbed a rickety exterior staircase to the second floor of the house and knocked on a glass-paneled door. From somewhere inside the apartment, they heard a radio playing Spanish music. An announcer came on, speaking Spanish. They knocked again.

"*Quién es?*" a man's voice shouted.

"*La policía!*" Carella shouted back. "*Abre la puerta!*"

"*Momento,*" the man said.

He came to the door in his pajamas. This was a little before noon. Striped pajamas. Red and white. Black hair tousled. Brown eyes bleary. Beard stubble on his narrow face. Peering through the glass panels, squinting into the sun, bored to tears, he said, "*Muestrame.*"

"Talk English," Meyer said to the glass.

"Choe me you bachez," the man said.

He meant Show me your badges.

Carella flashed his shield. "Are you Ramón Andros?" he asked.

"*Sí?*" Puzzled look on his face. "*Qué quiere?*"

"Talk English," Meyer said, louder this time.

"And open the door," Carella said.

Andros looked out at them one more time, pulled a sour face, and then unlocked the door.

"What do you want, man?" he said.

It came out, "Wah you wann, *loco*?"

"Okay to come in?" Carella asked.

Andros shrugged.

They moved past him into what they now saw was a long,

narrow kitchen. Sink, window, cabinets, stove, and refrigerator on the left, table and chairs on the right, radiator on the far wall alongside a doorframe leading into the bedroom. A teenage girl was sitting on the bed, the sheet tented over her knees. She was naked above the sheet. She did nothing to cover her breasts. The radio was on a night table alongside the bed. She kept tossing her head in time to the Latin beat. They wondered if she was stoned.

"Thees a ba' time, *loco*," Andros said.

They were beginning to understand him.

What he meant was, "This is a bad time, man."

"Want to close that door?" Carella said.

Andros shrugged again, went to the bedroom door, and closed it. From behind the door, the radio kept playing Spanish music.

"Have a seat," Carella said.

There were three chairs around the kitchen table, one on each end, one facing the wall. They pulled out the chairs and sat. Andros scratched his balls. This was his house, they guessed he was entitled. He had the bored air of a man who'd been hassled by cops more times than he could count. He'd come through it before, and he'd come through it this time, too. Whatever this was, he'd come through it. So he scratched his balls, and he yawned, and he waited.

"Denker," Carella said.

The brown eyes flickered.

Just a flicker. Like a snake's tongue coming out, now you see it, now you don't. Sudden interest—and then boredom again.

"Andrew Denker," Meyer said.

"Ees thotta name?"

Coming through loud and clear now: Is that a name?

"It's a name, yes," Carella said.

"Do you know him?" Meyer asked.

"No."

"We think you do."

"I don't know him."

"Then who's living in your apartment on Lewiston?"

"321 South Lewiston."

"Apartment 4C."

"Is that your apartment?"

He sat watching them through all this, not saying a word.
Then he said, "I don't know nobody named Albert Denker."

"*Andrew* Denker," Carella said.

"Him either."

"Then who's that in your apartment?"

"I don't know what apartment you're talking about."

"An apartment you're renting from Bridge Realty," Carella
said.

"On a one-year lease," Meyer said.

"Starting last July, right after you got out of the slammer."

He kept watching them.

"You feel like coming downtown with us?" Meyer asked.

"Why would I feel like coming downtown?"

"So we can sort this out," Carella said.

"What's there to sort out?"

"You seem not to know about an apartment leased in your
name."

"Who says?"

"A woman named Charlotte Carmichael of Bridge Realty.
Down near the Calm's Point Bridge, Ramón."

"I don't know this person."

"Okay, let's get out of our little peejays and into our street
clothes," Meyer said.

"Hold on a minute, okay?"

"We're holding," Carella said.

"What's this about, anyway?"

He sounded like Desi Arnaz asking "Wha's thees abou',
Lucy?" But they now understood him clearly, which showed
the benefits of a second language, darling.

"This is about a man named Andrew Denker," Carella said patiently.

"Who's renting your apartment on Lewiston," Meyer said patiently.

"Okay," Andros said, and nodded.

"Okay, what?"

"Let's say that's true, okay?"

"Let's say so," Carella said.

"So what?" Andros said. "It's against the law to rent an apartment?"

Ees agains' dee law to renn an apar'menn?

"No, but it's against the law to arrange somebody's murder."

"Pffffhhhhh," Andros said, and rolled his eyes. "Where did you get that from?"

"Do you know anybody named Martin Bowles?"

"Never heard of him."

"You never heard of him, you never heard of Denker, how about Roger Tilly?"

"No, who's that?"

"Do you have a hat, Ramón?"

"I have a hat, yes."

"Put it on. A coat, too. We're taking a ride down-town."

"Now, listen, hold on a minute."

"No, shithead, no more holding on. Get dressed, let's go."

"Okay, okay," Andros said.

"Okay, okay, what?"

"Suppose I know who Tilly is?"

"Okay, suppose you do," Meyer said.

"So what?"

"So he's dead, that's what."

Andros went "Pffffhhhhh" again.

"This is news to you, huh?"

"Absolutely."

"How well did you know him?"

"He was in Castleview while I was up there."

"When's the last time you saw him?"

"Up there. He beat up one of our people, that's why he was there."

"Uh-huh."

"His ass wasn't worth a nickel up there."

"What were *you* doing up there?"

"They framed me."

"Sure, everybody up there got framed."

"Sure, but this is true. They said I was running girls. Come on, *loco*."

"They were wrong, right?"

"Hey, of course."

"How so?"

"I done my time, okay? Why we bringing up all this shit?"

"Because we're still trying to find out how well you knew Tilly."

"I wouldn't even *talk* to that son of a bitch."

"You didn't like him, huh?"

"*None* of the Latinos liked him."

"So now he's dead."

"So go talk to the *other* ten thousand people could've juked him."

A glance passed between them. They knew in that moment that Andros knew nothing at all about the Tilly murder. Because whatever else had happened to him, he certainly hadn't been "juked," no one had stabbed him. Juking was what you did on the prison yard. The association was a natural one for Andros to make, but it told them that he knew nothing about the mechanics of Tilly's murder. Unless he was a hell of a lot smarter than either of them suspected he was.

"Ever hear of a woman named Emma Bowles?"

"Bowles?" he said.

It sounded like "bowels."

The detectives almost burst out laughing.

"Bowles," Meyer said, trying to keep a straight face. "Bowles."

"No, who's that?"

"Mrs. Martin Bowles," Carella said.

"I don't know this person."

"Okay, now let's hear about Denker."

"Denker," Andros said.

"Denker."

"I never met him."

"But you know him, right?"

"No, I don't know him."

"Ramón, let's cut the shit, okay? We *know* it's your apartment, and we know Denker's *in* it. Now how about it?"

"Okay, okay," Andros said.

"You said that before."

"Let's say I *did* rent the apartment to this Denker guy."

"Never mind let's say. Did you or didn't you?"

"More or less."

"What does that mean?"

"Not directly."

"Then how?"

"Let's say a friend of mine said he needed a place for somebody to stay."

"And the somebody was Denker, is that right?"

"The somebody was Denker."

"And who was the friend?"

"Why you need to know that?"

"Who's paying the rent? Your friend or Denker?"

"Denker. But through my friend."

"How much is the rent?"

"Twelve hundred a week. Cash."

"That's a lot of bread, Ramón."

"Well, nice apartments are hard to find these days."

"He could stay in a luxury hotel for that kind of money."

"But then he wouldn't have no privacy, *verdad*?"

"Okay, so who's your friend?"

"I don't want to get nobody in trouble."

"Fine, get dressed."

"What's the *matter* with you guys?"

Sounding like Desi talking to Lucy again.

They said nothing. In the other room, the radio station broke for a news broadcast. There was a lot of dial twirling in there until the girl finally found another station playing music. They waited. They had all the time in the world.

"Whatever this Denker did," Andros said at last, "*I* don't know, and my friend don't know, either."

"Who said he did anything?"

"You said somebody was arranging a murder."

Smarter than they thought.

"You know anything about that?"

"Nothing."

"You ever hear of Denker before he took the apartment?"

"Never."

"How'd your friend hear about him?"

"I don't know. He said he had this person was going to be in town a little while, he needed an apartment. That's all I know."

"You always rent that apartment to strangers?"

"It's not a stranger if a friend comes to me."

"You keep that apartment occupied most of the time?"

"There's always people need an apartment, one reason or another. It's a business investment," Andros said, and shrugged.

"A good one, I'll bet."

"I can't complain. There's no law against renting an apartment to somebody."

"Does your lease allow you to sublet?"

"It does."

"You're sure about that?"

"You want to see it?"

"We'll take your word for it."

"Anyway, even if it doesn't, that's civil, not criminal."

Much smarter than they thought.

"So what's your friend's name?" Carella asked casually.

"Why do we keep coming back to that?"

"We'd like to meet him. In case we need an apartment one day."

Andros pulled a face.

"So what do you say?" Carella asked.

"I say there's no way you can force me to tell you anything I don't want to tell you."

"That's true," Meyer said. "How old is the little girl in there?"

"Old enough."

"You auditioning her, or what?"

"'Cause you'd be looking at a Class-C if she's under sixteen."

"She's twenty-one."

"Has she got a birth certificate with her?"

"A Class-C can gross you fifteen."

"At your favorite hotel."

"So let's talk to her, huh?"

"No, we don't have to talk to her," Andros said.

"Find out how old she is."

"See how far we can go with this," Meyer said.

"So what's your friend's name?" Carella asked again, not so casually this time.

"Elena. And she's twenty-one, I told you."

"Not *that* friend. The one who contacted you about Denker."

"I forget his name."

"Okay, let's talk to the girl," Carella said, and shouted, "Elena! Put on your clothes and come out here!"

"She's twenty-one," Andros insisted.

"She looks fifteen," Meyer said.

From the look on Andros's face, he'd hit it right on the head.

"Let's *go*, Elena!" Carella yelled.

"Ramón?" she said from behind the door. *"Quieres que salga?"*

"Espera un momento," Andros said.

"Y bueno?" Carella asked.

"Su nombre es Gofredo Cabrera," Andros said.

His name is Gofredo Cabrera.

"Muchas gracias," Meyer said.

The social club was called Las Palmas, a name designed to evoke fond memories of palm trees and azure seas and whispering sands. But this section of the city was called *L'Infierno* by its residents, and it was a brick-and-concrete hell far from any sands, whispering or not, festering with poverty and drugs. In what had once been the apartment's bedroom, there was a small bar against one wall, with shelves behind it on which were some bottles of scotch and vodka, but mostly bottles of rum. And there was a microwave oven and a coffee maker on a small table, and there were several tables with chairs around them. Three men were sitting at one of the tables, playing cards and drinking wine.

This was now about three in the afternoon, there were no women in the club at this hour. The women would drop in sometime after dinner, to talk in Spanish with other neighborhood women, or to dance in the apartment's largest room, the living room, where there was now a record player and hardly any furniture. A blue curtain hanging in the doorway separated this room from the other one. This used to be the super's apartment when the building still had one. Now it was a social club, where people in the building came to laugh a little and drink a little and talk their native language.

The detectives were standing outside the front door, looking into the apartment. The man who'd opened the door for them had been sitting at the table when they knocked. His cards were still lying facedown on the table, in front of the chair he'd vacated. They had just identified themselves as policemen. The man wanted to know what they wanted.

"We're looking for someone named Gofredo Cabrera."

"Not here," the man said.

Faint Spanish accent, pale complexion, lean, handsome looks, small mustache under an aquiline nose.

"We were told he'd be here," Carella said.

"No," the man said, and shook his head.

"Know where we can find him?"

"No," the man said again.

"He's not in any trouble," Meyer explained.

"Mm," the man said.

"We'd really like to talk to him," Carella said.

"I don't know where he is," the man said.

"What's *your* name?" Meyer asked.

The man hesitated.

I'll be damned, Meyer thought.

"Are *you* Cabrera?" he asked.

The man's eyes darted nervously.

"Why do you want him?" he said.

"We have some questions."

"Just a minute," the man said.

He went back into the room, spoke softly in Spanish to the three men still sitting at the table, and then came back to the door and took a coat from the rack just inside it.

"Let's go downstairs," he said. "Get some air."

The air downstairs was virtually crystalline. Meyer and Carella fell in on either side of the man, flanking him, hands in their pockets. He walked with his shoulders hunched, the wind whipping his long black hair. He still hadn't told them who he was. There were names written on the brick walls everywhere around them, but they still didn't know his. If this were a movie, the graffiti-covered walls would have made a good backdrop for a location shot. The art director would have congratulated himself on having found something so riotously colorful against which to play a low-keyed scene, such *contrast*! So far, this real-life scene the detectives were playing was so low-key it was almost nonexistent. The man just kept walking along between them, hair blowing in the wind, shoulders hunched, lips sealed.

"In here," he said at last, and led them into a small *cuchi frito* joint with four red leatherette booths on the left and a green Formica-topped counter on the right. The place smelled of cooking fat. The man nodded to the short-order cook behind the counter, and then kept right on walking through the place, to a door at the back, and through the doorway into another room where a round wooden table sat under a hanging light bulb covered with a tasseled pinkish shade.

"Have a seat," he said, and motioned to the chairs around the table.

The detectives sat.

"You want some coffee or something?"

"No, we want Cabrera," Meyer said.

"Why?"

"Routine investigation," Carella said.

"What's your name?" Meyer asked.

"José Altaba."

"Why all the hocus-pocus, José?"

"I don't know what you mean."

"He means why'd you lead us halfway across the city on a day you could freeze your ass off, is what he means," Meyer said.

"To the back room of a crummy little . . ."

"I *own* this place," Altaba said, offended.

"Why couldn't we talk at Las Palmas?" Carella asked.

"Ears," Altaba said.

"Ears," Carella repeated.

"*Sí.*"

"What is it you didn't want anyone to hear?"

"There is a man there who wishes only harm to Gofredo."

209

It sounded like a direct translation from the Spanish.

"And this man was at Las Palmas, is that it?"

"*Sí*, that's it."

"So you didn't want him to hear any of this."

"Because he would twist it to his own use," Altaba said, and nodded. "Make it seem as if Gofredo was doing something wrong. Instead of being an honest businessman."

"Uh-huh," Meyer said. "And what *is* this business of his?"

"Not drugs," Altaba said.

"Who said drugs?"

"You guys always think drugs."

"What *is* he into?" Meyer asked.

"This other man would only use this to hurt Gofredo," Altaba said. "But I'm a good friend of his."

"So let's hear it."

"Guns," Altaba said.

"Guns," Carella repeated.

"*Sí*," Altaba said.

"*Selling* guns?" Meyer suggested.

Altaba nodded.

"So who'd he sell a gun to recently?"

Wanting him to say Andrew Denker.

"Somebody here to do a job."

"What kind of job?"

Wanting him to say murder.

"A big one."

"Like what? A bank heist? Something like that?"

Wanting it to come from him.

"No, no," he said.

"Then what?"

"I think you know."

"No, we don't know."

Like pulling teeth.

"Then what are you doing here?" Altaba asked. "If you don't know why you're here, then why are you here?"

"We're here because Cabrera found a room for somebody," Meyer said, and glanced at Carella who gave a faint, almost indiscernible nod. Run with it, he was saying. Tell him the truth, let's see where it takes us.

Altaba nodded, too. A big, knowing nod.

"Tell us," Meyer said.

"The same guy," Altaba said.

"The same guy *what*?" Meyer said, beginning to lose his patience.

"The guy he found the room for, this is the same guy he sold the gun to."

"Ahh," Meyer said.

"You got it," Altaba said.

"Who was the guy?"

"I don't know. All I know is he came to the club . . . "

"Who? What do you mean?"

"This guy he sold the gun to."

"Came to Las Palmas?"

"That's what I'm telling you."

"When?"

"After Christmas sometime. Right after Christmas."

"Was he white, black, Hispan . . . ?"

"White."

"What'd he look like?"

"Big tall blond guy."

"Okay, and?"

"And he ast for Gofredo. And the two of them went out together."

"Why do you think he was there?"

"For a piece, I told you."

"How do you know that?"

"'Cause Gofredo told me later he made a hun' fifty profit on the gun."

"What kind of gun, would you know?"

"A forty-five. A Colt."

"What else did he say?"

"Gofredo?"

"Yes. Did he say anything about a room?"

"He said he'd make another fifty on the room."

"What do you mean?"

"His commission. For helping the guy find a room."

"Did he say where he was going to get this room?"

"No."

"Does the name Ray Androtti mean anything to you?"

"No."

"How about Ramón Andros?"

"I think I heard that name."

"Where'd you hear it?"

"I don't know."

"Did Gofredo mention it?"

"Maybe."

"In connection with finding this man a room?"

"Maybe, I don't remember."

"Does the name Andrew Denker ring a bell?"

"No."

"Do you know anybody named Tilly?"

"Is that a girl?"

"No, a man. Roger Tilly."

"No."

"Roger Turner Tilly."

"Never heard of him."

"Who's the man at Las Palmas?"

"What man?"

"The one who'd like to get Cabrera in trouble."

"I can't tell you that."

"*Why* does he want to get Cabrera in trouble?" Meyer asked.

"Because Gofredo is fucking his wife."

"Ahh," Carella said.

"But you didn't hear this from me," Altaba said, and shrugged elaborately and innocently.

"Know where we can find Cabrera?" Carella asked.

"I wish I did," Altaba said. "I would tell you in a minute."

And suddenly they knew that the wife he'd been talking about was his own wife, and that the man at Las Palmas who wished only harm to his good old buddy Cabrera was none other than José Altaba himself, in person.

Altaba shrugged again, confirming it.

You came crosstown to the bridge that ran over the Diamondback River at its narrowest point, and suddenly the accents were no longer Hispanic. You were in Diamondback now, and Diamondback was black, although this was a misnomer in that none of these people were *black*, they were merely varying shades of colors as old as time and as rich as loam. Up here was where the thousand points of light never shone. Black mayor or not, black commissioner or not, up here was where the fire would come when it came, if it came.

Ollie Weeks survived up here by hating every black man who crossed his path. Carella and Meyer were cut of quite a different cloth, and what troubled them most was the thought that up here *they* might be the ones who got killed for Ollie's sins. So they drove carefully, not wanting to be responsible for the holocaust if it came, when it came. The car heater was on, but it contributed very little toward heating the car, what with the temperature outside hovering at the zero mark. Zero degrees Fahrenheit was about minus eighteen degrees Celsius. That was cold. That was unusually cold for this city. It sometimes got that cold here—as witness right *now*—but not very often and not for such long stretches of time.

Winter was beginning to get to them. In this kind of weather, they did not want to be shagging ass all over the city, chasing the killer or killers of a two-bit punk like Tilly. They did not want to be thinking up ways they could arrest Andrew Denker before he got around to killing Emma Bowles—if in fact he'd been hired to kill her at all. It *was* possible, after all, that he was *really* a private eye from the Windy City, here to protect the lady.

"What the problem is," Meyer was saying, "is we can't bust this guy unless we can prove Bowles hired him to do the wife. That's conspiracy. And if murder's the crime . . ."

"Or kidnapping," Carella said.

"Or kidnapping, right, then what we're looking at is a Class-C felony. But Bowles isn't going to come out and *admit* he hired him . . ."

"Of course not."

". . . and they won't let us have a goddamn wiretap, so where does that leave us?"

They were approaching the Eight-Three. Meyer pulled the car into the curb, alongside a blue-and-white. Before they got out of the car, they checked the street left and right to make sure nobody was about to go on a rampage, because in any rampage blind hatred could not distinguish shades of white or brown.

The Eight-Three looked exactly like the Eight-Seven, except that it was further uptown. The sergeant behind the desk could have been Dave Murchison, except that he was a little younger and not quite as paunchy. The walkie-talkies recharging on the wall alongside the Computer Room could just as easily have been taped with the words PROPERTY OF 87TH PCT. The iron-runged steps leading to the second floor had the same familiar ring to them.

And upstairs there were the same smells, the faint stink of urine as they passed the men's room, the aroma of coffee brewing in the Clerical Office, the stench of stale cigarette smoke as they approached the squadroom. The precincts in this city all looked and smelled alike. Even the new ones started to resemble the old ones before too long. There was a lot of crime in this city, and the station houses were used twenty-four hours a day. That was enough to make anything look older than it was.

Fat Ollie Weeks looked younger than he was. That was because he was fat. Fat people looked fat, but they also looked young. It was a phenomenon of nature. When they came in, he was talking to a black hooker at his desk. He motioned for them to take a seat, and then he turned to the girl again.

"Now, Marfelia," he said, "you know, don't you, that you are in very serious trouble here, don't you?"

The girl looked as if she knew she was in very serious trouble. Big brown eyes wide in a narrow fox face. Lipstick slash on her wide mouth. Hands nervously twisting in her lap and then tugging at the hem of a mini riding north. Thin legs crossed. High-heeled ankle-strapped pumps. She looked about nineteen years old, but Ollie was laying a lot of heavy muscle on her. Carella figured he knew why. What he was trying to arrange was a little tête-à-tête for later on. Let the girl go for now, but tell her she owed him one. Drop by when he got relieved, ask her to pay her dues to Big Fat Daddy here.

It was now almost four-thirty. Ollie actually looked up at the wall clock, checking the time, almost licking his lips, leaning in closer to the girl, whispering to her now. The girl kept nodding. She was understanding how much trouble she was in. She was listening to every word Ollie said. Ollie was her salvation. Yes, her head was saying. Yes, later. Yes, here's my address. Ollie was smiling like a crocodile about to eat a rabbit. He wrote something on his pad. The girl got up, nodded, said something to him, looked at the clock, and swiveled out of the squadroom on heels far too high for her.

Ollie came over to where they were sitting at the other desk.

"What can I do for you?" he asked, smiling.

"Get it all set up?" Carella asked.

"I don't know what you're talking about."

"You know what I'm talking about."

"Whatever you're talking about, it's none of your business," Ollie said.

"What do you know about a man named Gofredo Cabrera?" Carella said. Make this short and sweet, he thought, get the

hell out of here. The less time you had to spend with a cop
like—

"Who wants to know?" Ollie said.

"Two people who are shagging *your* fucking case," Meyer
said.

"Oh, listen how tough they're making them these days,"
Ollie said.

He meant Jews. Meyer wanted to kill him.

"Ever hear about interdepartmental cooperation?" he said.

"What's a fuckin spic got to do with anything went down
before?" Ollie said.

"Do you know him or not?"

"I know everything about everybody in this precinct. Even
a fuckin spic dumb enough to be living up here."

Up here.

That said it all.

There were rules up here. You stay on your turf, I'll stay on
mine. You come messin' up here, you got trouble, mister.

"Then you know who he is, right?" Carella asked.

"Sure."

"Who?"

"A penny-ante gun-runner."

"Who told you that?"

"Common knowledge. You guys work silk stocking, you
don't know what it is to . . ."

"Cut the shit, Ollie."

Ollie looked at him.

"You hear me?" Carella said.

"I hear you."

"So cut it. We're not silk stocking, and you know it. Just
tell us whatever you know about Gofredo Cabrera. If you don't
know anything, put us onto whoever does."

"I know everything goes on in this fuckin precinct," Ollie
said. "I'm gonna be *lieutenant* in this fuckin precinct one day,

so don't give me I don't know anything about Cabrera. What do you wanna know?''

"Whatever you've got.''

"He lives up here 'cause his business is guns. And niggers need guns. Period.''

"Have you got anything that would connect him to Tilly?'' Meyer said.

"No. Have you?''

"No, but . . .''

"Tell me, wise man.''

He was treading the thin edge of open anti-Semitism. A wise man was a rabbi. But Ollie knew that if he called Meyer ''rabbi,'' he'd be searching for his teeth on the squadroom floor. He was a cautious bigot, Fat Ollie. Meyer was close to hitting him, anyway.

"We think Tilly was hired to kill Emma Bowles,'' he said, controlling his anger.

"Ah yes,'' Ollie said, "Emma Bowles, ah yes,'' falling into his W. C. Fields imitation, hoping to charm Meyer out of his anger.

"And we think Cabrera sold a gun to the *new* boy in town . . .''

"Ah yes.''

"Andrew Denker . . .''

"Ah yes.''

"And also helped him find a room.''

"Wonderful connection, ah yes,'' Ollie said.

"We don't know how wonderful it is,'' Carella said, "but it's a connection.''

"Or a coincidence,'' Ollie said, abruptly dropping the Fields routine.

"Maybe not.''

"What'd Ballistics say about the gun killed Tilly?''

"A Hi-Standard Snub,'' Carella said.

"How does that tie with the gun this punk sold Denker?"

"It doesn't."

"Want to tell me what kind of piece it was? Or is that a state secret?"

"A Colt forty-five."

"Sure."

"Sure what?"

"Coincidence. The *guns* don't even match."

"Have you got any reason to believe Cabrera was tied to Tilly in any way whatever?" Meyer asked.

"None."

"Sold *him* a gun maybe?"

"I got no evidence of that."

"Or knew him in some other way? Dope maybe?"

"Why? Was Tilly doing dope?" Ollie asked.

"Not that we know of."

"So what's all this shit you're pulling out of thin air?" Ollie said, and looked up at the clock.

"She'll wait," Carella said.

"I'm in no hurry," Ollie said, and grinned again.

10.

She called him at a little before eight that Saturday night. She sat listening to the phone ringing on the other end, once, twice, gripping the receiver tightly in her hand, three times, and then his voice came onto the line—"Hello?"—startling her into silence for a moment so that he said, "Hello?" again, somewhat impatiently this time.

"Yes, hello, it's me," she said.

"Who's me?" he asked.

It occurred to her that this was the first time he'd heard her voice on the telephone.

"Emma," she said. "Emma Bowles."

"Oh, hello," he said. "How are you?"

She visualized him smiling, lying on a bed someplace. A rented room someplace. The lights out. Neon flashing downstairs someplace. He was living down there near the bridge someplace, he could probably see the lights of the bridge from his window, Calm's Point glittering in the distance. Lying on the bed. Smiling.

"The reason I'm calling," she said, and hesitated. "Well . . ." she said, and hesitated again. "You see, when Martin got home from the office yesterday, he told me he had to go out of town for the weekend . . ."

"Oh?"

"Yes. Up to Boston," she said.

"Must be cold up there," he said.

"Yes."

She hesitated again.

"Anyway," she said, "I was thinking of going to a movie tonight."

"What do you mean?" he said at once. "You don't mean *alone*, do you?"

"Well, yes, that's why I'm calling. I know how serious you are about your job, although with Tilly dead . . ."

"I am serious," he said.

"Yes, which is why I'm calling to tell you not to worry. In case you decided to call and got no answer. Because I told you I'd be home all day today . . ."

"Yes, you did."

". . . but that was before Martin decided to go out of town all of a sudden."

There was a silence on the line.

"I really don't like this," he said at last.

"Oh, I'll be fine, don't worry about it."

"I'm not so sure about that. What time does this movie start?"

"Nine-something, I'll have to look it up. But I'm sure you've made other plans."

"No, I haven't made any. . . ."

"Which would be perfectly understandable. I *did* tell you I'd be . . ."

"Yes, but I haven't made any plans, really. I'd be happy to come up there and . . ."

"Well, that's . . ."

". . . make sure you got home safe."

"That's very nice of you. Although, as I said, with Tilly dead there's nothing to worry about anymore."

"Well, I haven't seen a movie in a long time," he said.

"Well, if you really . . ."

"I'll catch a cab, be up there in half an hour or so."

"Well, all right," she said. "But really, I'd be perfectly safe by my . . ."

"Be no trouble at all," he said. "See you soon."

She heard a click on the other end of the line.

She put the receiver back on the cradle and stood by the phone, one hand on the receiver, the other holding to her mouth an Elsa Peretti lowercase letter *e* in gold. She nibbled on the *e* for an instant, and then let it drop on its slender chain to fall between her naked breasts.

Carmen Sanchez stood tall and loose-limbed in a blue spotlight that turned her long silvery gown to brilliant glare ice. A rhinestone clip twinkled on the right side of her head, caught in a mop of curly black hair that echoed eyes as black as midnight, sparkling in the cold blue beam, scattering reflected glints of light. She held the microphone in her right hand, its long cord trailing down one thigh and then curling behind her like a slender black snake. She had just broken a single chord into at least seven shimmering pieces, riding it to the ceiling of the club like a diatonic rocket, and following it with an expectant silence as deep and as dark as an ocean.

Smoke drifted up languidly on the air, blue in the light that bathed her. She looked out beyond the light, into the room, into the crowd, dark eyes slyly insinuating, microphone close to her mouth, lips opening in a caress around the single word that began the next song, the word hissing out of her mouth, her lips caressing it, whispering it onto the air and into the darkness.

"Kiss . . ."

From where they sat at the bar, Meyer and Carella listened and watched.

> "It all begins with a . . .
> Kiss . . .
> But kisses wither

And die
Unless
The first
Caress
Is true.

Kiss . . .
These lips that burn in a
Kiss . . .
Are only learning
To lie
Unless
The first
Caress
Is true.

So hold me tight and whisper
Words of
Love
Against my eyes.
And kiss me sweet and promise
Me your
Kisses won't be lies.

Kiss . . .
And show me, tell me of
Bliss . . .
Because I know I
Will die
Unless
This first
Caress
Is true."

The last word of the song hung on the air, drifted, faded, to be replaced by a silence as deep as the earlier expectant hush had been. And then someone shouted, "Yeah!" and the crowd leaped to its feet in thunderous applause. Carmen snapped the mike back onto its stand, and then, smiling graciously, she put her hands together as if in prayer and bowed her head in acknowledgment, the rhinestone clip tossing bouquets of glistening light to the audience. Still smiling, she swept the long silver gown around her long legs, and moved sinuously off the stage, one arm raised in a final salute, the blue light following her. The clock in a green neon circle over the bar read twenty minutes to eleven. Carella and Meyer nodded to each other and then got off the barstools and headed for the small curtained doorway to the right of the stage.

She knew they were here, she was expecting them.

They told her how terrific she was . . .

"Thanks, I appreciate it," she said.

. . . and then got down to business.

"The telephone calls that morning . . ."

"Here we go with the telephone again," she said, and looked suddenly very tired. She took a towel from where it was hanging on her dressing table, and draped it over her shoulders and the sloping tops of her breasts in the low-cut gown. Sitting before the mirror with its edging of small bright lights, she began taking off her makeup. Cold-creaming the makeup away, slowly revealing the shining face of a young and beautiful woman.

"Are you sure there were only two calls? The one that came in, and the one he . . ."

"Yes, I'm positive."

"Just the two calls, right?"

"What did I just say?"

Eyes watching them in the mirror. Eyeliner gone, lipstick coming off. A fresh-faced beauty underneath. Watching them.

"If we gave you some names, would you remember Tilly ever mentioning them?"

"How would I know? Try me."

"Ray Androtti," Carella said. "Or Ramón Andros."

"Neither one."

"How about Gofredo Cabrera?"

"No."

She took the towel from her shoulders and wiped her face clean with it. Rising suddenly and splendidly in the long silver gown and sequined silver slippers, she whisked across the room to a door, opened it, went into the bathroom on the other side of it, said, "I'll just be a minute," and closed the door behind her.

The detectives waited.

They could hear water running in there.

They kept waiting.

The water stopped running.

She was humming inside there now, the same tune that had closed her act. Kiss. Humming it softly. Some five minutes later, the door opened again. She was wearing a short skirt and a white blouse, low-heeled shoes, no makeup. She went over to the dressing table and began combing out her hair.

"This is Saturday night," she said, "I have another show at midnight. I usually go out for something to eat between shows. The food here is terrible."

"We won't be long," Meyer said.

"I hope not. 'Cause I work up a real hunger out there."

"What we want to know is everything you can remember about that second call."

"I told you everything I knew."

"Are you sure you heard Tilly say the name Bowles?"

"That's what I heard."

"Because if this is the man he was going downstairs to meet . . ."

". . . and if it had something to do with money," Meyer said, "you remember telling us the conversation had something to do with money, don't you?"

"Yes, I remember."

"Tilly wanting the rest of his money from Bowles."

"Yes, I think that's what they were saying. I told you, I was in the shower. . . ."

"No, you said you were dressing, don't you remember? This was after . . ."

"Either way, I wasn't paying too much attention to what Roger was saying on the phone."

"Well, let's go over it one more time, okay?" Meyer said.

"You know," Carmen said, "every time you guys come to see me, I'm on the way somewhere. And you always tell me this won't take long, this'll just take a minute, and it always takes forever. Only this time I just finished doing a show, and I'm starving to death, and I don't *want* it to take forever. I want to go *eat*, okay? You think you got that? I'm hungry, I'm famished, I'm starving to . . ."

"So let's go eat," Carella said, and smiled.

The movie let out at five minutes past eleven. It was a cold, clear starlit night, and Emma suggested that they walk back to the apartment. She had not worn her mink to the theater. Instead, she was wearing the long gray cavalry officer's coat and a gray woolen hat with a red stripe. Andrew was wearing the only coat he'd brought with him from Chicago, the camel-hair Burberry. Under that, he had on a tan Shetland sweater with a shawl collar, a brown wool turtleneck, and brown tweed slacks. He liked to look casually elegant, even if he was only going to a movie. He hoped she appreciated this. Even if it was a lousy movie. He was telling her he had not liked the movie because he'd found it unbelievable.

"All that stuff about the hooker," he said.

"I guess you know a lot of hookers," Emma said. "Your line of work."

"Well, I've run into a few of them, let's say that."

"What did you find unbelievable?" she asked.

As they walked rapidly through the windswept streets, he

reeled off all the inconsistencies he had spotted. She was amazed that he'd watched an essentially mindless film so carefully. When at last they reached her building, she said, "Thanks a lot for coming all the way up here, I really appreciate it."

"It was no trouble," he said.

The doorman had seen them now. He was walking toward the glass entrance doors, reaching for the long brass handle.

"Would you like to come up?" she asked.

"Good evening, Mrs. Bowles," the doorman said.

"For a cup of coffee or something?"

Sometime after midnight, the streets would begin to change. In the wink of an eye, what had at least *appeared* civilized would transmogrify into an alien landscape. But it was only twenty past eleven now, and the predators hadn't yet surfaced. The all-night deli around the corner from Clancy's was crowded with theatergoers, tourists, a few residents of the area, all of them enjoying a snack before toddling home to beddie-bye. Midnight was the witching hour. No one looked up at the clock on the wall opposite the door, but anyone living in this city had an internal clock that told him when the slime would come bubbling up out of the sewers. Best to be home before then. Best not to be touched by that slime. So they chatted nonchalantly, and they ate and drank with gusto, but the internal clocks were ticking away, and all these people would be out of here by twelve-thirty, one—because after that you had to be crazy. Only Carmen Sanchez kept an eye on the clock. She had a show to do at midnight, and she had to be in costume and made up by then.

She ate as if she hadn't had a decent meal in a decade.

Big hot-pastrami sandwich on a seeded roll, packed with rich red meat and dripping mustard. Huge platter of French fries smothered in ketchup. Sliced sour pickles smelling of garlic and brine. Celery tonic in a bottle, straws sticking out of it. Just as if she'd been born Jewish. The cops were drinking coffee. They watched her wolfing down the food. Meyer was wondering why she bothered getting *out* of her makeup when she only had to put it on again an hour later. Maybe she was shy, didn't want to be seen all dolled up in public. She didn't eat as if she was shy. She ate like the Russian Army.

"I'm positive the name was Bowles," she said, biting into the sandwich again, and then picking up a slice of pickle and biting into that and sipping at the celery tonic and popping a couple of fries into her mouth, a regular eating machine. Meyer watched her in wonder and awe.

"And there were only those two calls, is that right?" he said.

"Yes, that morning," she said.

"Well . . . were there *other* calls?" Carella asked.

"Well, sure, the phone rings all the time," Carmen said. "What do you mean, were there other calls?"

"I mean for *Tilly*," he said. "Not necessarily that morning."

"Sure. When he was there, he got calls."

"How often was he there?"

"Now and then."

"What my partner's asking . . ." Meyer started.

"I know what he's asking. The answer is no, we weren't living together, but yes, he came by every now and then."

"To spend the night."

"To spend the night, to spend a few days, whatever."

"Did you know he'd served time in prison?"

"Yes. But that was a bullshit thing, he beat somebody up."

"Hurt him pretty badly, from what we understand," Meyer said.

"Broke his nose . . ."

"Both his arms . . ."

"Sent him to the hospital . . ."

"Still bullshit," Carmen said. "Anyway, there are people who go to jail, you know, who are just as decent as you or me."

Neither of the detectives cared to argue this point. Carella looked up at the clock. So did Meyer. There was no detaining her this time. She had a show to do, and she had to be out of here by twenty-to. That was what she'd told them, and this time they'd honor it. It was now twenty-five past eleven. Carmen looked up at the clock, too, which made three clock-watchers in a place oblivious to time except for the ticking of all the internal clocks.

"Would you remember any of those other calls?" Carella asked. "The ones for Tilly?"

"Come on, guys, gimme a break, huh?" Carmen said, and bit into the sandwich again. A blob of mustard oozed out from between the slices of bread. "Oops," she said, and caught it with a paper napkin before it hit the tabletop.

"The night before, for example," Meyer said.

"Or anytime in the twenty-four hours preceding his death," Carella said.

"Any calls during that period."

"Any names you might have heard him mention."

They were still trying to put together a 24–24. The twenty-four hours preceding a homicide were important because if you could get a bead on what the victim had done, the people he'd seen, the places he'd visited, you might stumble across a murderer somewhere along the way. The twenty-four hours following the murder were important only because after that the trail got cold and the killer's edge widened. It was now five days since they'd found Tilly dangling from a basement pipe. And it was very cold outside.

Carmen was thinking.

"I got home late, you know . . ."

"Yes."

"Two o'clock or thereabouts. Roger may have been on the phone when I came in, I'm not sure. He was still watching television, so maybe it was someone on the *screen* who was on the phone, you understand?"

"Uh-huh. How about the next morning? You said you woke up and had breakfast . . ."

"Yeah."

"And then went back to bed for a little while."

"Yeah."

"After which you heard Tilly on the phone with two different people. Once with a car dealer, and the next time with Bowles."

"Right."

"And he said he'd meet him downstairs . . ."

"On the front stoop, right . . ."

"Right, in half an hour."

"But then Roger changed it to twelve sharp."

"Which is when Tilly went downstairs," Meyer said.

"Yes. Well, a few minutes before. Five to twelve. Around then."

"Okay. Were there any *other* calls that morning? While you were having breakfast, for example . . ."

"No."

"Or while you were in bed afterward. . . ."

"No, just those two calls."

"We know the first one was to a number listed to Arcade Motors. . . ."

"I don't know the name of the . . ."

"Well, we do. We checked with the phone company for any outgoing calls that morning or the night before. But the . . ."

"I only heard the man's name. Mr. Steinberg. I remember it because Roger had some other conversations with him. About the car he was looking at."

"What kind of car was he buying?" Carella asked abruptly.

"A Mercedes."

"Must've come into some money recently, huh?"

"We never discussed his business."

"What *was* his business?"

"I just told you we never discussed it."

"Then you don't know what it was, right?"

"I don't know what it was, right."

"You wouldn't know if it was dope or not."

"Is your partner deaf?" she asked Meyer. "If I don't know what it was, how would I know if it was dope?"

"Expensive car like that," Carella said, and shrugged.

Meyer glanced at the clock. Time was running out. He knew why Carella was reluctant to drop the dope angle. If, in fact, Bowles had not come uptown to meet with Tilly, then it had to have been someone else who'd been waiting downstairs to introduce him to Mr. Hi-Standard and his partner Mr. Snub. Buying an expensive motorcar tied in very nicely with selling dope. So Carella kept circling the dope possibility. Because if it wasn't Bowles and it wasn't dope, then it had to be a wild card. Something totally out of the blue, someone choosing a random victim, which nowadays happened more and more often. In which case, anybody in the whole damn city could have killed him. No wonder Carella was reluctant to let go of the dope angle. If dope was involved, there'd be people to talk to, paths to explore. In this city, dope always left a trail.

"But did you notice anything *unusual*?" Meyer asked, pursuing his line of reasoning out loud. "In the neighborhood? Around the building?"

"No," Carmen said. "Unusual?"

"Anything peculiar. During the twenty-four hours preceding the murder, I mean."

"No. Like what?"

"Someone watching the building . . ."

"No."

". . . or checking the mailboxes . . ."

"No."

". . . or asking questions?"

"No, I didn't see anyone . . . what do you mean? Asking who?"

"Asking the super . . ."

"No, nothing like that."

". . . asking people who live in the building?"

"No."

"You know, trying to get a *bead* on him," Meyer said, and shrugged, and looked at Carella. The clock on the wall read eleven-thirty-five. Carmen was finishing off the last of the fries.

"Did you and Tilly ever leave the building together?" Carella asked, picking up on Meyer's line of questioning.

"Yes?"

"Ever see anyone following you?"

"No."

"Ever have the *feeling* you were being followed?"

"No."

"Or observed?"

"No."

"Did Tilly ever mention any threatening phone calls or letters?"

"No."

"And you never saw anyone who looked as if he didn't belong in the neighborhood. . . ."

"No.

"I'm not talking about the twenty-four hours before the murder, I'm talking . . ."

"Well, yes, but . . ."

"Who?" Meyer said at once. "Who did you see?"

"Well, it wasn't so much a *person* . . ."

"Then what was it?" Carella asked.

"It just looked so *strange* up there," Carmen said.

"What did?"

"The limo," she said.

She was wearing a floppy black sweater, a gray flannel skirt cut just several inches above the knee, black French-heeled pumps, and what he assumed were black pantyhose. She stepped out of the pumps the moment she'd taken off her coat. Padding into the kitchen, she began measuring coffee into the pot, and then looked up and said, "Or would you prefer a drink?"

"Are you having one?" he asked.

"I rarely drink anything but wine," she said.

"I'll have a little vodka, if you've got some," he said.

He followed her back into the living room where she lowered the drop-leaf front of the bar and then searched among the decanters for the one containing vodka, studying the little hanging silver tags as if discovering them for the first time, squinting to decipher the lettering etched on them.

"I thought for *sure* we had vodka," she said, and knelt suddenly to open a pair of doors below the bar, her skirt riding up higher on her legs, the black nylon tightening over her knees. "Here it is," she said, and triumphantly held up a sealed bottle of Stolichnaya, swiveling toward him to display it, still kneeling, smiling. She rose in one swift motion then, like a dancer, the bottle in one hand, the other arm extended for balance. "How do you take it?" she asked.

"On the rocks, please," he said.

"I'll get the ice," she said, and put the bottle of vodka down and picked up the ice bucket. "Why don't you open it?" she said. "And put on some music."

He tore the seal on the vodka bottle and loosened the cap. Opening several doors on the wall unit, he located the digital disc player and a selection of discs on a shelf beneath it. Most of the discs looked like symphonies and such. He had lived his life by telling the truth only when it didn't matter. "I'm not too familiar with this kind of music," he said. "What would you suggest?"

"Try the Leningrad," she said.

"The what?"

"Shostakovich," she said. "The Seventh."

"Okay."

He searched through the discs, trying to find whatever it was she'd said, and surprisingly came across a Sinatra recording. "How about Sinatra?" he called to the kitchen.

"Oh sure," she said.

"Okay to put it on?"

"Whatever you like," she said, and came back into the room, cradling the ice bucket against her chest and holding a bottle of white wine in the other hand. "Do you know how that works?" she asked.

"I think I can manage it."

She put down the bucket, dropped three ice cubes into a short glass, and said, "I'll let you pour your own. You can open the wine for me, too, if you like."

"Sure," he said, "just let me get this going."

He had already turned on the power and was now studying the various little push buttons on the face of the player, each of them marked. He hit a few of them in succession, got the faint hum that told him the speakers were working and the disc was rotating, and then there was the sudden roar of trumpets as music boomed into the apartment. Emma grimaced and covered her ears with her hands, but he had already found the right control and was lowering the volume. The trumpets segued into muted trombones as Sinatra launched into the first tune.

"Nice," she said.

"Mm."

He peeled the yellow lead foil from the neck of the wine bottle, worked the corkscrew into the cork, and yanked the cork free. Emma handed him a stemmed glass. He filled it for her, and then took the cap off the vodka bottle and poured a hefty drink over the ice already in the glass.

"Let's drink a toast," she said.

"Sure," he said, and held out his glass.

"To openness," she said.

"To openness," he repeated.

"And honesty," she said.

"And honesty," he repeated.

They clinked glasses. He sipped at the vodka. She sipped at the wine. In the background, Sinatra sang of unrequited love.

"Openness and honesty," she said. "You drank to it."

"I did."

"Are you planning to kill me?"

He arched his eyebrows in surprise.

"*Are* you?" she said.

"No," he said, "I'm not planning to kill you. What kind of question is that?"

"Well, you just show up out of the blue . . ."

"I didn't just show up. Your husband hired me."

"But not to kill me, huh?"

"To protect you."

"Uh-huh," she said, and looked at him levelly. "Well, maybe so."

They were sitting side by side on the leather sofa now, turned to face each other, her feet tucked up under her, his legs stretched, his head resting on the sofa back. A new song had started. A bouncier tune. Saxophones and flutes repeating a catchy riff. Sinatra rode the riff in.

"Because, you see," she said, "Martin has another woman."

"Oh, come on."

"Well, it's true," she said.

"How do you know?"

"Little things. I love the way he sings, don't you?"

"Yes. What little things?"

"Unexplained absences, breaks in the routine, credit-card expenses . . . the usual. He's got another woman."

"You sound pretty sure."

"Yep."

"Do you know who she is?"

"Yep."

"Who?"

"A woman named Lydia Raines. She owns a flower shop on Parade, near Davidson. I've been in there. She didn't know who I was, may I help you, madam? I didn't tell her, either."

"How'd you get onto her?"

"We went to visit my sister in L.A. for Thanksgiving. She called me in December sometime, when she got her phone bill, asked if I'd made any long-distance calls while I was out there. Gave me a number listed on her bill. Three calls to the same number, right here in this city. All of them on the Friday after Thanksgiving. So I called the phone company here, and they gave me the name of the shop. I guess he was desperately *lonely* for her," she said, rolling her eyes on the operative word.

"Want to come work for *me*?" he asked, smiling, still playing the private eye.

"I'd be good at it," she said, and returned the smile.

"Have you asked him about her?"

"Nope."

"Think he'd admit it?"

"Nope."

Shoulders moving to the rhythm now, still tossing her head.

"Has he asked you for a divorce?"

"Nope. Let me freshen that for you, okay?" she said, and took the glass from his hand, and swung her legs out from under her and padded to the bar, swaying in time to the music. He watched her as she poured the vodka into his glass. Hips and shoulders moving to the beat. "He wouldn't divorce me in any case," she said. "He's got too much to lose."

She carried the glass back to him.

"There's lots of money involved," she said.

"Thanks," he said, and accepted the glass. She had poured it almost full to the brim. He suddenly wondered if she was trying to get him drunk. He almost smiled at the thought.

There were saxophones and flutes again, repeating the same figure that had started the tune. Sinatra rode in on top of them with a sustained note that seemed to go on forever. There was the sudden crash of a cymbal—and then silence.

"Lots of money," she said again.

"Kiss . . ." Sinatra sang.

"Oh God, I *love* this song," she said.

"It all begins with a . . ."

"Kiss . . ."

"Would you like to dance?" she asked.

"I'm not a very good dancer," he said.

"I'm not, either."

"Well . . ."

"So let's try it," she said, and opened her arms to him, and took a step toward him. He took her in his arms. His right hand rested lightly on the swell of her hip. Her left hand rested lightly on his shoulder. His left arm was bent at the elbow, her right hand in his hand. Their hands touched lightly. They began moving in time to the music. Cautiously. Feeling the beat. Moving tentatively into the beat.

". . . lips that burn in a . . .

"Kiss . . ."

"Nobody sings this better than he does," she said.

"Are only learning

"To lie

"Unless

"The first

"Caress

"Is true."

"By the way," she said, "I'm still not sure I believe you."

"About what?"

"Killing me. Being hired to kill me."

"When *will* you believe me?"

"Later," she said. "Maybe."

And stepped in closer to him.

His hand moved up to the small of her back. He realized all at once that she wasn't wearing a bra under the sweater, there was no bra strap crossing her back. And just as suddenly he felt her breasts against his chest, and her hand moved off his shoulder, and her arm circled his neck.

". . . against my eyes.

"And kiss me sweet and promise

"Me your

"Kisses won't be lies."

"The phrasing," she whispered. "It's his phrasing."

"Kiss . . .

"And show me, tell me of

"Bliss . . .

"Because I know I

"Will die

"Unless

"This first

"Caress

"Is true."

There were violins now, startling in that there hadn't been any on the previous two cuts, modulating into a different key for the bridge, swelling from the speakers, flooding the room, and then coming back to the original key for the final chorus. She tilted her hips into him.

"Kiss . . ." Sinatra sang again.

She lifted her face to his.

"And show me, tell me of

"Bliss . . ."

"Kiss me," she whispered.

"Because I know I

"Will die

"Unless

"This first

"Caress

"Is true."

Their lips met.

It was a kiss of death.

11.

At eight o'clock that Sunday morning, the thirteenth day of January, Meyer and Carella went downtown to where Executive Limousine kept its cars. The garage was in a narrow street on the Calm's Point side of the Old Seawall Tunnel, conveniently situated between a gasoline station and a company selling whole-sale tires. A painted sign ran across the top of the garage, the words EXECUTIVE LIMOUSINE running across it in black letters on a white field. Meyer wondered how many limousine com-panies in cities across the length and breadth of this fair nation were called *Executive* Limousine. Were there any limousine com-panies called Office Boy Limousine? Or Garbageman Limou-sine?

"Or Bag Lady Limousine?" he asked out loud.

"Huh?" Carella said.

"Just wondering," Meyer said.

There were three arched entranceways to the garage, all wide enough to accommodate the trucks that used to pull in here when the neighborhood was still part of the thriving Calm's Point Market. Those days were gone forever. Where now there were stacks of new tires outside the building on the left of Executive Limousine, and men rolling whitewalls inside to where auto-mobiles stood hoisted on lifts or jacks, there used to be rows of stands selling fresh fruit and vegetables trucked in from the farms out on Sands Spit or in the state across the River Harb. Where now there were self-service pumps and cars lined up bumper to bumper at the gasoline station on the other side of the garage, there once used to be stands of fresh fish pulled daily from the River Dix or netted far out on the Offshore Reaches, arranged neatly on ice each morning for restaurant buyers who sometimes came from as far as a hundred miles away.

Here in the surrounding side streets, Old World merchants once sold everything from furniture to plumbing supplies, dry goods to shoes, corsets to chandeliers. Day in and day out there had been the lively hue and cry of a loud and busy place of commerce. The area had survived the First World War, and the Crash, and the Depression, and the Second World War, and a handful of foolish adventures in the Far East and in Central America, but it could not survive crack. What had once been a thriving market was now a slum ridden and riven by narcotics. The tenements that had once housed shops on their street-level floors were now abandoned. Where people once had come to buy the goods that sustained their daily lives, they now came to buy the substance that was destroying them and America both.

Here was where the limousines were garaged.

The manager of Executive Limousine was a man named Marty Guido. They were in a glass-enclosed space that looked down on the constant automobile traffic moving in and out of the garage. In this city, the radio-car companies operated stretch limos and also what were called "black cars," even though many of them were actually white. These so-called black cars were town cars like Caddies or Lincoln Continentals. They ran you twenty-eight bucks an hour as opposed to the thirty-five for a stretch. Like sharks, the black cars and the limos were in constant motion within their sectors. If they parked, a zealous son-of-a-bitch cop would give them a summons. So they kept moving, waiting for the radio dispatcher to come up with a call in the neighborhood they were cruising. Behind Guido and the detectives, the dispatcher kept throwing out street locations, trolling for takers. The babble was constant. It sounded like code.

"Three-Seven Morris, who's up? Anybody up near Three-

Seven Morris? Let me hear from you, I've got a lady going uptown from Three-Seven Morris.''

On and on the dispatcher's voice droned behind them.

It was like trying to be heard in a steel mill.

"Roger Turner Tilly," Meyer said. "Used to work here as a driver.''

"Why, what'd he do?'' Guido asked.

"Nothing,'' Carella said.

"Then why you looking for him?''

"We're not looking for him. Do you know him?''

"I know him. He got in some trouble here a little while back. This was when I first started here.''

"That's what we want to know about,'' Meyer said. "The trouble.''

"Why?''

"Do you know what the trouble was?''

"One of the drivers called him a fag. So he beat him up. That was the trouble.''

"Yes, that was the trouble,'' Carella said. "Do you know who that driver was?''

"One of the Spanish guys.''

"We checked Tilly's record . . .''

"Who's headed out to B. Franklin? I got a pickup at United Airlines, who's running out that way? Anybody on the way to the airport? Or heading back? Anybody want a United Airlines coming into the city? Let me hear it, who wants it? Pickup at United, who wants it?''

Meyer waited for a lull.

"We checked Tilly's record,'' he said at last, "and apparently the driver he beat up . . .''

"A man named Hector Ruiz,'' Carella said.

". . . went back to Puerto Rico shortly after Tilly got convicted.''

"Yeah?''

"That's the information we have,'' Meyer said.

"So?"

"Did you know Ruiz?"

"I knew him."

"Is it true he went back to Puerto Rico?"

"Why you want to know?"

"Mister, what's troubling you?" Carella said.

"Nothing's troubling me. I get two cops in here asking about an employee, I'm naturally . . ."

"Oh?" Meyer said.

"Is Ruiz *still* an employee?" Carella said.

"He's driving for us again, yes. Which is why I want to know . . ."

"When did he get back?" Carella asked.

"October sometime, musta been."

"Just about when Tilly got out of the slammer," Meyer said to Carella.

"Is that when he started working here again?" Carella asked.

"October, November, in there," Guido said.

"Did he know Tilly was out of jail?"

"I never asked him."

"Did Tilly ever come around here again? After he got out?"

"Not that I saw him."

"Ruiz ever mention Tilly to you?"

"Never."

"Does he have many pickups on Ainsley Avenue? Up in Diamondback?"

"None that I know of."

"Any idea what he'd be doing up there? If it *was* him up there?"

"Whyn't you ask him yourself?" Guido said, and gestured through the glass panel toward where a black stretch limo was just pulling into the garage. Meyer and Carella started for the stairs just as the front door of the limo opened. A tall, burly man wearing a chauffeur's livery and cap stepped out onto the concrete. He took off the hat almost immediately, revealing a shock of intensely black hair that matched the thick mustache under his nose. He was walking toward a door marked MEN when Carella and Meyer came out onto the street-level floor.

"Mr. Ruiz?" Carella said.

"Hector Ruiz?" Meyer said.

"Police officers," Carella said, flashing the tin. "We'd like to ask you . . ."

Ruiz took one look and began running.

Straight out the middle arched door in the bank of three, hanging an immediate right toward the gas station, turning the corner there, and running for the river as Meyer and Carella came out of the building. They pounded along behind him, closing the gap as they cut through the gas station, angling off the corner just as Ruiz had, shortest distance between two points, Ruiz some fifty feet ahead of them now and still headed for the river.

There was a lot of early-morning boat traffic plying its way up and down the river or back and forth between Isola and Calm's Point. Behind Ruiz and across the river, the city's skyscrapers stretched upward toward a bleak gray sky. Smoke billowed up on the air from rooftop chimneys. Smoke floated up from the stacks of tugboats and ferries. Smokelike vapor trailed from the mouths of the men as they ran along the river's edge, passing joggers moving in both directions, none of them paying the slightest bit of attention to the man in black and the two men chasing him.

Ruiz was young and fast, and they never would have caught up with him if he hadn't taken a quick look back over his shoulder to see how close they were. In that instant—less than an instant, thirty seconds, ten seconds, the time it took for him to snap a backward glance at them and then turn his head forward again—he collided with a jogger coming from the opposite direction on his blind side. The jogger was a woman wearing red, and for an instant there was a checkerboard effect, Ruiz and the woman meeting in startled red-and-black collision, arms and legs flying as they both tumbled to the sidewalk.

"You stupid bastard!" the woman screamed.

But Ruiz was already scrambling to his feet.

He snapped another look over his shoulder.

This time he saw a .38 Detective Special three feet from his nose.

If a man began running when you yelled cop, that didn't necessarily mean he'd done anything. In certain parts of this city, the very sight of a blue uniform was enough to cause frantic scampering in all directions. So the detectives weren't particularly interested in learning why Ruiz had begun running the moment they'd announced themselves. On the other hand, Ruiz seemed perfectly willing to offer various inventive explanations for his curious behavior.

He first told them that he'd suddenly remembered leaving his wallet in a diner where he'd stopped for a cup of coffee before driving into the garage. Their sudden appearance had nothing to do with his sudden flight. It was just that he remembered about the wallet. This despite the fact that his wallet was in his back pocket, the sucker pocket in that any pickpocket could have relieved him of it by slitting the bottom of the pocket with a razor blade, but that was neither here nor there.

He then said it wasn't *that* wallet he was talking about, it was the wallet he usually kept in the limo's glove compartment, a wallet into which he normally placed all the signed vouchers from his trips. Not a wallet, really. More like a pouch. A soft leather pouch. This was what he'd *thought* he'd left in the diner, which turned out to be a mistake because there it was, right where it was supposed to be, right there in the limo's glove compartment.

On the way uptown to the station house, he told them that as a young boy he'd been frightened by two detectives who set fire to the mattress of the hooker who used to live next door to his family in apartment 44 at 7215 Corchers Boulevard in Majesta. He'd been afraid of detectives ever since. And now, in the ten A.M. privacy of the squadroom, surrounded by more detectives than he'd ever hoped to see in his entire lifetime, Ruiz told them that he'd begun running because he thought they were going to question him about the gypsy cab drivers who were getting shot all over this city, "This is some crazy city, eh, man?" he said, and smiled like one of the banditos in *Treasure of the Sierra Madre*. None of the detectives smiled back.

There were four of them, each one bigger than the other. Meyer, Carella, Hawes, and Brown. All of them looking stern and disapproving.

"This ain't right, you know?" Ruiz said. "Draggin' me in here, I d'in *do* nothin'."

"We think you did something," Hawes said.

Ruiz figured he was the meanest one in the bunch. Even meaner than the black cop. They were both about the same size. He wouldn't want to tangle with either one of them. He figured the bald cop was the easy mark. It was the bald cop who'd read him his rights and asked if he'd wanted an attorney. He told them he didn't need no attorney if he didn't do nothin'. He figured that was the smart way to play it. You ask for a lawyer, they right away think you done something.

"Tilly," Carella said. "Roger Turner Tilly."

He was thinking Ruiz could come up with a thousand and one explanations for why he'd run, and maybe nine hundred and ninety-nine of them would have at least a slight bearing on the truth, but a possible reason he wasn't yet mentioning was that he'd shot Tilly in the back of the head and strung him up from the ceiling. Which was a very good reason to run when cops came around asking questions.

"I don't know this name," Ruiz said.

"Hoo boy," Brown said.

"Let's start by telling the truth, okay?" Hawes said. "We'll all save a lot of time that way, okay, Hector?''

"Tilly," Ruiz said, nodding, seemingly thinking it over. "Roger Tilly, huh?''

"Roger Turner Tilly," Hawes said.

"The man who broke your nose and both your arms last March,'' Carella said.

"The man who sent you to the hospital," Brown said.

"Oh, him," Ruiz said. "What about him? He's in jail, ain' he?''

"No, he's not in jail," Carella said.

"Take it easy, fellas," Meyer said. "There's no need to jump all over the man this way.''

Playing Good Cop to all these big mean Bad Cops, all of them glaring at him as if to say, "Keep out of this, we know how to handle punks." Ruiz nodded to him in silent gratitude.

"You were spotted uptown, cruising in your limo," Carella said, expanding on the truth a bit in that Carmen Sanchez had not positively identified the driver of the limo that seemed to be casing the building on several occasions, "in the vicinity of ten-sixty-five Ainsley Avenue, are you familiar with that neighborhood?''

"I hardly ever go up there," Ruiz said. "You mus' be mistaken.''

"But you do go up there *sometimes*, huh?" Brown said.

"Very rarely," Ruiz said, savoring the word *rarely* as if it were a word he rarely used. "Very rarely," he said again, rolling it around his tongue like sweet wine.

"Were you up there on January seventh?" Hawes asked.

"When was that?''

"Monday, the seventh. Were you up there in your nice long limo?''

"No.''

"Around twelve, twelve-thirty," Carella said. "Looking for Tilly?''

"Tilly's still in jail, ain' he?"

The same line again, or a reasonable facsimile of it. The same bandito grin. Ruiz was very handsome, and he knew it. Thick black macho hair and mustache, grin like a gay caballero. Even with the broken nose, he was handsome. Maybe even handsomer than he'd been before Tilly rearranged it for him.

"No, he's not in jail," Carella said again, both of them circling the same old mulberry bush.

"He got out in October," Hawes said.

"When'd you come back from Puerto Rico?" Brown asked.

"I don't remember."

"Guido says you started working for him again in October, November sometime."

"If Guido says so, then it mus' be," Ruiz said, and shrugged, and smiled innocently at his good old pal Detective Meyer.

"The man's clean," Meyer said, "why are you giving him all this bullshit?"

"*Gracias, amigo*," Ruiz said.

"*De nada*," Meyer said, and patted his shoulder reassuringly.

"Why'd you come back here?" Carella asked. "Because you knew Tilly was out?"

"I thought he wass still *in*," Ruiz insisted.

"Because you wanted to pay him back?" Hawes asked.

"Get him for what he did to you?"

"Shaming you that way . . ."

"Little guy like that breaking your nose and your arms . . ."

"Big macho guy like you . . ."

"I don' know what you mean," Ruiz said, and again looked soulfully at Meyer.

"He doesn't know what you guys mean," Meyer said. "And neither do I. What if he *was* up there last Monday . . . ?"

"Thass right," Ruiz said. "What if I wass?"

"Does that mean he *killed* Tilly?"

"No," Ruiz said, shaking his head, "it don' mean I killed him. How could it mean that? I di'n even know he wass dead. I thought he wass still in jail."

"If you thought he was still in jail, why'd you shoot him?" Carella said.

"I di'n shoot nobody."

"Try this on for size," Hawes said, and suddenly tossed a tagged .32-caliber pistol on the desk. The gun landed with a solid thunk, slid across the desk toward Ruiz, and skidded to a stop, leaving a grayish-white residue behind it. Ruiz looked at it as if an abandoned bastard had suddenly returned home.

"What's that?" he asked pleasantly.

"What do you think it is?" Brown asked.

"It looks like a gun."

"Yes, it is a gun," Brown said.

"Mmm," Ruiz said, looking at the gun in wonder and amazement.

"It's a thirty-two-caliber Hi-Standard Sentinel," Hawes said.

"Mmm," Ruiz said again.

"Ever see that gun before?" Carella asked.

"Does the man look like someone who'd be familiar with guns?" Meyer asked testily.

"Ever see it?"

"No, wait a minute," Meyer said. "I asked you a question, Steve. Does this man . . . ?"

"I never seen that gun in my life," Ruiz said.

"Thank you," Meyer said.

"*De nada*," Ruiz said.

"We found that gun at the murder scene," Carella said, pointing to it. "Ten-sixty-five Ainsley Avenue, where Tilly was shot and killed."

"Right there at the scene," Brown said.

"Tilly hanging from the ceiling, a bullet hole in his head," Hawes said.

Painting the picture for him. Broad brush strokes.

Ruiz merely shrugged and looked at Meyer as if he didn't have the faintest idea what any of these people were talking about.

"Okay, let's go," Carella said.

"Go?" Ruiz said. "Go where?"

"Take some fingerprints," Carella said.

"What for?"

"Because we lifted some good prints from that gun, and we want to check yours against them."

He was lying. The gun had been covered with ashes, was *still* covered with ashes, and they hadn't retrieved a single good print from it.

"I don't have to let you do that," Ruiz said. "Take my fingerprints."

"Yes, you do," Carella said, "read your Miranda. Let's go."

"Anyway, how . . . ?" Ruiz said, and stopped short.

"How *what*?" Brown said.

"Nothing."

"What were you about to say? How what?"

"There's ashes all over it," Ruiz said. "How could there be fingerprints?"

"There were fingerprints," Carella said, lying again.

"And how do you know those are ashes?" Brown said.

"Well, you can *see* they're ashes," Ruiz said.

"No, it just looks like some gray shit all over the gun, how do you know it's ashes?"

"I just figured . . ."

"Yeah, what'd you figure?"

"It just *looks* like ashes, that's all," Ruiz said, and shrugged, and turned to Meyer. "Don' it look like ashes to you?" he said.

"Of course," Meyer said, and smiled encouragingly.

"*Hass* to be ashes," Ruiz said, more confidently now.

"But how'd you know right *off* it was ashes?" Brown said, closing in.

"Well, you said you found the gun at the scene, ain' that what you said?"

"Yeah?"

"So I figured there could be *ashes* down there, am I right?" he said, turning to Meyer, smiling again. "In a basement, am I right? There could be ashes. Depending on what kind of . . ."

"Who said we found it in a basement?" Meyer asked.

He was no longer smiling.

"Well, you . . ."

"Who said the word *basement*?"

Ruiz looked at Meyer as if his own mother had just stabbed him in the heart. He turned to the other detectives. None of them was smiling, either. The entire squadroom had gone utterly still.

"Well, you said . . ."

He was trying hard to remember what they'd said. Hadn't they said they'd found the gun at the murder scene? Down there in the basement? Tilly hanging from the ceiling? He was sure that's what they'd said. But—

"You want a lawyer?" Carella asked.

"Should I get a lawyer?" Ruiz asked Meyer.

Meyer wasn't permitted to advise him, but he nodded discreetly.

The clock on the squadroom wall read ten minutes to eleven.

Outside, it was beginning to snow again.

The world was white.

They had slept the morning away, and had made love again before rising, and now—at a little past noon—they came out into a fairyland of crystal peaks and minarets, spun-sugar towers and domes. In a city not particularly famous for its cleanliness, there was now a thick carpet of white that disguised and obscured. There was, too, a stillness that created a false sense of serenity. The few automobiles in the streets moved past silently on tires cushioned by the snow. Even the rumble of the train on the elevated structure in the distance seemed muffled somehow, as though the snow underfoot, the snow on the rooftops and chimneys, the snow still swirling in the air, had woven an acoustic cocoon in which the only sound was the murmur of a heart.

Andrew knew he had to kill her, he was being paid to kill her. He knew, too, that he should have killed her last night. Killed her after the second time they'd made love, while she slept on her back with an odd, pleased smile on her mouth, dark eyes closed, blonde hair against the pillow, should have killed her then. Taken a knife from the kitchen and slit her throat. Instead, he'd fallen asleep himself.

"Something?" she asked.

She was smiling.

She'd been smiling when they woke up this morning, and she hadn't stopped smiling since. Turned toward him expectantly now, arm looped through his, smile on her face, brows arched in anticipation, waiting for an answer. Something? she had said. Penny for your thoughts? And now she waited.

"I was just thinking of what we did last night," he said.

Which in a way was true. He'd been thinking of how he'd let pleasure interfere with business. Last night would have been the perfect time to do it. Bowles out of town, the lady's assassin right there in her fuckin bed. Last night was when he should have—

"What did you like best?" she asked, and hugged his arm.

"Everything," he said.

Which was also true.

He liked women, there was no question about that, but usually he wanted to go home after the second time around. Sometimes even after the *first* time. Wanted to get dressed and get out, thanks, it was great, see you around the bowling alley. Or if they were in *his* apartment, he wanted them to put on their panties and run for a taxi, here's the fare, darling, I'll call you. Next summer. Last night, all he'd done afterward was fall fast asleep.

"What do you mean by everything?" she asked.

Still clutching his arm. Snow flying everywhere around them, the city hushed. Snow clinging to the long gray cavalry coat and the blue woolen hat. Dark eyes squinted against the swirling snow. Face fresh and shining and wet with snow.

"Tell me," she said.

Lots of women liked you to talk dirty to them. While you were doing it, sometimes even after you'd done it. He knew the patter, knew what turned these women on, knew which obscenities to whisper in their ears, all the wetcunt talk, the bigcock talk, incitement to riot in the stillness of the night. Or better yet in broad daylight with a hand under a tablecloth and under a skirt, damptalk, he knew these women, he had met a thousand of these women in his lifetime. But he didn't think Emma was asking for an instant replay now, didn't think she wanted to buy his feelthy peectures, meester. She wasn't asking for that. He didn't know what the hell she was asking for, and he didn't care. He'd been hired to kill this woman.

"Cat got your tongue?" she asked.

Pussytalk? Licktalk?

Was *that* what she wanted?

"How far *is* this place?" he asked.

"Still five or six blocks," she said. "But it's worth it."

"I hope so," he said. "I'm starving."

"Best waffles in town."

"Long way to go for waffles," he said.

"But it's such a beautiful day," she said.

"Yes," he said.

"I forgot to ask you last night," she said, and turned away from him, looking off into the falling snow. "Are you married?"

"No," he said.

"You don't have to ask *me*, do you?"

"No, I know you're married," he said.

"Would you like it better if I weren't?"

"I like it fine the way it is," he said.

He hated this kind of talk.

"Have you ever been married?" she asked.

"Never."

"Ever come close?"

"Never. Never even thought of it."

"How about any serious involvements? Have you ever been seriously involved with a woman?"

He really *hated* this kind of bullshit talk.

"Well, I've known women I liked a lot," he said.

"When you say you . . ."

"Women I've been involved with, yes."

"Lived with?"

"One woman, yes."

"When was that?"

"Oh, a while back."

"How long were you together?"

"Two, three years, something like that."

"Don't you *know* how long?"

"Not exactly."

"What happened?"

"It just ended, that's all. Things end, you know."

"They don't have to, do they?"

"Well, it'd be very unnatural if they didn't."

"Still . . . there *are* people who stay together forever."

"Well . . ."

"Because they're good for each other," she said, and hesitated. "Because they love each other."

"Well, I guess."

"Did you love this woman?"

"I don't know."

"What was her name?"

"Katie."

"That's a nice name."

"Yeah."

"Who ended it? You or her?"

"She did."

"Why?"

"I don't know why."

"Well, there must have been a reason. . . ."

"No, I don't think there was a reason. It just ended, that's all. It was time for it to end, and it ended."

He'd never expected Katie to do what she'd done to him. Never. Twenty years old when he'd met her, a virgin, would you believe it? Hardly older than that when they started living together, taught her everything she knew. Katie Briggs. Dark-haired girl, part English, part Scottish. Brown eyes. Complexion like milk in a dipper. Beautiful girl. So he came home one night . . .

He'd been out playing poker the night Katie Briggs ended it. Left the poker game early because he wasn't feeling too hot, thought maybe he was coming down with the flu or something, and since he'd been losing, nobody complained when he told them he was splitting.

. . . came home that night and put his key in the door latch and walked in and found her in bed with two guys. One black, and one white, an equal-opportunity employer was young Katie. Naked and pale, with the black guy's cock in her mouth and the white guy's cock up her ass, that was the way Katie Briggs ended it, that was the way little Katie Briggs said farewell.

"Do you know what *I* liked best about last night?" she asked.

Back to last night again. Maybe she *did* want to tell him how much she loved fucking. You got some of these repressed house-wives, they wanted to tell you all their rape fantasies, all their fantasies about being fucked by the entire prison population of Joliet, Illinois. Maybe he'd figured her wrong. Go ahead, he thought, run with it, babe.

"What'd you like best?" he asked.

"Your gentleness," she said.

My *what*? he thought, and almost burst out laughing.

She was looking up at him. No smile on her mouth. Looking up into his face, searching his face, seemingly waiting for him to say something. He kissed her instead. When in doubt.

"I love you," she said.

This is going to be too easy, he thought.

"You understand he's a shmuck, don't you?" the lawyer said.

"Uh-huh," Carella said.

The lawyer had been appointed by Legal Aid to represent Hector Ruiz, who had decided on the advice of his good pal Detective Meyer Meyer that he needed an attorney after all, considering the fact that the police seemed to think his fingerprints were all over the gun that had killed Roger Turner Tilly. The lawyer was maybe thirty-seven, thirty-eight years old, and he was already going bald, which made him seem sympathetic to Meyer, who had gone totally bald when he was still very young. The lawyer was already trying to cop a plea even though a district attorney was nowhere in sight and he knew the detectives had no authority to strike such bargains.

"This is a macho thing with these people," the lawyer said.

His name was Morris Weinstein. He represented a great many Hispanic offenders, but he still referred to them as "these people." He also referred to blacks as "these people." He probably had no idea that a great many WASPS in this country referred to Jews as "these people." This was a funny country, America.

"He calls some shrimp a fag, and all at once the shrimp turns around and beats the shit out of him," Weinstein said.

"Must've been a big surprise," Carella said understandingly. He was thinking they were going to throw the fucking book at Ruiz for shooting and hanging Tilly.

"Terrible thing to happen," Weinstein said. "In terms of the macho sensibility."

"Yeah, terrible," Carella said.

"I'm thinking a 125.20," Weinstein said.

Meyer blinked.

"Manslaughter One," Weinstein said, as if they didn't know.

Meyer blinked again.

"In that this was a cultural thing committed under the influence of extreme emotional disturbance."

"Uh-huh," Carella said.

"Over which he had no real control," Weinstein said.

"Uh-huh," Carella said.

"So what are you thinking?"

"We're thinking Murder Two," Carella said. "In that he went uptown with the express purpose . . ."

"Well, we don't know that, do we?" Weinstein said.

". . . of putting a bullet in Tilly's head."

"Well, if you're going to put it that way," Weinstein said.

Carella tried to think of another way to put it.

"You have to understand these people," Weinstein said.

"Uh-huh."

"I read a book about Mexico," Weinstein said, "that explained wall-writing as a cultural trait. This is why you see so much graffiti in Hispanic neighborhoods."

"Is that why?" Carella said.

"Yes. It's a cultural thing."

Carella was happy to learn that writing on walls was a cultural thing.

"He's admitted to shooting Tilly," Weinstein said. "The important thing is to understand *why*."

"Yes, well, perhaps you can explain why at the trial," Carella said.

"Why are you being such a shit?" Weinstein asked.

"Because what we have here is a confession of murder," Carella said.

"Oh well, that," Weinstein said.

"Yes, oh well, *that*. You were there when he admitted seeing Tilly . . ."

"Yes, but . . ."

". . . standing outside the building waiting for someone . . ."

"We don't know that for a fact . . ."

"... forcing him to go down to the basement at gun-point . . ."

"Yes, but . . ."

"Shooting him in the back of the head . . ."

"Yes . . ."

"And then stringing him up."

"That's what I mean about the cultural aspect."

"Yeah, that's very cultural," Meyer said. "Hanging a man from the ceiling after you've shot him."

"As a matter of fact, it is."

"We've already had people hanging from lampposts," Carella said.

"What?" Weinstein said.

"Up here," Meyer said. "Young girls hanging from lamp-posts."

"Track stars," Carella said. "Hanging from lampposts."

"And it wasn't cultural," Meyer said.

"This *was*. Tilly had to be *punished*, don't you see? Not only shot, but *punished*, hanged from the ceiling as an example to others. Which is exactly why I'm looking for Manslaughter One. This man was in the grip of an emotional . . ."

"Bullshit," Meyer said. "He was in the grip of coming up here and shooting somebody in cold blood."

"Because this person had *humiliated* him. You heard him say that, didn't you? That he'd been humiliated?"

"Yes, we heard him say it. We also heard him say . . ."

"Humiliation," Weinstein said. "An important thing in the countries these people come from. Face. Losing face. The whole cultural macho thing."

"It's a pity that isn't the culture *here*," Carella said. "Because *here*, we're going to ask the D.A. for Murder Two."

"I guess I'll have to discuss that with him when he gets here," Weinstein said, and sighed deeply.

"Yes, you discuss it."

"Because you heard my client say, didn't you . . . ?"

"We heard him say he went up to Diamondback to blow Tilly away. Those were his exact words, to blow Tilly away. We've got them on tape."

"Exactly my point. Cultural bragging."

"Bullshit," Meyer said again.

"I'll admit to a Class-B and get him off with a year," Weinstein said. "He'll be out in four months."

They knew he was right.

12.

Forget the veined and bulbous nose, forget the razor nicks on his chin and cheeks, forget even the ill-fitting and somewhat rumpled suit. There was something more than his disheveled appearance that told you Frank Unger had long ago lost touch with anything more meaningful than alcohol. Lowell had not called him as a witness because he'd felt there was nothing positive he could add to their case. Santa Claus Addison was clearly taking a chance by calling him now. The man seemed bewildered at finding himself here in a courtroom, the center of attraction at this moment in time. Watching him as he was sworn in that Monday morning, Carella couldn't imagine anyone on the jury believing a word he had to say.

"Mr. Unger," Addison said, "can you tell me where you live, please?"

"At 7828 Harrison Street, apartment 24."

"How long have you lived in that neighborhood?"

"Fourteen years now. Be fourteen years in April," Unger said.

His voice was whiskey-raw, he had on his face an intense look of concentration, as if the very act of listening was difficult for him. Carella noticed that his fingers were nicotine-stained.

"Are you familiar, sir, with a liquor store called Empire Wines and Spirits at 7832 Harrison Street?"

"I am."

"Do you occasionally shop at that store?"

"I do."

"Mr. Unger, I ask you to think back to the night of July seventeenth last year, it was a Tuesday night, Mr. Unger, do you think you can recall back that far?"

"I think so."

"A very hot night, we were having a hot summer, do you recall that night?"

"Yes, I do."

"Mr. Unger, did you go to Empire Wines and Spirits that night at any time?"

"Yes, I did."

"Would you happen to remember what time it was that you went there?"

"Around nine o'clock."

"You recall that, do you?"

"Yes. I'd just given the cat some dry food—I like to make sure she's got food in her bowl all the time, there's just the two of us, you see—and I thought I'd have myself a little nightcap while I watched the ten o'clock news. What I usually do, I give the cat her dry food, and then I have a little nightcap while I watch the news. I usually go to sleep at eleven. That's my usual routine."

"But that night you say you went down to the liquor store."

"Yes. Because there wasn't anything in the house. I'd run out, you see. So I decided I'd go down for some. To the liquor store. I knew they'd be open till ten."

"And you say you went down at about nine."

"Around then. It's just a few doors up the street, you see."

"On the same side of the street as a bakery shop, isn't it?"

"Well, the shop's not there anymore."

"But there used to be a shop at 7834 Harrison, didn't there?"

"Yes."

"Called the A & L Bakery, isn't that right?"

"Yes."

"Right next door to the liquor store."

"Yes."

"Mr. Unger, how long would you say you were in the liquor store?"

"Oh, fifteen, twenty minutes."

"You got there at what time?"

"Five after nine? Ten after?"

"Well, which would you say?"

"Ten after, I guess."

"And you were there for . . . well, how many minutes? Fifteen? Twenty?"

"I'd say twenty. I like to talk to people. There's just me and the cat, you see."

"So you conducted your business there . . ."

"Bought a fifth of bourbon, yes."

"And talked to . . . well, who'd you talk to?"

"Ralph. The man who owns Empire."

"And you say you left about twenty minutes after you got there."

"Yes."

"Which would make it about nine-thirty."

"Yes, sir. Just about that time."

"You came out onto the street at nine-thirty, did you?"

"Yes."

"Did you hear anything at that time?"

"I heard shots."

"How many."

"Three."

"Where were they coming from?"

"The bakery shop next door."

"Did you see anyone coming out of the bakery?"

"I did. Almost knocked me over, in fact."

"*Who* almost knocked you over?"

"The man coming out of the bakery."

"You saw a man coming out of the bakery . . ."

"*Running* out of the bakery."

"And you say he almost knocked you over?"

"That's right. And told me to get the hell out of his way."

"Are you sure you didn't see *two* men running out of the bakery?"

"Positive. It was just the one man."

"Do you see the man sitting there at the defense table?" Addison said, and pointed to where Sonny Cole was sitting erect with his hands folded in his lap.

"Yes, I see him," Unger said.

"Is he the man you saw running out of the bakery shop at 7834 Harrison Street last July seventeenth at nine-thirty P.M.?"

"No, he is not," Unger said.

Addison walked to the defense table, picked up what to Carella—from where he was sitting—looked like a black-and-white photograph, and carried it back to the witness stand.

"Your Honor," he said, "I would like this marked for identification."

"Mark it Exhibit A," Di Pasco said.

"May I show it to the witness, Your Honor?"

"Yes, go ahead."

"Mr. Unger, I show you this, and ask if you recognize the man in the photograph?"

"Yes, I do."

"Who is he?"

"I don't know his name. He's the man I saw running out of the bakery shop."

"When?"

"On July seventeenth last year."

"At what time?"

"At nine-thirty P.M."

"Your Honor, I would like this photograph moved into evi . . ."

"Just a minute, please," Lowell said at once. "Objection, Your Honor. There's no foundation for admitting that picture as evidence. I don't know where it came from, I don't know who took it, I don't even know who the *subject*..."

"Let's approach," Di Pasco said.

Both attorneys went to the bench.

"Where'd you get that picture?" Di Pasco asked.

"From the New Orleans PD," Addison said.

"Who's it a picture of?"

"Desmond Whittaker. It's the mug shot taken at the time of his arrest."

"Well, really, your Honor," Lowell said, "I don't know if this came from New Orleans or Timbuktu. I don't know if it's a mug shot or a graduation picture. Without corroboration..."

"You don't *really* doubt its authenticity, do you, Mr. Lowell?"

"Well, Your Honor, all I know is it's a photograph. Where it came from, whose picture it is..."

"It came from arrest files in the New Orleans PD," Addison said. "And it's a picture of..."

"So you tell me. But until someone from the New Orleans PD can testify to that effect..."

"I can supply such a witness if the district attorney insists, but..."

"Well, yes, I do insist."

"... but that would require an adjournment," Addison said. "And, of course, a subsequent waste of the court's time."

"Do you *really* want him to provide that witness, Mr. Lowell? I can understand bringing someone all the way up from New Orleans if you sincerely doubt the picture's authenticity. But I must tell you, if you're doing this just to break Mr. Addison's chops..."

Addison smiled.

"... and mine as well, you might do better to let that picture move in unchallenged."

Lowell looked at him.

"What do you say?" Di Pasco asked. "Do we stipulate?"

"Sure," Lowell said, and sighed heavily.

"Good," Di Pasco said, and turned to the jury. "The parties have stipulated that Exhibit A may be moved into evidence," he said. "Mark it," he told the clerk, and then nodded to Addison.

"Let the record indicate," Addison said, walking back to the witness stand, "that Exhibit A is a photograph of Desmond Albert Whittaker, alias Diz Whittaker, taken by the New Orleans Police Department at the time of his arrest in Louisiana six years ago. Now, Mr. Unger," he said, "I'd like you to take another look at this photo, if you will."

Unger studied the picture again.

"Are you absolutely certain that Desmond Albert Whittaker is the man you saw coming out of the bakery shop at 7834 Harrison Street last July seventeenth at nine-thirty P.M.?"

"It is."

"Did he have a gun in his hand?"

"He did."

"And you say he was alone?"

"He was alone."

"Thank you, no further questions."

Lowell took his time rising. When at last he approached the stand, he appeared thoughtful and a trifle sad.

"Mr. Unger," he said, "you say you live alone, just you and your cat."

"That's right."

"Have you always lived alone?"

"No, I'm a widower."

"I'm sorry to hear that. When did you lose your wife?"

"Six years ago."

"Ah. I'm sorry," Lowell said.

He did, in fact, seem genuinely sorry, and Carella wondered why in hell he was garnering sympathy for a witness who—if the jury believed him—had just shot down their entire case. If Desmond Whittaker had been operating *alone* that night . . .

"Just you and the cat now," Lowell said.

"Yes."

"And you feed the cat his dry food every night before the news."

"Yes. Around nine."

"What time do *you* eat, Mr. Unger?"

"Well, that depends."

"Dinner, I mean. What time do you normally eat dinner?"

"Depends."

"Do you eat when you get home from work? Well, first . . . *do* you work, Mr. Unger?"

"No, I'm retired."

"Ah. Then you're home all day, is that it? Just you and the cat."

"Yes."

"How do you spend your time, Mr. Unger?"

"I have hobbies."

"Like what?"

"I clip things from the newspapers. I send away for things. I have hobbies."

"Do you drink, Mr. Unger?"

"Drink?"

"Alcohol. Do you drink alcohol?"

"Objection, Your Honor."

"Overruled. Answer the question, please."

"Yes, I drink alcohol. Everyone drinks alcohol."

"Well, no, everyone does *not* drink alcohol."

"Objection!" Addison shouted. "Argumentative, harassing the . . ."

"Sustained."

"Tell me, Mr. Unger," Lowell said, "just how much alcohol *do* you drink?"

"One or two cocktails a day."

"Cocktails."

"Yes."

"Mixed drinks, do you mean?"

"Yes."

"What'd you mix your bourbon with that night of July seventeenth last year?"

"I'm sorry, I don't understand the question."

"You said you bought a fifth of bourbon at Empire . . ."

"Oh. Yes, I did."

"To drink with the ten o'clock news. Did you, in fact, drink any of that bourbon when you went back upstairs?"

"Yes, I did."

"Well, with *what* did you mix it?"

Unger looked at him.

"Mr. Unger? Will you answer my question, please?"

"I didn't mix it with anything."

"Ah. So you drank it straight."

"Yes."

"So then you *don't* mix your drinks, do you? You drink your whiskey straight, isn't that more like it?"

"Sometimes I mix it, and sometimes I drink it straight."

"When you mix it, Mr. Unger, with *what* do you mix it?"

"A little water, usually."

"And that's what you call a mixed drink, hmm? Bourbon and a little water."

"Yes, that *is* a mixed drink. If you mix the bourbon with a little water, that's a mixed drink, isn't it?"

"But on the night of the seventeenth, when you went upstairs after having seen this man come out of the liquor store, you did *not* mix your bourbon with a little water, you drank it straight, didn't you?"

"Yes."

"How many drinks did you have when you went back upstairs, Mr. Unger?"

"I usually have a little nightcap when I'm watching the ten o'clock news."

"Yes, how many drinks?"

"One or two."

"Which?"

"Two."

"How many ounces?"

"Just a little nightcap."

"Well, what's just a little nightcap? A jigger? Two jiggers? A water tumbler . . ."

"No, no, certainly not a water tumbler."

"Then what? A juice glass?"

"More like a juice glass, yes."

"So after you saw this man in the street, and before you went to bed, you drank two juice glasses full of bourbon."

"Yes. Something like that."

"How many drinks did you have *before* you saw this man in the street?"

"I really don't remember."

"But you *did* have something to drink, isn't that so?"

"Yes, I usually have a little drink in the afternoon."

"Do you usually have a little drink in the morning, too?"

"Sometimes I'll have a little eye-opener."

"What time in the afternoon did you have your little drink on July seventeenth last year?"

"I don't remember."

"Was it just *one* little drink? Or was it *two* little drinks?"

"It may have been two."

"Bourbon?"

"Yes. I usually drink bourbon."

"Two *juice* glasses full of bourbon?"

"With a little water."

"I see, with a little water. *Mixed* drinks then."

"Yes."

"Did you have these drinks before dinner? With dinner? After dinner?"

"Well . . ."

"Or tell me, Mr. Unger, did you have dinner at *all* that night?"

"I don't remember."

"Well, do you sometimes go without dinner?"

"Sometimes."

"I see. Mr. Unger . . . before you saw this man or men coming . . ."

"Objection, Your Honor! Witness has stated he saw only one . . ."

"Sustained."

"Mr. Unger, can you tell me how many drinks you'd had during that morning and afternoon and evening and night of July seventeenth last year *before* you saw this man coming out of the bakery shop?"

"No, I can't tell you exactly."

"Can you *estimate* how many drinks you had?"

"No, I can't do that, either."

"Had you been drinking all day long, Mr. Unger?"

Unger said nothing.

"You're under oath, Mr. Unger. Had you been drinking all day long?"

"Yes."

"And *that* was when you saw this man coming out of the bakery shop. After you'd been drinking all day long."

"Yes."

"Mr. Unger, when Detectives Wade and Bent first interviewed you . . . you do remember them talking to you, don't you?"

"Yes, I do."

"Didn't you tell them you'd seen *two* men coming out of that bakery shop?"

"I don't remember what I told them."

"Well, let me refresh your memory. Would you take a look at this, please?" he said, and handed him a sheaf of papers. Unger read the pages silently. When at last he looked up, Lowell asked, "Can you tell me what you've just read?"

"It's a report on the conversation I had with the detectives."

"Is the report dated?"

"It is."

"What is the date on that report?"

"July eighteenth last year."

"And do you now recall stating that on or about nine-thirty the night before, you'd seen two black men running out of the A & L Bakery Shop toward you. Did you say that, Mr. Unger?"

"I guess I did."

"And did you further state that one of those men was carrying a gun?"

"I guess so."

"Yes or no, Mr. Unger? Did you make those statements?"

"Yes."

"But you now say there was only *one* man?"

"Yes. Anyway, I told them later . . ."

"Yes, what did you tell them later?"

"That I couldn't remember. When they were showing me all those pictures and the artist's sketches, I told them I couldn't remember."

"Yes, so you did. But now, all at once, you *do* remember. No further questions, Your Honor."

"Mr. Addison?"

"Yes, Your Honor, if you'll indulge me," Addison said, and approached the witness stand. "Mr. Unger," he said, "just two quick questions. Were you drunk when you saw that man coming out of the bakery shop?"

"I was *not*!"

"Thank you. And can you tell me why you're now so certain it was only *one* man you saw and not *two*?"

"Because I've given it a lot of thought since that night. And it's bothered me all this time that I might have been mistaken . . . that an innocent man might suffer for what somebody else did."

"Thank you, Mr. Unger."

Lowell came at him again.

No preamble, no politesse.

Just a tiger lunging out of a cage.

"Have you ever been drunk?"

"Yes."

"How many drinks does it take to make you drunk?"

"That varies. Inebriation depends on body weight, and I've weighed . . ."

"Five? Six? Eight? Twelve? A fifth? A quart? A half-gallon? How much liquor does it take to make you drunk?"

"I would say . . . I really don't know."

"How many drinks did you have that day?"

"I don't remember."

"Then how do you know you weren't drunk?"

"I know I wasn't drunk."

"You were drinking all day long but you weren't drunk?"

"I have a great tolerance for alcohol."

"I'll bet," Lowell said under his breath.

"Your Honor . . ."

"Strike that."

"Who's this innocent person you're feeling so sorry for?" Lowell asked.

"I don't understand the question."

"You said an innocent man might suffer for what someone else . . ."

"Oh. The accused."

"Samson Cole? The man being tried here for the *murder* of Anthony Carella?"

"Yes."

"You're afraid *he* might suffer for what his *partner* did?"

"Objec . . ."

"Are you aware that if *both* of them were in that bakery shop together, it doesn't matter *who* pulled the trigger, they'd *both* be . . ."

"Your Honor, I object!"

"I'll instruct the jury as to law when the time comes, Mr. Lowell."

"I apologize, Your Honor. And I have no further questions. But before Mr. Addison calls his next witness, and while Mr. Unger is still in the courtroom, may I ask that Dominick Assanti be recalled at this time?"

"For what purpose?" Di Pasco asked.

"Solely for identification, Your Honor."

"Call Dominick Assanti," Di Pasco said.

Carella watched as he was sworn in. He was wondering whether Lowell had made his point clear about the unreliability of Unger as a witness. He was also wondering why he hadn't hounded him on the fact that he'd changed his mind yet again on exactly whom he'd seen that night. Addison had tried to make it seem he'd come forward now for purely altruistic reasons. But wasn't it possible that he was identifying a dead man so that if the live one got off, he wouldn't come back to hurt him? Shouldn't Lowell at least have *mentioned* the fear of reprisal?

". . . ask you to look at Mr. Unger now, and tell me if he's the man you saw coming out of Empire Wines and Spirits on the night of July seventeenth last year?"

"He is," Assanti said.

"And is he the man who almost got knocked over by the two men you saw running from the bakery shop?"

"He is."

"How close to him were they?"

"Two feet? A foot? They almost knocked him over."

"Where was this?"

"On the sidewalk."

"Where on the sidewalk?"

"Under the street lamp."

"Brightly lighted, was it?"

"Very."

"Could *you* see all three of them clearly from where you were standing?"

"Plain as day."

"And of course they could see each other."

"Objection!"

"Sustained."

"Well, were they *facing* each other?"

"They were standing face to face, yes."

"Looking at each other?"

"Looking each other dead in the eye."

"Thank you, no further questions."

"Mr. Addison?"

"No questions. I would like Doris Franceschi to take the stand, please."

They were lunching at a little place across the bridge in Calm's Point. Bowles had chosen it because he was certain none of his clients or colleagues would be caught dead in a little Italian restaurant in a shitty neighborhood like this one. The restaurant was on the second floor of a clapboard building painted green, white, and red on the outside to resemble a gigantic Italian flag flapping in the wind. In the good old days, the people living in this neighborhood enjoyed the sight of that big flag announcing their heritage. Now the neighborhood was black and nobody cared what the green, white, and red represented. They only knew that some wops named Mariano ran a restaurant upstairs on the corner of Berris and Twelfth, and the stink in the air was garlic.

Bowles was in a very good mood. Perhaps because he'd consumed two gin martinis before lunch and was now working on the bottle of Pinot Grigio Santa Margherita he'd ordered for both of them. Andrew was wondering if perhaps Bowles's bimbo had accompanied him out of town this past weekend, which also might have accounted for the extremely fine mood he was in. Andrew was here to tell him that he wanted him to go out of town this *coming* weekend as well. Andrew was here to tell him that he planned to kill Emma this Friday night.

But for now, all was conviviality and camaraderie. Two good old buddies eating pasta and drinking good wine. Andrew wondered if Bowles had even the slightest suspicion that he'd spent the entire weekend with his wife, fucking her silly. Didn't leave the apartment until late yesterday, after Emma had called Boston to ascertain from her husband that he'd be catching a five o'clock plane. He wondered how Bowles might react to such news. Would he even care? Andrew doubted it.

"Did you have a good weekend?" Bowles asked.

"Yes, very nice, thank you," Andrew said.

"So did I," Bowles said, and winked. Actually winked. Andrew thought What a shmuck. Shoveling another forkful of pasta into his mouth now. Picking up the glass of wine, washing the pasta down. "Have you ever been in love?" he asked suddenly.

"Never," Andrew said.

This was a lie. He'd loved Katie Briggs with every fiber in his being.

"Pity," Bowles said. "You're missing a lot. I can't tell you what it's like to be with a woman who fills my days and nights with joy . . ."

Oh boy, Andrew thought.

". . . whose every glance is like a beam of sunshine . . ."

Boy oh boy oh boy, Andrew thought.

". . . whose very presence sets me tingling."

Linguini was hanging from the tines of his fork. He sucked it into his mouth. Andrew watched him chewing. Tall, slender man with dark hair and brown eyes, the handsomest man Emma had ever seen in her life, or so she'd said. He wondered if she'd changed her mind about that since the weekend.

". . . down on it like a peppermint stick," he was saying now. "Can't get enough of it. Emma doesn't know *how* to do it, or doesn't *care* to do it . . ."

That's what *you* think, Andrew thought.

Bowles picked up his wineglass and drained it. "I'll be happy when she's gone," he said, and signaled to the waiter to fill both glasses again. The waiter poured for them, put the bottle back into the bucket, and walked off. Bowles leaned forward. Lowering his voice, he said, "Do you know what I'm going to do when I'm free?"

"No, what?"

"*Really* free, I mean. I'm talking about months later. When I'm no longer a suspect. Maybe a *year* later, I'll have to play it by ear."

"If this works the way I want it to, you won't be a suspect at all," Andrew said.

"Well, just to be sure."

"I don't think you need to worry."

"Even so. Let's say six months, to play it safe. Six months afterward, I'm going to marry Liddy, that's her name . . . well, Lydia, actually, but I call her Liddy. Do you know what Lydia means in Greek?"

"No, what does it mean?"

"It means cultured."

"I see."

"And she *is*, too. Cultured," he said, and nodded, and picked up his glass again, and drank from it. It occurred to Andrew that his speech was becoming somewhat slurred. He hoped the man wouldn't get drunk. He wanted him to understand all the arrangements.

"Are you familiar with the Raines family in Chicago?" Bowles asked.

"No," Andrew said.

"I thought you were from Chicago."

"I am. But I don't know anyone named Raines there."

"Very wealthy banking family. Raines. Geoffrey Waincroft Raines was her father."

"I still don't know the name."

"Powerful family. Well, that was how we got onto you.

Lydia made a few calls to Chicago, asked a few discreet questions, and *voilà. Fait accompli.*'' He accompanied this last with a little gesture of his fork, as though waving a magic wand. ''The rich and the powerful,'' he said, nodding and digging into the linguini again. ''We'll make a good team. Her money, my money. Lots of money.''

Exactly the words Emma had used.

Lots of money.

The same words now.

''I'm plenty rich as it is, you understand . . .''

''So I understand.''

''But it never hurts to have more, does it?''

''Never does,'' Andrew said. ''Maybe I should raise my price.''

''Nosirree,'' Bowles said, and cocked a finger at him. ''A deal is a deal.''

''Just kidding,'' Andrew said.

''What was I saying?''

''Lots of money.''

''Before that.''

''Six months later . . .''

''Right, six months later I'll marry Liddy. And we'll go on a honeymoon to the South Pacific. I've always wanted to go to the South Pacific. Bali, Sumatra, Bora Bora . . .''

''Me, too,'' Andrew said.

''. . . Samoa . . . really? Is that one of your dreams?''

''Yes.''

''All those girls in nothing but grass skirts,'' Bowles said, and grinned. ''Well, not on my honeymoon, anyway,'' he said, and winked again, and again drained his glass.

''Better go easy,'' Andrew said, ''we've got a lot to discuss.''

''I'm fine, don't worry about it,'' Bowles said, waving away his caution. ''Who was it went down there? Gauguin, wasn't it? Emma would know, she used to be an art student. Got himself a harem down there, surrounded himself with all those young native girls. Little dusky girls in sarongs. You ever had yourself a little dusky girl?''

"Not in the South Pacific," Andrew said.

"But you had one, huh?''

"Several.''

"Are they as good as people say?''

"I don't know what people say. Women are women," Andrew said flatly. "Let's talk about your wife.''

Bowles looked around as if someone had fired a pistol.

"It's all right, the place is almost empty," Andrew said.

"The waiter's standing right there.''

"He barely understands English.''

"Barely is enough if people are talking about . . .'' Bowles lowered his voice. "About what we're about to talk about.''

Andrew looked him flat in the eye.

"Want to go for a walk then?''

"In this neighborhood?''

"You're the one who chose it.''

"No, I'd rather stay here.''

"Then let's get some coffee," Andrew said, and signaled again to the waiter.

Bowles commented on the fact that the cappuccino was frothy and lukewarm, not scalding hot the way some restaurants served it. Apparently he was a cappuccino expert. Andrew was drinking regular coffee, so he really couldn't appreciate what Bowles was saying. He hoped only that the lukewarm cappuccino with its milky white froth would help clear Bowles's head. He didn't want any mistakes here. Not with the timetable so tight. Not if this thing was going to work.

"Are you planning any other weekend trips?'' he asked.

Bowles was now on his second cup of lukewarm cappuccino. His eyes seemed clearer. His speech was no longer halting.

"When did you have in mind?'' he asked.

"I thought this coming weekend might be a good time," Andrew said.

Their waiter was standing at the bar, talking to the bartender. There were only two other people in the place, sitting over near the entrance door. He and Bowles were virtually whispering; Andrew felt certain they could not be overheard.

"When exactly?" Bowles asked.

"Friday afternoon sometime. I just don't want you there on Friday night."

"Is that when you plan to . . . ?"

"I think it'd be best if you weren't in the apartment on Friday night."

"We're talking about the Friday that's coming up, are we?"

"The eighteenth," Andrew said, and nodded.

"Well, yes, I think I may have some business in Miami that weekend."

"Good, go to Miami. Make sure you let someone know where you can be reached."

"I'll leave word with Emma."

Andrew looked at him.

"Oh," Bowles said. "Well, I'll . . . uh . . ."

All at once startled by the thought that this thing was really going to happen, someone was really going to *kill* his wife.

". . . make sure my secretary knows where I'll be staying. In case . . . uh . . . anyone needs to reach me."

"Go alone," Andrew said.

"What?"

"Don't take the bimbo."

"What?"

"Leave precious Liddy home. You won't need your little ray of sunshine in Miami. Now listen and listen carefully, because this is the last time we'll be talking until it's over and done with. I'll wait for you to get back, wait till the cops are through with you, wait till I get your call. Then I'll meet you at the pay locker, and we'll open it together."

"I still wish you didn't have to go into that safe."

"Do you want protection or don't you?"

"It's just . . ."

"If it looks like a burglar did it, you're home free."

"I just think meeting you afterward is risky. In case they're still watching me or something."

"Look, you can't have this both ways," Andrew said, his voice rising. "Either you trust me or . . ."

"Shhhh, shhhh," Bowles said, and glanced toward the couple sitting by the door.

"If you trusted me," Andrew whispered, "it'd be a different story. I'd leave the stuff in a locker, and get out of town the same night I did it, even before the police knew anyone was *dead*!"

"Shhh, come on," Bowles said again.

"But you want to make sure I won't stick you with a bunch of shit from the five-and-dime . . ."

"Well, no, but . . ."

". . . which is okay, I'd do the same thing. Just tell me where you *want* me to stash it. Name a place where there are lockers, anyplace you know where there are pay lockers, and I'll put the stuff there and meet you with the key as soon as I hear from you."

Bowles thought for several moments.

Then he said, "The Mayfair Building. There are helicopters that leave from there for Franklin, if you want to fly out right afterward. The pay lockers are on the forty-sixth floor."

"Good," Andrew said. "You have my number. I'll be waiting for you to call as soon as you're sure the cops are done with you."

He was lying.

The idea, of course, was to dress her so that she looked like the sort of woman who could turn a man's mind to mush. Calling her a woman was a stretch in itself in that Doris Franceschi— or Frankie, as Addison insisted on calling her—was but a mere sixteen years old, and entertaining lewd or lascivious thoughts about her could easily have landed a grown man in jail. But Addison's ploy was to treat her like a femme fatale, emphasizing the male name while advertising the contradictory femaleness of the witness sitting up there crossing and uncrossing her long, splendid legs.

Frankie was wearing a short, tight black leather skirt, and black stockings, and black high-heeled pumps, and a tight red silk blouse that was bursting with adolescent jewels. Every time she uncrossed her legs, the jury was afforded a quick forbidden glimpse of satin or silk, obliterated in the very next instant when once again she crossed them. Matching the black leather skirt and black stockings was long black hair that cascaded on either side of a pale white face with eyes the color of rich dark loam. Her mouth was full and sensuous, adorned with lipstick the color of the blouse. You could imagine Dominick Assanti losing himself in that mouth, imagine him getting dizzy with thoughts of Frankie as he remembered what they'd done together in her hallway.

Watching her, Louise Carella was thinking that if *her* daughter had ever dressed that way when *she* was sixteen, she'd have broken her head. Sitting beside her, Angela was thinking that after delivering twins, she herself would never look that way again—if ever she had. Carella was thinking that dressing her like an Ainsley Avenue whore wasn't going to help Addison's case—he hoped.

"Can you tell us," Addison said, "about what time it was when you and Mr. Assanti were in your hallway together?"

"It was sometime between a quarter to nine and twenty after nine."

"What were you doing during that time, do you remember?"

"Yes," Frankie said.

"Tell us," Addison said, and swung one arm wide to the jury, virtually bowing in her anticipated testimony. Nine men on that jury, three of them white, four black, and two Hispanic, all of them ogling young Frankie regardless of race, creed, or color. The three women watched her, too, thinking God only knew what.

"I guess we were necking," she said.

"By necking, do you mean...? Withdraw that. Frankie, tell us what you mean by necking?"

"Well, you know. Kissing."

"Were you doing anything else besides kissing?"

"Yes."

"And what was that?"

"Well, petting, I guess."

"How would you define petting?"

"Well, you know."

"If it wouldn't embarrass you, could you please tell us exactly what you mean by petting?"

"Well, it *would* embarrass me, actually."

"In which case I withdraw the question. As I understand it, then, you were necking and petting in your hallway for at least forty minutes."

"Yes."

"What happened then?"

"My father called me to come upstairs, so I went up."

"Where did Mr. Assanti go?"

"Home."

"How would you describe his condition at that time?"

"At what time?"

"When he left you."

"He was excited, I guess."

"He has testified that he was dizzy with thoughts of you. Did he seem dizzy?"

"Yes, he seemed very excited."

"Can you think of any other words that might describe his condition?"

"Agitated. Upset. Very excited."

"Upset about what?"

"Well, that I wouldn't let him . . . well . . . you know."

"So when he left you, he was excited, agitated, and upset."

"I'd say that's what he was, yes. Extremely excited."

"Did you see him again that night?"

"I did."

"When?"

"He came back about ten minutes later."

"Back to your house?"

"Yes."

"Was he still agitated at that time?"

"He was even *more* agitated."

"How do you mean?"

"Well, he was, you know, like babbling."

"Babbling?"

"Yes."

"In his excited state, did he tell you he saw two men coming out of the A&L Bakery?"

"No. All he said was he saw some guy with a gun."

"Were those his exact words?"

"Yes. Some guy with a gun."

"Thank you, no further questions."

Lowell rose slowly, nodding as he did, still nodding as he approached the witness stand. Frankie uncrossed her legs and then crossed them again. Lowell kept nodding.

"Miss Franceschi," he said, "am I correct in assuming that you were only fifteen years old in July of last year?"

"Almost sixteen," she said.

"Nonetheless, not *yet* sixteen."

"I was sixteen in November."

"So you were still three, four months away from your six-teenth birthday on that night of July seventeenth, is that correct?"

"Yes."

"You were fifteen years old, and you were necking and petting in your hallway for half an hour, forty minutes, whatever it was . . ."

"Yes."

"Which excited Mr. Assanti, you say . . ."

"Objection, Your Honor."

"Overruled."

"You've described him as becoming dizzy . . ."

"Yes."

"And agitated."

"Yes."

"And upset."

"Yes."

"Did *you* become any of these things?"

"No."

"You weren't dizzy?"

"I wasn't dizzy, no."

"Even though you were only fifteen years old, and you'd been petting for some thirty, forty minutes?"

"We weren't *petting* that long. First we were just necking."

"How long had you been *petting*, would you say?"

"Only fifteen minutes or so."

"*Only* fifteen minutes. Was this a usual thing for you? Petting in hallways?"

"No, it . . ."

"Objection, Your Honor!"

"Where are you going, Mr. Lowell?"

"Directly to Miss Franceschi's state of mind at the time, Your Honor."

"That had *better* be where you're going. Proceed."

"So petting in hallways *wasn't* a usual thing for you?"

"If you're trying to say . . ."

"Just answer the question, please. Was petting in hallways a usual thing for you, or wasn't it?"

"It was not. I was going steady with Dom, that's the only reason . . ."

"But even though this *wasn't* a usual thing for you, it didn't get you as excited as it seemed to get Mr. Assanti, is that right?"

"Well . . ."

"Is that right, Miss Franceschi?"

"I wasn't as excited as he seemed to be, that's right."

"How excited were you?"

"I was excited, but I certainly knew what I was doing."

"Were you *very* excited, as you testified Mr. Assanti was?"

"I suppose you could say I was very excited. But I still . . ."

"Were you *extremely* excited, as you further testified Mr. Assanti was?"

"No, I wasn't extremely excited. And, anyway, *however* excited I was, by the time Dom came back, I was completely in control of myself again."

"Had you not been in control of yourself earlier?"

"Yes, I was in control of myself earlier, too."

"Then why did you have to *regain* control of yourself?"

"I didn't say I . . ."

"You said you were completely in control again."

"Yes, but . . ."

"Which indicates you'd earlier *lost* control, isn't that right?"

"Only in that I was excited."

"Excited enough to have lost control, but not excited enough to be *extremely* excited."

"I didn't know there were different levels of excitement," she said, and nodded to the jury in prim satisfaction.

"Well, apparently *you* think there are," Lowell said. "There's just plain excited, and there's *very* excited, and there's *extremely* excited, and there's also agitated and upset. Those are all your words, all of them used by you to describe different levels of excitement. I ask you now, Miss Franceschi, isn't it possible that you yourself were in such a high state of excitement that . . . ?"

"Objection, Your Honor. *Anything's* possible. It's possible that the roof of this courtroom could fall in at any moment, it's possible that . . ."

"Yes, yes, Mr. Addison, sustained."

"Miss Franceschi, were you so excited that you misunderstood what Mr. Assanti was telling you?"

"No, I understood him completely. He said he saw some guy with a gun."

"What did you say to him when he told you that?"

"I said he should go to the police."

"And did he?"

"I don't think so. I think they found him later. On their own."

"After what *you'd* told them, isn't that right?"

"Yes."

"About him having witnessed the aftermath of the shooting."

"Yes."

"Now tell me, when Detectives Wade and Bent questioned you, did you know they were looking for *two* men?"

"No, I didn't know that."

"You do remember talking to them on the night of July seventeenth last year, don't you?"

"Yes, I remember talking to them."

"Well, didn't they ask if you'd seen two black men running from the direction of the bakery shop?"

"They may have asked me that, I really don't remember."

"Well, perhaps this will refresh your memory," Lowell said, and handed her a sheaf of papers. "Could you read these please? Take your time, study them carefully." He waited while she read the papers he had handed her. When she looked up at last, he asked, "Can you tell me what it is you just read?"

"It looks like a report on my conversation with the detectives."

"Yes, and do you now remember them asking if you'd seen two black men running from the direction of the bakery shop?"

"Yes, I suppose they asked me that."

"Did they or didn't they?"

"They did."

"Well, did you correct their misapprehension?"

"What misapprehension?"

"Did you tell them it wasn't *two* men running from the direction of the bakery shop, it was only one?"

"No, I didn't tell them that."

"You didn't feel it was necessary to correct them?"

"I told them what Dom told me, that's all."

"They asked if you'd seen two men coming this way . . ."

"Yes . . ."

". . . and you said your boyfriend told you he'd seen some guy running out of the bakery shop with a gun in his hand, isn't that right?"

"I told them what Dom told me, yes."

"But you didn't say anything like, 'By the way, it wasn't *two* men, it was only *one.*' Did you say anything like that?"

"No, I didn't."

"Because in fact, Miss Franceschi, you really understood all along, didn't you, that you were all talking about *two* men, only one of whom had a gun?"

"No, I didn't understand that at all."

"Well, did you understand them to be talking about *one* man?"

"Yes."

"Even though they clearly asked you about *two* men?"

"I thought they were talking about the man Dom saw."

"The man carrying the gun."

"Yes."

"Thank you, no further questions."

"Let's recess till tomorrow at nine," Di Pasco said.

13.

A cold, hard drizzle drilled the Tuesday morning streets, washing away most of what was left of the weekend's snow. Outside the courthouse The Preacher and his troops had gathered in support of today's star witness, Sonny Cole himself. The demonstrators were chanting, "Black Double Jeopardy, Black Double Jeopardy," which was not the name of a new game show, but was instead The Preacher's view of what was happening to Cole.

The Preacher's real name was Thomas Raleigh, but he had abandoned this slave-society appellation for the trendier Akbar Zaroum, which sounded vaguely African and which served him well in a day and age of heightened awareness of one's roots. Under whichever name he chose to use, it was estimated that he'd cost the city some $1,400,000 last year alone, for extended police coverage of his various marches, protests, and demonstrations.

"Black Double Jeopardy," he kept chanting into his bullhorn, "Black Double Jeopardy," and his followers behind him echoed the chant, bellowing it into the ice-edged drizzle, "Black Double Jeopardy, Black Double Jeopardy."

The chant had nothing whatever to do with reality.

Sonny Cole had been charged with two separate counts of first-degree murder. These murders had occurred in different locations, weeks apart. There were two different victims. He was now being tried for the murder of Anthony Carella. Next month, he would be tried for the murder of Dolly Simms. There

287

was no possible way anyone could even imagine he was being tried for the same crime twice—which was what the doctrine of double jeopardy aimed to prevent. But The Preacher operated on the theory that if you told a big enough lie often enough, people would accept it as the truth.

Wearing a long black coat and a red fez, rain-spattered dark glasses covering his eyes, long black hair slicked back, thick gold crucifix showing in the open throat of the coat, bullhorn to his mouth, Zaroum paced behind the blue-and-white police saw-horses set up on the street before the courthouse, chanting, "Black Double Jeopardy, Black Double Jeopardy." His follow-ers paced solemnly behind him, all of them wearing dark blue trench coats, blue suits, white shirts, and red ties, lockstepped into the cadence of the chant, "Black Double Jeopardy, Black Double Jeopardy."

The rain fell relentlessly.

Inside the courthouse, Sonny Cole was testifying.

He would have been a handsome man were it not for the scar on his face, running through his eyebrow and coming down his cheekbone to his jaw. Addison had advised against the hi-top fade Cole had groomed in jail, which the attorney said looked like a black flowerpot sitting on top of his head. Cole had styled his hair differently for the trial; he was now wearing it in a modified crew cut that made him look like a college student. To heighten the effect, he was wearing a gray tweed jacket with darker gray flannel slacks, a white button-down shirt, and a blue tie. He was also wearing eyeglasses, which Addison felt added a serious scholarly touch. Cole did, in fact, need glasses; without them he squinted, which Addison felt made a man look "mean and squinched," his exact words.

"Mr. Cole," he said now, "you have heard testimony in this courtroom regarding the events that occurred on the street outside the A&L Bakery on the night of July seventeenth last year, have you not?''

"I heard it, yes," Cole said.

His voice low. A pleasant voice. Deep. Well-modulated. The voice of a thoughtful, reasonable man.

"And you've heard testimony as to whether there was one man, two men, a dozen men . . .''

"Objection, Your Honor . . .''

"Sustained.''

"Hyperbole, Your Honor, forgive me,'' Addison said, smiling, spreading his arms wide in apology, "I withdraw the question. Mr. Cole, do you remember where you were at around nine-thirty on the night of July seventeenth last year?''

"I do.''

"Were you outside the A & L Bakery?''

"I was not.''

"Were you anywhere *near* the A & L Bakery?''

"I was not.''

"Can you tell us where you were?''

"I was on a bus coming from Greenville, South Carolina.''

"What were you doing in Greenville?''

"Just passing through, sir. Seeing a little bit of the United States.''

"And you say you were on a bus?''

"Yes, sir.''

"What time did you board this bus?''

"Oh, it must've been six o'clock or thereabouts.''

"Where were you going?''

"I was coming here, sir.''

"You were on a bus coming to this city, is that correct?''

"Yes, sir.''

"Can you tell us approximately where you were at nine-thirty that night? Which city, for example? Which state?''

"I think we were in Virginia by then. Passing by Roanoke.''

"When did you arrive here, do you remember?"

"At two o'clock on the afternoon of the eighteenth."

"As I understand it, then, you weren't even *in* this city on the night Anthony Carella was shot and killed."

"That's correct, sir. I was somewhere in Virginia around that time."

"How long is the trip from Greenville, Mr. Cole?"

"Twenty hours."

"And you boarded the bus when? I know you told us, but perhaps . . ."

"At six o'clock on the night of July seventeenth."

"And you were scheduled to arrive here when?"

"At two o'clock on the afternoon of the eighteenth."

"Which is when you did arrive."

"Yes, sir, give or take a few minutes."

"Where did this bus leave you off?"

"Union Terminal."

"Do you know a man named Desmond Whittaker?"

"I do."

"He is now deceased, isn't that so?"

"Yes."

"Did you know him on the night of July seventeenth?"

"No, I did not."

"When did you first meet Mr. Whittaker?"

"On the twenty-second of July."

"Which would have been five days *after* Mr. Carella was killed."

"Yes, sir."

"Where did you meet him?"

"In a cafeteria on The Stem."

"By The Stem, do you mean Stemmler Avenue?"

"Yes, sir, Stemmler."

"What was the occasion of this meeting? How did it come about?"

"We happened to be sitting at the same table, and we struck

up a conversation. He was from out of town, and so was I, we just started talking.''

''What happened then?''

''We went out looking for some girls.''

Addison nodded, went to the table where the evidence was arrayed, picked up the Uzi assault pistol, and carried it to the witness stand.

''Mr. Cole,'' he said, ''I show you this pistol and ask if you've ever seen it before.''

''I have,'' Cole said.

''Can you tell me the make and caliber of this pistol?''

''It's a nine-millimeter Uzi.''

''When did you first see this pistol?''

''Desmond Whittaker showed it to me.''

''When?''

''The night we met.''

''Which was when?''

''The twenty-second of July.''

''How did he happen to show it to you?''

''We were with this girl, and he showed the gun to both of us.''

Addison went to the defense table, picked up a paper there, and carried it back to the witness chair. ''Mr. Cole,'' he said, ''I ask if you have ever seen this document before.''

Cole took the document, studied it carefully.

''I have, yes, sir.''

''When did you first see it?''

''I only saw it once before now.''

''And when was that?''

''On the twenty-second of July.''

''How did you happen to see it?''

''Desmond Whittaker showed it to me and the girl.''

''Can you tell me what it is?''

''It's a bill of sale for that Uzi.''

''Objection, Your Honor!'' Lowell said. ''I've heard nothing about this until this very moment. My demand for discovery specifically asked for any physical evidence the defense planned to . . .''

''Your Honor, the document was recovered only yesterday from an out-of-state gun-shop owner. I regret this surprise . . .''

''It's a surprise, all right,'' Lowell said sourly.

''Let's see it,'' Di Pasco said. ''Come up here, both of you.''

Addison carried the document to the bench and handed it up to Di Pasco, who read it silently and then passed it on to Lowell.

''Your Honor,'' Lowell said, ''I cannot believe this turned up only yesterday.''

''I'm prepared to provide a witness who . . .''

''He's always prepared to provide a witness, Your Honor, but . . .''

''What witness?'' Di Pasco asked.

''The private detective who visited the gun shop in Memphis and found this copy of . . .''

''Oh, it's a *copy*,'' Lowell said. ''We don't even have the *original* here.''

''The original went to Whittaker at the time of the sale.''

''How'd you know where this gun shop was?'' Di Pasco asked.

''Your Honor, excuse me, but this is a *copy* of a document we've never seen . . .''

''Well, it looks like a good copy to me,'' Di Pasco said. ''How'd you get hold of it?'' he asked Addison, obviously impressed.

''Whittaker told my client he'd purchased the gun in Memphis. It was a matter of elimination, sir. Which is why it took such a long time to find it.''

''Well, I admire your tenacity, but I must tell you I look askance at this kind of last-minute evidence.''

''Your Honor, I would have provided it sooner, believe me, but the search was a long and difficult one.''

''Are you asking that it be moved into evidence?''

"I am, Your Honor."

"Your Honor," Lowell said, "this document should have been listed on the defense response to my demand for discovery."

"We didn't *have* the document at that time, Your Honor. The search has been an ongoing one."

"In any event," Lowell said, "lacking the testimony of the private investigator—and for that matter, the gun-shop owner as well—there's insufficient foundation to admit."

"Well, here we go again," Di Pasco said. "I'm sure Mr. Addison can call both those people if you insist, but do you honestly doubt the authenticity of this paper? Do we *really* want a costly adjournment?"

Lowell looked at him.

"It looks genuine enough to me," Di Pasco said. "Doesn't it to you?"

"It looks genuine, Your Honor, yes, but . . ."

"I'm prepared to call both the shop owner and the private investigator, Your Honor," Addison said. "The investigator lives here in this city. The shop is in Memphis, of course, but I'm sure we could expedite . . ."

"What do you say, Mr. Lowell?"

"I'll withdraw my objection," Lowell said, "provided we can verify that the document was not altered and that it was, in truth, uncovered only yesterday."

"How do you plan to do that, Mr. Lowell?"

"I'll have a detective in our office telephone the gun-shop owner at once."

"May we proceed while verification is pending?"

"If Your Honor wishes."

"Let's move it along then," Di Pasco said.

Lowell walked back to his table, where he leaned over and whispered something to his assistant. The assistant nodded gravely. Carella glanced at his mother to see if she'd noticed this. She had not. But Angela had. Their eyes met. There were questions in her eyes that he could not answer. At the table,

Lowell and his assistant sat stone-faced and silent as Addison elicited from his witness testimony regarding the bill of sale for an Uzi assault pistol legitimately purchased back in June, shortly after Desmond Whittaker was released from prison in Louisiana, Addison asking if this was the bill of sale Whittaker had shown him, and then asking Cole to read the serial numbers out loud, and then showing him the gun again and asking him to read the serial numbers on it, again out loud, which seemed to constitute incontrovertible proof that the pistol that had shot and killed Carella's father had belonged to Cole's partner and not to Cole himself. What they were trying to do was show that since the gun was owned by Whittaker, and since Cole was nowhere *near* the bakery on the night of the murder, then it had to be Whittaker who'd done the shooting. A man now *dead*, a man who could not possibly be questioned, had killed Carella's father. He felt Angela's eyes on him again. He did not turn to meet them this time.

"No further questions," Addison said.

Lowell approached the witness stand.

"So you were in Virginia that night of the murder, huh?" he said.

"Yes, sir."

"You didn't happen to save your bus ticket, did you?"

"No, sir."

"Threw it away, did you?"

"Yes, sir."

"Did you get a receipt for it when you bought it?"

"No, sir, I bought it right at the depot. Nobody gave me a receipt."

"How much did you pay for it?"

"A hundred twenty-three dollars and seventy-five cents."

"Give your name to anybody?"

"No, sir, I wasn't asked to."

"Meet anyone you knew in the depot?"

"No, sir."

"Or on the bus?"

"No, sir."

"What were you doing down there in Greenville?"

"Just passing through."

"Passing through from *where*?"

"I was down in Florida for a while."

"Where'd you stay while you were in Florida?"

"I slept on the beach."

"Uh-huh. Did you sleep on the beach in Greenville, too?"

"I was only in Greenville that one day. I caught a bus out that night."

"*Is* there a beach in Greenville, would you know?"

"No, I wouldn't."

"Can you tell me anything at *all* about Greenville?"

"Just that it seemed like a nice city."

"Can you tell me the names of any of the streets there?"

"No, I can't."

"Any of the hotels?"

"No, sir. I didn't stay at any hotel. I just walked around."

"Walked around, uh-huh. Can you tell me where the bus depot was?"

"No, I'm sorry."

"You just walked around and wandered into this depot, is that right?"

"No, sir. I knew where it was 'cause I'd come up from Miami by bus."

"I don't suppose you have that Miami ticket, either, do you?"

"No, sir."

"Miami-Greenville, you don't have that ticket."

"No, sir."

"Mr. Cole, do you have any proof at *all* that you were on a bus coming from Greenville the night Anthony Carella was murdered?"

"I'm sure people saw me on that bus, but I wouldn't know who they were."

"Did you talk to anyone on the bus?"

"No, sir."

"So we have just your word that you were on that bus that night."

"Maybe there's a record of the ticket someplace."

"Yes, maybe there is, but you don't have such a record, do you?"

"No, I don't."

"So we don't really know for sure, do we, that you took the bus that night and not the night before? Or two nights before? Or a week before? We have just your word for it, isn't that correct?"

"My word is good," Cole said, and suddenly there was a look of fierce pride on his face.

"A man of your word, are you?" Lowell asked.

"Yes, sir."

"Isn't it a fact, Mr. Cole, that you killed . . . ?"

"Objection!"

"Overruled. But I must warn the jury at this time . . ."

"Thank you, Your Honor."

". . . to consider the defendant's prior conviction only as it impacts on his credibility. It should not be taken as a propensity to commit this particular crime." He turned back to Lowell, and nodded to him to continue.

"Mr. Cole," Lowell said, "isn't it a fact that you killed an eighty-two-year-old man during a grocery store holdup in Pasadena, California, in nineteen . . ."

"That's what I was charged with."

"Well, you weren't only *charged*, you were *convicted*, weren't you? And *sentenced*, weren't you? You served *time*, didn't you?"

"I served time, yes."

"And you were paroled last year in April, weren't you?"

"Yes, I was."

"And you headed East and South, just seeing a little bit of the United States, isn't that what you said?"

"That's what I was doing in Greenville."

"And you ended up in this city . . ."

"Yes."

"Where you met Desmond Whittaker."

"Yes."

"Have you ever been to Washington, D.C.?"

"Yes."

"Isn't it true that you met Mr. Whittaker for the first time in *Washington* and not here in this city?"

"I met him for the first time in this city. In a cafeteria on The Stem. On July twenty-second."

"Isn't it true that you met him several weeks *before* Anthony Carella was murdered and that in fact you came here *together* from Washington, D.C.?"

"I met him for the first time in this city," Cole said again. "In a cafeteria on The Stem. On July twenty-second."

"Mr. Cole, when you were arrested on the night of August first last year, were you in possession of a nine-millimeter semi-automatic pistol?"

"I was."

"I show you this Uzi, and ask if it is the gun recovered from you by Detective Randall Wade that night."

"It is."

"The same gun, is it? You're sure about that?"

"Yes, it's the same gun."

"When did this gun come into your possession?"

"It was *not* in my possession on the night of . . ."

"I didn't ask you when it was *not* in your possession. I asked you when it came *into* your possession. You're under oath, and you're a man of your word, so how about answering my question?"

"It came into my possession that very day."

"August first last year?"

"Yes."

"Have you ever fired this gun?"

"Never."

"When you were arrested that night, did you turn this gun on Detectives Wade and Carella?"

"I turned *to* them. I didn't turn the *gun* on them."

"But you had the gun in your hand, didn't you?"

"Yes."

"So when you turned, the gun also turned, didn't it?"

"I suppose it did."

"Were you planning to fire it?"

"No."

"You just had it in your hand to . . . well, why *did* you have it in your hand, Mr. Cole?"

"For self-defense."

"Ah. Then you *did* intend firing it."

"I'd already been *shot*, damn it!"

"Please answer the question. Did you intend firing that pistol at the arresting officers?"

"No, I did not."

"Tell me, Mr. Cole, do you know how to use this gun?"

"I've seen guns like it."

"Answer my question, please."

"I could figure out how to use it if I had to."

"Mr. Cole, do you or do you not know how to use this pistol? Please answer my question."

"I do."

"Even though you've never fired it?"

"Guns are pretty much all the same, one like the other."

"No more questions," Lowell said.

Addison came back to his witness.

"Mr. Cole," he said, "I have only one other question." He lowered his voice. "Did you kill Anthony Carella?"

"I did not."

"Thank you. I have no further questions. The defense rests its case, Your Honor."

"I just want to clarify one point, Your Honor," Lowell said, and approached the witness stand again. "Mr. Cole, are you saying that before the night of August first you had never even held this pistol in your hand?"

"That's what I'm saying."

"Thank you, I have nothing further."

"All right then," Di Pasco said, "I'd like to recess till one o'clock this afternoon, at which time we'll hear your closing arguments. One o'clock suit everybody?"

"Yes, Your Honor."

"Yes, Your Honor."

"This court is recessed," Di Pasco said, and slammed down his gavel.

As Carella did every evening when he got home, he was now telling Teddy everything that had happened at the courthouse that day. Explaining trial procedure in sign language wasn't an easy task, but he went through it dutifully, augmenting his faltering fingers with speech so that she could read what he was talking about on his mouth as well.

He told her that the way a criminal trail ended was first the defense attorney made his closing argument and then the D.A. made his, after which the judge charged the jury, explaining the law to them and the possible verdicts they could reach in the case under consideration. It had taken Lowell an hour and a half to tell the jury what he had told Carella and his sister at the Golden Lion last Friday, before which Addison had taken a full two hours to tell them what a wonderful person of sterling character was his client Samson Wilbur Cole, who—as Addison had proved—was nowhere near the city on the night of the Carella murder, and moreover did not come into possession of the evidence pistol until two weeks *after* the murder was committed.

Di Pasco then told the jury that each witness's testimony should be weighed carefully and with the greatest solemnity as to the reliability and credibility of the witness, and urged them to put aside all thoughts of sentencing or sympathy, allowing only the evidence they had seen and heard to govern their verdict. He explained further that if they decided Samson Cole himself had not pulled the trigger on the night of the murder, but had in fact been acting in concert with another during the commission of a felony when the murder took place, then he was as guilty as whoever may have done the actual shooting, and should be found so by the jury. He reminded them again of the oaths they had taken as jurors, asked them to be fair-minded and open-minded in reaching their verdict and warned them again—as he had at the beginning of the trial—not to discuss the case with anyone but themselves while they were in deliberation. In conclusion, he wished them good luck in reaching a true verdict.

"Lowell said it may take a week, ten days," Carella said, signing, "or they might surprise everybody and decide earlier. He's known juries to come back in less than an hour."

Teddy nodded, watching his fingers, alternately watching his lips.

"But he said usually the longer a jury's out, the more likelihood there is of a compromise verdict. There's no hard-and-fast rule, they can come back in ten minutes and say guilty, or they can come back next week and say not guilty, there's really no way to gauge it."

How will you, she started to sign, but he anticipated what she was about to say, and overrode her flying fingers with his own, talking at the same time.

"He'll beep me when it looks close. The lieutenant has a car and driver standing by for me. We'll ride the hammer all the way downtown."

He was telling her they'd use the siren. She knew the expression. She nodded. Then, her face grave, she asked, *What do you think the verdict will be*?

"I don't know," he said.

They went to see Emma Bowles the very next morning.

She was just coming out of the building as they pulled up in the car. Wearing red tights, black leg warmers, black jogging shoes, a short black parka. No hat. Blonde hair glistening in the sunlight. It was one of those cold, clear, crisp days that made this city seem livable even in the wintertime, the sidewalks and streets spanking clean after yesterday's rain, all vestiges of sullied snow gone. The doorman outside started waving them off until Meyer lowered the visor to show a placard with the city's Police Department logo on it. He came over apologetically then, and asked if they'd move the car just a little bit up, away from the canopy and the front door. Meyer got out to run after Emma. Carella moved the car and then caught up with them.

She was walking very fast.

She explained that she went to aerobics three times a week, on Tuesday, Thursday, and Saturday, and walked on all the other mornings but Sunday, when even the Lord rested. She smiled when she said this, and then conversationally asked the detectives if they did much walking. Carella admitted that they didn't walk too often, except when they were tailing someone. Emma said they should both make sure they got plenty of exercise, it was paramount to one's health. That was exactly the word she used. Paramount. Both detectives were already out of breath, trying to keep up with her.

"What we wanted to tell you," Meyer said, "is that we've arrested the man who killed Tilly . . ."

"Oh?"

"Yes. Got a signed confession from him, he was arraigned Monday morning."

"That's wonderful," she said.

"It clears up a few questions, anyway. At least now we know your husband didn't have anything to do with Tilly's death."

"The reason we're *really* here, though," Carella said, "is to tell you what progress we've made regarding this Denker person."

"Denker?" she said.

"She doesn't know his real name, Steve," Meyer said.

She turned to look at Meyer on her left and then immediately turned to Carella, not missing a step, long legs reaching for pavement, fists pumping.

"The man your husband hired," Carella said. "The so-called private eye."

"But he *is* one," she said.

"Well, we don't think so, ma'am," Carella said. "The Chicago phone number he gave you is listed to someone named Andrew Denker, which we're assuming is his real name. We know he started shopping for a gun practically the minute he arrived here . . ."

"Yes, he told me he has a gun."

"He's got one, all right," Meyer said. "A Colt forty-five, which he bought from a small-time dealer in Diamondback. Guy named Gofredo Cabrera, who also put him in touch with someone who rented him a room downtown."

"Yes, he told me he was living somewhere near the Calm's Point Bridge."

"321 South Lewiston," Meyer said, nodding. "Apartment 4C."

"Anyway, we figured if we requested a search warrant for the gun, it'd be denied," Carella said. "Insufficient cause—we were already turned down on a telephone tap. So all we can do, really, is keep an eye on him, make sure he . . ."

"Keep an eye on him?"

"Yes. Ask the lieutenant to . . ."

"But how?"

"Well, get some detectives assigned . . ."

"But he's gone."

Both of them almost missed the beat.

Emma kept running as if she hadn't just dropped a bombshell. They kept running beside her, flanking her, each turning to look at her.

"Back to Chicago," she said.

"How do you know?" Carella asked.

"He told me he was leaving. He said with Tilly dead, my husband saw no further need for his services."

"When did he tell you this?"

"Yesterday afternoon."

"And you think he's already gone?"

"He told me he was catching a plane late last night."

"To Chicago?"

"Yes. To Chicago."

"Shook hands, said goodbye . . ."

"No, nothing that formal. Just came by to say he'd be leaving, it'd been a pleasure working with me, he hoped everything turned out all right. But you know . . ."

They waited.

"I believe you, of course, I'm not suggesting that your information is wrong. But I think he really *was* a private detective, and I think he really was trying to protect me. I don't know why he used a false name, *if* he did . . ."

"He did," Carella said.

" . . . but perhaps there was a reason for it. In any case, he's gone now. So even if he *did* pose a threat—which I doubt—he no longer does."

"Unless he was lying," Carella said.

"Did he say which flight he was taking?" Meyer asked.

"No," Emma said. "But, really, why would he . . . ?"

"To put you off guard," Carella said.

"I think you're wrong. I think he was here to do a job, and when my husband told him he was no longer needed, the job ended."

They had reached a Stop sign at the end of the road. Carella figured they'd come at least a mile and a half from her building. The sign was obviously a turnaround point for her. As if obeying it, she stopped for an instant, breathing hard, head lowered, sucking in great gulps of air. At last, she looked up at them. Apparently continuing her thought of a moment ago, she said, "Things do begin, you know . . . and then they end."

"Well," Carella said, and for a moment didn't know quite what else to say. "If you should need any further assistance . . ."

"No, I'll be fine," she said. "I'll be alone this weekend, but with Tilly dead . . . well, I'm sure there's nothing to worry about anymore."

"Just in case you should need us," Meyer said, "you know where we are."

"Thank you," she said, "I appreciate that."

There was a small, sad smile on her face.

The superintendent at 321 South Lewiston told them he wasn't in the habit of checking on the comings and goings of his tenants and didn't know whether the man in apartment 4C was still there or not. Nobody had told him anybody was leaving, and it wasn't none of his business anyhow.

"Do you have a passkey to that apartment?" Meyer asked.

"I do, but . . ."

"Think you could let us in, take a look around?" Carella asked.

"Not without a search warrant," the super said.

"Five, ten minutes is all we'd need," Meyer said.

"I wouldn't give you five, ten seconds," the super said.

"Thank you," Carella said, and hoped he didn't sound unappreciative.

* * *

A call to the phone number on the Darrow Investigations business card got a recorded voice that was presumably Denker's. It said:

"Hi, I'm back in Chicago, but I'm out just now. If you leave a message when you hear the beep, I'll return your call as soon as I can. Thanks a lot."

Carella did not leave a message.

Instead, just as he'd suggested to Emma Bowles, he went into the lieutenant's office and requested a round-the-clock on Denker's building, just in case he hadn't left the city at all and was merely laying down smoke.

The lieutenant went in to see Captain Frick, who was in command of the entire precinct and who normally wasn't too terribly bright. This time, he seemed to make sense.

"Why are we still fucking around with this?" he asked.

"Well, sir, there were two murder attempts, you know . . ."

"Yes, but the man who made those attempts was himself killed later on, wasn't he?"

"Yes, sir."

"And we've already got the man who did it, haven't we?"

"Yes, sir, but . . ."

"So who *is* this woman, the governor's wife or something?"

"Well, no, sir, but . . ."

"I had a nickel for everybody had attempts made on their lives in this city, I'd be a rich man. People are *really* getting killed every fucking day in this city, I can't waste men on somebody who *might* get killed. The request is denied. Drop the case, mark it cleared."

"Yes, sir, cleared," Byrnes said.

"That it?"

"That's it, sir."

"I'm busy," Frick said.

14.

His beeper went off at a quarter to four. He was at the water cooler; the insistent piping voice of the instrument startled him. The call had to be from Lowell; no one in-house would be beeping him while he was right here in the squadroom. He called back at once. Someone picked up on the second ring.

"Hello?"

Lowell. The unmistakably British-sounding voice.

"Hello," Carella said, "what is it?"

"How fast can you get down here?"

"Twenty minutes. Have they . . . ?"

"From what we can tell, it'll be any minute now."

"I'm on my way," Carella said.

The men and women of the jury filed in at twenty minutes past four.

Carella tried to read what was on their faces. Throughout the course of trial, when they were mere supporting players to the stars on and around the witness stand, he had paid scant attention to them. But now, suddenly, they were center stage, walking into the spotlight as a group and solemnly taking their chairs in the jury box. The foreman had a mustache. He had not noticed that before. Two of the three women were wearing eyeglasses. One of the black jurors was wearing an outrageous tie. All of the jurors, male or female, white or black, Hispanic or Asian, wore expressions that were completely blank.

Judge Di Pasco turned to them as soon as they were seated.

"Ladies and gentlemen of the jury," he said, "have you agreed upon a verdict in this case?"

"We have," the foreman said. He was a tall black man wearing a dark suit, a white shirt, and a burgundy-colored tie. His hands were shaking.

"Please return the papers to the Court," the clerk said.

"Mr. Foreman," Di Pasco said, "what is the jury's verdict?"

Carella caught his breath.

"We find the defendant not guilty," the foreman said.

Carella felt as if he'd been hit in the face with a closed fist.

Lowell was immediately on his feet.

"Your Honor," he said, "may I respectfully request that the jury be polled?"

Di Pasco nodded to the court clerk. At the back of the court-room, Sonny Cole's supporters, most of whom did not know him and many of whom would not have cared to meet him in a dark alley at midnight, were slapping each other on the back in congratulation.

"Juror number one," the clerk said, "Franklin Jonathan Miller, how do you find the defendant?"

"Not guilty," the foreman said.

"Juror number two, Maria Catalina Perez, how do you find the defendant?"

"Not guilty."

And now Carella sat stunned and silent as the names were called and each member of the jury rose in turn to respond to the clerk's question, how do you find the defendant, the answers seeming to resound into that paneled chamber, rising to its vaulted ceiling, not guilty, cascading down onto the grinning faces at the back of the courtroom, not guilty, rushing down through the center aisle, not guilty, not guilty, and settling at last on Carella in a final fading roar where he sat feeling oddly embarrassed and utterly alone, not guilty, not guilty, not guilty.

* * *

The night could not be trusted, winter could not be trusted.

What had started as a bright and sunny day was now, at eight-forty P.M., bitterly cold. Meyer and Carella stood in their heavy overcoats outside the Smoke Rise building where murder had been committed, talking to the Chief of Detectives, who had come all the way uptown on this one because he was afraid of what the media might make of it.

Blue-and-white radio cars were angle-parked into the curb across the street from the building. Directly in front of the building's green canopy, an ambulance was backed into the curb, its rear doors open. Grayish-blue exhaust fumes floated up on the night. Uniformed cops with nothing to do stood around near the front door. Monoghan and Monroe, who had got here ten minutes before the chief arrived, were talking to the doorman, trying to appear actively essential to the investigation.

The Chief of Detectives was named Lou Fremont, and he had been appointed only recently by the new commissioner, an act of conciliation in that he was both white and a man who had come up through the ranks right here in this city and not in some little Southern town where the only action on a Saturday night was the blinking of a traffic light on Main and Cucumber. Both Meyer and Carella knew Fremont from when he'd been in command of the Seven-Three in Majesta. A gruff, no-nonsense man in his late fifties, he had a reputation for being short of temper and quick with his fists. But he knew what it was like to be a street cop, and they knew he would go to bat for them if this thing got out of hand. What they were all worried about was something called Prior Knowledge.

"Said somebody was trying to kill her, huh?" Fremont asked.

"Well, someone pushed her off a subway platform," Carella said. "And later, he . . ."

"What'd you find out about that?"

"It's a complicated story, Chief."

"I'm not going anyplace," Fremont said. "Are you going someplace?"

"No, sir."

The chief nodded. He was anticipating the media saying the police had known there was murder in the air, the woman had come to them after a murder attempt, and now there was an *actual* murder, never mind *attempted* murder. Twist this around a bit, it could look like they'd been negligent in their investigation. Thank God it didn't involve race. All they needed was another goddamn racially motivated incident in this city.

Carella was telling him how the guy who'd shoved her off the platform had tried to run her down later on and had finally ended up dead himself, the victim of a shooting. This was—

"What shooting?" Fremont asked. "Where?"

He told the chief all about Roger Turner Tilly hanging from the ceiling in a Diamondback basement—

"Hanging? I thought you said he was shot."

"Shot first, hanged later," Carella said.

"In Diamondback? That's the Eight-Three, isn't it?"

"Yes, sir."

"Then how'd you get . . . ?"

"First Man Up, sir."

"Because the woman came to see you on the murder attempts?"

"Yes, sir."

"*Two* of them, I'm now hearing. I don't like this, I can tell you that."

"Yes, sir. We were looking for Tilly because she'd identified him as the man who'd tried to run her down. So when Tilly turned up dead, there was some question about whether or not FMU applied here."

"I would say it did."

"Well, Lieutenant Byrnes wanted to check that. But meanwhile, he advised us to stay on the case."

"Do you think this might be the same person?"

"Sir?"

"Who killed Tilly and did this one?"

"Oh. No, sir. No, we've already *got* Tilly's murderer. He was arraigned Monday, and the judge denied bail. It couldn't possibly be the same person."

"Good work," Fremont said.

"Thank you, sir."

"But I'm still worried about Prior Knowledge here."

"Yes, sir."

"I know it's a stretch . . ."

"Well, yes, sir, I think actually it might be."

"But the media has ways of making something out of nothing, you know that."

"Yes, sir."

"She *did* come to you . . ."

"Yes, sir . . ."

"And now . . ."

Fremont shook his head.

"What's it look like upstairs?" he asked.

Meyer filled him in on what it looked like upstairs. The safe broken into, tool marks around the dial and the edge of the door, victim lying on the—

"Where is this? The safe?"

"In the master bedroom, sir," Meyer said. "Closet in the master bedroom."

—victim lying on the floor just inside the bedroom door, shot in the face at close range. Three spent cartridge cases recovered, as well as two bullets that went right on through, exiting at the back of the head, the other bullet presumably still someplace inside the head.

"Anything left in the safe?"

"Dry as a bone, sir."

"Any idea what was in it?"

"We found a list in the desk drawer, yes, sir."

"How about the casings and bullets? What do they look like?"

"Forty-fives," Meyer said. "Clearly stamped on the casing. Remington forty-five Auto Colt."

"Better run them down to Ballistics right away."

"Yes, sir."

"Because what I want here is immediate action. *Immediate.* Before those television assholes get on our backs."

"Yes, sir," Carella said.

"What we were thinking, sir," Meyer said, "is that the perp may be someone we've had under investigation."

"Oh?"

"Yes, sir."

"Let me hear it."

They told him about Andrew Denker, alias Andrew Darrow, who'd presented himself to Emma Bowles as a man her husband had hired to protect her—

"I don't like that," Fremont said, shaking his head. "That brings us right back to Prior Knowledge again."

"Well, we don't know for sure that this man was actually hired to *kill* her, sir. What we *do* know is he bought a Colt forty-five when he got here . . ."

"What do you mean got here?"

"From Chicago?"

"Any record on him there?"

"No, sir."

"Do you know where to find this guy?"

"Well, we have him at an address on Lewiston, but his answering machine says he's back in Chicago."

"Doesn't mean a thing, nowadays you can change a message long-distance."

"Yes, sir, that's what we . . ."

"All you have to do is push a few buttons on your phone and then do the recording."

"Yes, sir."

"Get a search warrant, go . . ."

"We were turned down on a wiretap, sir, we figured we'd wait till we get the Ballistics report."

"Hell with Ballistics. You've got your stamped casings, you *know* the gun was a forty-five."

"Yes, sir."

"So get your warrant, and then go toss this guy *and* his apartment. Because I'll tell you, the sooner we wrap this one, the happier I'll be."

"Yes, sir."

"Did you talk to the doorman here?"

"Yes, sir."

"What'd he have to say?"

"Nothing much, sir."

"A man gets in here, pumps three slugs in a person's face, he had to get in one way or another."

"Yes, sir."

"So did he see anyone going in or out?"

"No, sir."

"Did you describe your man to him?"

"Yes, sir."

"And he didn't see him, huh?"

"No, sir. But he was . . ."

Monoghan and Monroe came wandering over, hands in their pockets, hats tilted low like gunslingers.

"Evening, Chief," Monroe said.

"Evening," Monoghan said.

"Uhm," Fremont said, and nodded curtly.

"Doorman didn't see anybody suspicious going in or out," Monoghan said. "But he says he was . . ."

He fell silent all at once.

The ambulance attendants were coming out with a stretcher.

The men all turned to watch them.

The resident intern followed the stretcher out of the building.

He was wearing a black overcoat over his hospital whites, a stethoscope hanging out of his pocket.

There was a black body bag on the stretcher.

Carella's application for a search warrant read:

1. I am a detective of the Police Department, currently assigned to the 87th Detective Squad.

2. I have in my possession several bullets and spent cartridge cases recovered at the scene of a murder that took place in apartment 12A at 907 Butler Street, this night of January 17 inst.

3. The stampings on the cartridge cases indicate that the bullets were manufactured for use in a Colt .45-caliber automatic pistol.

4. I have information based upon my personal knowledge and belief, and facts supplied to me by a normally reliable source, that a man named Andrew Denker, alias Andrew Darrow, now residing in apartment 4C at 321 South Lewiston Street did sometime at the end of December, illegally purchase a pistol of the same caliber and description as the pistol used to fire the aforesaid cartridges.

5. Based upon the foregoing normally reliable information and upon my personal knowledge, there is probable cause to believe that a pistol in possession of Andrew Denker may constitute evidence in the crime of murder.

Wherefore, I respectfully request that the court issue a warrant in the form annexed hereto, authorizing a search of the person of Andrew Denker and the premises at 321 South Lewiston Street, apartment 4C. No previous application in this matter has been made in this city or any other court or to any other judge, justice, or magistrate.

This time, the warrant was granted.

They decided that the best time to hit the apartment was immediately. They further decided that if Denker was the man who'd committed the murder, then it would be risky if not foolhardy to go in with insufficient numbers. Cops were heroes only on television. In real life, they had wives and children and they wore bulletproof vests when they were about to take a door.

Meyer called Inspector John Di Santis, the Emergency Service commander, and told him they needed a six-man backup on a No-Knock warrant. Di Santis asked him when. Meyer said right now—which was already a quarter past ten—and they arranged to meet around the corner from Lewiston at eleven-thirty that night. The plan was to go in silently and undetected, the E.S. cops assaulting the door in ceramic vests and armed with riot guns, the detectives and their search warrant immediately behind them.

At twenty past eleven, Meyer and Carella were parked at the curb on Geurtz Avenue, in front of a bar named Ballantine's, waiting for the E.S. team to arrive. A leggy young girl wearing a short blue coat over blue stockings and a pleated blue mini came out of the bar and waved back to someone inside. "So long, Daisy!" a man called, and the girl went off up the street, humming softly to herself. The night was silent again. They waited. Carella looked at his watch. There were sirens in the city. There were always sirens in this city, but there seemed to be a great many of them now, shrieking to the night. On the radio, they heard Molly O dispatching cars and ambulances to the airport.

"Must be something," Meyer said.

A moment later, Di Santis radioed them.

"This is Inspector Di Santis," he said. "A plane coming in from Baltimore just crashed at Franklin, we need The Truck out there and every available Emergency Service unit. Can this thing wait till later tonight?"

"We'll get back to you," Meyer said.

The two men sat in the car, talking it over.

Carella blew his nose.

Meyer said, "We wait till later, he may be gone. If he isn't gone already."

"Yeah."

"Never mind Chicago, he could've moved to anyplace else in this city."

"Except he doesn't know we've got the address here."

"Yeah, but . . ."

"I'm saying he doesn't know we're onto him. He's got no reason to run."

"Except murder."

"Which is sometimes a reason to stay put. Till it all blows over."

"Yeah."

"So what do you think?"

"Let's go do it," Meyer said. "Get it over with."

Carella looked at his watch.

"Yeah, let's go do it," he said, and sighed.

"You all right?" Meyer asked.

"Yeah, I'm okay."

His father's murderer had walked out of a courtroom a free man, but he guessed he was okay.

They went around the corner to Denker's building and looked up the facade to the row of fourth-floor front windows. Not a light was burning. They went into the building then, and stood in the entrance hallway downstairs, trying to warm up a little. The temperature outside was four degrees Fahrenheit, which Carella figured was about minus sixteen degrees Celsius. That was cold in any language. He and Meyer were both wearing bulletproof vests under their coats. The vests made them look bulkier than they actually were.

These weren't the virtually foolproof ceramic vests that you wore when some lunatic was shooting down from a rooftop with a high-powered rifle. These paneled Kevlar-and-cotton vests weren't nearly as effective, and many cops refused to wear them because they hampered movement. But Carella and Meyer had good reason to believe that the man upstairs—if there *was* a man upstairs—had committed murder. They were here, in fact, with a warrant that authorized them to search for the .45-caliber Colt automatic that had been the murder weapon. They would have felt happier with the Emergency Service backup they'd been promised, but that was ancient history.

They had taken off their gloves. Meyer was blowing on his hands. Carella had his hands in his pockets.

The glass panel in the upper half of the building's entrance door was frosted over except for an uneven circle at its center. Through the clear patch of glass, the detectives could see an occasional automobile passing by, its headlights cutting through the darkness outside. It was almost midnight. They hoped Denker would be in bed, asleep, secure in the knowledge that everyone thought he'd already vacated the apartment. Their warrant came equipped with a No-Knock provision. They had fought like hell to get it, finally and in desperation showing the supreme court magistrate an eight-by-ten black-and-white photo of what the .45 had done to the victim's face. The judge finally agreed that a No-Knock might be advisable in this instance.

"How you doing?" Meyer asked.

"My fingers are still a bit stiff."

"Take your time," Meyer said. "If he's still here, we're okay."

He was wearing a woolen watch cap over his bald head. His cheeks were still red from the bitter cold and the wind outside. His blue eyes seemed brighter against the rawness of his face.

This had been the coldest winter he could remember, starting early in November it seemed, and bludgeoning the city with on-and-off single-digit temperatures ever since. Carella was wearing a pea coat and blue jeans over long underwear. No hat. L. L. Bean boots. Outside, a traffic light changed. The clear patch on the frosted-glass panel segued from green to yellow to red. Meyer kept blowing on his hands. Vapor plumed from his mouth. The patch of clear glass turned green again.

"Ready when you are," Carella said.

The guns came out.

It had taken them half an hour to drive here from the Eight-Seven. When they left the station house, Sergeant Murchison said from his perch behind the muster desk, "Be careful out there." He'd been watching too many television reruns. Life imitating art. Though most often art imitated life, and occasionally art imitated art—all too successfully.

They did not need to be told to be careful. They went up those steps like wayward husbands sneaking home after a night on the town. Gun hands hanging loose at their sides, no need for a state of extreme alertness yet, not until they reached the fourth floor, Denker's floor. Denker didn't know they were coming, it wasn't likely he'd be out in the hallway in his pajamas. So the climb to the fourth floor was cautious but not timid, quiet but not altogether still.

Denker lived in apartment 4C.

For all he knew, he was home free. Tonight would be surprise time; they had him cold. If he was still here.

Apartment 4A dead ahead now, at the top of the stairwell.

A nod from Meyer.

An acknowledging nod from Carella.

They peeled off to the right. Guns up now. Muzzles pointing toward the ceiling, butts close to their shoulders. Moving silently down the hallway, gliding past apartment 4B, Johnny Carson inside cracking jokes with Ed McMahon, 4C at the end of the hall. Both men moved up close to the door.

Meyer put his ear to the wood.

Not a sound in there.

He kept listening.

Carella raised his eyebrows questioningly.

Meyer shook his head.

From apartment 4B down the hall came the sound of *The Tonight Show*'s orchestra. Doc Severinsen in his funny clothes playing expert trumpet. Big-band sound behind him. Meyer kept listening.

Still nothing.

He backed away from the door.

Nodded to Carella again.

Carella nodded back.

What they were about to do was called Taking the Door. It was the most dangerous thirty seconds in any policeman's life. The most frightening, too, though the men here in the hallway merely seemed serious and apprehensive. Meyer was standing to the right of the door now, the gun in his right hand tucked in against his shoulder, ready to roll himself around the doorframe and into the room behind Carella the moment he kicked the door in. Carella was standing some three feet away from the door, arms widespread like a diver bouncing on a board, gun in his right hand, eyes on the knob and strikeplate, a nod to Meyer, knee coming back like a coiled spring, foot lashing out to hit the door flat and just to the right of the knob, a grunt when his foot made contact, and then the door splintered and the lock tore loose and metal screws and slivers of wood sprinkled the air.

Carella followed his own momentum into the room, gun fanning the midnight air, Meyer immediately behind him and to his right, a wedge of light from the hallway spilling into the darkness.

"Police!" they shouted simultaneously, and four shots came crashing out of the black.

They both threw themselves headlong onto the floor, and then rolled away in opposite directions because the guy in here was a killer who knew the tricks of the trade. Unsurprisingly, his next shots chewed wood out of the floor, where he'd guessed they'd be this time around—five, six, seven, and silence. Not *exactly* where he'd guessed, but close enough to cause Carella to break out in a cold sweat. Another shot, a muzzle flash deep in the blackness ahead. Silence again. Eight slugs gone. Your typical Colt .45 carried seven in the magazine. Add another one in the chamber and that came to eight. That's all there'd been, goodbye, Charlie. And now the solid click of a new magazine being shoved into the gun butt. And silence. Carella scrambled to his knees behind what he now discerned was a stuffed easy chair.

He could not see Meyer in the darkness. He did not call out to him, nor did he shout a police warning again. Denker knew they were here and he knew they were policemen. What he *didn't* know was where they were. Neither of them had fired yet. No muzzle flashes to reveal their location. The light spilling from the hallway came only so far into the room. Beyond that, blackness. And Denker waiting with seven more bullets in the gun now, all stacked up in the magazine.

Outside on the street, an ambulance siren. Doo-wah, doo-wah, doo-wah, doo-wah. The bridge to "Over the Rainbow," ask any musician. Carella scarcely dared breathe. He was waiting for his eyes to adjust to the darkness. Problem was, Denker's eyes were *already* adjusted to the darkness, and now he was waiting for them to make just a single move, show so much as a fingernail and he'd empty his gun in their faces.

A doorframe took shape.

Denker was in the room beyond that doorframe. A bedroom most likely.

Carella could see nothing in that room.

Pitch-black in that room, Denker waiting with the gun in his hand. Or were there two guns? Or even more. He'd reloaded, but that didn't necessarily discount the possibility of more than one gun. Count seven shots, rush the room, and discover he's also got an Uzi in his lap. Problems, problems. Meanwhile, there wasn't anything to count. Denker wasn't firing again, not just yet. Didn't want to reveal his position. Mexican standoff here. Two cops pinned down in the darkness, Denker afraid to fire for fear they'd locate him. The trouble was they didn't have all night here. If there was a window in that room—

"Denker!" he shouted.

Silence.

Had he already split? Out the window, down the fire escape, lost to the night?

"Denker!" he yelled again.

Two shots came out of the blackness, the first one almost tearing off Carella's head, the second one knocking plaster out of the wall behind him. From somewhere across the room on Carella's left, Meyer immediately opened fire, zeroing in on the muzzle flashes, although Denker was smart enough not to be where he'd been only seconds earlier. Neither was Carella where he'd been.

In the time it took Meyer to snap off four rapid shots, Carella was on his feet and racing to the doorframe. He stood to the right of the bedroom door now, flattened against the wall, wondering if Meyer could see him there.

"Meyer!" he yelled.

"Here!"

"We go on three!" he shouted.

"Got it!"

Silence.

Denker waiting in the dark. Five cartridges left in the automatic, *was* there another gun in there? Waiting for them to rush the room on the count of three, not knowing that these men had worked together for years and years and that when one of them yelled "We go on three!" it meant nobody was going anywhere, everybody was sitting tight right where he was, the words *we go* negating the whole damn thing. They were not going to storm that door on the count of three, they were merely

321

hoping Denker would begin firing on three and would shoot himself out of yet another magazine.

Silence.

Outside on the street, another ambulance siren. Busy night tonight. Carella was hoping they wouldn't need an ambulance here. Or a body bag. Especially not for Denker. Better to take him out of here without any leaky holes in him. Carry him out of here on a stretcher and some shyster lawyer would start the Wheels of Technicality rolling even before the ambulance attendants got down to the second floor. As it was, the detectives would have to justify the use of deadly force, convince the people downtown that they hadn't used the gun as a means of apprehension but had opened fire only in self-defense. This city, you sometimes felt everybody was trying to make the job more difficult than it actually was. All they were trying to do here was arrest a killer.

Meanwhile, they waited in the darkness, hoping the trick that had worked for them a hundred times before would work again for them now. Knowing, too, that even if it *did* work, even if they managed to fool Denker into emptying his gun at an empty doorframe, he might reload before they'd moved a foot into the room, or—worse yet—he might cut them down with a *second* gun.

"Stand by!" Carella shouted.

Denker had to know he was just outside the room, standing to the right of the door. Denker had to be waiting to blow him away the moment he stepped into the frame. But nobody would be there.

"One!" Carella shouted.

Silence.

"Two!" he shouted.

More silence.

"Three!" he shouted, and Denker opened up.

He was taking no chances. He fired two shots to the right of the jamb, where he knew Carella had to be, another shot straight down the middle, where the other cop *might* be, and the last two to the left, where the other cop might *also* be. Five shots altogether, plus the two he'd fired at Carella's head earlier, which made seven for an empty magazine. There was a click and then another click and then Denker yelled "Shit!" because nobody'd been counting but us chickens, boss, and now he was in it up to his nostrils. Nobody had to yell go, nobody had to give any kind of signal to storm that room right this minute, both cops knew this was it, there'd be no second chance if they blew this one. Denker was starting to slide a fresh magazine into the gun when they rushed him. Meyer kicked him in the balls, and Carella rabbit-punched him at the back of his head. The magazine fell to the floor, but Denker swung out backhanded with the empty gun, catching Carella just below his right ear and sending him reeling back across the room.

"Freeze!" Meyer shouted, but nobody was freezing.

Denker whirled on him with the gun, the barrel clutched in his fist now, wielding the gun like a hammer, its butt in striking position, moving up fast on Meyer who stood in the gunfighter's crouch they'd taught him at the Academy all those many years ago, and who said again, very softly this time, looking down the length of the gun directly into Denker's eyes, "Freeze," and this time the single word stopped Denker in his tracks because maybe he'd seen what was in Meyer's eyes and figured he'd rather take his chances with twelve good men and true. Or women, for that matter.

He dropped the gun.

Carella snapped the cuffs on him.

They were all breathing very hard.

Nellie Brand had been to a late party and had just fallen into a deep sleep when her boss phoned. Her boss was the district attorney. He told her the Eight-Seven had made an arrest in the Bowles case, and she'd better get uptown right away because it looked like real meat. This was at a quarter to two in the morning. Mumbling, Nellie lumbered out of bed, stumbled to the bathroom, and stood under the shower for a full ten minutes before she began feeling moderately alive again.

An assistant D.A. was no less an authority figure than a doctor; both had to look well-dressed even when making a house call in the middle of the night. Nellie wore her sand-colored hair in a breezy flying wedge; all she had to do was use the dryer on it, and run a comb through it. She put on black pantyhose and bra, a pale pink long-sleeved blouse, a gray woolen pants suit, and black pumps with low heels. No jewelry but her wedding band. She inspected herself in the mirror on the back of the bathroom door. All things considered, she looked reasonably representative of The Law. She kissed her sleeping husband goodbye, put on a down overcoat, took from one of its pockets a blue woolen hat that matched her eyes, and pulled it down over her ears. She locked both locks on the apartment door, and then went downstairs to look for a taxi.

When she got to the 87th Precinct that morning, it was almost two-thirty.

Miscolo offered her a cup of coffee he'd personally brewed in the Clerical Office, but she'd been up here before and she politely declined. Carella diplomatically suggested that perhaps they should send out for some Danish, and while they were at it get some coffee delivered, too. He called the order in to a deli on Culver Avenue. The food got there half an hour later.

They sat drinking coffee and eating cheese Danish at three o'clock in the morning. There was something almost cozy about it. The squadroom was piping hot, radiators hissing, windows melting frost now that someone had turned up the thermostat. They'd worked together before, these three. They knew each other and liked each other. Carella had poured his coffee from its cardboard container into his personal squadroom mug, marked in red nail polish with the initials S.C. Meyer's mug was marked M.M. Nellie drank from a plain white guest mug. They sat around

Carella's desk as if it were a kitchen table. The coffee was very hot and very good. The Danish was good, too. This was nice. Three people here or there in their thirties, all of them more or less in the same business, all of them just sitting here eating and drinking at three o'clock in the morning while Andrew Denker cooled his heels in a holding cell downstairs.

"So what've we got?" Nellie asked.

"Everything but the ballistics report," Carella said. "We're waiting for that now. I was promised a quick comeback."

"Which means next month," Nellie said.

"Usually, but I said we had a prisoner here we were waiting to question."

"When was this?"

"When I messengered the stuff downtown. Twelve-thirty, a quarter to one. As soon as we got back here."

"What'd you send them?"

"Denker's gun, and some spent cartridge cases and bullets."

"That his name? Denker?"

"Andrew Denker," Meyer said, nodding. "*Andrew*, not Andy. He doesn't like to be called Andy."

"A contract player from Chicago," Carella said.

"Very expensive hit men there," Nellie said.

"We've got expensive ones here, too," Meyer said.

"Why don't you give Ballistics another call?" Nellie said, turning to Carella. "Goose them along."

Carella looked up at the clock.

"I just don't want some shyster saying we held him too long before questioning," Nellie said.

"Sure, but . . ."

"So if we can speed them along . . ."

"Well, there's only one guy working this time of night," Carella said, and looked up at the clock again. "And he promised me."

"What time did he say?"

"Three-thirty, four o'clock."

325

"I sure would like that make before we start the Q and A."

"I think we're okay even without it," Meyer said.

"Because then we can go in blazing. Without it . . ."

"I think we're okay even without it," Meyer said again.

Nellie turned to him.

Meyer figured she hadn't heard him the first time around.

"How do you figure?" she asked.

"Long story," Carella said.

"You got a taxi waiting?" Nellie said.

"Better get the file," Meyer said, and eased himself off the corner of Carella's desk, and went across the room to where a row of green metal filing cabinets stood against the wall. He pulled one of the hanging file folders from the second drawer, carried it back to the desk, and took from it a thick manila folder. Hand-lettered onto the front of the folder was the name BOWLES, EMMA. Carella opened the folder. He took a single sheet of paper from it and handed it to Nellie. She was looking at a standard Complaint Report form, the likes of which she'd seen at least a thousand times before. This one was dated December 28. Since midnight, today was the eighteenth day of January.

"She came in three weeks ago," Carella said.

Nellie nodded.

She was reading through the vital statistics on the form. White female, full name Emma Katherine Bowles, maiden name Emma Katherine Darby. Married to a man named Martin Bowles. Lived right here in the Eight-Seven, on the outer fringes, up near Smoke Rise. Age thirty-two, weight one-twenty, height five-seven. Blonde hair, brown eyes. No visible scars, birthmarks, or tattoos. No regional accent or—

"Anybody named Carella up here?" someone said from the slatted wooden railing that divided the squadroom from the corridor outside. A uniformed cop was standing there, holding a manila envelope in his gloved hands.

Carella signaled to him. "I'm Carella," he said.

The cop fiddled with the catch on the gate, came into the

squadroom, and walked directly to Carella's desk.

"I need your signature," he said.

The printing across the face of the manila envelope read IDENTIFICATION SECTION—BALLISTICS. Carella signed the receipt slip fastened to the envelope. The cop tore off the top yellow copy, waved vaguely, and went out.

The room was suddenly very still.

Carella unlooped the little red string from around the little red cardboard button, lifted the flap of the envelope, and pulled out several typewritten forms. He was looking at the report on Denker's gun and the cartridges and bullets fired from it. Meyer was standing on his right, Nellie on his left, both of them slightly behind where he was sitting. All three silently read the report.

"Let's go get him," Nellie said.

15.

He was much better-looking than Nellie had expected. You hear somebody's a hit man from Chicago—with a handle like *Denker,* no less—you expected some kind of gorilla. A big unshaven guy still wearing the threads the state gave him when he was released on parole. The cold, flat eyes of a professional killer. A thin-lipped mouth. Broken nose, lotsa muscles, no brains. That's what you visualized.

But *Andrew* Denker—who didn't like to be called *Andy*—was a tall, well-dressed, slender blond man with an easy, pleasant smile and a gentle voice. When she entered the interrogation room, he was in quiet conversation with a man wearing a brown sharkskin suit. Nellie heard no dems, deses, or doses. Denker was altogether attractive. She was quite taken aback.

"Mr. Denker," Carella said, "we'd like to ask you some questions now. Before we do, though, I want to be sure you still understand what your rights are. Earlier tonight, we . . ."

"Speaking of rights," the man with Denker said, "my client's already been here . . . how long have you been here now, Mr. Denker?"

"They entered my apartment illegally at . . ."

"We had a warrant," Carella said.

"No-Knock," Meyer said.

"I'm Nellie Brand," Nellie said, extending her hand to Denker's lawyer. "District Attorney's Office. I don't believe we've met."

"Harvey Keller," he said, "Legal Aid," but did not accept her hand. "Miss Brand, *I've* been here for an hour and a half already, and my *client's* been here since . . . when was it, Mr. Denker?"

"About twelve-thirty," Denker said.

Keller looked at his watch.

"That makes it more than three hours already, three hours and ten minutes to be exact, and no one has told him *why* he's here or what he's been charged with. I believe you're familiar with the section in Miranda that . . ."

"He hasn't been unduly detained, Counselor," Nellie said. "And with his permission, we'll start the questioning as soon as we're sure he still understands his rights."

"What am I doing here, anyway?" Denker asked, and smiled. His eyes met Nellie's. An invitation in those eyes. He was a man accustomed to using his charm on women.

"Detective Carella?" Nellie said, ignoring Denker's steady gaze. "Would you read Mr. Denker his rights, please?"

Carella read Miranda by rote.

Denker affirmed that he still understood all his rights.

"Mr. Denker?" Nellie said. "Are you willing to answer our questions now?"

"What's this in relation to?" Keller asked.

"A homicide that occurred last night, the seventeenth of January."

"Am I to understand you'll be charging my client with murder?"

"That is our intention, yes, sir," Nellie said.

"So why should he answer any questions?"

"He doesn't have to, of course. You know Miranda as well as . . ."

"I would advise you to remain silent," Keller said.

"Why?" Denker said. "I didn't do anything. I have nothing to hide. Besides, I'd like to put on the record that these two officers broke into my apartment and began shooting at . . ."

"Mr. Denker, excuse me, sir," Nellie said, "but before you say anything else, would you please affirm that you're willing to answer our questions?"

"I would still advise . . ."

"Yes, I'll answer any questions you have," Denker said.

He was slumped casually in a wooden armchair, long, slender fingers laced across his chest, long legs extended under the table around which they all were sitting. A one-way mirror was on the wall facing him, but no one was in the room behind it. A detective from the Photo Unit was running the video camera. A police stenographer sat behind a stenograph machine, taking backup notes. Nellie read the date and time into the record and named everyone there present. "Mr. Denker," she said, and the Q and A began:

Q: Can you tell me your full name, please?

A: Andrew Nelson Denker.

Q: And your address, please?

A: 321 South Lewiston, Apartment 4C.

Q: Is that a permanent residence?

A: No, I make my home in Chicago.

Q: How long have you been in this city?

A: I got here on the second. Right after New Year's Day.

Q: What is your occupation, Mr. Denker?

A: At present, I'm unemployed.

Q: What is your *usual* occupation?

A: I do various jobs.

Q: Of what sort?

A: Well, I usually do bodyguard work.

Q: Mr. Denker, did you present yourself to Emma Bowles as a private detective from Chicago?

A: Yes, I did.

Q: Why did you lie to her?

A: To put her at ease. I thought she might feel more secure if she thought I was a licensed detective.

Q: But you're *not* a licensed detective, are you?

A: No, I'm not.

Q: Did you also give her a false name?

A: Yes.

Q: And a false business card? With a false address on it?

A: Well, yes. But the telephone number was my own. In case she decided to check on me.

Q: Why did you go to all that trouble?

A: Well, I like to maintain a private identity.

Q: I see. Did you maintain this private identity with Martin Bowles? Or did he know you were Andrew Denker and not Andrew Darrow?

A: He knew, yes.

Q: Did he also know that you're not a licensed detective?

A: Yes, he knew that, too.

Q: But he hired you, anyway.

A: Yes.

Q: *Why* did he hire you?

A: To protect his wife.

Q: To *kill* his wife, isn't that what you . . . ?

A: Excuse me, Miss Brand.

Q: Yes, Mr. Keller?

A: Mr. Denker has indicated that he will answer any questions you may have, and his willingness to cooperate should be noted on the record. But when you begin hurling reckless accusations . . .

Q: Sorry, Counselor, would you like me to rephrase what I just asked him?

A: Surely, if this were a court of law, a judge would . . .

Q: Well, this isn't a court of law, but I will rephrase the question. Mr. Denker, did Martin Bowles hire you to kill his wife? Is that okay now, Mr. Keller?

A: Yes, thank you, Miss Brand.

Q: Would you answer the question, please?

A: Martin Bowles hired me to *protect* his wife.

Q: Not to kill her?

A: No, not to kill her.

Q: I see. Mr. Denker, does your line of work require possession of an automatic pistol?

A: Sometimes, yes.

Q: Do you now possess such a pistol?

A: Yes, I do.

Q: I show you this Colt .45-caliber automatic pistol and ask you if this is your pistol.

A: Yes, it is.

Q: Do you have a license for this pistol?

A: No, I don't.

Q: Wasn't this pistol in your possession when it was taken from you by force last night?

A: Yes, it was.

Q: But you admit not having a license for it?

A: That's correct.

Q: Mr. Denker, I show you a report from the Ballistics Section, comparing bullets and cartridges test-fired from this gun with bullets and cartridges recovered at the scene of a murder committed on the night of January seventeenth. Would you take a moment to . . . ?

A: May I see that, please, Miss Brand?

Q: Certainly, Counselor. Please have the record indicate that Mr. Keller is reading a Ballistics report dated January eighteenth and signed by Detective/First Grade Anthony Mastroiani.

(Q and A resumed at 3:52 A.M.)

Q: May I show this to Mr. Denker now?

A: Please.

Q: Mr. Denker, would you take a look at this, please?

A: Thank you.

Q: Have the record show that Mr. Denker is now reading the same Ballistics report.

(Q and A resumed at 3:56 A.M.)

Q: Mr. Denker, have you now read the report?

A: I have.

Q: Do you understand what it says?

A: I do.

Q: It says, does it not, that the test cartridges and bullets fired from this pistol . . .

A: Well, there are expert witnesses who'll tell you . . .

Q: I'm sure you know all about expert witnesses, but the report nonetheless states that the test cartridges and bullets fired from this pistol match exactly the bullets and cartridges recovered in apartment 12A at 907 Butler Street on the night of . . .

A: Mr. Denker, I would strongly advise you to keep silent at this time.

Q: Mr. Denker? Do you understand what this report says?

A: I don't care what it says. It has nothing to do with me.

Q: Mr. Denker, this gun was fired by you at two detectives attempting to arrest you . . .

A: I thought they were burglars.

Q: This gun was taken from you by the arresting detectives, and it now turns out it's the *same* gun that was used in a murder that took place last night. How do you explain . . . ?

A: I don't have to explain anything. This isn't a court of law. I can stop this anytime I want to.

Q: Mr. Denker, I show you certain items confiscated in your apartment tonight at the time of your arrest. Do you recognize these?

A: The previous tenant probably left all that in the closet.

Q: You're saying that whoever had the apartment before you occupied it . . .

A: Yeah, that's probably what happened.

Q: Left behind a hundred thousand dollars in T-bills and cash, is that it? Plus jewelry worth . . . do you have that list, Mr. Carella?

A: (from Carella) Right here.

Q: Thank you. This is a typewritten list of the contents of the safe in the Butler Street apartment. I believe the detectives found it in a desk drawer . . .

A: (from Carella) The living-room desk. Kneehole drawer.

Q: It itemizes jewelry worth some fifty thousand dollars. The *exact* jewelry, piece for piece, that was found in your apartment. The serial numbers on the T-bills match as well. Now, Mr. Denker . . .

A: That's it. No more.

Q: Am I to take it that you wish the questioning to stop at this point?

A: (from Mr. Keller) You heard the man, he said no more. What does no more mean if it doesn't mean no more?

Q: Fine. If that's what you want, that's the way we'll play it. But you know, Mr. Denker . . . turn that off, will you, please?

The camera operator hit the OFF button. The room was silent now. When Nellie spoke again, her voice was soft, almost gentle. Not the murmur of a threat in it. But Carella knew what she was about to do, and he watched her in silent admiration.

"If I can just offer a few words of advice," she said. "Off the record."

"Sure," Denker said, and smiled confidently.

"I know you're from Chicago, so perhaps you don't understand how the law works here in this state. I can tell you we've got a very strong case with the murder weapon and the . . ."

"Well, that's for a jury to decide, isn't it? Whether a case is strong or not."

Still smiling confidently.

"Well, I think it's a very strong case, both the murder weapon *and* the jewelry. So I can tell you we'll be going for Murder Two—which is as high as we can go in this state

335

unless you've killed a police officer or a prison guard or . . . well, we won't go into all that just now. Murder Two will be the charge, and I'm sure the grand jury will indict on what we've got, and if we get a conviction . . . which I'm sure is a lock with everything we've got . . . then the minimum mandatory sentence'll be fifteen to life, and the mandatory max'll be twenty-five to life, all depending on what judge you get. We've got some pretty tough judges in this city. And, of course," she said, almost casually, "you'd be serving your time in a state penitentiary."

She paused for just a moment, and then repeated the words.

"A state penitentiary, Mr. Denker."

And allowed them to sink in.

"Now I don't know if you're familiar with the state penitentiaries in this fine country of ours," she said, "but I don't think you'd find any of them very much to your liking."

"I'm willing to take my chances," Denker said.

"Oh, I'm sure you are. Good-looking white guy . . ."

The operative word was *white*.

The fear word.

Carella was still watching her, listening to her intently. There was something professionally cold-blooded about her performance, almost chilling, but there was also something extremely seductive about it. He wondered what being married to her was like.

"Man who takes such good care of himself," she said, "dresses so beautifully . . ."

"Thank you," Denker said, but he seemed to be paying more attention now.

"Very confident of yourself, I'm sure you think you'll be able to handle yourself just fine in a prison population where all at once you're the minority group."

Playing on the fear again.

"Maybe a ratio of ten to one, Mr. Denker, black to white, Hispanic to white, that's what you're likely to find. Streetwise hoodlums serving hard time, that's what you'll find in a state

penitentiary. Running the show. Calling the tune. A topsy-
turvy world, all at once. Your ass'll be grass, Mr. Denker.
Literally."

"Now see here," Keller said.

"This is all off the record," Nellie said.

"Even so."

"I think Mr. Denker is listening, though. Aren't you listening, Mr. Denker?"

"What's the upside?" he said.

Carella saw her eyes flash almost imperceptibly. She knew
she had him hooked now, and she was going to reel him in.

"The upside would be a federal penitentiary."

"Uh-huh."

"Something like Danbury or Allenwood."

"Uh-huh."

"A country club."

She let this sink in, too.

"Now I don't know what you may have done anyplace else
but here," she said. "I *know* you did that murder last night, and
I'm going to nail you for it, believe me. But if we can clear up
anything else while we're at it, then maybe we can talk a shorter
term in a federal pen, that's entirely up to you."

"How short?"

"Well, I don't know what you've done yet, do I?"

"Nothing here."

"Except for last night."

"I haven't said anything about last night."

"Okay, so where?"

"Chicago. Mostly."

"Let's concentrate on Chicago then, okay? Let's say . . . I'm
not asking you anything yet and I'm not making any promises
either . . . but let's say you've done some things we can clean up
for the feds there . . ."

"Like what? I'm not saying I *did* anything . . ."

"I understand. This is all off the record."

"But like what kind of things did you have in mind?"

"Well, considering your line of work . . ."

"I told you I'm a bodyguard, is what my line of work is. What kind of things did you have in mind?"

"Loan-shark collections?" Nellie said, and shrugged. "Laundering drug money? A little extortion here and there?" She shrugged again. "We'd be asking you to testify against anyone you may have done such work for. If there was anything like that, stuff I could talk over with the people in Chicago, it might help me get what you're looking for."

"What is it you think I'm looking for?"

"Let's say ten to life in a federal pen, how does that sound to you? *If* I can swing it."

"I'm not saying I *did* any of these things, you understand. . . ."

"I realize that. Besides, we'd have to clear up all the details of the case here before I could even . . ."

"No way. Talk to your people first. Tell them I can maybe give you the kind of stuff you want, and then find out if you can get me a federal pen. And ten to life sounds high."

"Let me make some phone calls, okay?"

"Sure. I'm in no hurry," Denker said.

Nellie nodded, said, "Give me a few minutes," and left the room. Denker sat with his hands folded on the table before him, studying them. The clock threw minutes into the room. The video-camera operator passed wind, mumbled, "Sorry," and then yawned. When Nellie came back some ten minutes later, she said, "Depending on what you've got for me, I think I can get it down to eight-and-a-third to life. Want to play?"

"You *think* you can get it down?"

"I can *promise* you the eight-and-a-third, okay? Provided this is real meat. The feds don't like being jerked around."

"Give me a Queen-for-a-Day letter," Denker said, leaving no doubt in anyone's mind about his professionalism.

"Nothing in writing," Nellie said flatly. "What do you say?"

"How do I know . . . ?"

"We can always go the other route," Nellie said, and shrugged in dismissal. "Some state pens are better than others."

Denker looked at her.

"So what do you say?" she asked. "Are we done here, or are we just beginning?"

"What do you want to know?" he said.

"The stuff here first."

"Okay."

She nodded to the camera operator. He hit the button.

"Did Martin Bowles hire you to kill his wife?" she asked.

"Yes."

"When was this?"

"I called him from Chicago."

"*When*, Mr. Denker?" And then, more gently. "Please tell us when, won't you?"

"On the thirtieth of December."

"And said what?"

"That I understood he had a job for me. Someone had recommended me for a job he needed done down here."

"You both knew what that meant, did you?"

"Yes, we both knew what that meant."

"What happened then?"

"We arranged to meet."

"Where? Here in this city?"

"Yes."

"When did you actually meet with him?"

"On January third."

"Where?"

"In a restaurant downtown. In the Old City. Near the Seawall down there . . . is that what you call it, the Seawall? His office was down there, he wanted me to meet him down there. But not in his office. He was too smart for that. It was very cold that day, in fact much colder than Chicago had been when I left, I was surprised. Here in this city . . ."

Everything is still decorated for Christmas, the trees still hung with lights, the shop windows brimming with merchandise on sale now that the giving season is over. This is a few days after the start of the new year. The city looks extravagantly beautiful, a dazzling snow princess in silver and white. The restaurant is one of those places that seem phony because they're so real, genuine wooden beams that went back to the British occupancy, or so Bowles tells him, leaded-glass windows, a copper-topped bar, all of it looking exactly the way it must have looked in the eighteenth century. Denker almost expects their waiter to be wearing white stockings, knee breeches, and a powdered wig.

They sit in a booth with high wooden sides, private and apart.

They are here to discuss murder.

Bowles tells him he's an investment broker up for a promotion with his firm, he'll be a partner by the first of May if all goes well. He is a man in his late thirties, Denker guesses, exceedingly handsome, with dark hair and brown eyes, wearing an elegant gray business suit on this very cold night in January, drinking first one martini and then another, looking almost cheerful as he tells Denker that he wants his wife killed.

"Why?" Denker asks.

"You don't need to know that, do you?" Bowles says.

"You're right, I don't," Denker says.

Business is business, he thinks. He himself has been nursing a vodka on the rocks for the past half hour now. When murder is the topic, he likes to keep a clear head. Only amateurs drink when details are being discussed. Denker is a pro.

They look at the menu . . .

Bowles orders the prime ribs, Denker the lamb chops . . .

. . . and return to the problem at hand. It seems that Bowles has been trying to dispose of his wife since shortly after Thanksgiving, having hired a man who claimed to be an expert but who, in fact, turned out to be the world's worst bungler. In the middle of December, the man made a blatant attempt to shove

Emma under a goddamn subway train with half a dozen people watching. And just last week—and this is what prompted Bowles to start looking elsewhere—he tried to run her over with a car. Now Emma knows for *sure* that someone is after her. . . .

"What do you mean? Did she suspect *before* then?"

"She told me she thought someone was following her, yes."

"I see."

"And she was right, of course. The man I hired *had* been following her."

"Uh-huh."

"Waiting for his opportunity."

"To push her under a subway train."

"Brilliant, wasn't it?"

"Or run her over with a car."

"I know this might make your job more difficult."

"Might?"

"Her knowing she's been targeted."

"Mmm."

"But I'm willing to pay you well. Provided . . ."

"Did your people in Chicago tell you what I normally get?"

"Only a ballpark figure. They said I should discuss the fine-tuning with you."

"Uh-huh. What was the figure they gave you?"

"They told me fifty thousand. Ballpark."

"They told you wrong. Ballpark. They haven't been keeping up with the times."

"Well, I must tell you, fifty . . ."

"No, I must tell you, Mr. Bowles. Fifty was what I got five years ago. Even adjusting for inflation . . ."

"Well, obviously I was misinformed."

"Does that mean I don't get to eat my lamb chops?"

"It means we're here to talk. I'm used to making multi-million-dollar deals every day of the week, Mr. Denker. Tell me what you want and we'll discuss it."

"I'll tell you what I want, but we won't discuss it. There's no room for discussion. I normally get seventy-five, half on agreement, half on delivery. But someone has already fucked up here, and your lady's on emergency alert. For all I know, she may have gone to the police already. . . ."

"I understand the risks involved. How much do you want?"

"A hundred grand. Half now, half on delivery."

"Agreed."

"Good."

"Provided."

"Provided *what*?"

"Provided you make it look like an accident."

"I have to pay for your mistakes, right? You and the dumb guy who tried to shove her under a train."

"No, *I* have to pay for the mistakes. Through the nose, it seems. Have we got a deal or haven't we?"

"We've got a deal."

"Good. When can you start?"

"When do I get the first half?"

Q: When, actually, *did* you start?

A: On the seventh.

Q: Of January?

A: Yes.

Q: And last night . . . well, tell me about last night.

"Mr. Denker," Keller said, "I would still advise you to . . ."

"Do *you* want to go to a fucking state pen?" Denker said, whirling on him.

Nellie wondered what he was thinking in that moment. The job had gone wrong, true, and often this seemed a good enough reason for a criminal to *explain* what had been planned, show the brilliance of the plan, demonstrate how fate had conspired to fuck it up. But so far he hadn't explained anything except the details of how he'd been hired. No confession so far, nothing but the gun so far, all they had so far was the gun. And the jewels, of course. Maybe enough to convict him, maybe not, you couldn't tell anything with juries nowadays. Nellie wanted to put him away for a long, long time; the man was a murderer. But she was willing to settle for the eight-and-a-third she'd prom-ised rather than risk a jury trial and the attendant possibility that he'd walk entirely. All she wanted to do now was get her confes-sion, get whatever other Chicago shit she needed for the feds, seal the bargain, call it a day.

"How'd you get in the building?" she asked, almost ca-sually.

But he was silent now.

Q: Mr. Denker?

A: (Silence)

Q: Can you tell me how you got in the building?

A: I . . .

Q: Yes. Go ahead.

A: I thought . . . at first I thought I'd cause a diversion, some kind of diversion to get the doorman away from the front door, but suppose I set a fire up the street or something and he just didn't pay any attention to it? I mean, I haven't been in this city long, but it's plain to see that the people here just don't *give* a damn. You can be . . .

. . . slitting somebody's throat in the street, they'll tip their hats and walk right on by, this is *some* city, I've got to tell you. So the more I thought about a diversion, the more it looked like it wouldn't work. What I did, I watched the front door of that building all day Tuesday and Wednes-day, and I recognized there was a routine the doormen followed, and that it would just be a matter of working myself into that routine. For example, the afternoon guy comes on at three-thirty, and he gets relieved at eleven-thirty. Now three-thirty was too early for me to go in, and eleven-thirty was too late, I wanted it finished and done with by eight o'clock, latest. Out of the apartment and the building by eight o'clock, latest.

Watching the front door, I realized that the afternoon guy took a coffee break an hour or so after he came on, four-thirty, five o'clock, around then. Locked the inner lobby door, walked to the McDonald's up on Woodcrest, came back with coffee in a container. Didn't take his dinner break till seven-thirty or so, which was too late for me, I wanted to be in the apartment long before then. So all I had to do was wait for him to take his coffee break, and then let myself into the building. Once I was inside . . .

Q: How did you let yourself in?

A: I had a key.

Q: A key to the inner lobby door?

A: Yes. And also the keys to the apartment. There are two locks on the apartment door.

Q: Where did you get all these keys?

A: Emma gave them to me. I spent a weekend with her when Bowles was out of town. That's when she gave me the keys.

Q: So you waited for the doorman to take his dinner break . . .

A: His *coffee* break. Watched him walking up the street . . .

Q: And then you let yourself in the building. . . .

A: Yes.

Q: What time was this?

A: Around twenty to five.

Q: Did you go directly upstairs to the apartment?

A: Yes.

Q: Was there anyone in the apartment when you got there?

A: No.

Q: The apartment was empty?

A: Yes.

Q: You let yourself into the empty apartment . . .

A: Yes.

Q: Used the keys Emma Bowles had given you . . .

A: Yes.

Q: And then what?

A: I marked the safe, used a chisel to mark the safe, you know, make it look like an amateur was trying to bust into it, and then I opened it with the combo Bowles had given me. And I cleaned it out. Took all the cash and the T-bills and the jewelry. And then I sat back to wait.

Q: Was this a spur-of-the-moment thought?

A: Ma'am?

Q: Taking all that stuff from the safe.

A: No, no, that was part of the plan from the beginning.

Q: Why was it necessary to . . . ?

A: To make it look like an interrupted burglary.

Q: I see. So you burglarized the safe . . .

A: Yes. Well, no, I didn't have to *break* into it, if that's what you mean. I already had the combination, Bowles had given me the combination.

Q: But you did open the safe . . .

A: Yes.

Q: And you did remove the contents . . .

A: Yes.

Q: And took the contents with you when you left the apartment . . .

A: Yes.

Q: . . . and the building.

A: Yes.

Q: Tell me, Mr. Denker, how did you get out of the building?

A: Down the fire stairs to the basement and then out the doors leading to the alley.

Q: Where did you go then?

A: Up to Woodcrest Avenue, where I caught a taxi downtown.

Q: To your apartment?

A: Yes, ma'am.

Q: Let's get back to right after you'd opened the safe and removed its contents. You said you sat back to wait . . .

A: Yes, ma'am.

Q: For what?

A: For the moment when I actually had to do it.

Waiting is always the most difficult time. He is waiting to do murder. The contents of the safe are in a dispatch case on the bedroom floor, and he is sitting on the edge of the bed, facing the bedroom door, waiting to hear the click of a key in the front door lock, the click that will tell him to thumb off the safety catch on the .45. It is getting late, he is beginning to wonder if he's made a mistake, beginning to wonder if he'll be sitting here all night, waiting for nobody to come home.

His watch reads a quarter past six.

A hundred and fifty thousand dollars' worth of jewels, cash, and treasury bills in that dispatch case.

He sits waiting.

Tapping his foot.

Waiting.

Remembering what happened in this bed.

Waiting.

It is twenty minutes to seven when he hears a key in the front door latch. He thumbs off the safety. He gets off the bed. Takes up a position just inside the bedroom door, to the left of it. He hears the front door being closed again. The click of the thumb bolt as it's locked. Sound of the closet door opening. Closing again. Footsteps coming through the apartment. You and me, he thinks. Footsteps closer now. Closer. *Now*.

"You!"

Eyes opening wide in surprise.

"Me," he says, and fires.

Q: How many shots did you fire?

A: Three.

Q: All to the head?

A: All to the head.

Q: You shot Martin Bowles three times?
A: I shot Martin Bowles three times.
Q: You killed Martin Bowles?
A: I killed Martin Bowles.

The basic plan, of course, was already in place. Nothing much had to be changed. Simply shoot the husband instead of the wife. Because it was a much better deal, you see.

Certain very definite advantages to be gained from doing it this way. *Dollar* advantages. If he'd gone through with it the way Bowles wanted it, he'd have gotten the second half of his fee, *plus* the jewels, which he'd never planned to return, anyway. So that would have come to a hundred in cash, total, and maybe thirty for the fenced jewels.

But the way they talked it over that weekend when Bowles was away, the way they'd finally planned it, there was going to be a lot *more* money involved. Lots of money. Forget the thirty the jewelry would bring—if, in fact, it really did bring that much. If he fenced it, which was still the plan, by the time they discounted it, he might end up with twenty-five, maybe less, maybe only twenty. That didn't matter because they'd get what the jewelry was worth, anyway, the minute Emma filed an insurance claim. This *was,* after all, a felony murder. Her dear husband *had* been killed during the commission of a burglary. And the jewels were insured against theft, so the fifty thou would come back to Emma in the long run, and coming back to Emma was the same as coming back to him.

"She told me she wanted to marry me," he said, and smiled. "Can you imagine?" And shook his head in wonder. "Why not, I told her. Good-looking woman, why not?"

Marry her and forget the lousy fifty and some change for the jewels, forget the hundred in cash and T-bills, that was all chicken feed. The *real* money would come when Bowles's will was probated.

Lots of money, she'd told him.

Most of which Bowles had inherited from his father, all of which would go to Emma as sole beneficiary.

Marry all that money.

And the beauty part was that the inheritance would never be questioned because nobody would even *guess* that Emma had been involved in any way. Last night, while a burglar was killing her husband, she'd been nowhere near the apartment. She had in fact . . .

"She told us she'd been out to dinner with a girlfriend," Carella said.

"Exactly," Denker said.

"Yes, we checked. An early dinner. Her alibi's a good one. She was nowhere near the apartment when you killed him."

"Which is exactly the way we planned it. I told Bowles I wanted him out of town on *Friday* night, I was going to do it *Friday* night, *tonight*. But instead I did it *last* night. He never expected to see me there in a million years. I think he realized what was happening a second before it happened. But by then it was too late, wasn't it?"

"It was too late, all right," Carella said. "Do you know what else she told us when we got to the apartment last night? After she came home, and found her husband dead, and called the po . . ."

"I know exactly what she . . ."

"She told us, *again,* that she thought you'd already gone back to Chicago. Told us, *again,* that she'd said goodbye to you on Tuesday afternoon."

"That's right. That was my alibi. I was gone, I was in Chicago, it was a burglar who killed her husband. That's what we worked out together. She was *supposed* to tell you . . ."

"Well, she did. And she also said your relationship had been strictly business . . ."

"Right . . ."

" . . . and whereas she wasn't sorry her husband was dead, she couldn't see how you'd had anything to do with it."

"She was supposed to say that, too."

"Good, she did. And, of course, *she'd* had nothing to do with it, either. *She* was out having an early dinner with a girlfriend. How much money would you say was involved here, Denker?"

"In the will? A million-six."

"That's a lot of money."

"Sure. Well, that's the only reason I went into it. She kept talking about love, but I was counting all that money. It was a good plan."

"Still is," Carella said.

Denker looked at him.

"But guess who'll end up with all of it," Carella said.

Denker kept looking at him.

"The recovered jewelry, the cash, the T-bills, the million-six in the will . . ."

Denker was already shaking his head.

"Yes," Carella said, nodding.

"No."

"She set you up, Denker."

"No, she didn't."

"Yes, she did. She used you."

"You're wrong."

"Just a few questions, Denker, set it straight."

"Sure."

"Did she ever once mention that we knew of your existence?"

"No, how could you . . . ?"

"Because she told us all about you, you see. We began tracking you almost from minute one."

Denker looked at him.

"Did she mention that we knew you'd bought a gun?"

"No, she never . . ."

"Didn't mention that, either, huh?"

"No, but . . ."

"Because she also knew *that*, you see. That you'd bought a gun. We'd given her that information."

Silence.

"A Colt forty-five."

Silence.

"She let you use a gun we *knew* about, Denker."

Another silence. The silence lengthened. He was realizing that the gun was the only real thing that linked him to the murder. She'd known they were onto the gun . . . but she hadn't warned him.

"But . . ."

He shook his head.

"She wanted to marry me," he said.

Carella said nothing.

"She told me she loved me," he said.

Carella still said nothing.

"For Christ's sake, we *planned* it together!" Denker shouted.

"Can you prove that?" Carella asked.

"Well, no, but . . ."

"Neither can we."

It was six o'clock on Friday morning.

Dawn was yet almost half an hour away, but there was already a faint reddish stain on the horizon to the east. Denker had been taken away in handcuffs. Nellie Brand had all she needed, and now she and the two detectives sat in the squadroom drinking fresh coffee they'd ordered from the all-night deli on Culver. They were trying to figure how they could bring Emma Bowles into this. They couldn't see any way to do it.

"We can't use his confession to implicate her," Nellie said.

"No, we can't," Carella said.

"That's the law."

"That's the law," Meyer said.

"Otherwise everybody and his brother'll say somebody else put him up to it."

The squadroom was silent. The clock ticked loudly into the stillness.

"Can *you* see any way to charge her with anything?" Nellie asked.

"No," Carella said.

"No," Meyer said.

"So that's it," Nellie said, and drained her cup. She looked up at the clock, stretched, and said, "If I leave for home right this minute, I'll get half an hour's sleep before the alarm rings."

The two detectives said nothing.

"Cheer up," she said.

Carella nodded.

Nellie shook hands with Meyer.

"Good night," she said. "I'll talk to you."

"Good night," he said.

She extended her hand to Carella. He took it.

"Good night," she said.

"Good night, Nellie."

Their eyes met.

"Come on," she said. "Half a loaf is better than none."

Carella nodded.

He was thinking that yesterday afternoon Samson Wilbur Cole had walked out of that courtroom a free man, and today Emma Katherine Bowles was walking, too. He was thinking that nowadays if you got anywhere near half a loaf you were lucky. Most of the time, all you got were the crumbs left on the table.

"Come on, Steve," she said softly.

For an instant—but only an instant—it seemed as if she might lean in to kiss him gently and comfortingly on the cheek. The moment passed. She released his hand.

"See you guys," she said, and went out of the squadroom.